BEYOND THE TIDES

CLASSIC TALES of RICHARD M. HALLET

EDITED BY FREDERIC B. HILL

Down East Books

An imprint of Globe Pequot
Trade division of The Rowman & Littlefield Publishing Group, Inc.
4501 Forbes Blvd., Ste. 200
Lanham, MD 20706
www.rowman.com

Distributed by NATIONAL BOOK NETWORK

Library of Congress Cataloging-in-Publication Data
Names: Hallet, Richard Matthews, 1887–1967, author. | Hill, Frederic B.,
    editor.
Title: Beyond the tides : classic stories of Richard M. Hallet / edited by
    Frederic B. Hill.
Other titles: Beyond the tides (Compilation)
Description: Lanham, MD : Down East Books, [2022] | Includes
    bibliographical references. | Summary: "A selection of tales in the vein
    of Joseph Conrad, Jack London, and Rudyard Kipling written by a Maine
    literary lion"—Provided by publisher.
Identifiers: LCCN 2022007259 (print) | LCCN 2022007260 (ebook) |
    ISBN 9781684750443 (paperback) | ISBN 9781684750450 (ebook)
Subjects: LCGFT: Short stories.
Classification: LCC PS1784.H14 B49 2022 (print) | LCC PS1784.H14 (ebook) |
    DDC 813/.52—dc23/eng/20220503
LC record available at https://lccn.loc.gov/2022007259
LC ebook record available at https://lccn.loc.gov/2022007260

For Ben, Emmett, and Will
Sapere aude

CONTENTS

PREFACE

"I suppose only a few seconds of any man's life are actually pivotal. These are the seconds in which he makes up his mind to some kind of volte-face which shapes his course anew."

Richard Matthews Hallet wrote those words in his entertaining autobiography, *The Rolling World*, in describing a key moment in his adventurous life—when, at age nineteen, he was working a summer job as a policeman in a Boston-area amusement park.

He was applying that maxim to his sudden realization that he might not measure up to his hero, heavyweight boxer John L. Sullivan,[1] after being knocked out cold by a razor-wielding thug while patrolling the amusement park.

At the time, in 1906, Hallet was a sophomore at Harvard and earning summer money at the Mayflower Grove, where he often ran into the gregarious and boastful Sullivan, now retired, terribly overweight, and living off his reputation. Sullivan enjoyed provoking Hallet, squeezing his muscle and calling it "an oyster on a broomstick" and telling him, "Me lad, you'd better get on a vessel and go to sea."

Hallet attributed that challenge, and his youthful admiration for the sea-going adventures of his uncle Richard Willis (Will) Jackson, to his decision after graduation from Harvard Law School four years later to sign on as a lowly seaman aboard a windjammer headed from New York to Sydney, Australia, "in quest of a backbone."

Will Jackson, the older brother of his mother, had survived numerous near-death experiences in his nautical travels across the globe in the

1880s. As a young man, Hallet had read Jackson's many letters home about his exploits, including the heroic tale of a shipwreck in the far Pacific.

Hallet's voyage to Australia turned out to be even more consequential. Returning in June 1912 from several shipboard adventures, trekking across Australia, and living off his wits in England, Hallet was days away from accepting a position with a prestigious New York law firm.

On the weekend before he was to report to the law firm, Hallet went to visit his family in Cambridge, Massachusetts. There he found a letter from the editor of the *Saturday Evening Post*, George Horace Lorimer, offering him $250 for a story he had mailed from London—"The Black Squad," a lively account of working as a boilerman on a steamship from Sydney to London. (Note: $250 in 1912 is approximately $7,036 in 2021 dollars.)

Hallet's story described "the literal hell of a life [he'd] led in the boiler room"—"I saw black, thought black, spit black, the base of my brain was enclosed in a black fog"—with an abrasive crew of misfits and "the impenetrable wall between firemen and first-class passengers." A noted preacher said every clergyman should read the story to strengthen "their conception of hell's fire."

It is no small coincidence that one pivotal moment in my own life that led me to change direction was a visit to my mother's first cousin, Richard Hallet, in January 1965. That visit to his home in Boothbay Harbor, Maine, during a Christmas holiday led to a beneficial turning point—for me—that dramatically altered my life's course.

In January 1965, I was a first-year law school student at Boston College and quite miserable. After a brief and unsuccessful fling with professional baseball following graduation from Bowdoin College, I had set my latest career goal on the law—and found it, except for a course on criminal law, numbing.

Over several hours, lunch with Hallet and his wife Mary, and a game or two of chess, "Uncle Dick," then seventy-seven, subtly but persistently suggested that I should try journalism. "You write well," I remember him saying, though we had exchanged no more than three or four letters. "You have a good education, and newspapers just might be your calling." Providentially, he then quoted Henry Louis Mencken's warning not to stay in the newspaper trade too long, or one's creative processes will get "jammed up."

Within a month or so, I had visited a half-dozen newspapers on the East Coast, from Boston to Washington—including the *Baltimore Sun*, where a friend had provided an editor's name and an introduction.

By March, I had resigned from law school and, after several interviews, was offered a job as a reporter at the *Sun*, then one of the leading newspapers in the United States—and the paper of H. L. Mencken. Looking back today, after twenty years as a police reporter, investigative reporter, foreign correspondent, and editorial writer at the *Sun*; two years as foreign affairs director for a respected Republican senator (Charles McC. Mathias Jr.); and then twenty challenging years in the State Department, I realize how lucky I was to have found my pivotal moment in Richard Hallet's living room on a chilly winter day in 1965.

This collection, then, of a number of his short stories, is a long overdue "thank you" to an inspiring mentor and, more important, a truly outstanding writer who never quite made it to the top ranks of American literary circles and salons but was certainly near the top in the 1920s, 1930s, and 1940s.

In addition to his novels and autobiography, and a half-dozen more unpublished novels, Hallet wrote nearly two hundred short stories for the most widely read magazines of the period: *Saturday Evening Post, Harper's, Atlantic, Collier's, Everybody's, American Legion Monthly*, and so forth. He wrote seventy-nine of them for the *Saturday Evening Post* after publication of "The Black Squad," regularly sharing billing on the front page with the likes of F. Scott Fitzgerald, Ernest Hemingway, William Faulkner, Will Rogers, P. G. Wodehouse, H. G. Wells, and two of his fellow Maine authors, Kenneth Roberts and Ben Ames Williams. (Fitzgerald wrote sixty-five stories for the *Saturday Evening Post* between 1920 and 1937 and credited the income from the *Post* with enabling him to pursue his successful literary career.) A 1930 story, "Zimbolaci's Daughter," ran next to a long article on "The Dole" by a British parliamentarian named Winston Churchill.

Hallet, whose literary heroes were Joseph Conrad, Jack London, and Willa Cather, first came to national attention in 1916, when his "Making Port" was selected as one of *The Best Stories of 1916* by the anthologist Edward J. O'Brien. O'Brien, in fact, termed it "the best short story" of the year. Like many of his tales, "Making Port" was drawn from Hallet's personal experience—about an old salt Hallet encountered during his very first shipboard adventure, a romantic but unlucky seaman who always seemed to choose the wrong ship in a long, Sisyphean struggle to return home to Liverpool.

O'Brien, who said he preferred stories that "rendered life imaginatively in organic substance and artistic form," praised the "subtlety of [Hallet's] substance as lucidly conveyed through deft characterization, clearly revealed atmosphere, and richly colored speech. The story ranks with the best of Conrad."

Other contributors to that 1916 collection included Robert Frost, Sherwood Anderson, Edith Wharton, and Theodore Dreiser. Critics then and later often drew favorable comparisons between Hallet's writing and that of Conrad, London, Herman Melville, and Stephen Crane.

O'Brien chose several of Hallet's stories for his collections in later years: "Rainbow Pete," "The Harbor Master," "To the Bitter End," "Misfortune's Isle," and "The Gulf Stream." A 2000 edition of *The Best American Short Stories of the 20th Century*, edited by John Updike, cites four Hallet stories in its index: "Making Port" and the first three of these five.

The noted critic Bernard De Voto commented, "For years, I have delighted in Hallet's stories because of their expertness, their gorgeous colors, their humor, and above all else, their zest." Another, J. B. Kerfoot, promoting upcoming stories for *Everybody's* magazine, said of his writing, "Hallet is one of those rare individuals who can talk to us—talk to us, mind you—with a pen in his hand. . . . Listen to him while you read."

It has been very difficult to select the stories for this book. I'm sure other readers would have chosen many I have left out. My overriding objective was threefold: to find stories that were appealing to read—both today and eighty to one hundred years ago; that are representative of his craft; and that were significant milestones in Hallet's writing career. Thus, this collection includes "The Handkerchief": his first published story, in the November 1909 issue of *Cosmopolitan* magazine, when he was an undergraduate at Harvard. He was paid $60. It is clever, with tragic irony, but might not have made the cut if it were not his first. I left out several other pieces that drew O'Brien's plaudits because they struck me as overwrought and/or too long.

One must remember the context in which these stories appeared in the leading magazines of the day. There was no television in the first four decades of the twentieth century, no social media. Contributors had dozens of popular magazines to write for, and though most paid by the article and not by the number of words, they had few limits imposed on their imaginations.

But what an audience. The *Saturday Evening Post* (still published today with six issues per year) had a weekly distribution as high as nearly seven million—plus Norman Rockwell on the cover many weeks!

And other writers read these magazines. A biographer of Eugene O'Neill wrote that O'Neill regularly read the *Saturday Evening Post*, and the playwright's main character in *The Hairy Ape* was heavily influenced by a young seaman in Hallet's story "Ticklish Waters." Hallet's tale, about a World War I Atlantic crossing of a troopship carrying horses and soldiers and facing threats from submarines and spies, was based in part on his own experience as a merchant marine officer on such a ship. It ran in two successive issues of the magazine in September 1918.

Hallet also met several famous writers in his travels around the world. He crossed paths briefly with Joseph Conrad in a London publishing house (without knowing it until later), and the first editor of his debut novel, *The Lady Aft*, was a young Sinclair Lewis.

Many of Hallet's artful and engaging stories are just too long to include in this book. One example is "The House at Craigenside," an entertaining tale of intrigue and Oriental magic in the misadventures of New England sea captains. Written as a prospective novel, it was serialized in the *Saturday Evening Post* over four issues in 1917, its first part featured on the cover. *The Canyon of the Fools*, his only novel made into a film despite repeated interest in adapting others, was serialized in seven issues of the *Post* in 1921.

The stories I have chosen break down mainly into two general categories: vivid tales of the sea, both in the days of sail and in the midst of war, often built around shipboard tensions and tumult; and stories of Maine and New England and their small town values and rivalries—with a fair dose of romance. A few more reflect his worldly travels and experience "looking for material" while "on the wallaby" (on the road) in the outback of Australia, digging copper in Arizona mines, and prospecting for gold in Canada.

The final selection, "My Uncle's Footprints," is one of only two articles in this book, a *Saturday Evening Post* piece on his World War II visit to the small atoll in the Marshall Islands on which his uncle, Will Jackson, my great-uncle, was shipwrecked in 1884.

Throughout his life, Hallet paid tribute to his uncle Will, who, as the youngest and lowest-paid seaman, led the rescue of the captain and all twenty-seven members of his ship, *Rainier*, after it wrecked on an uncharted coral reef. At the time, stories spread that the islands were inhabited by cannibals, though that was not the case. Yet Jackson's adventures after that incident, dodging one calamity after another in seaborne travels around the world, fascinated his nephew, who grew up in Bath, Maine, and Cambridge; to Hallet, Jackson remained "the eternal symbol of Maine." (Richard Hallet was the son of Andrews Hallet and Alice Jackson, the younger sister of Charles T. Jackson, my mother's father and my grandfather. Will Jackson was Charles and Alice's older brother.)

A few final words on Hallet's approach to writing: To become an author, a writer, he recommended a perceptive eye, an empathetic heart, and an organizing brain—as well as extensive travel.

More extensive coverage of the remarkable career of Richard Matthews Hallet follows in the introduction—excerpts of an outstanding profile written by Richard Cary in the *Colby Library Quarterly* in 1967 on Hallet's eightieth birthday, two months before his death.

Richard Cary, a native of New York, was a professor of American literature at Colby College, author or editor of thirteen books, and head of its Special Collections department. He focused on Maine authors.

Cary's profile covers the landscape, from Hallet's birth to his later life, when, as a correspondent for Maine newspapers, he reported on World War II in the Pacific, taught courses on writing at Bowdoin and Bates Colleges, became a regular contributor to *Down East* magazine, and campaigned through news columns, editorials, and radio broadcasts for various reforms in Maine. Hallet's editorials highlighted the need for an institute on maritime affairs in Maine and drove the establishment of the Maine Maritime Academy.

Mr. Cary's profile also led me to the memorable remarks of the central character in Conrad's early novel *Youth*. It is the Marlow of Conrad's later novels who opened his young eyes to the allure of "the good strong sea, the salt, bitter sea that could whisper to you and roar at you and knock the breath out of you" as he sat on a ship at a dock in Indonesia—and observed:

> *Only a moment; a moment of strength, of romance, of glamour—of youth!*
> *. . . A flick of sunshine upon a strange shore, the time to remember, the*
> *time for a sigh—good-bye! Night! Good-bye . . . !*

Closing the circle, my son Alex and I adopted this striking description of the fragility of life—*A Flick of Sunshine*—as the title of our recent book on the daring and heroic life of Richard Willis (Will) Jackson, who provided such an early inspiration for Hallet to pursue his own stirring and full life. Addressing the *Boston Herald*'s annual book fair in 1938 as his autobiography was being published, Hallet said, "I know I went to sea trying to emulate Will Jackson." Another pivotal moment!

NOTE

1. John L. Sullivan was the first boxing superstar and one of the world's highest-paid athletes of his era. Recognized as the first heavyweight champion, he reigned from 1882 to 1892. He even fought a few bare-fisted battles during his career, although gloves were far more common. Due to a life of overindulgence in food and alcohol, he died at age fifty-nine.

EDITOR'S NOTE

In placing Hallet's stories in some order, I have set them chronologically, as written and published, with a few exceptions.

I have chosen to place first my two personal favorites, "Beyond the Tides" and "The Anchor." They are marvelously clever and well-told tales about two very different subjects: an aging sea captain's strong character and will, and the dangers and personal rivalries aboard a steamship facing the threat of German U-boats while crossing the Atlantic in the middle of World War I. Both reflect Hallet's wealth of experience and gift for storytelling at a young age (the first written when he was twenty-five, the second at age thirty-two). The two stories display quite strikingly his keen knowledge of ships and the sea, his personal service aboard maritime ships in the midst of war, and even his hand-to-mouth adventures traveling across Australia barely a year after graduating from law school.

I have put next to each other two pieces drawn from that colorful and risky experience going "on the wallaby" Down Under with his friend Frank Hyde: "With the Current" and "The Razor of Pedro Dutel," for obvious reasons. And I put toward the end Hallet's own favorite, "The Devil Takes Care of His Own," mainly because it did come later in his life (age fifty), though it was drawn from his early worship of and frequent collisions with the famous heavyweight boxer and braggart, John L. Sullivan.

INTRODUCTION
RICHARD MATTHEWS HALLET:
ARCHITECT OF THE DREAM
By Richard Cary

From *Colby Library Quarterly Series* VII,
No. 10 (June 1967)

Road's End on Spruce Point in the morning of a spring day, white light deflects off the blue waters of Boothbay Harbor and picks out the equally blue eyes of a large man slumped in a deep chair, deep in the room. Books in long files dominate the walls, and tables are stacked with reading matter of many descriptions. Out of this deceptively passive atmosphere rises a voice with the quality of a subdued gale, rich and easy and glad, the voice of a born yarner. Remembering seas and heights and horizons of yesterday, and the lives of sailor, sheep shearer, line rider, stone breaker, oil drillman, hobo, gold miner, copper mucker, policeman, stoker, trapper, naval officer, author, and war correspondent he has lived.

FAIR HARVARD

On July 20, 1887, Sylvanus Cobb, Jr., Maine author of *The Gunmaker of Moscow* and some thirteen hundred other fictions, died. On the next day, in Bath, Maine, Richard Hallet was born. From this congruence of mortal events Richard's father adopted the notion that Cobb's disembodied soul and his dint for literature had transmigrated into the body of his brawny new offspring. His fabled Uncle Will Jackson wrote to inquire how much Richard weighed and whether he had the makings of a sailor.

Five years later, the Hallets were living in Cambridge, Massachusetts. Here Richard attended Cambridge Latin School, absorbing the heavy curriculum of classics and developing the tendency to allusiveness that was to mark his style thereafter. From the first, his father nudged him toward reading and writing. "I had to write . . . the old rascal . . . gave me stuff to read when I was a kid that stirred up what was already in my head. Stevenson, Kipling and Fenimore Cooper, etc."

His Certificate of Admission to Harvard in 1904 indicates that "he passed with credit in Elementary Latin, History, Algebra, Chemistry, and Advanced Greek." With these credentials, and an enabling scholarship, he took his place in the class of 1908. The bulk of his courses were in history and economics, he audited philosophy, but most memorable to him was freshman composition with its required daily theme. In a registration of eight hundred, he received one of only three A grades awarded. This he attributes to his job as guide in the Venetian palazzo on the Fenway which housed the art treasures of flamboyant, iconoclastic Isabella Stewart Gardner.

Within Harvard's halls he also heard Jack London indict the softening effects of civilization and was stirred by his call for literary roughage.

To lay away some money for college expenses, Hallet took a summer job as a policeman at Mayflower Grove, an amusement park in Bryantville, Massachusetts, which comprised a pineboard hotel, a lake, a theater al fresco, and a carousel, largely patronized by shoe operatives from Brockton and cordage workers from Plymouth. Here the Harvard innocent . . . underwent some eye-widening experiences among the "worldly" chorus girls who embellished the syncopated musical comedies and vaudeville acts. Here too he met John L. Sullivan, thenceforth one of his heroes and a prime source of literary provender. The Boston Strong Boy, now retired from the prize ring and weighing in excess of three hundred pounds, often wandered into the park from his nearby farm. When Sullivan first spotted Hallet the policeman, he seized his biceps in massive fingers and roared: "What's this for a muscle? It's an oyster on a broomstick!"

On an idle Sunday afternoon during his sophomore year, Hallet was moved to write a short story which he called "The Handkerchief." With the intrepid spirit of his nineteen years, he dispatched it to *Cosmopolitan* and expectantly checked results in the return mail.

He was destined to wait considerably longer. On November 17, 1908, an assistant editor of the magazine wrote: "We must apologize for the length we have retained 'The Handkerchief,' but it was held up for further consideration. We shall be glad to make use of it if $60.00 is a satisfactory price for the manuscript." Satisfactory! Hallet turned half a dozen somersaults and began reckoning the size of his future fortune. All he need do of a Sunday afternoon from now on was to pound out a story and earn $60, which would carry him through college handsomely and over any other conceivable economic shoals. It was an illusion that served him well. In the face of rejection after rejection in following years, he mumbled stubbornly to himself, "By God, I did it once and I can again."

Hallet does not have a copy of "The Handkerchief," nor can he in fact recall anything about it except that it was "a pretty wild sort of mystery story." *Cosmopolitan* promised its readers "a little masterpiece of a short story—the kind that made DeMaupassant famous." It does display an element of de Maupassant in the reflexive denouement, but Hallet goes one turn better, swiftly transposing a sudden access of horror (a corpse) into a romantic symbol of impotence (the handkerchief).

While still at Harvard, Hallet had another unusual fling at professional writing. *The Arena*, once a robust monthly, had come on sallow days. For several issues before it ceased publication, Hallet ground out most of the editorials and non-fictional content. He thinks now that this may well have hastened the end.

THE LAW, LEARNED HAND, AND THE SEA

Hallet disclaims high rank in his class, but there is ample testimony that his colleagues and the administration rated him "an exceptionally bright student." Bright enough, assuredly, to be accepted into the Harvard Law School, to attain his degree in 1910, and to be chosen as secretary by Judge Learned Hand,[1] then thirty-eight years old and rising through the hierarchy of the Federal District Court for Southern New York. Hand impressed Hallet, physically and mentally. "He had the jaw of a lion, the eye of a gazelle, and a memory of iron." Their talks would start with law and invariably digress into literature, philosophy, politics. In those metropolitan days, Hallet's dinner often consisted of a five-cent beer and cuts of ham and hardboiled eggs from the free lunch counter of the Gaiety Bar on Broadway. "There I would spear an egg as nonchalantly as if I had no need of eggs at all, as if I were a successful businessman eating an egg in a fit of absentmindedness, or just because it happened to be there."

He submitted stories and ruefully read editors' comments linking him with Meredith and Conrad—and declining the manuscripts. He wrote mainly of outdoors and the sea, although he could not then tell a capstan head from a martingale. He delved into Kipling, London, and Conrad, and liked Galsworthy, Maurice Hewlitt, and Hardy. He was vaguely dissatisfied with his lot. In June 1911 Judge Hand decided to close his chambers and go to Europe for the summer. This was Hallet's Rubicon and he crossed it unflinchingly—he would go to Europe too. Hand arranged for him to ship on a square-rigger belonging to the Standard Oil Company—"so I shipped on the windjammer and never got back to the law at all."

What conglomeration of motives impels a man, basically intellectual, to opt for the strenuous life? For Hallet, the mixture included his legendary Uncle Will Jackson, who "surely started me off on the sea adventures," and John L. Sullivan, who looked upon his slim frame and admonished, "Me lad, get on a vessel; you'd better go to sea." There was the fascination of the faraway—"the wide sweep of the bay, the glittering sands, the wealth of green infinite and varied, the sea blue like the sea of a dream, the crowd of attentive faces, the blaze of vivid colour"—in Conrad's *Youth*, a ten-cent volume plucked from a bookstall in Cornhill during law school days. And there was the ineluctable message from within, "a feeling in me that my spine was soft and that I must go looking for trouble." He mulled over Trollope's recipe that the way to write is to drop a piece of sealing wax in your chair and stick to it; rubbed it against Scott's dictum that it is better to do something worth writing about than merely to write something worth reading. He concluded that "to write, you must first have something to write about, if not adventures of the soul, then adventures of the body."

Thus it was that with two Harvard degrees he put to sea as an ordinary seaman on a baldheaded bark, the *Juteopolis*. For him, as for Conrad's young Marlow, it was no mere shipboarding. "O Youth! The strength of it, the faith of it, the imagination of it! To me she was not an old rattle-trap carting about the world a lot of coal for a freight; to me she was the endeavour, the test, the trial of life."

AUSTRALIA

The *Juteopolis* left the port of New York with a million gallons of case oil and touched Sydney 124 days later. A reporter pictured Hallet on arrival as the biggest man forward, hair unbrushed, face unshaven, mustached and goateed, wearing a Crimean shirt, soiled pants, and no shoes. Conditions aboard having been less than ideal, Hallet and his mate jumped ship and plunged into the wilderness. They trekked for the next five months, covering approximately a thousand miles through thick brush, down roads built by convicts, and along the Murrumbidgee River. Such adventuring without much planning is known as "on the wallaby" in Australian, or on the road, looking for work.

They fought midges and black flies, dodged bulldog ants and venomous snakes, slept under the open sky or in bush tents, and when it rained, they broke into empty huts or inns. To survive, they took jobs shearing sheep, driving bullocks, breaking rock, and punching rabbits. "At night I used to sit beside a campfire, chew my pencil and put down what had happened during the day, in the form of a sort of tale. Kipling said that was the way to do it."

After a time, they built a sixteen-foot bateau, roofed it with a tin whisky advertisement that flaunted a white horse striding a blue ground, and launched it into the Murrumbidgee. It was prophesied they would last half a day at best among the river snags; they managed to stay afloat three weeks before collapsing against a sunken gum tree near Wagga Wagga. Here they abandoned the craft and struck south for the city of Melbourne.

Hallet took lodgings in a trolley car barn containing twenty cots for which a larger number of drunken sailors vied nightly. He cajoled a hundred sheets of paper from the editor of the *Melbourne Argus* on the promise to deliver an account of his exploits in the back blocks, rented a typewriter with his last five shillings, and, working day and night shifts, produced "The Seaman's Book of Swag." (A swagman, Hallet explains, is a floater who carries all his earthly possessions on his back.) The *Argus* turned down the script as too colloquial, but it found haven in the *Herald and Weekly Times* for the life-saving sum of thirty golden sovereigns. Two other stories of note germinated in this era, including "With the Current."

CONRAD, CANADA, AND COPPER MUCKING

Hungering for new pastures, Hallet signed up as a stoker on the British steamship *Orvieto*, bound for London. In temperatures ranging to 140° Fahrenheit, he shoveled coal while the ship plowed through the Indian Ocean, the Red Sea, the Suez Canal, and the Mediterranean, stopping at Naples and Toulon before discharging him at Tilbury on Thames. The literal hell of a life he led in the boiler room—"I saw black, thought black, spit black; the base of my brain was enclosed in a black fog"—the abrasive sociality of the crew, the impenetrable wall between firemen and first-class passengers, all these he etched in baleful detail in "The Black Squad." He tried first to sell it to *The London Times*; in his sea garb he could not get past the office boy. Next, he went to *Nash's Magazine* in Fleet Street. As he climbed the dingy stairs to the editor's office, he passed a stocky man in brown tweeds and brown beard, whose unusual eyes pierced him with a glance. The editor, an American, skimmed hastily through Hallet's story, shook his head, and said: "You should take a leaf out of the book of the man who just left." "Who was he?" "Joseph Conrad." And then Hallet knew that the man walking downstairs was the very man who long ago had unwittingly ordained that silent rendezvous.

Shortly afterward he mailed the manuscript to *The Saturday Evening Post*, with return address to Cambridge, Massachusetts, and thought no more of it. He bicycled for an interlude along the South Coast, joined an archaeological expedition to the west of England, then settled down to research at the British Museum. There he wrote an article on Dartmoor, "Archaeology for Amateurs," which the *Times* also turned down. When further freelancing produced not a red pence, he took another job as a fireman in order to get back to New York. Judge Hand supplied him with a letter of recommendation to a prominent admiralty law firm. Hallet was promptly hired, and he agreed to start work on Monday. That weekend he went to see his family in Cambridge. On arrival, he found a letter from George Horace Lorimer offering to buy "The Black Squad" for $250. This was June of 1912. The *Titanic* had gone down in mid-April, with a loss of over fifteen hundred lives, rousing public curiosity in the workings of great ocean liners. To this day, Hallet insists that it took a major disaster to sell his story.

Whatever the propellant, Hallet resolved then and there that literature, not law, was his game. He never reported to Burlingame & Beecher (the law firm). For a spell he stayed in Boothbay Harbor, writing incessantly in long yellow pads on a marble-topped table shaded by a lobster cactus. In this atmosphere of swooping gulls and flowing waters, he began to make some headway. In 1913, two of his stories appeared in *Harper's* and one in *The American*. Henry Mills Alden, then a silver-crowned patriarch among editors, asked that he be permitted to abbreviate "The Foreign Voyager," promising he "would cut like a priest, not like a butcher." Hallet was in need of just such a trimmer. These early stories about prideful idealists who are beached by time linger too fondly over details of description which contribute little to inner development. Characters lean to eccentricity, and action to melodrama.

At this time, Hallet first met Mary Holton under circumstances that found him accoutred in a pair of crepe-paper angel's wings and holding a basket of artificial flowers. He was sure she thought him asinine. In the longer run she learned he was neither ass nor angel, and eventually consented to become Mrs. Hallet. In this period, he also completed his first novel, *The Lady Aft*.

Restive as ever, he took to the Canadian woods with a hardy cousin, four flitches of bacon, some patented camp food, and a surveyor's map of the region. In this wasteland of lakes and rocks, of wild animals and a few tribes of nomad Indians, they trudged, often aimlessly, hoping by some miracle to stumble upon gold. One night, Hallet fired at a wolverine or Indian dog that was trying to swipe bacon from their kettle of beans. Soon two armed Northwest Mounted Police materialized out of the void and informed them it was against the law to fire any weapon within Kenora Township limits during wartime. So it was that Hallet discovered the onset of World War 1. He and his partner had breached the forest shortly after the assassination at Sarajevo; it was now November. He sold nothing in 1914, and hove off to Chicago after fresh material with $10 in his pocket. He hitched rides in boxcars, hauled trucks along railway platforms, ate with hoboes, slept with sheep and made innumerable notes. Through the beneficence of a *Chicago Tribune* editor who paid him $50 for a story ($49.50 went for fare and four bits for ham sandwiches), he rode in elegant style out of the Midwest capital southward.

Soon he found himself in Arizona in company of a Swedish butcher, a deserting soldier, a Mexican miner, and a burro named Yim, once more in pursuit of the elusive yellow metal. When the search petered out, he made for the town of Globe, site of the Old Dominion Copper Company. Through the intervention of the local bank president, who was too canny to lend him money on the dubious security of an unfinished manuscript, Hallet secured a job in the pit. He mucked for four months and recounted the hazards of working on the twelfth level— equivalent to one of Dante's lower circles—in an essay, "Shooting Off the Solid." Daily, when his stint at the mine ended, he wrote news copy, editorials, and obituaries for *the Arizona Record* until midnight. With what time remained of the twenty-four hours, he persisted at his fiction. Proceeds from the copper-mucking article (*The Saturday Evening Post* paid $400) finally enabled him to head back to Boothbay Harbor and another term of concentrated writing.

THE LADY AFT

Hallet topped off his first novel between the time he returned from London and before he set out on his continental hegira. The story concerns a lawyer's clerk whose forebears had built ships and sailed them boldly down the salty reaches. Like Melville's Ishmael, the clerk finds the constraints of land overbearing and takes to sea. Like Melville's *Pequod*, this ship is a microcosm of the world's motley of human types, shapes, shades, and sizes. To complicate the normal politics of a ship's crew, Hallet inserts the captain's daughter, a capricious maiden whose difference the men try hopelessly to assimilate into their habitual hostilities. Instinctively they shy from the allure and torment of her presence, for they agree that women poison ships: "It ain't what she does. It's what she is." Her only ally among these sea-worn cynics is the young naif, known simply by the epithet, The Stiff. Hallet's use of anonymity insinuates a sense of universality, for this fumbling, name-less hero, without knowledge or experience but with ageless pluck, personifies the eternal thrust toward life, the priceless foolhardiness of every youth who must ram his head against the wall of the world and thus come to uncover for himself the meaning of existence.

The Lady Aft, then, is Hallet's bildungsroman, his chart of progress from unfledged lawyer to aware, self-determined manhood. The movement is symmetrical: from defeat in a fistfight, through the climax of a murderous squall, to victory in a fistfight, sheathed in a Conradian mood of brooding mystery and menace. Day-by-day life in the forecastle is realistically portrayed, there is a good deal of rough masculine humor, and character is evoked by sudden dips into the psyche rather than by slow unfoldment. Hallet's point of view is that of stage manager, denoting his control by numerous sententious asides. Most effective is the language which rolls like drops of golden brandy on the tongue, heady in color, rhythm, alliteration, and in the electric quality of Stephen Crane's muted hyperboles. Regrettably, the resolution is somewhat forced and implausible; *the lady aft* too facilely stripped of her secrecy and absolved of her duplicity. Today, Hallet calls it "a mighty bad piece of work," but on July 3, 1915, Rudyard Kipling wrote that he had read *The Lady Aft* "with great interest." The book had preceded Hallet to Arizona and was, indeed, the reason he had no difficulty obtaining his position with the *Record*. Curiously, the review in that newspaper had said "he writes like a young Kipling."

DOMESTICITY AND EARLY FRUITS

Three short stories published in *Everybody*'s during 1915 braced his courage to the sticking point. These are a far remove from their antecedents in *Harper's*. The scene is Australia, Hallet and his partner are on the wallaby to Melbourne, local color abounds, the tone is bantering, and the loose plots collapse on comic reversals. In italics, the editor advises his clientele to "listen to him while you read." Justifiably, for Hallet handles the vernacular here like lyric poetry. The year 1916 was a big one in a host of ways. *Everybody*'s bought more stories and the *Atlantic Monthly* printed "Archaeology for Amateurs," a rollicking record of his search for dinosaurs among the tors of Dartmoor.

Magazine editors began courting him for manuscripts; Doubleday and Macmillan sent feelers about book publication. Small, Maynard &

Co. brought out his second autobiographical novel, *Trial by Fire*, which he hoisted from his brief season as a fireman on the *James M. Jenks*, a Great Lakes iron ore freighter. As in "The Black Squad," Hallet vivifies the hell pit of below-decks and poses a contrast with the passengers who occupy cabins. The confrontation of Cagey, the anthropoidal stoker, and Avis Wrenn, an heiress, presages that of Yank and Mildred Douglas in Eugene O'Neill's *The Hairy Ape*, produced six years later. In *Trial by Fire*, Hallet's consuming love for the music of words is still salient although he curtails his usage in the tenser scenes and holds descriptive passages to reasonable bounds.

In the latter part of 1916 Hallet wound up his revisions of "The House of Craigenside" and sold it to *The Saturday Evening Post* for $2,000. Of this sum he lent $500 to a relative, and thereupon proposed to Mary Holton. "Do you think we can make it on $1,500?" he asked. She did. They were married in Boothbay Harbor in November. Lorimer ran the novel in four installments during February and March the following year. It opens in portentous Poe-sque fashion: the landscape of an eerie mansion on the encroaching dunes of a lonely coast, a house with a hooded personality fostering a grim drama of ancient guilt and vengeance. The narrative is encased in a frame—unfortunate Conrad carryover—sustains a high pitch, and totters under excessive description and lateral commentary. It was not issued as a book.

On October 9, 1916, anthologist Edward J. O'Brien wrote "May I formally ask your permission to reprint 'Making Port' in my new book to be entitled *The Best Short Stories of 1916*? I have selected it as one of the best twenty American stories after reading about twenty-five hundred stories published in America during the past year." If 1916 needed anything more to qualify as Hallet's annus mirabilis, this was it.

O'Brien dedicated the volume "To Richard Matthews Hallet," and said in his critical summary: "'Making Port' is, in my opinion, the best short story of 1916. It is elemental tragedy played out worthily against an eternal background, with an intimately human foreground of intensely realized personal experience. Mr. Hallet's style, always mannered, is here at its simplest and best, and the subtlety of his substance is lucidly conveyed through deft characterization, clearly revealed atmosphere, and richly colored speech. The story ranks with the best of Conrad, with whom Mr. Hallet shares much in sympathy, although their literary methods are very different." No small praise when one observes that this volume also carries "The Lost Phoebe" by Theodore Dreiser, and stories by Sherwood Anderson, Robert Frost, Amy Lowell, and Edith Wharton. In his annual Roll of Honor, O'Brien scores Hallet's "The Quest of London" as a "mannered piece" yet espies "a transition from euphemism to style," a style which is becoming "adequate to the richness of his substance. . . . It is told with all the prolixity of a sailor in the forecastle."

The Best Short Stories of 1917 includes the misinformation that Hallet was born in Yarmouthport, Massachusetts, but it also includes "Rainbow Pete" among the best twenty stories published that year. Applying what he defined as his test of substance—"how vitally compelling the writer makes, his selected facts or incidents"—O'Brien chose this brawling ballad of gold-hunting in the Canadian barrens on the strength of its "incorrigibly romantic mood. Mr. Hallet casts glamour over his creations, partly through his detached and pictorial perception of life, and partly through the magic of words. . . . Some figment of the marvelous and the mystic invests every tale so far told by the young Maine dreamer who dropped Blackstone and set forth, eyes ablaze, for lands that shimmered over the wide seas. . . . Full of danger and promise."

WORLD WAR I

Hallet's idyll of connubiality and growing renown was abruptly punctured in the spring of 1917 by America's entry into the war. Forthwith, he went back to Harvard, satisfactorily completed a six-week course at the Navigation School and qualified as third mate on steam vessels of [unlimited] tonnage for [whatever] oceans. Notwithstanding, he made his first trip as Junior Officer on an interned North German Lloyd liner with a cargo of nine hundred horses and one hundred mules. After assorted contretemps with leaks, the beasts, rabid seas, threats of submarines and ships in the night, they debarked at St. Nazaire, reposed briefly in France, and returned without animals or incident. Boothbay Harbor, though agog with shipbuilding, was too tame to engross him. He passed the course in navigation given by the Recruiting Service of the United States Shipping Board and was certified as a deck officer in the U. S. Merchant Marine. His next assignment was on a Seattle freighter which was being rebuilt in dry dock at Hoboken. Hallet capitalized this layover time by scribbling away at a story about Aronowsky and the rammed ship *Tankard*, "The Anchor."

Hallet's ship this time loaded locomotives, "Iron horses instead of the flesh and blood variety." Under convoy they made for St. Nazaire again. In a cafe there, halfway through a chess game and a bottle of Medoc, news came that the Armistice had been signed. Thence to Brest for oil, to Bermuda, and once more Boothbay Harbor, the lobster cactus and the yellow pads.

The war year and its immediate successors were especially prolific for Hallet. While he was still in service *The Saturday Evening Post* published "Ticklish Waters." Subtitled "A Tale of an Ocean Pussyfooter," it describes without flourish the tribulations of a novice navigator on a ship transporting horses during wartime. At supper, the captain of Hallet's current ship, now plowing across the Atlantic, held up a copy of the story and proclaimed to his gathered officers: "This was written by a man of vast knowledge and experience." One of the mates laughed. "Captain," he said, "do you know that the man who wrote it is your third mate on watch upstairs?"

THE LORIMER SUNROOM

The products of this intensive period found their way into the pages of *Harper's*, *Collier's*, *Century*, and the *Pictorial Review*, but primarily into *The Saturday Evening Post*, which offered ten of his titles between February and November 1919. The first two, couched in supple, anecdotal prose, examine the condition of the merchant marine fleet and the insufficient provisions of the Merchant Seamen's Act. The eight stories draw upon his recent naval travels and recollections of New England coastal waters, towns, and inhabitants. The modification in Hallet's approach is instantly notable: his diction is less grand, his characters less postured, his story line more casual, his point of view steadier. The Atlantic crossings doubtlessly took some of the flutter out of his wings, but Hallet is quick to acknowledge the sure hand of editor George Horace Lorimer, who for the next seventeen years, acted as literary counselor and physician. "Lorimer's motto was 'story above style.' He liked things well-written, but mere felicity of phrase would get you nowhere with him." Lorimer advised Hallet on composition and viable topics and turned down enough of his effusions to make him toe the mark.

In these postwar years a new note was rising in American literature, and it became clear that sultry queens of Zanzibar with blood-red rubies on their breasts were no longer on call. Hallet wheeled around for a sharper look at reality, now the mode, and sought to ensnare truth—that "sad hamperer of genius"—in less luxuriant locales and language. "Limping In" and "Everything in the Shop," for example, limn austerely the perils of wartime passage along the northern sea lanes. "To the Bitter End," "The Mountain and Mahomet," "Inspiration Jule," "The First Lady of Cranberry Isle," and "Bluebeard Shadrach" run their courses in an environment not specifically labeled but definably the Maine seaboard. Hallet's immediate invention was Hat Tyler, a powerful, brash, irascible captain of her own boat, and antecessor of Tugboat Annie. With her pindling husband Jed and a set of salty Down-Easters, she bustles through several risible predicaments. As a radiating center, Hallet provides the Tall Stove Club, a rendezvous where local legends are born and maturate. The pace and structure of these tales are relaxed, colloquial talk is dominant and effectively furthers the narrative and characterization. While Hallet was not falling in with the New Realism, he was assertedly in tune with a New Regionalism. This new feet-on-the-deck factuality was hearteningly recognized. Edward J. O'Brien singled out "To the Bitter End" as one of the best twenty American stories of 1919 and republished it in his annual volume. Among *The Best Short Stories of 1921* is listed "The Harbor Master," a tale of hapless passion which relentlessly entwines a solitary scapegoat over two generations.

A BACKWARD GLANCE

Hallet once took comfort in Pascal's observation that the men who write long books are those who will not take the time to write short ones. This may explain the surprising reversion of his 1922 novel, *The Canyon of the Fools*, a distinct throwback to the days of gold fever and copper mucking in Arizona, and to the ways of callow exuberance. This romance in the roughneck Southwest-Mexican border tradition boils over with familiar ingredients of the genre insofar as action, intrigue, landscape, love, and flashy types are concerned. The old overplus of pictorial description reappears and the narrator's viewpoint is unduly magnified.

Although Hallet culls a multitude of details from his own experience (several sections of this novel are reproduced with only scantling adjustments in his autobiography, *The Rolling World*), he gives freer rein to his daydreaming propensity than heretofore or hereafter. McCarty, who quickly earns the soubriquet El Romantico, declares unequivocally that "Realities were only the springboards from which I launched myself in long dives through the mellow ether of fancy." In the final analysis, one lays this book down with the nagging suspicion that it is a gigantic hornswoggle.

HEYDAY AT THE *POST*

By 1924 Hallet was back in the Lorimer sunroom. For the next dozen years, he appeared almost exclusively in *The Saturday Evening Post*, approximately fifty times. This represents his climb to glory through the medium he felt most at home in—the short story. He had by now, consciously and intuitively, worked out a credo and a craftsmanship best suited to his gifts. That these also suited George Lorimer and his enormous constituency of readers during the *Post*'s golden era is a happy convergence of appetites. From the mid-Twenties through the mid-Thirties, Hallet begot a trim, satisfying succession of short narratives. Several characteristics infiltrate all of them, some of the properties emerge and mature in a predictable cycle, but variety and a surpassing sense of the quixotic in human experience stamp these as capital instances of the storyteller's art.

The first subdivision of stories may be called encounters by the sea, uncoilings of events in an atmosphere of schooners and islands, rogue ships and the all-encompassing ocean. There is talk of silver mines in Patagonia, of India, and Chinese chop dollars, but they are incidental to the nearer dramas on board. Description serves stronger effects than mere picturism—the creation of mood or the substantive backing of action and character. A calm of composition reigns in both verbal expressiveness and narrative evolution. A more remarkable transformation, however, becomes manifest: the arena in which these actions transpire is no longer one of sparkling, devil-may-care masculinity but one of normal community interchange in which women are present as a matter of course and manage to preside by exercise of their natural sagacity. Most often, adventure is the foreground tincture, and resolution of an embroiled courtship, the overtone. Important too is the emergence of a saltwater Solon, usually an aged captain who has roamed all the seas and continents, and who saves the impulsive young from their follies.

The first in this brightest epoch of Hallet's career is "The Gulf Stream," which won O'Brien's tribute of three asterisks in *The Best Short Stories of 1924*. Others in this bracket are "A Streak of the Mule," "The Horoscope," and "The Cloud Shooter." Acute readers responded most vocally to "Gambler's Gold," wherein the hero blithely climbs ships' masts and swims a mile with $20,000 worth of gold dust snugged around his waist. One metallurgist gravely informed Hallet that such an encumbrance would weigh something like a hundred pounds. Hallet's only recourse was Herbert Spencer's rueful assertion that the greatest tragedy in nature occurs when a theory is slain by a fact.

The largest in number and most ample in substance are Hallet's score of stories about the Maine seacoast and its natives. No actual, and few fictive names are assigned to the shore hamlets, yet the aura of wharfs, ketches, gulls, bridge houses, coves, town meetings, checker games, fish aprons, and corncob pipes is inevasibly Maine. The Inlet recurs as a generic focalizing feature, as do the waterside kitchen and the church dance. Plot consists of adagio movements rather than hectic enterprises; actions indicate personality rather than being merely theatric. Violence is not totally eliminated; it more frequently happens offstage, and its reverberations bear less crucially upon the key issues. Authentic parlance meaningfully augments characterization, and there is no discursive narrator-persona. Disclosures of small mysteries or disentanglement of misunderstandings come about at the close with seeming inadvertence and with a shrug of good-humored chagrin. These Maine stories are ritualistic courtship' comedies enacted toward the consummation of a female-oriented domesticity. Men bluster, toss orders, and behave like masters of their fate, while women hold their peace, their tongues, and gain the final victories. Male reluctance or rebellion is of negligible avail; the result is unvaryingly the same: the female of the species, with a Gioconda smile, envelops the male in silken webbing.

Hallet's titles are slyly metaphoric: "The Kitchen Democrat," "Tame Crow," "The Winter Kill," "Husband in the Dark," "Tick-A-Lock Iron Bars," "A Bad Washing." "Foot-Loose" is perhaps the most exquisitely artful. Inch by inch and irrevocably, the cocksure seafarer is meshed in matrimonial bonds. "Bottomless Pond" is an extended analogy of the unfathomable depths of a woman's mind—at least to a rational man. In this story, Hallet touches fleetingly on a theme endemic in local-color fiction: the contrast of natives and outlanders.

In March 1928 Hallet was invited by the Secretary of the Navy to observe the western fleet in its Pacific maneuvers. He boarded the *California* at San Francisco and for the next three months shared the official ventures and made shift with a few of his own among the Hawaiians and Japanese. He had intended to write a comprehensive report of the trip but so many prohibitions were imposed on publication that he canceled his plan. Among these resplendent isles and titillating people, however, his addiction to the romantic was once more awakened.

On his return in June he retreated to a log cabin on a hilltop, over-looking the harbor and blocked out a dozen stories around the character of Captain Arad Wilkins, sending him on the good ship *Water Witch* from Salem to such parts as Honolulu, China, the Fiji Islands, Sumatra, the Caribbean, Chile, Manila, Morocco, and Zanzibar. Wilkins, a resourceful Yankee of the early nineteenth century, broke many a lance in the trade for pepper, horses, sandalwood, and birds' nests; tiffed with pirates, head-hunters, convicts, slavers, opium dealers, revolutionaries; and dallied with not a few dusky beauties. "Trader's Risks" was the first of this series to appear. "Misfortune's Isle," which revolves around a sensuous woman and a upas tree with lethal capacities, was (selected) for the O'Henry Memorial Prize Stories of 1930, and by another promi-nent anthology of contemporary short stories.

He turned then to the real, larger-than-life John L. Sullivan, idol of his college years. Around certain incidents in the life of pugilism's first world-known heavyweight champion, Hallet wove a sheaf of stories, three of which were published in the *Post*. By a method which may be called fictionalized factuality, Hallet revivified the Sullivan-Corbett bout, and intricated the popular ballad "Throw Him Down,

McCloskey" with one of Sullivan's early brawls. Best of the three, and Hallet's favorite among all his short stories, is "The Devil Takes Care of His Own," founded on Oscar Wilde's visit to Boston and his advocacy of a destitute resident sculptor, John Donoghue. In his lecture at the Music Hall—replete with sunflower in buttonhole—Wilde fulminated: "In young Dennis O'Shaughnessy [Hallet's pseudonym for Donoghue], of whom you know nothing yet, you have a man who can whip up the horses of the sun and yet know how to curb them. You have a man whose idlest thoughts are unborn bronzes, a man whose delicate fingers are brains, yet you prefer to adulate a brute whose brains are his fists." A committee of abashed civic-minded art lovers was formed, raised sufficient funds, and awarded Donoghue a carte blanche commission. The Homeric (and utterly true) irony is that Donoghue chose to do a statue of . . . John L. Sullivan.

Hallet's final stories in the *Post* are of the latter tradition. Major General Andrew Jackson, Washington Irving, and Jefferson figure in one; Daniel Webster in another; a third, "The Crowbar," introduces the book *Michael Beam* and the bitter question of sovereignty which afflicted state and federal banks in the early 1800s, a character and controversy Hallet expanded to novel length three years later.

MODUS OPERANDI

From the lengthy questionnaire Hallet diligently filled out for several books on writing, and numerous remarks in personal interviews, a reliable diagram of his literary ways and means may be drawn. He loved to write, did not write easily, but cannot think of anything else he would rather have done. He usually started at eight in the morning and stayed with it for five hours, more when he was going well. He composed in long-hand on legal-size yellow sheets, then typed a first draft. Thereafter began the painstaking job of revision, "three or four times, often next door to complete rewriting." He averaged two thousand words a day. Before initiating a story, he would research the materials meticulously; for *Michael Beam* he accumulated two reams of notes before setting down the first word.

Authorship, Hallet discovered, requires: 1) a perceptive eye— the ability to spot details and use them tellingly; 2) an empathetic heart—the power of suffering and exulting with one's characters; 3) an organizing brain—the skill to bring together and relate the elements of narrative in a satisfying pattern. To become a good writer, Hallet decided, one must travel extensively and yet must also remain at home: "I remember that once I went to the Crossroads of the World after an idea, and then came back and found it in Salem. But if I had gone to Salem in the first place, I wouldn't have found it there." He is in consonance with the view of Poe and T. S. Eliot that the act of creation should carry you out of yourself, make you "forget for a time the 'everlasting, tormenting' ego." One should read the classics for inspiration and guidance, and be on guard against his contemporaries, for the tendency is to simulate those you admire most: "I dogged Conrad nearly to my undoing."

Hallet sought to please himself foremost in the development of effects, yet he considered the potential reactions of his audience, for "stepping out of your own skin and into the skin of a reader" constitutes a valuable transaction in self-criticism. Although Hallet deferred to the formularies of his craft in a course on writing short stories which he gave at Bowdoin College in the winter of 1935–1936, he distrusted the implications of technique. Unavoidably, cultivation of particularized forms and methods leads to dehydration of natural expression and a surfeit of subtleties and complexities. In his estimation, technique ruined Henry James and debased the later efforts of Conrad and Kipling. To the aspiring writer Hallet offers this axiom: "A little technique is as good as a lot."

Prior to the writing of a story he mapped out a fairly definite sequence of events and a denouement. He found that the first-person point of view made for smoother narrative flow but for greater difficulty in compounding plot. Nonetheless, plot was not his cardinal concern; he utilized it to illustrate and intensify character. Indeed, plot often unfurled from character, as in "Foot-Loose," where the old man who predominates in the beginning practically disappears as the younger protagonists come to the fore. "A plot," says Hallet, "attracts facts and characters as a magnet attracts iron filings." Characters and action contribute reciprocally to the plot, quickening the pace and deepening the theme. To achieve optimum impact in a short story "it should be picked up like a puppy, a little bit ahead of the middle." Writing is essentially a lonely business, as Hallet himself often attests.

SLAPHAPPY HOLLYWOOD

In 1923, *The Canyon of the Fools* was purchased, filmed, and released in movie houses throughout the country. Featuring Harry Carey and Ethel Clayton, not inconsiderable stars of that time, it enjoyed a modest success at the box offices. Thereafter producers perused *The House of Craigenside*, "The Harbor Master," "Beyond a Reasonable Doubt," "The Figurehead," and "Gambler's Gold" for motion picture possibilities and, with elaborate unanimity, rejected every one. Not the least daunted, Hallet set out for California in November 1933 to hawk a scenario on the life of John L. Sullivan. He took up residence in Pasadena and received favorable publicity in the local and Los Angeles press. He called on studio after studio in the Celluloid City and made absolutely no headway against the impervious ranks of subordinates who prevented his dealing directly with key personages. So he tried other tacks. One of his scripts had been submitted to Darryl Zanuck. After an interval without news, Hallet implored his agent, "Let me have a talk with him personally." The agent shook his head morosely. "Zanuck doesn't see people." Nevertheless, he did arrange through a friend of a friend to waylay Zanuck at a polo game. When the climactic moment arrived, the friend of a friend, captain of Zanuck's team, "was boiled to the whites of his eyes. Zanuck was not ten feet away, but he might as well have been on the planet Mars."

HOME BASE

After Lorimer's retirement from the *Post* at the end of 1936, editorial policies and preferences underwent rather rapid change. The standard *Post* favorites developed by Lorimer over the past quarter-century found entry to the magazine less and less regularly. One by one they shifted to other sources or took up new mediums. Hallet began to freelance close to home. In 1937 he sold several features to the *Portland Press Herald*. "Windjammer," recollections of square-rigger days drawn from his journey on the *Juteopolis*, ran in ten consecutive issues. His tingling vocabulary, jaunty point of view, fetching anecdotes, and lucid exposition created a general demand for more. Before long he was engaged full time by the Gannett newspapers in Portland to write editorials and special features for the *Press Herald* and the *Sunday Telegram.*

Hallet plunged into his assignment with typical vigor and versatility. His editorials nipped at the state legislature for its action or lack of action on highway construction, industry, education, civic improvement, development of airfields and shipyards; he analyzed state politics, upheld Maine ships and shipbuilders, examined innovations at the four major Maine colleges, and re-evaluated the state's natural resources of lumber, potatoes, granite, lobsters, mineral deposits (aluminum, asbestos, gold), fish, game, and the tides at Passamaquoddy. He expatiated on finance, reviewed books, interviewed Fritz Kreisler and Gene Tunney, and revived forgotten fragments of Maine history, legend, and lore. He wrote about Walt Disney, about the filming in Maine of novels by Mainers, and about the native movie director John Ford; he scrutinized the career and works of Maine authors, including Harriet Beecher Stowe, Laura E. Richards, Edwin Arlington Robinson, Booth Tarkington, Kenneth Roberts, Ben Ames Williams, Mary Ellen Chase, E. B. White, and John Gould. For a time, his daily column appeared under the catchall title of "Maine Tide Rips." He did half-hour broadcasts over the Gannett radio station in Portland, during which he described special events and held palavers with celebrities in sports, politics, and the arts.

In 1938, Houghton Mifflin issued Hallet's autobiography, *The Rolling World,* a distillation of at least one hundred notebooks he had compiled on the run and of his unrecorded mercurial memories. In a panoramic, though not necessarily chronological unrollment of episodes, he reanimates his most lustrous moments at Mayflower Grove, in Canada, Australia, England, Hawaii, the American Mid- and Southwest, on the Atlantic in wartime, in France, and at the port of maximum sanctuary, Boothbay Harbor. With fire and love and sly self-deprecation, he retraces his circumambulations of the globe with dappled companions casually met. Max Miller said, "There is a lot of Joseph Conrad in Hallet, and a little of Jack London." Others collated him with Ulysses, Sinbad, Marco Polo, Davy Crockett, Mike Fink, Daniel Boone, Homer, Horace, Gauguin.

Of all the recommended worthies, Conrad and Ulysses bear closest affinity to the Hallet of the autobiography. The fury that ejaculated him from the static parish of a law office into the vortex of the world was the same that goaded young Marlow: desperate realization that he must snatch his chance, for to every man fate vouchsafes "Only a moment; a moment of strength, of romance, of glamour—of youth!" And, like Tennyson's wayfarer, the compulsion that kept Hallet going lay in his iron resolve "To strive, to seek, to find, and not to yield." The autobiography takes off at a spanking pace but slows to a ruminative pause every time Hallet returns to Boothbay Harbor. While in transit he avidly subjects his bookish preconceptions to the rasps of experience and howls gleefully as one disillusionment succeeds another. Immobile in Maine, he meditates on the ethics and intricacies of authorship, instructive, exploratory, profound without being ponderous. If this autobiography is sometimes intoxicated and sometimes parched, so is Hallet's life as he led it. So, indeed, is life.

Richard Hallet's response to this activation was *Michael Beam*, published by Houghton Mifflin in 1939. Although Hallet considers himself more capable in the short story form, he rates this novel as the best work he has done. True to his fashion, he amassed a thousand pages of notes before writing a page of text. The extent and precision of his research is perceptible in every detail of his place names, topography, flora, fauna, speech rhythms, descriptions of dress, artifacts, occupations, amusements, and in his grasp of prevalent ideas and attitudes. Upon these he overlays long intimacy with the outdoors, his knowledge of Indians, camping, hunting, trading, cruising, of the customs, the rough relationships, and the strategies of survival. And yet, for all this amalgam of lore and wisdom, he would have spawned another egregious blunder had it not been for his thirteen-year-old son. Hallet promised to help him build a cabin in the pine grove adjoining the house in Boothbay Harbor if the youngster would listen to him "talk out" the novel. Between the sawing and the hammering, this pact was sacramentally observed. At one exigent point in the plot, Dick junior remonstrated, "What, they only had one axe in the blockhouse?" Dick senior gulped, and inserted a mitigatory paragraph.

Michael Beam is a diorama of the American frontier's surge westward to the upper Illinois River; a hopeful epic of the founding of towns, the establishment of religion and the press; a bloody report on the subjugation of Indians; a tartan of stressful loves and loyalties. Michael—tough and tender, passionate and principled—is outlawed when he "takes a crowbar to the Constitution," smashing the door of the United States Bank at Chillicothe in defiance of Justice John Marshall's decree that no state bank may tax a federal bank. This is the act that triggers Beam's flight to the wilderness and the frenetic complications of love and war that ensue from his presence there. After Beam saves the life of Red Bloom, an enticing Indian girl, the states' rights issue recedes and is supplanted by a webwork of conflicts—racial, societal, familial, and personal. To the intransigence or resolution of these dissensions Hallet steadfastly bends his attention, while keeping the adventure at full tilt.

One agrees with Hallet that this book is the sum of his best writing. In fibrous and fitting diction, he delineates a virginal setting, populates it with characters devoid of quaintness, and engages them in actions well within their compass. The tempo is consistently brisk, the author entirely inconspicuous. Individual scenes rise superbly above the surface narrative, the most beautifully textured being Michael's first meeting with Red Bloom. Kenneth Roberts called Hallet "an artist in everything he does," and Ben Ames Williams paid the maximal compliment: "*Michael Beam* is a book to be read a sentence at a time." Six major studios evinced interest in the story but Hallet's Hollywood bugaboo held out. *Michael Beam* was never filmed.

PRO BONO PUBLICO

In the years preluding United States entry into World War II, Hallet campaigned in the Gannett newspapers for vocational training in secondary schools, for physical fitness, civil defense, and other aspects of preparedness. For his zealousness he was appointed to the Maine Port Authority, to the Maine State Defense Committee, and made Chairman of the Maine State Salvage Committee. His most durable contribution, however, was to point up the imperious need of an institute in Maine for the training of merchant marine. He secured the cooperation of Representative Ralph A. Leavitt of Portland, who introduced a bill in the Legislature for the establishment of such an institute in Castine; and so the Maine Maritime Academy came into being. Hallet was nominated 2nd Vice-President and served on the Board of Trustees for a decade. In the interstices between civic obligations he kept his hand in with stories about John L. Sullivan in *The Boston Sunday Herald* and *American Legion Monthly*, an essay in *Writer's Digest*, five in *The Christian Science Monitor*, half a dozen in *Technology Review*, and one in *Science Digest*.

In the 1938–1939 season, Hallet went on a lecture tour. He had several formal speeches prepared, "but mostly I wound up just yarn-spinning." One of his auditors wrote appreciatively of the "racy drawl, native mother wit, and acid scraps of philosophy." The University of Maine conferred upon Hallet in 1940 the honorary degree of Doctor of Letters in recognition of his "splendid achievements as an author who is closely identified with the State of Maine."

After the United States drifted irresistibly into war, Hallet was accredited as a correspondent with Admiral Nimitz's Pacific fleet. From April to August 1945 he sent back daily dispatches to *The Portland Press Herald* and *The Kennebec Journal* from Honolulu, Pearl Harbor, Kwajalein, Okinawa, Guam, Iwo Jima, the Marshall Islands, the Marianas, a number of infinitesimal atolls, and the cryptic "Somewhere in . . ." He described as much of naval operations as he was permitted, but the bulk of his reportage had to do with the condition, thoughts, and messages home of individual Maine men stationed in these areas. While on this tour, Hallet made particular pilgrimage to Ujae, a tiny island in the Marshalls sacred in his mind as the site of Uncle Will Jackson's legendary shipwreck. On her maiden voyage in 1883, the Bath ship *Rainier* struck an uncharted reef and went to pieces in a riotous sea. Under a blistering sun, using breadfruit trees as the frame, with planking and spikes from the ruined ship's decks, the redoubtable Jackson and his mates built a new ship, all the while ringed by naked cannibals whose king superintended the work with an empty Prussian needle-gun under his arm. Hallet's return to this site was memorialized in his final appearance in *The Saturday Evening Post*, "My Uncle's Footprints" (March 30, 1946), and in *Down East*, "The Wreck of the *Rainier*" (October 1954).

EARTHBOUND

Hallet published just two magazine fictions during the war: "The Trail of Bambi" in *Collier's* and "Dark Kingdom" in *Argosy*. His only other imaginative work was his last novel, *Foothold of Earth*, a teeming canvas of Maine spirit in the early war years. Into this book he poured the stored apperceptions of a full and kinetic lifetime. His protagonist, Jason Ripple, leads us through three separate but coexistent areas: the harborside, the farm, the high seas. Hallet was of course thoroughly steeped in all three levels, and his exposition of their figurations and influences is expert. While avoiding the clichés of local color voguism, he endows Roger's Inlet with a prodigal complement of physical details and inhabitants. We are immediately acclimated among rotting ships, doves hopping on roof shingles, humped footbridges, and the smell of sour oak; indoors, the aromas of gingerbread, apples, and frying eggs, or the pungency of sulphur, damp carpet, and shriveled flowers. We are inducted into mazy small-town interrelationships in which even juvenile speaking contests are fraught with the politics of inherited spite. Felicitously, Hallet sketches in all the specialties of color, sound, odor, speech, and costume to imbue his place with vitality and uniqueness.

After his return from the Pacific, Hallet's by-line graced the magazine section of the *Portland Sunday Telegram* over vivacious stories about tugboating, iron horses, Maine authors, civic prospects of Portland, native, birds and fish, industry, spring, lobsters, and legends. He wrote a series in the *Press Herald* on the histories of Maine rivers, and from November 1949 to June 1950 a daily installment of "The Story of Maine," a title he chose in order to elude the dull connotation of a formal history. Planned as a text for school children, it conjures interest through its pulsing characters and momentous encounters, "the blood and bone and skin and hair" of history, not its dreary dates and diplomacies. Yet there is no manhandling of facts; Hallet submits two years of research as warrant of its accuracy. Another encyclopedic project in the *Press Herald* was his "Men of Maine," a gallery of 130 biographical vignettes which ran from November 1951 to May 1952. Each segment of some five hundred words is enlivened by sprightly quotations and humanizing anecdotes about such Mainers as William King, General Henry Knox, Henry Wadsworth Longfellow, Elijah Lovejoy, Samoset, Edwin Arlington Robinson, Ferdinando Gorges, and Jeremiah Chaplin, Colby's first president.

In 1951, arthritis began incapacitating Hallet to the extent that he retired from the Gannett newspapers within a year. He composed thereafter four articles for *Yankee* magazine but reserved his major labors for *Down East*. Beginning with the first issue of this magazine in September 1954, he contributed thirty-four essays on the subjects of a gold hoax, destroyers, Bill Nye, Hannibal Hamlin, Kenneth Roberts and his water dowser, Senator Margaret Chase Smith, and another great Maine lady, opera singer Emma Eames, the last in August 1963. This seemed to mark the close of Richard Hallet's active career as a writer. But, like his own "man of many bells," he rang out plangently in May 1967 with an article on Sir William Pepperrell, also a Mainer and also indefeasible.

AFTERGLOW

Thoughtfully, Hallet abstracted the title of his autobiography from Alexander Smith's emblematic lines:

> *The soul of man is like the rolling world, One half in day, the other dipt in night; The one has music and the flying cloud, The other, silence and the wakeful stars.*

Until the terminal sentence of *The Rolling World*, Hallet wrestled with the riddle of identity. "Are they facts, or only shadows of my dream of living? Is the past a treasury of facts, or only the cradle of a dream? Who am I that sit writing of my battle with the facts? . . . flame-thrower . . . or the cuttlefish that squirts ink to throw a cloud round him and baffle his pursuers? . . . Nobody can answer that." Nobody. Least of all one's self.

> *AT ROAD'S END on Spruce Point in the afterlight of an autumn day, graying air settles elegiacally over the book-filled room. Echoes slide along the walls and expire in cushioned nooks. Momentarily the large man with blue eyes, now deepened to black, sits silent in an eddy of retrospection. Remembering red shacks at Canberra, John L. Sullivan, Canada, the belly of the Orvieto, Ujae, Lorimer, a monochrome law office, Arizona, Cambridge, a second-hand book stall, and Joseph Conrad in Youth: "A flick of sunshine upon a strange shore, the time to remember, the time for a sigh—and good-bye!—Night—Good-bye."*

NOTE

1. Learned Hand was a highly respected judge for more than fifty years after his graduation, like his clerk/secretary Hallet, from Harvard and Harvard Law School. Widely considered one of the most outstanding jurists never to reach the Supreme Court, Hand was first named to the U.S. District Court for the Southern District of New York in 1909, and then he became a judge and eventually chief judge of the U.S. Court of Appeals for the Second Circuit—initially by President Calvin Coolidge. He served on that court until he died in 1961. Hand delivered one of the most famous comments on liberty in 1944, during a celebration of I Am an American Day, at the height of World War II:

Liberty lies in the hearts of men and women; when it dies there, no constitution, no law, no court can even do much to help it. While it lies there it needs no constitution, no law, no court to save it. And what is this liberty which must lie in the hearts of men and women? It is not the ruthless, the unbridled will; it is not freedom to do as one likes. That is the denial of liberty and leads straight to its overthrow. A society in which men recognize no check upon their freedom soon becomes a society where freedom is the possession of only a savage few; as we have learned to our sorrow.

The spirit of liberty is the spirit which is not too sure that it is right; the spirit of liberty is the spirit which seeks to understand the minds of other men and women; the spirit of liberty is the spirit which weighs their interests alongside its own without bias.

EXCERPT FROM *THE ROLLING WORLD* (AN AUTOBIOGRAPHY)

by Richard M. Hallet

*After jumping ship (*Juteopolis*) in Sydney, Australia, in 1912, Hallet and his friend, Frank Hyde, went "on the wallaby"—walking, hiking, and canoeing through the back country to Canberra, taking any job they could find: sheep shearing, digging holes, breaking rock for new roads. Returning to civilization (in this case, Melbourne), down to their last five shillings, they landed in Mrs. Walters's rough lodgings in Little Collins Street. And Hallet, the fledging writer, saved the day.*

Hallet sold a series of articles about their adventures, titled "The Seaman's Book of Swag," to a Melbourne newspaper. Other than a short story ("The Handkerchief") he had sold to Cosmopolitan *magazine as a Harvard sophomore in 1909, Hallet's success renewed his confidence that he indeed might be a writer. A few days later, Hallet and Hyde took jobs as stokers on the steamship* Orvieto, *headed for London, and Hallet's account of working in the hold, with temperatures often hitting 140 degrees, produced "The Black Squad," purchased by the* Saturday Evening Post. *The graduate of Harvard and Harvard Law School never entered a law office.*

CHAPTER 5: THIRTY GOLD SOVEREIGNS

We came to Melbourne finally. By train, too, which was not quite in accordance with the terms of the wager. Our shirts were charred, but we still had our canes with ram's-horn handles, and the filmless kodak hanging by a strap from Frank's shoulder was the badge of our respectability. We lived high at first and spent all of Thomas Cook's money. Then, when we were down to our last five shillings, we went to lodge with a Mrs. Walters, in Little Collins Street. She was a severe, competent little woman with a very good head of hair and searching blue eyes. She had to make up her mind about a lodger the instant he presented himself; and she told us that she seldom made mistakes in a man's character.

"I knew the minute I saw you I could trust you," she said.

Frank Hyde told her that we were bullock-drivers and stake men, fresh from the capital city of Canberra. He completely enchanted her by confessing in a whisper that back of everything we were journalists from America.

"Not those American journalists!" she cried.

Yes. No other than those far-famed men, whose deeds would be known to the latest generations. Mrs. Walters was impressed. She was, to use Frank's phrase, transmogrified. She showed us our quarters. Mrs. Walters's lodgers lived in what had been a trolley-car barn, and the rails still ran in under big sliding doors; but there was a smaller door cut for lodgers who were smaller than trolley cars.

There were about twenty cot beds in there, and drunken sailors contested for these nightly, with severe and separate oustings. Mrs. Walters fed her lodgers in a little restaurant just across the street. Steak and kidney pudding, steak and kidney pie, ale and figs, made the staple of her diet. Pitchers of ale, brought in from the Rose of Australia bar, went sloshing up and down the long tables. It was all very homelike and companionable, but we didn't linger long at table that first day. We had other fish to fry.

We were journalists and we sought out the editor of the *Melbourne Argus*—the Hundred-Eyed. We offered him an option on our magnum opus, to be called "The Seaman's Book of Swag." He closed with us at once, and gave us, to bind the bargain, a hundred sheets of typewriting paper.

A typewriting agency agreed to rent us a typewriter for our five shillings, but it required references, and we were forced to take our troubles to the American Consul. I have forgotten his name, but I am certain that his reception of us was kindly, though a trifle non-committal. Consuls are chopping blocks in a vagabonding era. He took the journalist story with just the right pinch of salt, too, because, although he offered me a pair of shoes, he was forced to say that he really didn't know us from Adam, and certainly couldn't identify us as correspondents of the *New York Herald*.

Just in the nick of time—because he was on the point of deciding that the proper course for a diplomat was to show us the door—I spied on his desk a fat book known to me of old. It was a Harvard catalogue. Making up that catalogue used to be one of my jobs when I was inching my way through Harvard. Our Consul was a Harvard man.

Epic moment! Romantic and practical moment too, important for literature—my kind of literature—because if it had not arrived, I should not have got that typewriter into my hands. And as the pen was once mightier than the sword, so now the typewriter is more potent than the tank. The Consul convinced himself that he was standing in the presence of another Harvard man, and he went with me to the agency and vouched for me. He dubbed me journalist at last and put the working tools of my profession into my hands.

The agency's boy followed me through Melbourne streets, dragging the typewriter on a little truck. When he came to my residence, the car barn, he whistled low, but he had had his orders. He left the typewriter with me, and I found a box to perch it on. Now I was happy. The great cat of letters lolled on a narrow bed, waiting for the mouse of literature to come out of its hole.

And the mouse came out, and looked at me, and went back into its hole again. I knew what I wanted to say, and still I couldn't say it. I agonized, and fished round in the chaos of things unbegun. Was it true, as Emerson had said, that thought was only a pious reception? Or was it more practically the sweat wrung from action?

I knew only that the lightning flash of an immortal thought must precede the rolling thunder of a mighty line; and I was stopped on the threshold. I never did find out the secret of the glib literary mechanism. Is it posture? Mark Twain used to write lying in bed, fresh from sleep and while the dew was on the rose. But then David Graham Phillips wrote at midnight, standing up to a high reporter's desk. Is it temperature? Bossuet composed his "Funeral Orations" in a cold room, with his feet in a tub of cold water—on the principle, I suppose, that if the blood was driven out of his feet, it had a better chance to find his head. And ideas, naturally, swim in the blood; the brain is only the anvil where they take their final shape. Is it odors? Schiller wrote "Wilhelm Tell" with an apple rotting on his desk.

As for "The Seaman's Book of Swag," it struggled to the light under a heavy cloud of British shag—that "infinite tobacco," Carlyle's receipt—and under a cloud of oaths directed at me, for my noisy chattering, by fellow-lodgers who came staggering in from the port of Melbourne at any and all hours. But my partner stood guard, and the work proceeded.

Every afternoon we went into the Rose of Australia bar to drink beer and chat with the barmaid, whose great hero was Ned Kelly the bushranger. Kelly had been kind to the poor and had worn boilerplate around his chest. He knew how to ghost too. Romantic girls served him in the capacity of bush telegrams and tipped him off when the police were near.

"He was a proper man, Ned Kelly," our barmaid told us.

When he was caught at last and turned off, it was here in Melbourne jail, and turnkeys would still show you the black beam from which Ned Kelly swung. On his way to execution, sobbing women besieged him and pelted his coach with white roses.

As for the black beam from which he swung, we ran into an old friend of ours who had lately been living and working in its shadow. This was our friend, the port bos'n of the *Juteopolis*. Coming out of the Rose of Australia, we found him sitting on the sidewalk, begging, with his poor silver-spotted hands thrown all out of joint, and his mustache no longer clotted with molasses.

"'elp a poor sailor, sir, that's just out of jail," he moaned.

We stared. The mighty seaman who had ruled the port watch, the whole ship, with a rod of iron crouched at our feet, crying piteously that the wire poison had struck through his blood and crippled him.

"Bos!" we cried.

He got up with a lithe, easy motion, and took our hands in a crushing grip. He was a little fatter than he had been on the high seas; but the silver spots of him were unchanged, and his beautiful red eyes still had their famous glare. His health was never better, he said; and he turned back with us into the Rose of Australia and drank beer thirstily.

By fits and starts, we got his story. Like ourselves, he had jumped the ship in Sydney. Having shivered that cold month at sea, running down the easting, he stole the Captain's over coat as he was leaving, and sweated with it under tropic suns, staggering north to Newcastle, and, like ourselves, crossing water to confound the dogs. Safe in Newcastle, he had shipped out for Freemantle on the West Coast. His month in Freemantle he had spent in jail—for what crime he couldn't say, unless it was the crime of being a sailorman ashore. Next he had shipped on a coasting brig for Melbourne, and coming ashore here to this very Rose of Australia bar, had fallen again into the hands of the police, and was just now out from doing his customary month in Melbourne Jail, under the black beam.

"How do they do a man in there?" we asked the bos'n secretly; for the shadow of the place had fallen on ourselves now, since we owed Mrs. Walters more than we could pay.

"It's all right. The guards are grafters," the bos'n said. In Australia a grafter is a man of sterling principle, a prince.

"How's the food?"

"Boscar."

The food then was good.

"How heavy are the mauls?"

"Ten pound."

Ten pound. Mere splinters. We told the bos'n scornfully that in the back blocks we had swung fourteen-pound mauls.

"Fourteen pound! That'll make the skin of your hand slip like a bloomin' glove," the bos'n said aghast.

It was marvelous and a little unnatural to be standing here, man to man, beard to beard, talking on equal terms with the great man under whose frown we had quaked for so many months. We felt constrained and a little abashed to touch on money matters with the bos'n; but we did finally pluck up and ask him if the begging yielded a satisfactory return.

"Gor bli' me, no," he said. "A beggar's got no standing 'ere at all."

"Then why don't you ship out?"

There were no ships in the port of Melbourne, the bos'n said. Or none except a French brig, and the bos'n couldn't speak the language of the frogs. He cried out that he was headed for the jail again, as fast as ever his two feet could carry him; and more docile than we had ever dreamed of seeing him, he agreed to come along and share our lodging.

But by now, although the manuscript of "The Book of Swag" was piling up, so was our debt to Mrs. Walters. We used to go in and yarn with her of an evening. We told her stories of the duck-billed platypus that we had found and made a pet of, on the banks of the Murrum-bidgee; and of the ship's pig that ate flying fish and sprouted wings of its own and flew away. We told of the fifteen-foot carpet snake that had crawled out of the belly of a dead bullock by moonlight and held us in a trance with its weavings; and of the tiger snake that Frank had killed with a paddle. We told tales of the *Juteopolis* and of the albatross with twelve-foot wingspread that had hung off the mizzen yard ready to puncture our skulls with its pink beak; and of how we had caught it on a codline baited with pork. We had one of its wing bones with us now, and Frank brought it out for Mrs. Walters's inspection.

"You and your stories!" Mrs. Walters said. "Fair words butter no parsnips."

Her insight amounted to clairvoyance. Fair words. Her blue eye struck its frost into our veins. Fair words, was it? It began to look as if she might have to take her pay in just that currency. I had suddenly sick-ened of fair words myself and had to lash myself to the least sentence. The whole composition had gone flat and wrote itself against the grain.

Now, too, when we sat at Mrs. Walters's table, we had the bos'n to think of as well as ourselves. We hadn't produced him, of course. The ice was too thin, and he stayed in the car barn with his back to the wall. We smuggled over to him sultana rolls, split lengthwise with our sheath knives, and filled with scraps of meat, tasties from the steak, and kidney pudding.

And the bos'n was grateful to us. He never once left the shelter of the car barn. We had got a paper-covered novel for him called "Belinda's Passion," and he lay propped on an elbow, reading it through a pair of much-taped hexagonal spectacles. As fast as he read a leaf, he tore it off; in this way he never lost his place. "Belinda's Passion" dwindled and dwindled and got kicked and scuffed around the car barn. The bos'n's lips moved, shaping the scarlet words. He breathed stertorously, chewed the ends of his red mustache, and dripped sweat into his red brows.

Everything now hinged on the success or failure of "The Book of Swag." And it was growing plainer and plainer to me that that magnum opus was as heavy as a fig pudding. I was finding bitter truth in that

Italian proverb that words are women, deeds are men. Words were coy and resisted new arrangement. Thinking, when it was not a pious reception, was much more like pulling a cat along by its tail.

The agency rescued me at last. The week was up, and the agency sent its boy with his truck, and instructions to get five shillings more, or take the typewriter away. He took the typewriter, and I finished twenty pages of "The Book of Swag" in longhand.

I took this child of my flagellated brain—that diseased sweetbread, Frank called it—to the office of the Hundred-Eyed. *The Argus.* Is there a better name for a newspaper than that? I felt all its hundred eyes on me, when the associate editor reached for my manuscript.

"Young man, I can only say I hope you've turned the trick," he said.

In exactly twenty-four hours, he passed it back to me with a relinquishing gesture.

"You didn't quite turn the trick," he murmured regretfully. He, personally, had read the thing with pleasure, but the editor had come a cropper over it. "He thinks it's too colloquial."

The associate—he was in a red and blue striped blazer and cricket cap and was just departing for the cricket field—leaned towards us and whispered, "He's rather a solemn ass, you know."

He looked enormously relieved to have this judgment of his immediate superior off his chest. A solemn ass. The associate had told nobody else. It was no doubt a great accommodation to him to have us lend him our ears for this pronouncement—but it put no florins in our pockets. Buttered no parsnips, in short.

We felt the shadow of the Black Beam of Ned Kelly floating over us, but there was another shot in our locker. There was another newspaper in Melbourne, the *Melbourne Herald and Weekly Times*. The editor proved to be an American, from Detroit, and he promised us a decision by the next night.

We didn't go back to Little Collins Street. We didn't dare. Mrs. Walters would be sure to nab us now. The news of our rejection by the Hundred-Eyed must have run like a fluid into every nook and cranny of the city. People were whispering behind their hands at the discomfiture of the celebrated journalists.

"There they go. That's them with the ram's horns screwed to their waddies. Claiming to be rock men, and one day breaking rock used them up. Fourteen-pound hammers were too heavy for them. They'll get a chance at ten-pound hammers now. Journalists my eye! They're bloody himpostors. Jail's too good for them."

We slept on a wharf-end and spent the next day in the Melbourne Public Library. I sat in an alcove reading "Gulliver's Travels" and thinking about ten-pound hammers. We wondered what the bos'n might be doing. Not eating, surely, any more than we ourselves.

At five o'clock we were sitting across the desk from our editor, who sat gauging us and smoking his bulldog pipe in little sips. There was an apple on his desk, left over from lunch; and the eyes of the journalists were chained, enslaved by the childish appeal of that red apple.

Then the editor dropped his bomb.

He said: "I like this stuff of yours. It's damned excellent, that goes without saying. But on the other hand, gentlemen, you must realize that out here in the Australian bush, so to speak, we can't pay New York prices, nor even London prices."

Prices! We were talking price! I looked at Frank, and he was looking down his nose, like a man turned to stone. I thought that he might blow the gaff, and I muttered idiotically that we might be willing to listen to Australian prices. I felt a flush all over me, like a girl at her first ball.

And here's a curious thing. If the editor had rejected me, I should have spoken evil of him—on the sidewalk. But he had accepted me, and I felt that I ought to warn him that his judgment had gone galley-west, that the whole business was a swindle. I was nearer a jailbird than a journalist, and I felt like shouting out to him that if he bought this manuscript, he was liable to lose his job.

But I got hold of myself. If he wanted to pay a couple of pounds for it, that would clean us up with Mrs. Walters, and nobody the wiser. Or say three pounds. I inched up on him mentally and decided to make a last-ditch stand for three pounds. Yes, it would have to be three pounds or jail.

And then the editor put his pipe down on the desk with a definitive little click.

"Thirty pounds is our top for this material," he announced in a conversational tone. "After all, gentlemen, we are a young country."

A young country. Was there no stronger word in English? Young! Glorious! Golden! Thirty pounds! No wonder they shod their horses with golden horseshoes. I was afraid the elephant (tattooed) on Frank's belly might run amok, and I didn't dare to look at him.

"Thirty pounds is ample," I said softly.

The editor shot me a beam out of his sympathetic blue eye.

"We shall be very glad to print you," he said.

The time never was before, and never came again, when just this feeling of hilarious triumph flooded through me to the marrow-bones. Sam Johnson had written a piece to pay for his mother's funeral, but then, win or lose, there would have been a funeral. I had written myself out of jail and made partly good the most colossal of Frank's lies. I was a journalist at last, and when everything was on a shoestring too. I wanted to throw myself on that man's neck, and still I couldn't risk being too effusive. I mustn't let him see that a mere matter of thirty pounds could blow the man down. I tried to think how a journalist would act who had sold a story to the papers.

I heard my editor saying, "I should imagine you've had a lot of fun doing this thing. What I like about the stuff, it's free and easy. It's colloquial."

Colloquial. It's a pity the Hundred-Eyed couldn't have been dragged in there on his belly to listen to that word. But I was too transmogrified even to appreciate his praise of "The Seaman's Book of Swag." I couldn't think later how I had got out of that man's presence, but I found myself in the Rose of Australia bar, drinking with Frank, and poking crackers through the cockatoo's cage bars.

We came out of our delirium far enough to remember the bos'n, and we went back to the car barn. He was still there but looking ravenous.

"Gawd strike me blooming well blind!" was all he said when we showed him the thirty golden sovereigns.

We took him into Mrs. Walters's restaurant. It was the clear quill, as they say in my native State of Maine. She didn't speak, but she watched our every mouthful. The bos'n ate his steak and kidney pie with relish and washed it down with ale. Gape and swallow, as John L. Sullivan used to say.

Mrs. Walters sat perfectly still, with her knees under the cash box table. She had resigned herself to think that for once she had been mistaken in her reading of a lodger's character. And then I stood before her and showed her the thirty golden sovereigns stacked in two stacks in the palm of my hand.

"You and your sovereigns," she said, and flashed a look at us out of the corner of her eye. She thought we had cracked a crib, but all the same her faith in human nature had come back.

"There is still corn in Egypt, ma'am," my partner said. He looked as if he had done nothing all his life but feed sugar to the ponies.

"I said from the beginning that you two gentlemen were grafters," Mrs. Walters said. She used grafters of course in the fine Australian sense, but the word did strike a little chill through us. Her total bill was two pound ten, and we gave her three sovereigns and our blessing.

"I suppose you'll be shipping out again," she said. "There's a ship docked today at the Steam Packet Navigation Company's docks."

THE BOOK OF SWAG

An Overland Cruise: Sailors on the Wallaby

From the *Melbourne Herald* (July 26, 1913)

(This is the account of the adventures by road and river in Australia of two Americans, who, "for to admire, and for to see, for to behold this world so wide," shipped before the mast from their native land, and travelled from Sydney to the Murrumbidgee [river], carrying their swags. What they saw on the journey is here set down for the enjoyment of those others, stay-at-homes or wanderers, who have resisted or yielded to the invitation presented to every man at least once in his life—"The Call of the Open Road.")

NO. XIV

Then, harsh necessity, we went to work. The job was on top of a mountain where two circular reservoirs were being sunk. Porthos [Frank Hyde, Hallet's sailing mate] got us this job, and I remember his coming back, consequential as a turkey cock, and saying in voice of brisk finality, as of one who has done a thing, and done it up brown, that he had "fixed" it for the two of us at nine bob a day.

THE GANGER'S HOMILY

It was a monstrous climb. We went up with the "ganger [foreman]," who swung along at the easy gait of custom. He was talking about Sydney, and how he used to be a navvy [laborer] there, and loved fast horses, and played his money on the races. Easy come, easy go. Some men never conquered the weakness, but he had, and see where he was now. Well, see where he was now. He had certainly attained a high position: you could say that for him. Little gasps, chortles, served him for all answer, and he went on. The path became a sheep trail; the sheep trail ended in a vast side hill of broken rock. The ganger sprang along on magic heels.

At length, dirty, disheveled, heaving, we jumped down into the rockbound circle of granite where we were to work. First, we were set to filling rotten-bottomed little drays with dirt and chipped granite. This was easy; we recovered breath. But then the ganger appeared at the edge of the pit, and swung down two gleaming yellow-handled mauls, and advised us to break up the stone a bit, to "make it easier put into the cart." Thus, speciously, we were introduced last to the real Botany Bay, and came to grips with the last turn that human toil can take—breaking rock.

SMITING THE ROCK

This rock was the healthiest of granite; it had no grain, no crack in it. The maul was not a formidable thing at first. It weighed fourteen pounds when I began to use it; but it went ahead in a ratio truly geometric.

"Aha," I thought to myself, "this is the real thing at last. This is Might, this is Toil;" and the ringing of the maul fell on my ears Titanic, and indeed I was become a Titan.

I felt like that recumbent picture of brawn which customarily heads an article on commerce. The broken granite gleamed in black and gray; all about me other men were smiting, bronzed arms lifting in air, the mauls falling, ringing, rising and again falling on the impenetrable stuff. There were perhaps a dozen navvies in the pit, gray-shirted, impervious, silent and hard as the very stone they wrought in. Some were huge, and some were not; but one and all the mauls swung in a tireless, machine-like unison, the granite fell into gleaming fragments, edged like a saw.

"Granite," as Porthos said gloomily, "that you could polish into as pretty a tombstone as a man would care to have over his head."

Meantime, I hammered and hammered at one vast fragment that defied me. Never a crack appeared in its powdered surface; I might as well have tried to halve Gibraltar. I began a little wildly to rise up on my toes and swung the maul almost in a full circle. Each blow that landed stunned me to the heart; the song of the maul rang continuous in my ears; but the rock remained intact.

After a time, I felt the whole palm of my hand slip; and a stream of blood ran down the handle. If I could not break rock, it seemed I could break blisters; and so, begun, that work at least went nobly on. At length one of the navvies took pity. "A new chum," thinks he, and sidles over to me, where I stood exhausted over the metal, sweat blinding me.

THE THICK OF IT

"Let's lift 'er, a bit, mate," says he, "if you don't mind?"

He waited in a subtle spirit, to see whether his suggestion of aid might not have fallen on the long ears of professional conceit.

"Right-O!" I gladly said, and we bent and prized the thing over. He fumbled about for a small stone, in a leisurely way, and there he had one edge of the confounded thing over vacancy.

He took the maul and began on the one spot with slow disinterested strokes. "Hunh—hunh"—with each stroke he grunted; the air came so out of his lungs with the least effort. He seemed not to think—yet all at once he said. "Rome wasn't—hunh, hunh—built in a day." Stroke. Stroke. He didn't care if it never cracked. This was precisely how a navvy was paid to serve a stone. If it wouldn't come in pieces at this, it would have to be drilled and fused. That was all. Stroke. Stroke. The rock parted—he turned over the larger of the pieces and began upon that without comment. I watched him a moment. He was not as large as I; seemed no heavier; yet he would go on at this gait for maybe thirty years yet—shivering granite under blazing suns. He had not even any respite of loading the cart; his job was breaking stone, and he broke stone. It was no mental effort for him; he knew precisely what to anticipate, what "slant" to take at it. Every muscle in his forearm knew and leaped with the direction of the maul, and he had grained himself into the work as all these atoms, black and gray, had grained themselves into the granite.

THROUGH THE MILL

It is a trade to grow up in, navvying; seasoned timber will alone avail. But hah, the bitter seasoning; that period of slender and exulting youth which must be blasted, as the very rock is blasted, by the initial stages of their toil. The hardening will come; something obdurate and flint-like in the body; but by then the spirit, too, will have hardened, and come by slow degrees into the bald and impenetrable condition of the remorseless stone itself. The driver of the dray was in that early stage; a youth of nineteen, with lean, corded arms; strong with a forced maturity of strength. He looked at my hands, flooded with blisters, torn with false holds taken on rotten granite.

He said, "Your hands'll be sore in the morning. Them's terrible lookin' hands. Mine used to be that way. But you get 'em hard."

He spread his out, and they were indeed hard. He could light a match and burn it out in the center of his palm without pain.

STONE-DRILL

"Your back'll be sore, too," he went on, "an' your neck, an' your arms. You'll be sore all right: You won't see 'ow you're goin' to get another day through. You'll wish t' hell one o' them stones had dropped on yer today, tomorrow, you will. I did. It's a 'ard gyme, navvyin' is."

He turned his face, a boy's face, a mere oval, brown, beardless, glinting with soft down, towards the sun; his heavy wandering blue eyes filled with a kind of satisfaction. "It's nearly noon," he said.

Respite! He lived for these times when he might drop his maul and jump out of the pit. But this was only the seasoning; another year or two and there would be no movement in his soul, with the dropping of the picks and mauls; and in some far time, he might clamber out of life itself as he clambered now out of this pit, and look about him with dead eyes at some space that might be splendid beyond mortal dreams. For by then he would be a man no longer; but a thing that could swing a maul more cleverly than yet devised machines, the gleaner among rock, the irreg-ular, the bit of human filler which no fertility nor deftness of thought will ever do away with quite in the hard amalgam of civilised results.

THE TOLL OF TOIL

We had lunch at a shilling each at Ruddy's—soup, beans, mutton, and rice with syrup.

"Sticks to the ribs," said a wild and blue-eyed engineer of this last. And the stuff gleamed fair as dawn on his wan moustache. By this time, I could hardly lift a knife and fork, let alone a maul; and a bearded old navvy, who had his camp nearby in an angle of stone, gave us liniment out of a bottle "to soften 'em up," he said.

It softened 'em up right enough; you could have dissolved granite in it. We went back to it again; but the afternoon went poorly enough. The sun sank; the pit, which had been at white heat all day, filled with cool shadow. Then the thought struck me to go up and tumble down a few rocks edging the pit, and I did this. One of them bounded about six inches over the head of another rock, whereupon an antique drill-man, wrinkled as a sheep, stopped his maul, and said, losing nothing of his phlegm:

"'Ey, myte, I don't want ter cross yer, but 'ave you any flamin' wish to go up in little pieces?"

I disclaimed any such flaming wish.

"Tyke a look at that 'ere rock," he said, and I took a look at the rock I had just missed. A white fuse curled out of the top of it.

"One little jar, an' 'eavenward we go," said the drillman.

He spat on his hands and—hunh—hunh—he was off again. He seemed to suggest that one place would do as well as another; whole or parted, in big or little pieces, he cared not for himself. He was altruism in his kind advice.

As for me, I came very cautiously down, and began to shovel loose stone into the dray; I found no more innovations for the job.

RELEASE

When the shadow reached the water tank, the ganger said, "Go home," in a loud voice, and the gray navvies gathered their tools, and climbed out silently, lighting pipes, drawing on coats, gazing, thoughtfully into the sun. We went a little way down the mountain and sank down on a stone. We looked at one another with glazed eyes, smoked, basked in the red sun. Suddenly the top of the mountain exploded like a volcano; a rain of small stone fell around us. The ganger was getting off his night shots. Presently, he joined us.

"Blowed?" says he.

"Blowed," says Porthos.

"Aye," says he, "It's not too good, this. I've 'ad navvies out 'ere wot was professionals from Sydney, rock-men as I know could swing a maul; and they wouldn't sty 'arf an hour. 'Not good enough,' says they, and down the mountain with 'em."

"It's down the mountain for us," says Porthos.

"Goin' to quit?" says the ganger curiously. "You did all right today."

"Here today, and gone tomorrow," says Porthos. "Look at these hands. Yes, something whispers faintly in my chest that I've looked my last on that hole up there. Look at those hands."

"Good Lord," said the ganger. "Them is hands."

"They was," said Porthos. "Twenty-two," he prompted the ganger's count of blisters. "I'm a moving ruin," he said.

A FAREWELL VOW

We got down somehow, tumbled into the boat and slept, too tired to cook supper. We slept until noon next day, side by side, logs. We had begun to come to before that, moved, groaned, and postponed the waking point. When we did awake, we collected our day's wages, slid in the boat, and began to paddle feebly away from that mountain. As we limbered up a little, we paddled desperately away from it. By noon we had it in a green haze, and by night in a purple one.

We took a solemn oath over the pancakes not to commit a crime, neither to kill a sheep. strangle a turkey, nor lift a bag from the river's bank. For in Australia the convict—so our information ran—does but one thing—he breaks stone.

(To be Concluded.)

POSTSCRIPT

Hallet's series of fifteen articles, titled "The Book of Swag," was published in the *Melbourne Herald* nearly a year after he left Sydney on the ship *Orvieto*, a 554-foot twin-screw steamship, for London in 1912. Beginning June 12, 1913, they were published through July 26, 1913. The full series of articles is available on Trove, the online service of the National Library of Australia: *https://trove.nla.gov.au/search/category/newspapers?keyword="the%20book%20of%20swag"&sortBy=dateAsc&l-title=1190*

A BATH BOY WHO IS MAKING A NAME
IN THE FIELD OF LITERATURE

Richard Matthews Hallet.—An Account of His Wanderings
and Adventures and of His Work With the Pen
Now Bringing Him Fame

Early newspaper article about Hallet's rising literary fame.

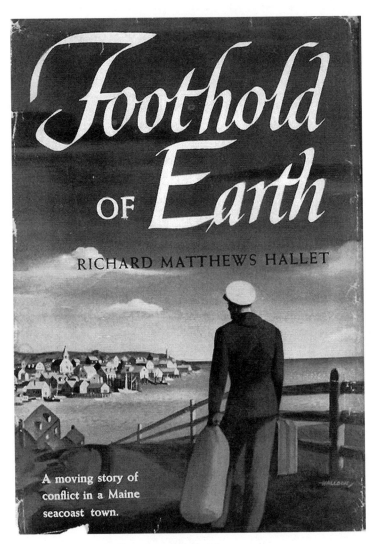

foothold
of Earth

RICHARD MATTHEWS HALLET

A moving story of
conflict in a Maine
seacoast town.

The cover of Hallet's last novel.

Hallet (left) and fishing companions Lowell Thomas (noted broadcaster) and Commander Donald McMillan (famous explorer). (*Collections of Maine Historical Society*)

Hallet at five years of age. (*Courtesy of Susan Hallet Witt*)

The boxer John L. Sullivan.

Judge Learned Hand.

Illustration of the four-masted, 310-foot steel barque *Juteopolis*, owned by the American Oil Company, which Hallet sailed on to Australia. (*Courtesy of South Australian Maritime Museum*)

Illustration of the *Orvieto*, a two-stack, 554-foot, twin-screw steamship that carried 350 passengers. (*Courtesy of South Australian Maritime Museum*)

Frontispiece illustration to the Hallet novel *Trial by Fire*.

"He made no effort to stir up the men against the old man. . . . But they all knew that death hung over that ship." Illustration for Hallet's "On a Calm Sea" in the *Saturday Evening Post*.

"It looked like a fatal blow to my prestige when it appeared that I must come ashore on the shoulders of a squat, muscular Marshallese." Illustration for Hallet's "My Uncle's Footprints" in the *Saturday Evening Post*.

Hallet at a copper mine in Arizona.

Richard Willis (Will) Jackson. (*Collection of Editor*)

Harvard Law School graduation, 1910. (*Courtesy of Susan Hallet Witt*)

Mary Holton Hallet. (*Courtesy of Susan Hallet Witt*)

Richard Hallet and family in Boothbay Harbor, 1936. (*Courtesy of* Portland Press Herald)

Published Weekly

The Curtis Publishing Company

Cyrus H. K. Curtis, President
C. H. Ludington, Treasurer and Treasurer
J. Martin, General Business Manager
William Boyd, Advertising Director

Independence Square, Philadelphia

London: 6, Henrietta Street
Covent Garden, W.C.

THE SATURDAY EVENING POST

Founded A°D¹ 1728 by Benj. Franklin

Copyright, 1917, by The Curtis Publishing Company in the United States and Great Britain

George Horace Lorimer
EDITOR

Churchill Williams, F. S. Bigelow,
A. W. Neall, Associate Editors

Walter H. Dower, Art Editor

Entered at the Philadelphia Post-Office as
Second-Class Matter

Entered as Second-Class Matter at the
Post-Office Department
Ottawa, Canada

Volume 189   PHILADELPHIA, FEBRUARY 10, 1917   Number 33

THE HOUSE OF CRAIGENSIDE

By Richard Matthews Hallet

ILLUSTRATED BY HENRY RALEIGH

Behind the Rusty Pendulum Was a Little Pug-Nosed Idol of Green Jade

HIS house of the Craigenside had loneliness and terror written plain on its pillared front—for it is certain that houses, whether by chance or of design, do convey something of the mysteries of human expression. It was a solid, four-square house, flanked by funereal cedars, and bearing on its roof and within its pediment a quantity of ship's scrollwork. The pediment itself was supported by six marvelous, fluted pillars with ornamented capitals; and in front of each of these pillars crouched a teakwood dragon, with mouth wide open and battered wings half raised. These were the spoils of one of Jared Craigen's last adventures in the East; and they formed a guard very suitable for a house of that tradition.

The ground in front of the house had been graded into terraces, which descended to the river's bank, and were connected by short flights of stone steps, worn monoliths which the action of frosts had cracked and upheaved from mossy beds.

The house sat fairly on the six feet of a grassy dune, with Hedley's River flowing past on one side and the sea encroaching on the other. Thus the view everywhere was of water and sand, and more water and more sand. The sand appeared to copy the action of the water, as if the same sad devils of unrest had prompted it, and so it took the shape of ribs and ripples where the water teased it into animation, and farther inland reared it in sharp, white, sphinxlike mounds, whose crests and curves reflected with strange faithfulness the lineaments of the winds which fled across them. Made up of material blown about and sorted by the wind, these glittering Æolian drifts were never constant, and so the coast could never establish itself in equilibrium with their activities.

The prevailing winds in Dockport blew, at the time of which I

dunes encroached on that house of doubtful omen. They allied themselves with the winds to form sand blasts which poured against the hand-carved seraphim on the roof and rendered the expressions on those wooden faces indecipherable. In tiny grains and invincible atoms the sand sifted in upon those sunken floors. It was hurled through cracks in the splintered paneling of the great front door, and found a resting place in the folds of Oriental stuffs which hung within. It rattled into the maw of the huge fireplace in the sitting room, fled into the wide mouths of two old brass-mounted dueling pistols which lay crossed on the mantelpiece, and was prevented from insinuating itself between the window sashes only by means of huge rolls of red cloth stuffed with sand and laid close to the panes.

"It takes sand to fight sand," Mercy Cobb said gloomily to me one day with a glance out of the window at the menacing dunes. "They are coming to snatch at my old body," she would add in lower tones, "like raveling hounds, but I'll defeat 'em or I'll yet. Not that it makes a difference to me where men lay my old bones when I am done with them—and the Lord have mercy on my soul that day—but I vow I have sat here so long looking at them that I have an appetite against them, as some people have an appetite against onions."

She sat there, as almost always, in a great rocking chair with a wide horsehair back. She was a stern little old lady with an implacable nose and sallow features. She dressed always in some stiff black material that shimmered, that crackled. She was an old lady cramped into a beetle's case. On her head she wore a flat black ribbon fashioned into a knot exactly square. Like the lady in a hideous old crayon portrait which hung yellowing in the hall, she wore on her withered lip a slight but perfectly defined black mustache.

Front page of the February 10, 1917, edition of the *Saturday Evening Post* featuring the Hallet story "The House of Craigenside," in the first of four parts. (*Courtesy of SEPS; Curtis Licensing, Indianapolis, Indiana*)

Hallet in Mexico. (*Courtesy of Susan Hallet Witt*)

Hallet enjoys time with his granddaughter Susan at his home in Boothbay Harbor.
(*Courtesy of Susan Hallet Witt*)

Cover of Hallet's autobiography, *The Rolling World*.

BEYOND THE TIDES

From *Harper's* (May 1913)

Colorful story of an elderly sea captain watching—and deciding to do something about—the decay and imminent demolition of his ship of five decades in a Down East harbor, now drawing more attention as the subject of a painting by a young artist. The artist's focus on the decrepit ribs and rot of the old ship contrasts with the captain's memories of her early construction and glorious, full-rigged voyages—and his own determination to even the score.

Old Captain Hodges, sitting in Gardner's Sea-Grill, gazed stonily through wrinkled window-panes on a cold November harbor. There were three or four others in the Sea-Grill, but this solitariness or inner vision of Captain Hodges had struck them silent. They seemed waiting nervously for the return of the spirit to its worn clay, even questioning if it would come back at all.

By his silences, his brief bullyings, his foreign curios, old Captain Hodges was known and commended for a character.

"He's a character, all right," people said; and indeed, so necessary was the observation that people sometimes made it who were characters themselves, if you come to that. And since in no way did Captain Hodges account for his silences, people said again that he was a great thinker, who had been known to sit for "seven square hours" at the Sea-Grill, glaring over the warped table, his big legs, which were bowed slightly, doubled under it, and his fingers gripping the handle of his

queer cane. This cane in its whole length was nothing more than vertebrae from the spine of a shark, wired together, with the cruel beak of an
albatross fixed to the top.

And now, with the leisure of one who could think for seven square
hours at a time, Captain Hodges lit his pipe. Oblivious of the oppressive
tension of the place, he drew thickening clouds from that brown bowl,
his big nose hanging over it with solicitous, expanded nostril.

All eyes were turned with a painful and involuntary interest upon the
captain's nose, thus so intimately associated with his pipe. There was a
dull movement of feet under the cramped tables, a creaking of chairs, a
harrowing cessation of social experience. And then the captain spoke.

"Any pancakes, Lem?"

"Sorry, Cap'n, but I'm out of mixture," said Lem, his lean form
drooping apology. "Got a nice swordfish here."

Captain Hodges said nothing to the swordfish; and then a young man
with mighty forearms and a stupid face, thinking to widen this rift in the
silence, said, "Fallish, ain't it?"

"Damned if it ain't," said another.

But again, the tyranny of Captain Hodges's secret thought overcame
them. They sat looking at him with constraint and dumb pity. They
seemed to know that they could not expect enlightenment from one
who had known the world as he had; who had been beaten down, blow
on blow, to this. Yet a man does not sit thinking seven square hours for
nothing, and this time they partly knew the reason. Knowing it, they
held their tongues.

Captain Hodges rose to go. He made a pause in putting on his coat,
to fix a contemptuous eye on a little sloop which was coming in with
paradoxical speed, in view of its slack sail. Everybody knew what
Captain Hodges thought of little sloops with cowardly engines up their
sleeves. Usually he roared out something about them. To-night he said
nothing, but drew the coat over his vast, shrunken shoulders, tapped his
cane once or twice on the wooden floor, as if to feel it solid under him,
and went out. Those who were left in the Sea-Grill, relieved from the
pressure of his inscrutability, kicked the chairs around, yawned, struck
matches, and burst into speech.

"Takes it hard, don't he?" said the young man with bulging forearms.

"An' so would you, Harry," said the thin, woeful man opposite him,
"if you'd sailed a ship for fifty years, fair an' foul."

"So I would," said Harry, abashed, feeling that his youth had played him into the hands of wisdom.

"Not that I blame Jed an' Martin," said the other. "It was their chance. They wouldn't've took the lease of the railway if they hadn't had the *Bessie K. Whitehead* in mind. They knew it was bound to come."

"No, you can't blame Jed an' Martin," said the young man. "It's a pretty smart move for them."

"I dunno's he blames 'em in his heart," said the thin fellow, teasing his mustache. "He had nothin' to say, of course. His int'rest in her is down to a sixty-fourth, I hear, not enough to qualify him for master. He had hard luck those last voyages, and had to sell. Put his money in that mine."

"They say he was a Tartar when he was younger, Roddy," said young Harry.

"An' so he was," said Roddy, with the mysterious reserve of a man who knows things which he had better not have known. "Black Taylor himself warn't nothin' to old Cap'n Hodges when he was riled."

Roddy was popularly thought to have gone a voyage with Captain Hodges when he was younger. But people generally, even though they hadn't sailed with Captain Hodges, said in round terms that he had been a Tartar, if only because it seemed so little likely to people who saw him for the first time. He looked gentle enough, a trifle morose, but quite "moderate"—tractable, even. You might have said he would "hear reason" if any man would. Yes, but there were people in the town who knew better and said nothing. It was these soft-spoken men who had their way on the sea. And look at his nose. Wasn't it plain from his nose, to go no further, that the man must have been a Tartar? He was old now; nobody knew how old—like a wreck that the sea had cast up here, after all those years. But who knew what he had been in those years if not those who had gone to sea along with him?

"But it is hard," said the young man. Folding his forearms on the table, he gazed at them proudly.

"It won't make much difference to Cap'n Hodges long," said Lem. "Nothin' won't make much difference to him long. His heart, y' know. Doc Elwood says he won't last the winter out."

"All the same," said the young man, drearily, still gazing at his forearms, "it's hard."

"Damned hard," said Lemuel.

Captain Hodges, leaving the wharf and leaning heavily on his cane, took the road to Baker's Landing. The crook in his legs gave more than a seaman's rock to his shoulders; his walk was a gigantic toddle. He looked straight before him frostily at the rough road, where the mud had partly frozen in deep rolls. The board walk creaked and sank under him, and now and then his cane stuck in a crack, and he stopped to pull it out absently. Once a spasm of pain twisted his wry old face, and it was quite a minute before he could go on again.

Passing the ship-chandler's, Captain Hodges paused to look down a narrow alley to a little white house with shells against the door. A tall girl was leaning there, talking to the ship-chandler, a sturdy fellow who hung absorbed over the dilapidated fence. She had brown eyes, with brows which arched radiantly as small surprises dawned upon her. A man might guess how big surprises would illuminate her.

"Uncle Ira," she called, joyously, to old Captain Hodges. He paused on his cane.

"Going over to the railway?"

"Yes, Fan," he said, gently.

"Tell Jed I can't come now, won't you? He'll be 'most wild, poor fellow, but I can't help it."

Captain Hodges nodded, and went on past Baker's Landing to the deserted premises of Smalley & Co., ship builders. Stepping into the abandoned shipyard through a twisted door in a high, weather beaten fence, he paused again. Smalley, and Smalley & Co., had died years before, and the town with them. Or rather, like the spouse of an Arabian prince of old, the living town had gone down into the grave with Smalley.

In the spongy yard gray, rotting rounds of crooked spars lay half-embedded, and strange outworks huddled on the waterfront—rusty boilers, crabbed anchor-flukes, and nameless iron parts, with blunt-ended bolts and savage cogs. The innumerable chips were gray, and in the half-twilight showed soft and vague, like feathers, as if a monstrous bird had been plucked over the place. Grass and burdock marked the roadways. By the ways and falling scaffolding, where many a stanch keel had rested, rose a broad flight of heavy wooden steps, worn and scarred and ashen, now black and ruinous against the west. Step by step they rose into the cold sky, ending in nothing, like, aspirations which time has brought to naught.

Yet it was from these ways that the *Bessie K. Whitehead* had taken the water, it would be close to seventy years gone, now; and by these steps that a boy—old Jared Hodges's shaver—had climbed timorously up to look down into the vast empty hold of the new ship, this hold mysterious and deep, smelling of the pines, scattered with trunnels and shavings and shining wire nails and tufts of oakum, and braced with new iron, which showed dull black and formidable against the yellow ribs and timbers. What a thrill of confidence in her he had had, looking forward through the gloom of her 'tween-decks to where those giant ribs, yellow, bolted, with hewn surfaces revealing the stroke of the broad-ax, began to thicken and straighten up along the sheer. And the fine satin finish to the rounds of the masts, cold to his cheek, around which he could not put his arms. Sooner should the rooted pine fall than these. Then it had seemed to this little chap—old Hodges's shaver—as if everything in the world could be stowed down there, and as if so strong a ship must last forever.

He knew better now, standing there, forlorn and vast and withered, with his youth behind him, and the youth of his ship behind him. For, looking to the extreme end of the shipyard, he could see this very ship, so invincible to his boy's vision of might, now drawn out on the marine railway, propped, pilloried, at her last gasp. She was old, seared, gaping; each poor mortal crack and outline of her proclaimed her ended. Her sticks curled forward; her stays were slack. There were lurking horrors in the darkness of her underbody which the sea had covered. She wasn't seaworthy.

Captain Hodges, leaning on his cane, with the strong beak of the albatross protruding from his withered fist, bent his bleak eye upon her. Now that she lay out of water, he had to accept the inevitable fact. Any time this last five years a proper inspection must have forced her out of service. But he had fought for her, excused, concealed, lied, staving off this moment as he could, until at length she came to be known as a ship where even the cook had to jump back and forth between the galley and the pumps, and the fact of her decay stood forth beyond all subterfuge.

Now they had her trapped, laid bare, all the secret vices of her patent and damning. Even so, if they would only haul her up and have done with her, he could still think of her as in the past and glorious. Though it might wring his grim old heart, which had wasted emotion or founded sentiment on nothing but his ship, he could have put up with that. But they weren't content with that. They were going to degrade her, make her over, squeeze the last ignoble utilities out of her collapsing hulk.

Putting his cane forward, he picked his way across the shipyard, among the boilers and the sunken cranes, darkly meditating, under the stern post of the *Bessie K. Whitehead*. The tide was lapping in over the slimy rails on which the dock rested; dark masses of reluctant weed turned with it, wavering, hanging from the heavy blocks of rough granite, which, bracketed in iron, held the wooden frame of the dock under the tides as it slid out on the rails. If anything, this dock was older, more decrepit even, than its occupant.

Brume and dankness hovered under the dismal bottom of the ship, and this bottom was heavily marked in ways which only Captain Hodges could explain. Her lines had lost their liveliness. She sagged aft; it was plain to any eye. A raw breath came from her, like an exhalation from that whole grim bulk, which still forced upon the mind its suggestion of inalterable might.

Captain Hodges put out his hand to the black timbers, where they dripped, and drew from the stolid immobility of the ship's side a half-comforting assurance. He followed with his eye the uneven seams, covered in places with slime and barnacles; the heavy boldness of the curves, the something jowl—like and steadfast in them yet. These people were so cursed afraid of pumps nowadays. She could keep the sea out still, and what more could be asked of her? He impressed himself with her resources.

In the clear light of the late afternoon his ship hung over him, immense, assembling for him at a blow, with her decrepitude, all those hard years which had brought him to this, and her to this. They had had an equal span, it seemed. He had never thought of outlasting her; never even unconsciously pitted his mortal expectations against hers. It wasn't to be thought that a man could outlast a ship, a thing ribbed and bolted, and with that appalling purport. And yet here he was, outlasting her in spite of all.

Captain Hodges, lost in heavy shadow, indistinct, like a visionary guardian, looked along the port side of her, and up at the cockbilled yards, and the great shears, crossed and lashed, which were to send down the masts to-morrow. From there his roving eyes twinkled and contracted as they turned to the still harbor, which lay in the fading light, minutely accurate, like a steel engraving. These were the points he had known always; the dark, ragged pines, the low rocks, where the tide ran forever in and out, marking the centuries in inches. That calm coast, low-lying under its pines and birches, was like no other coast he knew, and he knew them all. The red buoys at their low slant, like fingers raised in warning, were unchanged from his youth. From farther out reverberations were borne into him of the sullen tongues of the bell—buoys, salt-incrusted iron wardens of the coast, eternally tormented into lonely utterance. Cold, tide-worn, impervious, this featureless vicinity had submitted to the birth of ships and their passing, the birth of men and their passing, and given no sign. Shaking his head, he moved away, leaning more aged-ly than ever on his cane, wrapping his fingers about those strange pink jaws, deeply creased, shut with meaningless tenacity.

All at once, looking up, he became aware of a young man sitting on a stool beside an easel, smoking. Captain Hodges's soul smoldered wrathfully when he thought of artists. He could never see how it was they stood alone, brought up families—that sort of thing. They appeared to do nothing. This one, a light-hearted fellow in light flannels and a green felt hat, sat swinging one leg over the other and singing a snatch out of a popular ballad. Now he cocked his head at his easel, and again lifted it to brood over the darkening outlines of the ship, with a visible joy in that artistic wreck. Let her dislimn, he would have told you, for the soul shines forth triumphant through the last vestiges of what is mortal. The masts, with their gaunt rake forward, showed her aspiring to the end.

It was indeed bare ruin that he had laid upon his canvas, while he could still see to work; and old Captain Hodges, leaning over him, saw how he had traded on her weaknesses for his effects. He had accentuated that sag aft, so that it seemed as if only by a heartbreaking effort could the old ship hold her integrity at all. He had robbed the hull of what ruggedness it still possessed; and he had even, forestalling time unwarrantably, broken out a section of the bulwarks forward. The ship staggered up out of the green depths of his canvas, not as if suddenly stricken, but as if quietly overtaken by mischances numberless, lapping her round like the tides, leaving each its incalculable mark.

"You call it a ship?" said old Hodges, thickly, clutching at his cane, and raising the point of it to the canvas.

"What is left of one," cried the young artist, gaily. "As good a subject as I've seen in many a day. That hull alone, below the waterline, would torture a man out of conceit with himself. You see what I'm after"—bringing the bottoms of his palms together slowly—"the slack bulge of it—the gaping seams—that rough, mottled look, like the withered hide of some dead sea-monster—and there, those brownish stains dribbling down from the ports. If I can only get that look of something losing semblance, bursting open, crumbling. And the isolation, the look of a thing wrecked, cast up beyond the tides, hungering still for its element. Really, that's it, you know—beyond the tides. She's old. . . . Oh, the mockery of words!" said the artist, thinking of the surer felicities of paint.

"Aye, she's old," said old Captain Hodges, and he turned his deep-set little eyes wistfully upon her. They had lost their twinkle. She was old. He had not known till now how old.

"No doubt she was a gay ship once," said the artist, hilariously. "And when she was, I shouldn't have looked twice at her. Now she's old, she's a joy. With a soul in her."

"A soul," said old Hodges, deeply, looking at her. "Something, you take it, that isn't in the wood altogether now?"

"Why, yes," said the artist; "something of the sort." He was content to be vague, like all his sketchy tribe.

Old Hodges turned, looking across the harbor again. A little north of Baker's Landing the hull of an old coaster lay smoldering on the beach. They were burning the iron out of her. As night fell and the flame brightened he could see, through a red chasm in her side, the great gutted, ruinous hollow of her; those rows of charred ribs relaxing, and the iron of the hull glowing, rising into sight as the wood burned and blew away, day by day, week by week.

And suddenly his gray eyes held a wicked twinkle; and tapping his grisly cane forward among the gray chips, he lost himself in the gloom of the ship's side. Laboriously balancing himself on his crooked old legs, he got himself to the deck.

A tall young fellow with shirt open at the throat lounged against a capstan, reading a paper. Hearing the captain's cane on the deck, he looked up.

"Hello, Cap'n Hodges!" he said. "Fine evening."

His eyes softened with pity, and he could find nothing else to say. With the aged figure of this former master of the ship before him, he shuffled about uneasily, looking at the black, oily deck.

"Tough on the old fellow," he was thinking, like those others. But old Captain Hodges, aloof, bleak, with his small, steely eyes twinkling in his shriveled head, called out no spoken sympathy.

"Watching her, Jed?" he said, gently, lifting his cane and rubbing the ugly beak with a massive thumb.

"Why, yes, Cap'n," said young Jed. "We aren't taking any chances. This is a big thing, you know."

"Yes," said the captain. "You've got your hands full. Foremast coming down to-morrow?"

"Going to try to get it down," said Jed. "It's a good-sized contract."

"Man-sized," agreed the captain. He took a turn or two thwartships.

"Saw Fan in Martin's doorway as I came along," he said, presently. "Talking with the ship-chandler."

Jed darkened.

"Shouldn't let the ship-chandler do me out, Jed," said the captain, cunningly.

"She was coming down here," said Jed, angrily.

"Reckon she's detained," said old Hodges. "Better look her up. I'll watch the ship, Jed. Ship-chandler's a dangerous character."

Jed hesitated. "It's mighty good of you, Cap'n," he said, irresolute. The captain leaned on his cane, admirably indifferent.

"One watch more or less," he murmured, "out of fifty years. . . . But just as you say, Jed."

"I'll do it," said Jed, suddenly, the menacing possibility of the ship-chandler deciding him. "'Bout an hour, Cap'n."

He vanished over the side. Old Hodges watched him out of the dusk of the shipyard. Turning slightly, he could see, below, the lean face of the artist, yellow over the glow of a match. He was lighting his pipe again, no doubt content to sit there and drink in the various shadows of the falling night.

Leaning his cane against a binnacle, Captain Hodges fumbled in his pockets for a moment. Then he went forward at that rocking gait of his and lowered himself painfully down the hatch amidships. But before he was altogether out of sight, he checked himself and looked up the mizzen at the black yards dangling there, untrimmed, against a crescent moon. He blinked once or twice and drew down his head into the blackness.

In a quarter of an hour he came on deck again and resumed his cane. But now he was no longer the same man. Craft and guiltiness were in those little eyes, and he darted a quick look across the deserted shipyard.

"Jed will suffer by it," he murmured. "But Fan's a smart girl. They don't know."

He walked aft uneasily and put his hand on a spoke of the idle wheel. Looking through the maze of spars at the great black shears forward, crossed, as if in a damnable compact to undo the ship, he drew a deep breath, and the Tartar came out plainly in his rugged face. You could see then, if not before, that he had been master of his ship. Rousing himself out of that terrible speculation, he made for the ship's side, at his snail's pace, and yet with a suggestion of haste. But in the moment of putting his foot over he spied on the main hatch a small gray cat.

"God bless me!" he said, suddenly; and, forgetful of his haste, he withdrew his foot from the gangway and went cautiously toward the hatch. With bold, unwinking eyes, the cat allowed him to come very near; and then, with a prim consciousness of the futility of his chase, removed noiselessly to the other side of the hatch, and, sitting down there, again regarded him, without reproach, but by no means concili-ated to the point of surrendering her person.

With rigid steps and deepening anxiety, he followed her from point to point of the ship, crooning to her with a queer sort of desperate patience.

"Kitty, kitty, kitty!" he called, in a cracked high voice, intent upon capture. The little cat, poised upon the bulwarks, lured him on, mingling her elusiveness with coy promises of ultimate submission.

Then Captain Hodges stood still; sweat gleamed on his wan temples; and the cat, sliding toward him along the rail, fawned upon him, arching her back, and agitating her throat with a noise of kettle drums. He reached out his hand and seized her.

"Pretty kitty!" he said and dropped her into the pocket of his coat. Suddenly a kind of spasm ran through him; he stopped, listening, but there was no noise, except the creak of a yard on its truss, swinging idle. Picking up his cane, he went over the rail and into the blackness of the ship's side again.

Emerging, he found the artist still smoking his pipe and communing with the night. "Been looking her over?" said that young man, lightly.

"Aye," said the old man, and now his voice was tremulous and his whole manner haunted and expectant, "and for nigh on sixty years."

The artist whistled. Old Captain Hodges bent toward him fiercely.

"I sailed that ship from boy to master," he cried. "She's my own ship. I know her. No one else."

He stopped over that thought, glowering. Yes, he could be said to know her, certainly. As he had known no other mistress, so his ship had known no other master over fifty years. This had been a strange union of intents and purposes. All those years he had cherished her, watching her through storms, fogs, channels, lifting his eyes to her yards, fingering her taut gear, rising and falling with her in the same concession to the seas and the same defiance of them. On her beam-ends, with the main-yard in the water, he could still trust her; as in quiet harbors, when he paced her deck, brooding, aching for the sea-winds again which should set her creaking, and laying over like the thing of life she was. And now, in his old age, she was condemned, a relic, with this young fool making a picture of her bones.

"A bit of a crab with the wind on the quarter, maybe," he began again, gustily, "but with the yards braced up there wasn't a ship to touch her in the Western ocean. She had wings, man. She'd go still if they'd let her. She's strained aft, and she needs a new mainmast, but she'd go yet. She'd lay over to it with any of 'em. Give me four men to a watch, and I'd bring her into 'Frisco now ten days ahead of the fleet."

He spoke as if there were still a fleet, as if the ringing of the mauls had just knocked off in the shipyard of Smalley & Co. He looked back swiftly toward the ship which rose blackly over them. The old coaster, nothing now but the red heart of a ship, a moldering skeleton, with glowing ribs warping open, in serried ranks, sent a red path across the water, tingeing their faces faintly red and giving the night shade a stain of purple. The face of old Captain Hodges, coming out of gloom, worked strongly, and his eyes, strangely small and fixed and deadly, caught the light from the burning ship.

"She only wanted a bit of going over," he mumbled. "Good for ten years with a bit of going over. But they wouldn't have it."

His head fell a little, and he clasped one hand over the other on his cane, with his arms straight before him. In that posture, and for a brief instant, he seemed stripped of his age, and to stand on his two legs with the old sturdiness.

"She's done her work, and they won't let her alone," he cried, in a passion of sympathy. "She was a proud ship—a proud ship, I say. I could show you—records. She's led steam the way before now. And now what? Now what? They're sending down the sticks tomorrow. They'll use the hull for towing coal. A barge."

The old man drew a staggering breath, and in that moment the artist, without being told, could see that he had been a Tartar.

"But they won't do it," the captain said, coming closer and talking in shrill whispers. "They won't do it. I've put her beyond the tides, as you say, young man. Beyond the tides."

He looked at the ship over his shoulder with a strange, torturing expectancy. The artist, who had been bending over his kit, stopped at these last words, which were his own, and so had about them an arresting quality. At that moment his eyes were on the captain's queer, foreign cane, and it seemed to him that the long, narrow beak leaped out of the dark, snapping at him. At once he saw that the worn bone had reflected a light behind him, and he turned quickly.

In that very instant it appeared as if the old *Bessie K. Whitehead* brimmed over fore and aft with flame. The flicker on the cane had come from near the mainmast, but, with the speed of thought, the ship was a burning ship from stem to stern. Her timbers, many times dried and drenched in oil, offered no resistance. The young man stood staring helplessly, and old Captain Hodges, swaying on his cane, gave forth a crazy chuckle.

As the light grew, the heavy outlines of the ship showed dumb and cumbrous through those flying cavalcades of fire; and the yards, dripping small bits of burning gear, gave an effect against the masts of twisted crosses blazoning against the pale night sky of the north. The old ship, catching the spirit of her last moment, seemed to snatch at the chance of flame for her adornment; and the flame purged her of age, and set her roaring and shining and throwing down upon the flat, gray harbor the sinister light of that enthralling beauty.

The young artist gasped, "Good God!" and took a stumbling step or two toward the yard gate, but old Captain Hodges, pouncing on him, held him with his invincible bony fingers.

"Let be!" he cried, turning his puckered face from the heat, already grown fierce. "She's gone . . . like a ship . . . beyond the tides."

His grip slackened, he took a step or two, stiffly, and, supporting himself on his cane, sank down upon a box which lay against one of the outposts to the railway. At that moment the mainmast, already eaten out with dry rot, reeled under the corroding touch of fire, and fell, moving a vast yellow fan of flame against the night, crushing the railway super-structure and lapping the heavy bulwarks over as a man might fold a sheet of paper.

"Fore t'gallan' downhaul!" shrieked old Hodges then, casting his eyes aloft, and his voice had a full body, as a voice must have to run against sea winds. But this was a voice out of the past; in a moment his head fell back, knocking against the post, and he was still. The artist, standing irresolute and horror-struck, saw a sudden movement of the old man's right-hand pocket, and directly the long, woeful head of the cat appeared from under the thick flap. The little animal, struggling out, fell to the ground and fled out of the heat, but old Hodges was without movement, his tuft of a beard pointing upward, and his cane with the albatross head fallen against his side.

The glowing ship burned his still face with dread insistence, but he did not flinch. They were alike, the skipper and his ship, beyond the tides.

THE ANCHOR

From *The Century* (March 1919)

A powerful, engaging tale of a clash between a young captain and a jealous, older third mate aboard a supply ship struck by a German U-boat's torpedo in the mid-Atlantic during World War I. Hallet employs humor, irony, and his personally gained knowledge of the dangers of mid-ocean naval encounters to set the stage for a struggle of command in a moment of crisis. Told by a surviving second mate, the story also reflects Hallet's living-off-the-land trek across Australia, as well as his lifelong fascination with the frequent ambiguity between known facts and the truth.

I had this tale straight from the second mate of the wrecked ship *Tankard*. He was an Estonian by birth, by the name of Aronowsky. Captain Wilkinson of the *Tankard* had called him the grandest liar in Christendom before taking leave of him; but for my part, I think he was telling the truth. He was the sort of man who had to tell the truth, indeed, or forfeit all those grimy papers that gave him standing as a political being. He carried them all in a brown envelop, even down to his birth certificate; and if he lost even the least of them, he would find himself at once in a very ugly fix, and might even be deported, he feared. So long had he been subject to the probe of official eyes, tongues, fingers, all but pinch bars, that the habit of telling the truth, walking a chalk-line, and having documentary evidence to bear him out had become the least of his precautions.

"I don't usually say more than I have to," he told those of us who were loafing in the shipping offices, waiting for a ship. "Not to them, anyways," and he jerked his head toward the captain's room. This policy of silence under probe dated from his first exile from Russia, when he had traveled the length of his native state on a flat-car laden with frozen beeves in two long rows, the whole covered with tarpaulin. At sidings he had to bear with a soldierly practice of thrusting bayonets, like darning-needles, through the concealing canvas in search of just such as he. All Russia was divided into the hunter and the hunted. Once the cold steel had pierced the calf of his leg, but he had not cried out. Indeed, he had the presence of mind to wipe the bayonet clean of blood with his coat as it was being withdrawn from his wound.

"If I had so much as whimpered," he informed us, "I would never have been assigned to lucky Wilkinson's ship, and you would not be hearing from me now."

"You say Jim Trojan was third of this ship?"

"His second trip, I believe."

"He was a hard case as I remember him."

"He had taken orders too long to be able to give them, however," said Aronowsky. "To look at him, though, you would say he was one of those chaps who drive nails with their fists and pull them out again with their teeth."

He had been a seaman too long to make an officer out of him, Aronowsky said a couple of days later. By this time, we had begun to form a picture of the man without getting a hint as to the cause of the disaster. He had a hairy barrel of a body, copiously inked, big red paws, pitted cheeks. There was a white slash across his back. He was a hard case and looked as if he had been sewed together as many times as a sack.

On the other hand, Captain Wilkinson—Lucky Wilkinson—was a lank, cool devil, as gentle as a woman, corn-silk hair tumbling over his ears, a wide mouth, wedge jaw, and quizzical wrinkles in the corners of his blue eyes. Every time Trojan saw him coming, his voice dropped into the back of his throat, and he went into ambush directly. He was afraid of authority. All the days of his hard life it had been his custom to tremble in the presence of the "old man," and he trembled now before this old man, Wilkinson, an old man ten years younger than he was himself, and with nothing like his sea experience. The chance of war had forced Trojan into this fix. The authorities had pounced upon him, taught him the rudiments of navigation, and converted a swaggering boatswain into a timorous third mate.

Directly he got upon the bridge he was beset by nervous terrors, like a girl at her first ball. Having climbed to that dizzy height, he felt as if somebody had kicked out the ladder from under him and left him to his own resources, unsupported and without counsel, hanging over that blueblack abyss, and charged with the safe conduct of two hundred souls.

"If you make a mistake, you're a criminal," he said with awe.

His fears were legion. If he sighted smoke, he was visited by the moral certainty that a raider was bearing down on him. If a sail was reported, that was submarine camouflage. If he saw a light at night, that was a submarine again, and he sent a man post-haste to break the slumbers of the old man.

To be sure, once the captain took the bridge, nothing that he did seemed right in Trojan's eye. Wilkinson's judgment was faulty, and Trojan's could not be that, because he never allowed himself to exercise it. If the old man showed running-lights, that was folly; but if he refrained from showing running-lights, why, that was folly multiplied a thousand times. If he stayed below, he was neglecting his ship,—"We might all have beer, at the bottom a dozen times for all him,"—if he appeared, as he often did at night, walking about in silk pajamas of robin's-egg blue, with purple frogs, then Trojan said that the old man was ready to jump out of his skin through sheer nervousness. If so, it must have been the nervousness bequeathed to him by Trojan; for the third mate, as soon as he saw Wilkinson, and knew that nothing thereafter could be charged against him, and that if he appeared in court, it could only be in the capacity of a witness, mysteriously recovered all his faculties, and muttered that the old man had better stay in his bunk and leave the business of shoving the ship along to men who had got their knowledge out of something bigger than a book.

Still, when Wilkinson was by, the dumbness of his sailor years came over him and clouded him. He would speak his mind, and yet he could not. The bullying ring was out of his harsh voice; his throat was thick; he was sheepish and even reverential in his attitude.

One night he (Trojan) was certain he had seen a black object right ahead. Sweat stood on his forehead and ran down his pitted cheeks. He grasped the handle of the engine-room telegraph, thinking to give her "Full astern;" instead, he let his hand drop again and cried out:

"Wake the old man!"

He stared again; the black object was not clear to him now, and by the time Wilkinson was at his elbow he was not sure of it at all.

"Well, what is it this time, Mr. Trojan?"

The captain's voice sounded wide-awake, as calm as the clock ticking behind his ear; but the words "this time" were hard to bear.

"I thought I saw something, sir."

"Saw what?"

"I don't know, sir."

"Where was it?"

"Right ahead."

"In the path of the ship?"

"Yes, sir."

"Then we have rammed it by now, I suspect." The captain's voice had good-natured satire in it.

Trojan muttered something like:

"Be on the safe side."

"Yes, of course," said Captain Wilkinson.

A wave of sheepish subjection to authority, a sort of mental paralysis, attacked the brain of the watch-officer. That erstwhile expansive personality stood miserably dumb, enfolded in darkness.

Wilkinson still lingered. His lower jaw sagged. His strong teeth gleamed white. By the side of his enormous watch-officer he looked like a fairy prince. He put his mop of yellow hair aside, and adjusted glasses to the bridge of his nose.

"There is positively nothing there," he said at length. "Watch the steering close, Mr. Trojan, and call me if you need me or if any marked change in the weather occurs."

At midnight Trojan hissed in the ear of the second mate:

"This old man is a scholar."

Trojan could say no worse of a man than that he had a feebleness for books. Say what you would, there was a lurking cowardice in resorting to the printed page. It was taking an undue advantage of a man who had a manly, bracing contempt for all books.

"A scholar?"

"Yes. He has never been in a real pinch. I would like to have that article on the deck of a windjammer just once."

"The old man began life in sail."

"He ought to have ended it there, I say. Snooping around, dousing himself with perfume! He is a dangerous man to have on a ship, I tell you. They will end by smelling us out, with that man shedding flavors the way he does."

It was true that Captain Wilkinson liked strong scents. An ethereal violet wake trembled away from him when he walked. He laved himself with scented soaps and shook geranium powders into his bath.

"He is soft, too," whispered Trojan. "Going to get married, hey?"

"Yes, this time home. Lucky man, I say. Have something to come home for."

Soft and book lover! The indictment was heavy indeed, but the old man did not suspect, did not dream, that he was hateful in the third's sight. He thought Trojan worshiped him. And, indeed, the fellow never let an indiscreet word escape him when the captain was near. He took pains to conceal his hatred. He seemed to fear for the life of his grouch. Even when the old man found him putting the cook's dog ashore and interfered, Trojan did no more than acquiesce, though in that instance he was plainly in the right of it. A ship in submarined waters is no place for a dog. It was that prenuptial softness of Wilkinson's that had urged upon him leniency in the case of the cook's three-legged yellow cur, a mangy, cringing, hollow-flanked phenomenon, which was sometimes averred by the crew not to be a dog at all, but merely the incarnation of the cook's yellow streak.

"I was afraid we might stumble over it in the dark, sir," Trojan said worshipfully.

"Ah, I see. Put the poor devil in the 'tween-deck."

The Yellow Streak went into the 'tween-deck. For the most part he lay stretched out on the hatch there, massive head watchful between crusted paws. Wilkinson sometimes flung a scrap of meat down there when he came up with his after-dinner cigar. The old man was at peace with the world, a lucky captain who had never lost a ship, had never seen a periscope, and who was going home to marry the finest woman in the world.

"Yes, up to that time I had rather have had that man's luck than a license to steal," Aronowsky said, after due deliberation. "He told me himself that if he could make another trip without taking the covers off his guns, he would begin to think of heaving them on the dock.

Everything fair, a good crew, the engines kicking out ten and a half, fair skies, and the ship sliding on as if she had had fat laid along her keel."

And yet all was not well with him. Trojan had grown bitter. On the very last night indeed,—the last night of the *Tankard* as a surface ship,—during what would have been the first dog-watch in the old days of two mates, Trojan found himself looking with all his eyes in at the lee door of the captain's room. He was viewing the old man's uniform, which hung from a series of pegs on the port side. They were very tasty garments, but all wrong, according to Trojan; mysteriously and dishearteningly wrong, like everything that appertained to the old man. He had for Wilkinson an antipathy in all its comprehensiveness. He hated him for his uniform, for his scents, for his yellow hair, for his prospects of bliss, for his loose-jointed "Lord-of-creation" walk, and even for the way in which he sat down to table, giving, what Trojan called, "a nasty look all round him first." Most of all he hated him when, in the dead vast and middle of the night, he was forced to call him to the bridge for consultation. Bitterly he longed to conduct his watch through to an end without leaning on that crutch; but at the first sign of weakening he grappled it to him.

Now, as he stared at that cap, with its high, stiff crown, its blue cover, its gold braid, its impressive eagle, he gave way suddenly to the compelling itch in his fingers, lifted down the cap, and settled it on his brows.

A voice from behind said crisply:

"A very good fit, Trojan."

The wretched third snatched it from his head and dropped it in his tremulous eagerness to get it back on its hook. Wilkinson was not annoyed; indeed, his voice was friendly and half pitying. He said:

"You ought to have been wearing that cap long ago, Mr. Trojan, with your experience. All you lacked was the will power to buckle down and learn the few essential propositions. You had all the rest."

Trojan made a respectful noise in his throat, but his hate increased many times.

And now came the night of the disaster, for disaster had to claim that lucky ship at length. The Fates mercifully snipped her thread off short.

Aronowsky, the original narrator, paused here, and looked about him at the loungers in the shipping office, his eye lighting on first one, then another, of that stolid group. Nearly all of them had lumpish chins and steady, far-seeing eyes, without any sort of guile observable in them; good square heads of the kind to which destiny had first entrusted and now reconciled him.

"It was a far cry from the press report of it," he said cautiously. "That, as I say, was Captain Wilkinson's mistake. They naturally went to him first, and it would have looked bad for me to contradict his story.

"The newspapers had reported the ship torpedoed in the usual fashion, at about two o'clock in the morning, you will recall, by a torpedo coming against her on the port side; but that, fortunately, she was kept afloat for nearly an hour by the lucky chance of that fatal shot taking effect slightly above the water-line."

"These people must have thought we were hit by a flying-fish," the second mate observed thoughtfully.

"You say she was not torpedoed, then?"

"No; certainly not."

"Still, you felt a jar?"

"A jar, man? I thought the ship was split. It was a collision, and next door to a head-on collision, too. We were rammed on the port side just aft of the collision bulkhead, ripped open as neat as a prong of ice could slip into her belly, laid open like a fish on a slab. I don't know what craft did it to this day. How should I know? It was black, black. I couldn't see these five fingers in front of my face. No lights either. Black out. Light tight. We were stealing along in the dark, like thieves up an alley."

Trojan had been moaning all along about the lack of lights, and so it was no surprise to him at least when the ship suddenly went short over to starboard, as if she had been cuffed over by the tail of some emerging leviathan. It was precisely eight bells—midnight; the second mate was in the act of relieving Trojan but had not actually received the course from him. Both officers were standing together in the port wing of the bridge. Aronowsky was thrown sharply to his knees. He thought at first, of course, that she had been torpedoed, although the sensation, when he later collected himself enough to describe it, was rather that of being hooked to the heart; as if she had been first penetrated, and then brought up short by some monstrous barb.

As soon as he heard anything at all, he heard Trojan calling in his thick tones to the spare quartermaster:

"Wake the old man!"

He was reaching out again for that discarded crutch, and this time in a perilous hour, certainly. He had not had time to turn the ship over formally to Aronowsky, and the responsibility was still his. His first impulse in these circumstances was to summon that masterful object of his aversion to the bridge. Next he cried harshly: "She's all gone for'ard—all gone. What do you make out there?"

They stared ahead. Was she in truth hopelessly broken open? The throb of the engines was still audible, at least. Aronowsky stared through the dark at some object like a hideous snout that seemed to be nuzzling his ship's flank there on the port side, a moving horror, as if a gigantic snail were drawing itself the length of the ship. He stood rooted in his tracks by an absurd misgiving lest this catastrophe to the ship might be attributable to a supernatural source.

"That was a bad moment," he confessed. He stood there, helpless to see what had happened, unable to make out anything ahead of his own nose, and the heart in his breast like a bomb treacherously tucked in there by the enemy, swelling up and getting ready to burst.

And suddenly the clawing ceased, a black shape reeled away from the port side, and the ship came back a trifle from her extreme list to starboard.

All this had occupied very few seconds. They found that the lank form of Captain Wilkinson had interposed between them.

"Who is here? Mr. Trojan, Mr. Aronowsky?" he called rapidly. "We have been laid open on the port side by some confounded trawler, I believe. It's not serious. Mr. Aronowsky, go into Number Two at once, and see if water is making there. I think the blow was above the water-line. Wake the mate and tell him to stand by those collision-mats. Mr. Trojan, notify the steward to bring what mattresses he has, turn out the crew. Muster them forward to plug the gap. Quartermaster, let her go west half south. Not too much wheel. Steady, my boy!"

At the same time he signaled, "Slow ahead," on the telegraph, and immediately after stopped the ship.

Aronowsky, who had already tumbled somehow into Hold Number Two, felt the cessation of that pulse like the failure of his own heart, he said. He had expected it, however. And now he could see at a glance the whole extent of the fatality. The empty hold was like the humming shell of a crustacean; it was full of boomings, viperous hissings, slobbering sounds, unreal; it quaked like the belly of a stringed instrument.

A strong, cool current of air touched his sweaty brow. To his horrified gaze, the hole in the port plating looked bigger than the ship herself.

"I am honest with you," the Estonian stated slowly. "That hole seemed to fill the whole sky, and I could see solid water jumping up, and stars beginning to show beyond that. A fresh wind blew right in on me. That is how we were fixed."

The second mate felt as if he had been disemboweled personally. He looked up out of the hold with a dismayed gasp, forced out of him by the cold rush of water about his knees as much as anything, and he was reassured by hearing the calm voice of the captain giving an order to the boatswain. From first to last Wilkinson did everything that mortal man could, even threatening the seamen with loss of their papers if they did not stand by the boats until the mates came to order them lowered away. This had a tonic effect. Like Aronowsky, they were mostly men whose right to set foot anywhere on the naked earth was curiously conditioned on their ability to produce papers, bits of salt-stained, sweat-stained wood-pulp, testifying to facts and intentions of various kinds. Without these to show, it would be better, or at least less tedious, to die forthwith, as any seaman will understand.

Aronowsky returned to his muttons. The furrow in the *Tankard*'s shell-plating, he found out, began just aft of the collision-bulkhead, near the prow of the ship. It was three or four feet out of water at that point; the plates were bent sharply out, and the heavy U-bars out of which the ribs had been wrought were twisted in ghastly fashion.

"You would as soon expect to see a skeleton floating as that ship," said Aronowsky. The tear in her flank went deeper as it went aft, until, at the extreme after part of Hold Number Two, water was coming in with a nasty choked-back sound, as if it couldn't come fast enough to satisfy itself—the sound of water coming through the neck of a bottle, in short. It went streaming across the 'tween-deck hatches right merrily and had the effect of sinking the ship to starboard every instant. She was altering her trim now as well and had every intention of going down by the head, if Aronowsky was any judge. He felt terribly skittish about staying where he was in ignorance of developments, and he confessed that nothing but the cool voice of Captain Wilkinson stayed this sort of panic.

And just then an entirely new phase of the mystery took him literally off his feet. This was the violent doubling of some hard object about both his legs at the knees, under water. He threw both arms out in going down, and so discovered that what he was tangled up in was nothing less than about two fathoms of chain cable.

The mind of a seaman is very orderly in its reasonings, and proceeds on the assumption that there is a place for everything, and that everything should be in its place. It seemed to Aronowsky nothing short of pure delirium to run afoul of chain cable lashing about in that part of the ship, where no chain had ever been before. Had the chain-locker been crushed in? And if it had, surely there was not force of water yet to float out iron chain!

A swirl of water shifted him along the deck. His outstretched hand brought up against a junk of iron. He bent his fingers around it. It was the palm of an old-fashioned anchor.

Aronowsky took time to be surprised again. An anchor! His delirium was growing on him. In falling, he had shattered his electric torch, but he used his fingers with the agility of a blind man. The palm of that anchor had wedged itself into the web framing, that giant rib of wrought iron to which was tacked the bulkhead, or steel partition, running athwartships directly under the bridge.

He could now read the history of this case complete. That beam-trawler, or whatever she was, had punched the crown of her port anchor clean through the *Tankard*'s plating forward; next, the palm of the anchor caught on, just as it might have on a mud bottom, took an inside bite, and plowed along in the breast of the ship, parallel with the water. After two fathoms or so of chain had run out, a knot of it must have stuck in the hawse-pipe, breaking off there finally. But those tormented links had hung for just long enough to cook the *Tankard*'s goose, ripping through her plating as if it had been sleazy cloth, snatching out cold rivets, and in general opening the ship outwardly, as a can opener opens a can of tomatoes. The web framing was the first thing it encountered strong enough to stop it; but by that time a rapidly increasing strip was being torn out of the ship's hide, and the lower edges of the strip were under water.

The lower hold was still whole, however. Aronowsky saw at one glance that the thing to do was to get tarpaulins across those hatches, and the battens wedged in with good nine-inch oak wedges, before the incoming water could float the hatch boards clear of the hatch-opening. The lower hold, free of water, offered a reserve of buoyancy; with that maintained, the 'tween-deck might fill, and still the ship remain afloat. With the whole compartment flooded, it became a narrow question for mathematicians. Aronowsky would not answer for her.

At this point James Trojan joined him, followed by a group of men bearing mattresses on their shoulders. But when they saw the hole, these stopgaps slid from their fingers.

"Where's the mate?" cried Aronowsky.

The third mate's face thrust toward his with a savage jerk.

"Monkeying with those outside window-curtains."

"Are they coming down over the hole?"

"Lord, no. They are ripped into shreds. Seamanship! I knew how it would be with that—article on our hands. That was one of his grand ideas, I suppose."

These window-curtains were, in fact, an invention of Captain Wilkinson's, a sort of modified collision-mat. They were rolls of reinforced and wired canvas held to the rail of the ship and weighted with heavy slice bars at their bottom edges. These weights were added with the idea of preventing the inward spout of water from pinching the mat against the plates before the hole should be fully covered. Unluckily, whatever their merit, they had been planned with a view to the ship's being driven in; and here, by some nightmarish chance, she had been plucked open instead. The cruel, curling points of the rent plates pierced those window-curtains as fast as they could be rolled down and gnawed them to ribbons.

"The hole cannot be plugged?"

"Not in a week."

"Then we have got to get tarpaulins over this hatch. Quick! Get your men together. There's no time to lose."

Time was lost, notwithstanding. Trojan stumbled over something.

"What's that?" he cried, groping. "There's some damned fish rolling around here."

He was wrong. It was the cook's Yellow Streak, a fact of which they were reminded by hearing the cook yell down to them to pass up his dog and give it a chance at the lifeboats. At the same time Captain Wilkinson called from the bridge in stentorian tones, "Pass that dog up out of there!"

"We've no time, sir," cried Aronowsky; but his voice was lost in the increasing uproar.

"He's captain," cried Trojan, savagely.

"Do as he says. Pass up the dog." And he set about taking steps to do it with a malicious gleam in his eye.

"We couldn't have known it at the time he came aboard," said Aronowsky, "but it was that cook's Yellow Streak that lost the ship."

He had more than a tinge of personal misgivings in the matter. Perhaps he should have turned a deaf ear to his captain in the circumstances. At all events, the time lost in rigging a tackle to pass that forlorn specter of a dog out of the 'tween-decks was the time which should have gone to stretching the tarpaulins over the hatch. For the hatch is ever a ship's weakest member. Let the sides be never so strongly bolted, if the hatch fails, all fails. With a canvas well stretched across it, and tucked under the battens, it can resist the probe of the water; but boards relying merely on their weight are soon floated free. In the case in question they spun away from the strong backs like tiddly winks. A croaking chasm lay under Aronowsky's staring eye; his last hope was gone. Water began to fall into the lower hold with a deep roar. A puff of hot air and wheat dust came out. Aronowsky coughed.

"She's gone," Trojan said huskily. "The ship's gone."

"Yes, there is nothing more to do now. She will sink in ten minutes, hey?"

"Or less time. Lower your boat, I am going to tell the captain to abandon the ship."

"He has lost her by his own fault," hissed Trojan.

It was true that she was lost. The hold was filling almost as quickly as a bowl could be filled out of a pitcher.

"I never saw water move in faster than it did aboard that ship," Aronowsky said, with his serious expression deepening, as if to reassure those who doubted him as to his complete candor. There was a strong drama in the perfect calm which he employed in narrating to us how he had gone back to the bridge and told the captain there was nothing to be done now but abandon ship.

Such a moment must cut any true seaman to the heart. That ship never left the ways which had not power to strike into the breasts of the men who walk her decks a sentiment of affection. If they cannot love her for her performance, they can still love her for the lack of it. If they cannot admire, they can pity; and pity is akin to love.

"What are you saying?" said Captain Wilkinson. He laid his thin hand on Aronowsky's shoulder like a brother. He was still in his sleeping-suit of robin's-egg blue.

"The lower hold is gone, sir."

"You were not able to cover the hatch in time."

"No, sir."

"The devil! My collision-mats were no good either."

The captain leaned over the dodger.

Water was certainly not very far away. The forecastle head was under; the ship shuddered; the roar of the cataract falling into Number Two prolonged itself into a death-rattle, and the shift forward in the ship's trim could be felt from moment to moment.

"I have pumped out all the starboard tanks," Wilkinson said. "She doesn't come back."

She would never come back.

"Very well. Can you get her west half south now, boy?"

"It's no good turning that wheel over now, sir," interposed Aronowsky, gently. "The rudder will be out of water."

"I expect so. Get your boats overboard, Mr. Aronowsky; abandon ship. I am signaling, 'All finished with the engines.'"

The voice of the lucky Captain Wilkinson broke a little over those words. It was a signal very necessary to be made. Without it, deep in the bowels of the ship there was a hand which would not be absent from the throttle till death relaxed its grip. All finished with the engines! An ironic signal on the whole. It would be a marvel if the engines didn't leave the beds of their own accord the next instant, to plunge into the boilers, and out again at the drowned eyes of her.

A weird silence floated through the ship, broken by a thin, despairing cry from nobody knew where—the voice of one imprisoned, evidently. Aronowsky could scarcely bring himself to leave the bridge. The old man was staring down into that abyss with a fascinated smile.

"I hope you are coming away, too, sir," Aronowsky ventured timidly.

"Yes, yes. Go to your boat," said Wilkinson. "I only had half a notion—"

He had half a notion that the ship might not sink at all. Aronowsky lingered to bring him out of that trance. It was a fearful moment, plucking at the sleeve of that lean, abstracted devil, and wondering if he was out of his head. The second mate felt as dizzy as if he had got up on the roof of a house and was going to pitch forward over the cornice. He had time for a curious thought—the instant of curiosity that prompts a man not to flee, but to embrace death. Once before he had felt it, when the head of a deadly snake was raised within three feet of him. There was death to be had for the asking. He could reach out and touch it, join hands with it, and almost did; but, after all, he wasn't quite curious enough.

"I will take the chronometer, sir," he said.

Wilkinson nodded, still very much taken up with the ship's behavior forward.

"I can't carry him bodily," the second mate reflected; and he decided to save his own skin, if such a thing might be. He beat a hasty retreat by the port ladder. In the chart room the lights were turned up, and in the midst of a mass of crumbled charts stood Trojan. The angle of the deck was steep, but not unnatural. It hardly seemed as if in three more minutes that well-appointed refuge would disappear under the waves. Indeed, it hardly seemed as if Trojan thought so. While Aronowsky was lifting the chronometer out of its cupboard, and laying its strap over his shoulder, the third mate was standing deep in thought, or perhaps tranced by the very deadliness of a peril which was revealed only by a sharper inclination of the deck under his feet.

"You had better get your boat away," said Aronowsky, sharply.

"He has given the order to abandon ship?"

"Yes, certainly."

"You heard him?"

"I still have ears."

"Then let me tell you something."

"Well?"

"He is no longer captain of this ship."

"You refuse to leave, then, as ordered?"

"I refuse to recognize his authority."

"Will you recognize the authority of the Atlantic, then?"

Trojan returned no answer. The second mate suddenly perceived what had been claiming the man's attention all this while. It was the coat and hat of Captain Wilkinson's uniform, hanging at a weird angle from a hook under the megaphone-rack. The cap was fitted with a wired crown, formal and tyrannizing to a degree. Aronowsky left him with a last yell of warning.

He had not left himself too much time. The men in his boat were getting restive and with every good reason. They had been withheld from cutting the falls only by the insistence of a big Swede, Iverstrom, who was visible in the stern-sheets in the act of making a forbidding gesture.

Aronowsky had a warm rush of brotherly feeling for that impassive sailor.

"You never know your friend," he said soberly, looking at us with a puzzled expression. "I had bawled that man out only the day before for something or other, and yet he took a chance on his own life to wait for me. He would have knocked every man in that boat on the head, if necessary. And all the while I thought he had a grievance."

As soon as his boat was water-borne, Aronowsky sheered her out with an oar, and cried to the Swede:

"Capsize the after block."

They were free of the ship in another instant. Could he now pull clear of that vast, declining shadow of a ship, so like a cold phantom or inverted dream of floating through blackness upside down? A duty remained. As second mate, he was bound to see to it that all the boats were clear. The ship was gone, but in his opinion the organization of the ship's forces remained. That was what distinguished man from the lower animals, of course—the power to maintain invisible hierarchies of authority in the face of anything. He could not, for his part, agree with Trojan that the captain was no longer captain, once he had given the order to abandon ship. That view was widely held, however, as he knew.

He shot his boat under the *Tankard*'s stern.

The night had lightened appreciably. At once he saw a boat bearing down on him, loaded to the rails. Jim Trojan was standing at the tiller.

"The crazy fool had put on the captain's coat and cap," Aronowsky said wonderingly. "He denied the old man's authority, and then robbed him of his uniform. Not that Wilkinson would have thought anything of it. In point of fact, as it turned out, he came straight aft from the bridge, not looking into the chart room at all. But the odd thing was, Trojan actually looked more like a captain at a little distance than the captain did himself. He was roaring orders with all his lungs, too. Good old Jim Trojan!"

Once he had got the ship fairly sunk under him and taken to a boat, he wasn't afraid anymore. What had scared him was the notice that she might sink.

He meant to pass directly under the stern of the *Tankard* and away; but the heavy beam sea brought him closer than he had planned, so close that in another second the rudder loomed fairly over their heads. Still fixed in its gudgeons, it was jammed over to the extreme of starboard helm. The propeller was visible. Its rusty blades, eaten away at their tips, looked as frayed as the wings of an aged dragonfly. They had ceased to turn, of course. They were all finished with the engines, you will remember.

Aronowsky had time to note that a dim amber wake-light was still burning at the stern rail; next that Trojan, with his steering-oar, was making a serious effort to veer out from that descending mass of steel and iron. He continued to be drawn toward the *Tankard*, however, and he was too busy to note that Captain Wilkinson, coming aft at the eleventh hour, had vaulted the rail of the doomed ship, swung down by the rudder-chain, and seated himself on the lip of one of the propeller blades. In his pale sleeping-suit he was a figure of enchantment. He cried out:

"Look out below I am going to jump."

"There is no room here," cried Trojan, wrestling with his oar, and fighting hard to slide out from under that slight figure dangling from a strut. He had murder in his eye at the prospect of being robbed of his first unquestioned command—the command of the ship's boat, the ship having been abandoned. His struggle was vain. The captain of the erstwhile *Tankard* dropped beside him as light as a thistle and shouted to the rowers:

"All together, now!"

The rowers needed no urging to pull away heartily; in two seconds they would have done so, but two seconds were lacking to them. The very heel of the sinking ship, the strut which furnished a socket for the rudder, hovered, descended, checked a little, and ended by nipping the edge of the thwart ever so gently. The ship's nethermost plates, dented, slimed with gray-boot topping, were close at hand. Suddenly the rower nearest the rudder began to shriek, thresh about, and gasp for breath. Some part of his clothing had been nipped, and he thought the ship meant to sit on him outright. He abandoned his oar, but before it could slide clear it was caught in a thin, white hand.

"Steady my man!" said Captain Wilkinson. "It will lift in a second."

There was a general mistrust of that proposition, however. And indeed, if they did not drown, it was only because the wheel of their exciting fortunes offered them a better chance of being blown to pieces. The ship had all this time been going down quietly by the head, until, at about the time Captain Wilkinson dropped clear of the screw, a neat little cataract began to pour into the boiler-room through the open grating which ran thwartships just abaft the bridge.

You can imagine whether those hot, fat boilers took kindly to that rush of cold water. They blew up virtually at a touch. Thereafter for a space the men in the boats lay as still as little lizards stunned by hail-stones. Still, the immediate effect of this lucky chance was to raise the sinking stern a foot or two, and the pinioned life-boat drifted away; but no thanks to the glassy-eyed persons rolling on her thwarts, be it added. They had lost half their oars: chaos had come again. They were too dazed to take in what was going on around them. The altercation which had sprung up between their captain and Jim Trojan seemed a part of the general madness.

"So you want to drown us all, do you?" Trojan was shouting, holding out his face to within a foot of the old man's. "First you sink the ship under us and then you drown us. All for a lousy dog. If you had done as I wanted—"

"Sit down there!" said Wilkinson, with an imperious gesture. He was quite unruffled. He thought that Trojan had gone out of his head.

"Sit down, hey? Who are you to tell me to sit down? Tell me that."

"I am captain here, I presume, my man."

"You are? Do you think you are captain? You gave the order to abandon ship, I understand."

"I did, yes," replied Captain Wilkinson.

"Good. And now you come into my boat and want to lord it over me here. You're no better than a sailor here. I'll show you who's in command here, sir. Take an oar. Take an oar, by God! before I break you in two pieces."

Captain Wilkinson passed a hand patiently through his corn-silk hair. His invincible sanity held him from any rash act. Trojan stood over him with apelike malice in his eye; but the old man was not cowed. He merely saw that he would have to humor that madman. He sat down and took an oar.

"Since you are captain here, give your orders," he said, watching him narrowly.

"I am through taking them; I know that," said Trojan at white heat.

"If you give them now, you are a mutineer."

At the word "mutineer" Trojan half faltered, as if he felt or foresaw that in some mysterious way he would be punished for venturing to take command of anything, even a small boat. And he was right in so thinking.

For it was precisely at that moment that they heard a guttural voice cry out of darkness in excellent English:

"There's our man—the commanding officer."

This voice was close above; a submarine in an awash condition had to be within ten feet of them.

"She got all the credit in the papers for sinking that ship, but, as I have told you, she had nothing to do with it," said Aronowsky. "She merely happened by, and saw a chance to bag a life-sized captain out of an open boat. Just as good as a scalp to a submarine commander, you know. In the colonies, when you kill a rabbit, you have to exhibit its ears to collect the bounty."

Trojan was yanked bodily out of his boat, braid, coat, cap, and all.

Captain Wilkinson felt a heroic necessity upon him. Standing up in the sternsheets, he called out mildly.

"You have got the wrong man. That man is out of his head. The shock has driven him crazy. I am captain of that ship."

And Trojan, from the deck of the submarine, only laughed contemptuously. It was his chance to escape from death, or worse than death, and he rejected it.

"Don't ask me to account for it," said Aronowsky. "It's my belief that he had got so wrapped up in the part that he couldn't shake loose from it, even to escape that horror. Or maybe he was trying so hard to keep the old man from knowing how he hated him that he just couldn't keep from doing him a favor even at the very last. It was a favor, you know, considering that Captain Wilkinson was going to be married to the finest woman in the world, distinctly a favor. Because the destroyers were going to blow that U-boat into kingdom come in a very few minutes."

Poor old Trojan swelled out inside that braid. He turned to his captors.

"Take a look at us," he said bitterly. "Which of us looks like a captain of a ship? Convince yourself."

They turned a flashlight first on Trojan, next on the heroic Captain Wilkinson. There could be only one answer.

"They took Trojan, of course," said Aronowsky. It was a fleeting triumph. A search light leaped out of nowhere and was crossed by another. It was like the nervous play of rapiers in the hands of good swordsmen; and it could end in one way only.

"We were not done with shocks yet," the Estonian related soberly. That destroyer came tearing across the water like scissors ripping through cotton cloth; naturally she had her eye on one thing, the precise spot where that submarine had submerged. A fleck of phosphorescence was there, a floating silver blotch as large as a lily-pad; nothing more. That destroyer picked up speed from one crest to another, darted ahead like a pickerel, dropping something that all at once tore a hole in the water with a shocking concussion. The second mate felt as if he were bleeding at every pore. He grasped the gunwale of the boat like a man in a dream; and his grip was weak, as it might have been in a dream. It was worse even than the detonation of the ship's boilers. Captain Wilkinson, staring hard at the water around him, cried:

"She will never come up again."

They stared and stared, forgetting in their rapt search to send up a signal to the destroyer. Captain Wilkinson, clutching his second officer hard around his arm, whispered, with a heave of his shoulders:

"Do you see now? He knew all along what was the matter with us. He knew from the first that we had been torpedoed. We wouldn't listen to him. He knew more than all of us put together. He put himself in my place—to save me. I knew he was devoted to me, but I could not have anticipated that."

Captain Wilkinson sank to a thwart and buried his face in his hands.

"He even had presence of mind to slip into my coat and cap," he murmured. "My God! what a man!"

Aronowsky saw something bitterly ironical in the fact that it was too late for Trojan to hear this confession of his captain. For his part, he thought it best not to say anything at all, not at that time. But the captain could not be silent. He had remembered a wandering detail of Aronowsky's report to him upon the loss of the lower hold.

"What was that you were telling me about an anchor? It sounded wild at the time, I remember."

"Yes, wild," repeated Aronowsky. "The fact is, water was coming in there so fast that I—"

"No matter—torpedoed. Only this morning he told me what a lucky man he considered me," Wilkinson said heavily. "He was attracted to her, and he had only seen her photograph, too. And there I was ready to twist his neck off his shoulders! That's what cuts."

Aronowsky was silent. There was a movement among his listeners.

"So what do we know, after all, in this world?" he continued. "Do you know, my opinion is that the truth can never be put into words any more than fragrance. The fact is nothing, and the motive can never be got at."

"So how do we know you are telling the truth now?"

"I have convinced myself that I am an accomplished liar," he said complacently. "That's the healthy view to take."

"How was your story received, then?"

"My story?" Aronowsky bent toward us impressively. "It was never told. It is told now only between ourselves. The less said of that anchor, the better. As it was, Wilkinson never had full confidence in me after that, and I had to ask to be put on some other ship than his. He took the view that if I had made an accurate report in the first place, Trojan might never have been called on to make his sacrifice. Altogether, it was a matter that wouldn't bear looking into."

He tapped the breast-pocket behind which bulged his papers—citizenship paper, war zone passes, licenses, passports, identifications, birth certificates, testimonials.

"I shouldn't want to forfeit these," he said.

THE HANDKERCHIEF

From *Cosmopolitan* (July 1909)

His first published article, written as a Harvard sophomore. Once published and paid $60, Hallet sustained his writing ambition for several years by citing this early success, saying, "If I can do it once, I can do it again." A dark tale of intrigue and competition between two brothers, competing for the hand of a young woman, told by two observers over drinks in a London club.

In a little corner of Bohemia, ripe with the memories of old tales well told and old wine fittingly uptilted, Aymar and Gaunt, of the law firm of Gaunt and Aymar, sat out the late night hours. The racking case of Frost vs. Morrow had that day gone against them in the lower court. In the youth of the evening they had grumbled together over the strong coffee and the black cigars, hatching plans for the appeal in a meaningless rack of legal terms—meaningless to Philip, their waiter, who said nothing and supplied their wants with unobtrusive handiness. As the night advanced, however, and the wine struck inward, the talk mellowed, and flowed into less technical departments.

"There are other things in life than the cases," said Aymar sagely; "things the law-reports hold not a hint of."

"You have the better knack of words," said Gaunt. "Proceed."

"There is a gentleman at the fourth table to your right," said Aymar, "who is worth a second glance. Look thou discreetly, Freddy, and if the good wine dissolves the clouded lining of my spirit, I will unfold a tale." He wet his lips with the warming fluid in his glass. "'Tis the only prescription in life," said he, and his keen eye glowed anew with every sip. He pulled his shoulders into a more formal jointure with his spinal column.

Freddy swiveled about in his cane chair and glanced discreetly as he had been told. A vast gentleman sat there with bowed head, a dead cigar in his hand. His figure was all drawn together in conformity with the curtains of unconsciousness about his soul. He had gone to sleep. He had no beard, but a great mustache, the iron-gray extremities declined. A square chin grazed his shirt-front; the hand that held the stale cigar seemed white and slender for so big a frame. From the great bulk of him and his imposing presence one felt that here was not a man to pity even in his suffering; a strong soul that might face its torment calmly.

"A splendid presence," said Gaunt at length, facing back toward his companion.

"A burnt-out hell," said the other grimly, and went on with a narrator's gusto, in a mellow, wine-driven voice, to spin his tale:

Oramel Osmyn was the first of two sons to fortify the last mortal bulwark of the great family of Osmyn. "Osmyn & Osmyn, Wine-Merchants," for quite a century the faded sign had creaked over the unwashed windows of the house of Osmyn. In all that time the business instinct of the line had not once faltered; the firm had stood without a quiver the fastest pace that competition could enforce; its accounts were founded on the rock of a great business intuition; bad times and good, it stood the test, rose triumphant out of the worst depressions of the trade, and expanded under the rays of returning confidence to heights no others had before aspired to. To Jeffrey Osmyn, in the very middle of the panic of '37, was born a son to reenforce him in the wine trade. News of it came to him just as he had plunged unshaken through the surf of those wild times. A grim smile ran along his powerful jaws, expressed itself in sudden bunchings of the stolid muscles of his face, and vanished in the stress of more immediate considerations. He knew in his soul that his son would be as untiring a fighter as himself.

Confidence was never lacking to that iron man; he read in the infant's face the promise of his own great jaw and crushing will and fed his hopes with prophecies. A second son followed within a year—a sickly child, that would not last out its infancy, the doctors said; to him he paid no heed. His wife died with the second birth.

Osmyn's hopes, unlike his cash-accounts, were built upon illusion. The elder of the two, growing up, turned out curiously to have inherited the husk of greatness only; the jaw, the head, the deep and vibrant chest were there, and that was all; the rest was weakness, the more emphatic for the deceptive aspect of an inner strength the poor youth bore about with him. He had neither will nor mental energy: a tender spirit, he held no promise, in his father's view, from boyhood up—a sensitive-plant, in this crude family of cactuses, that could no way flourish with them. He was cast out of his father's plans at an early age; the elder Osmyn, though misgiving the slender thread, was forced to base his hope upon the younger brother Randolph, who, under the pleasure of the best medical science, had weathered a sickly infancy only to embark on a sicklier period of youth. He was a thin-lipped, unkind fellow, who had imbibed all his father's contempt for the incompetence of his brother. Mentally he was from the same mint as his father; the two coins rang to the same note. They preserved the even greatness of the Osmyns. Cold precision and an iron temper attached themselves in the son, as in the father, to an unfailing business sense; and while Oramel was left to skulk his time away at college, Randolph was already taking over the destinies of the great wine trade that throve so solidly in Garter Street. He widened the firm's connections, placed the whole concern upon a broader gage, reached out of the wine trade into the operations of the street, and, fusing with his father's crushing energy a more formative, constructive genius, opened the doors of the house to a more compre-hensive prosperity than it had ever known. The elder Osmyn was content, he knew that now he left the vital forces of his work intact; and from looking to his son, in the beginning, as a means to a great end, he regarded him, as he grew old, with a more personal affection—if such a sentiment could thrive in a soul so bleakly self-regarding. Neither of them had ever a word for the wretched Oramel. They had cast him defi-nitely out of the house of Osmyn, with a good allowance and a greater scorn. If possible, the younger of the partners felt for the poor outcast the livelier contempt. A derelict he came into the world, thought he, and a derelict he might drift on and out of it.

A quite incredible reversal. My word, the elder was the more imposing of the two. His very eye bore a command in it; he stood erect, beheld himself a general in action, and was the most retiring of mortals. He had gone to college almost with relief, for though the poor fellow misdoubted the strange world that he was hastened into, he had dwelt so long in the range of that cruel disapproval that he could fortify himself against the direst change that should withdraw him from his father's scrutiny. At college he found himself a slow, secluded youth. If he had been despised in the bosom of his family, how, he argued, could he look for favor in the candid presence of these strange associates? He shrank to and from his classes with a dark and corrugated brow; his great physique and the gloomy airs with which he wrapped himself about gave him a certain atmosphere of mystery. Those kindred souls who might have been attracted to the inner nature of him were frightened by his austere carriage; while his bolder classmates took him for a cynic, or some heavy soul in torment, and so passed him by in silence, and presented to his eye the surface of a wild youth, riotously lived.

His inability to mingle drove him in upon his own reflections; and here he brewed a devil's draught of black and morbid thoughts and let the whole outpour into the infertile strata of his mind. Isolation more complete there never was; despair more bitter never puddled the clear spirit of misguided youth.

Out of this chaos of self-pity there arose at length a kind of egoism. Most youngsters pass this trouble off in harmless superficial radiance; it appears like an eruption on the surface of the character and dies commonly with youth. Not so with young Osmyn. He bled inwardly of it. His self-respect revived unhealthily; I think he was the worse of it in time.

Oramel knew no girls at college, danced no dances, played no games of love. However prettily he talked with the lady of his dreams—and romance had sprung full blooded with his egoism and played dim harmonies that deepened his tragic spirit—my lady in life reacted like a dire alembic on his mind. He gazed on living beauty with a recoiling and a closing brain; his repartee was frankly the most unenlightened balderdash. He drew apart; acted out in the lowest of spirits a continual tragedy of loneliness and grief.

From this portentous shadow his egoism afforded him but one relief. He used to leave his room by night and walk the then deserted streets under cover of darkness. And strange to say, the outer blackness seemed to lift away the blackness from his heart. At such times he felt himself alone with the universe and master of its destiny. He towered in his mind to heights unheard of; the statesman, the poet, the artist walked abroad in him, in the consciousness of a great work greatly done. For he could even coax himself during these walks into a gladsome retrospect, the feeling of a past magnificently lived, with things of moment achieved. He thought of the physical shroud in which he walked as some kind alien cloak, in which a great spirit, clogged and hampered by its former clothing, might revel and expand into the infinite ether.

Enough of this sad etching. The main effect was little altered when its subject fell in love. A gentle lady she was, of far too flexible a nature— a Miss Thorley, daughter of the head of Thorley & Crew, of the wine trade also. Oramel had met her in his long vacations and seemed to sense in her a kindred spirit. They took little silent drives together and tea afterward at the Circassian, with a waiter to grin over the uncommunicative genius of the tete-a-tete. They had, indeed, little to say; they were sadly dull people. Randolph, glancing out his office window on a June morning, marked them at their driving with a silent leer; then he steadied his mind on the problems of the trade—problems now almost of commercial empire, under his keen manipulation.

The trouble came with a depression in the wine trade. Thorley & Crew were setting a hot pace in that quarter. Randolph's speculations were already vast; he had no wish to face the constant menace in his father's business, which had been his springboard into high finance. He determined in a moment to marry Miss Thorley and forestall attack from that direction. He spoke to his father about it curtly over the wine.

"Thorley & Crew are making it warm for us in the Madeiras," he said, his thin face showing like a piece of crumpled paper in the gloom. "We will have a bride into the house."

"Miss Thorley?" questioned the elder Osmyn, and laughed loudly, shaking the dusty glass pendants on the candelabra.

"Why not?" retorted his son. "Old Thorley feels himself as hard pushed as we; and if I could let down the strain in this quarter, I could turn to copper with a freer hand."

"The house of Osmyn is rather going out of wine," said old Osmyn, but looked not ill pleased. The two of them had talked thus far with scarce a recognition of the presence of the elder son. But Oramel now rose, trembling in his place, and with a white face, whiter than his brother's, and words coming from his lips with a dry huskiness, stammered out a profession of his love for the lady they tossed so freely over the dessert.

"Sir," he gasped, "I have the honor, sir—Miss Thorley—I love her, sir—with your permission, I had thought—the lady consenting—"

Old Osmyn's laugh and the thinner rasp of his younger son rang out together.

"You love her, sir?" shrieked the elder Osmyn, in the middle of it. "You have a damned rusty way of showing it. Does the lady know it?"

A spurt of anger banished Oramel's confusion. "She does more, sir; she loves me in return."

This flat retort took Randolph rather in the wind. He and his father crossed glances. The love of Oramel was but a joke; but it was plain old Thorley would never marry the lady against her positive preference. A lack of love would not have been a bar—but here was different matter for consideration.

Jeffrey Osmyn gave a cruel chuckle. "Well, well," he said, "after all, he is of the blood. It would do to tie them to the house of Osmyn."

Randolph made a strange reply. "It would do," he said, "but I have my own desire for her." The other two were struck into a dead silence. Randolph chewed and twisted the end of his cigar with his thin lips.

"Here is a snarl," said Jeffrey. "I'd not have thought you had that side to you at all, Randolph. But you've earned her; and by the powers of business, you get her."

"Will you ride roughshod over the lady's own desires?" questioned the luckless Oramel. "Sir, I have said that she loves me." His great figure and commanding eye resolved even his father's presence into something lesser, but the voice quavered like a child's. "God knows I am a poor enough clod," he said. "You've always thought me so; I've always acted out the part. But here I might have got a little happiness in a dull life, and you would have that out of me at a turn of Randolph's finger."

"You have heard him say," grumbled the old man in his beard, "he loves her, too."

"And how will that avail him, think you," poor Oramel was fighting on, "if she on her part neither loves nor can respect him?—as she could not if he took her in the teeth of her desires."

"They are not over-strong, I should have said," returned his father.

"And there you do her great injustice," said his elder son; "she is the purest spirit alive."

"Enough," said the other. "I will have no argument. Randolph wins."

Full-blooded passion rose and beat in Oramel's thick brain for the first time in his life, and for the last. "Why, then," he roared out, "I will take her in the face of you." And with a wild movement of uncontrollable anguish and despair he hurled himself into his chair and cupped his chin in his trembling hand—a thing he did instinctively when much excited. There was another deep silence in the room. Randolph refused to take a hand. The old man reddened under the slow fire of the first wrath his son had ever wakened in him—had ever been man enough to waken in him. He lowered his voice to a deep, hollow tone. In that gloomy room these three distorted spirits fought out the issue to its hideous conclusion.

"So-ho!" grunted the huge voice. "Well, then, take her; but you will take no substance from the Osmyns. And you are a fine-fixed lad to earn a living. Do you figure your wife in a blue calico at the washing? How long would she last under your guidance, think you?"

The anger had quite died out in Oramel; his chronic weakness flooded back into the centers of his being. He dashed his head to the table, flung his arms about it, and wept, great sobs that tore out from his shoulder-blades. There was something almost comic in this unreserved display, as if the heavy business in a melodrama had been sorely overdone. Old Osmyn's words spat out a withering disdain.

"When you have unglued the table with your tears, maybe you will feel the better of it—what?"

The partners left him to his misery.

Oramel had been correctly gaged. He had had one vital moment put before him and had failed to occupy it to his credit. He could now in prospect join a black future with a black past. He wrote a short pitiful note to his abandoned lady; it would be sacrilege to inquire fully into its incoherence. Enough that it shook the last puff of spirit from the sails of that fair vessel. The lady was quite resigned to marry Randolph at a word from Gordon Thorley.

Oramel was not present at the wedding, but he sent a pretty handkerchief, of some sort of soft Eastern stuff—perhaps for her to dry her tears upon, in sad reflection upon the giver. Six months or so later he presented himself suddenly before his brother's wife, as portly and as dull as ever, with the same awful majesty in his demeanor. He haunted the place for a week or more, never intruding at all on Randolph's wife; merely exchanging indeed half a dozen words with her at table. But somehow Randolph, who knew that he had not secured his wife's heart with her hand, conceived a tearing jealousy of his brother. At the end of the week he had the poor derelict down to the counting-house, dealt him out a letter of credit, and banished him to Europe.

Oramel lived abroad in his old black spirits; the greatness of his failure oppressed him like a shadow of some huge monument of woe. Night and day, year following year, he dwelt secluded in that shadow, and had not nerve enough to make an end. He haunted the cloisters of cathedrals; he peered into carved sarcophagi, with the mud dry at the bottom, and thought upon the boon of infinite repose therein. He sidled so through all the watering-places of the Continent, returning at last to drink tea and agitate his dark conscience in the slow current of London life. Many a person, marking the great figure and the iron jaw, mistook him for a bank-director, or perhaps, noting his brow, for a member of the opposition, and passed in envy, never questioning his greatness. Such lengthy suffering it were a horror to depict; to live, for all but Oramel, impossible. The nervous impulse of the suicide never lurked within that self-despising brain; the course that nature had laid down for it, that would it pursue. It was a great many years, certainly, that Oramel existed with his own reflections, and in all that time they ran upon the one topic. He had been disallowed a correspondence from the first, his quarterly remittance being dispatched to Randolph's London bankers. He had ceased, in the midst of life, to be a social atom.

Randolph, after his marriage, throve marvelously in his business ventures, but had as little joy in his domestic life as Oramel had fore-told. His wife pined gently. He never openly ill-treated her, but his passion for her died quite sharply with her loss of beauty; and finally, he sent her abroad to some mild climate. The business pace that he set would drive a stronger man than he into his grave. The elder Osmyn was long since dead, and after the great consolidation Randolph broke rapidly. He fell back in his chair at dinner ultimately, and the butler, coming in, looked down incredulously on the crumpled figure, to see so terrible a spirit finally inert.

The lawyers plowing through the papers of his vast estate found record of a brother resident in England and had word through to Oramel of Randolph's death. The news came to Oramel like a blazing light in his darkness. This was a solution he had never contemplated. He, like the butler, had half believed that Randolph, with his masterful energy, was scarcely mortal. He had grown gray and rather corpulent in all his misery, but if he looked in the glass he saw at least as much to charm her in his dull face now as there had been in youth. He knew that she was never angered by his weak defection; hoped perhaps that he might build his love anew upon those gentle premises. What reason soever brought him, he came back as tamely as a homing pigeon.

I had my office then in Garter Street. I hadn't got before the juries then; didn't even have the chance to lose cases that I have now. A step on the stair was like a hammer at my heart. I used to open Blackstone and dangle a little monocle I had for the purpose from a gold chain. It was on a dusty May morning, with a streak of sun lighting up Blackstone's definition of *primer seisin*—I can remember the thing as vividly as that—when I heard that solid step at my door, and saw that solid presence in the room. The big face was dull, but had a strained look, as of a past horror not lived down. His eye had a queer depth to it. It was a far cry that morning to get down to business; I had been out late the night before—there had been revelry and inspiration, and I was writing upon a rather turgid poem which I had provisionally named "The Wild Thin Edge of Beauty." However, I pulled a professional face, and dashing the similes out of my head, "If you were to go carefully over the whole ground," I said, "I should be the better fixed to frame a theory."

The poor gentleman passed briefly over his exile. "I came back," he said. "She was the one friend—God!" He groaned deeply, put his huge unshaven chin in his left hand, and went on. "I was directed," he said, with the horror growing in his eyes, "to the safe-deposit vault—a key was given me. It had been Randolph's wish that I should open it." His eye glared, but presently glowed amiably again, like newly poured champagne. "Death is but a passing, a change," he said, as if to fortify himself. "It was his wife's corpse within the vault."

I was a bit upset, you may believe, but it occurred to me at once that this was not a law case. And very shortly somebody came tumbling into the room in a good deal of a flurry, took my client by the arm, and led him out into the hall. The newcomer bobbed his head in again for a minute.

"Daft," he said, "but quite harmless. A gentle old idiot." And bobbed out.

Aymar drank deeply; the memory of it had palpably affected him.

"What might he have found in the vault?" said Gaunt.

"Oh, yes!" said Aymar, "I found out later. It was more his corpse than hers—the dead body of his manhood. The lady herself had died quite properly in the Azores, years before. Oramel would have known nothing of that. The vault contained only a crumpled silk handkerchief of foreign make."

THE BLACK SQUAD

From the *Saturday Evening Post*
(August 24 and 31, 1912)

A vivid tale of the tough grind of stokers on a steamship from Australia to London—with temperatures in the boiler room touching 140 degrees. Hallet worked as a stoker on the ship Juteopolis *to pay his way home from Sydney. This story's publication at age twenty-five with a handsome (for the time) $250 was the turning point in Hallet's decision to reject a career in law and pursue a life of adventure and literature.*

PART I

The beginning of this was in Australia. Three months before I had jumped a windjammer in Sydney and had all this time been coming down the road to Melbourne. Your new chum has a great place in the back country, and I lived well and wrought not much. But there is a kind of subsidence of personality in towns—a fine figure will become a mean one over night; a cold word will shrivel an imposing port; and a bitter wind sap the promise of a bed for the night which a sheltered roguery, basking in good esteem, will quite possess. Be that as it may, I had short shrift at the Apollo Inn, where I had sat me down, as I thought, to write my memoirs. Rogueries of the Road, I think I was to have called them; and there was to have been a fine dash and revelry about them too—but that's aside.

The truth is that, as I was coming down Flinders Street one dingy morning, with the heroic sixpence in my pocket, I passed the port bo'sun of that windjammer. We turned and stopped. He was an impudent little figure customarily, with red whiskers and a glowing red face that might have just dropped hot from some perverted Vulcan's anvil—but now he smiled because he suspected me of the sixpence; and there was about him a sheepish and liberated air, which he at once explained—a little proudly. He had been in jail twenty-eight out of thirty days ashore, it seemed. He felt a trifle jubilant to have wrung bed and board out of an ungrateful country all that while! Then there were the baths—daily! And you were only required to swing a ten-pound hammer. He had spent worse hours in chain lockers.

"What's the shipping?" I asked. A Norwegian bark and a French one. A few jobs at painting. He was going "on the coast."

"There's a job trimming a mail steamer at the port of Melbourne," he said; "but I'm no man for that. I'm no fireman. Too near hell as it is to be toasting my toes before my time!"

"Then that's for me," I said. I provided him beer and turned my steps toward the port of Melbourne. An able seaman is one thing and an able fireman quite another. If I was to get out of Melbourne in any honest fashion I should have to ship as trimmer.

I shipped as trimmer. The job was mine for the asking and a little pounding from the doctor; the trimmer's job is, so to speak, on its knees. I put my gear—a slim collection—in the forecastle of the four-to-eight; looked into the messroom, but not for long—and failed in an effort to get a mattress. I slept finally on the steel slats of my bunk.

I was prodded in the ribs. An elderly, very touchy person, with white hair, held a slip of paper. He read my name off.

"That you?" he shouted.

"Yes."

"Engine room!" he screamed and vanished.

I rolled out stiffly and went down into the engine room. This irascible old fellow was there before me, with his black cap at a commanding angle. He was called storekeeper, though he appeared to have nothing in his store but oil lamps and a great yellow brick.

The noise of the engines was such that it was impossible to hear him until after a third or fourth repetition, a thing that greatly inflamed him and that was probably the cause of his ruined disposition. A fellow

victim, who had told me hurriedly on the way down that he was going
to join a deserted wife—his own—in Freemantle, was set down with
the brick between his knees and a rasp with which to scrape off dust
for polish. He was a slight youth, with fair mustache—a waiter; and
nothing could be more melancholy than to see him sitting there clasping
that brick, sweat blinding him, those great, bright flawless rods, blurred
with grease and steam, plunging all about him. Surely his wife could
want no better demonstration of his renewed affection for her! This
devotion sanctified him.

The storekeeper put in my hands a three-cornered steel scraper, an
old shovel and some strips of burlap, and bade me dig the grease out
of the deckplates, beginning with the tail of the shaft and working
forward. The shaft is laid in a long, narrow alley, and is an uncom-
panionable thing. It spins its whole sleek, fat, shining length without a
murmur; strange varicolored frying greases lie under it, mottled with
pale, leprous bubbles. This shaft is rigid, infallible, greedy of work,
incommunicable. A lone-somer place than that long alley I cannot
remember to have seen!

When I had been clacking a couple of hours over the diamond
impressions in the plates, depositing black grease in the shovel, the
storekeeper stood over me again.

"Put on a coat," he said, "and go up and sign the articles."

Four of us had joined the ship in Melbourne and we met to sign
articles in the purser's office. We made a humble group, standing there
with our dusty caps off, unkempt and huge in this magnificence, before
a plump, white presence—the purser's assistant. We stood on plush and
leaned on rosewood, answering questions. This assistant was young and
peremptory—dispatch was what you read in his poised pen.

"You've been to sea before? You know the articles?" he shot at us
seriatim in a keen voice. We nodded; yet we never have known—never
shall know—the articles. They form the vague but artful bond which
binds us to the tyrant of the seas. We have heard them mumbled over
in consuls' offices. We understand that whisky and firearms must not
be brought aboard; bowie-knives and knuckle-dusters are forbidden;
assault is five shillings for the first offense and ten for each succeeding.
We cannot be asked to go farther south than the eighty-fifth parallel—
that is, we cannot be forced to go hunting for the South Pole. Beyond
this, we know simply that they tie us up somehow; that if we do not do

as we are told the company has so framed the articles that we shall get the worst of it. Well, what's a payday more or less? We affect a supreme indifference to these articles; we sign them to humor the plump assistant—or because we are there, and it would be childish to refuse. As with all simple people, our sense of tort is quicker than our sense of contract.

I took advantage of this business to have a word with the second engineer. Two hours had unequivocally fed me up on the shaft and its vicinity.

"I shipped as trimmer, sir," I said. "Am I not to get a chance to . . . er . . . trim?"

He laughed shortly. "Your first trip, I see," he said. "You'll get your chance to trim."

I went back to the shaft. Presently the storekeeper was standing over me again.

"Put away your gear," he said, "and wash up. You're in the four-to-eight."

Now the four-to-eight is generally conceded to be the best watch of the three. As the men put it, you have "all day off and all night in." This is specious. There are two terrific intervals—dawn and dusk—when you are neither "off" nor "in," but unmitigatedly "on." It is either broad day or black night when you come off; and for five weeks you will not see the sun rise or set, but only a waxing or waning light at the top of the ventilators.

During that "all day off" I acquired a mattress, a plate, a knife and fork, an empty; baking-powder tin—to drink out of—and an active distaste for Tasmanian tiger, an animal arching his back over that first dinner table, the men supplying him with growls. Tasmanian tiger is no other than stewed rabbit—an incomprehensible dish, I take it, though there were Olivers among us who called for more; but these had been on watch—and the body of a stoker roars for fuel like a furnace.

At seven bells I put on my working gear—dungarees, a gray shirt, a black cap, a sweatrag knotted about the throat. Weak tea, piping hot, made its appearance. A great noise arose in the galley, where the men were threatening the frightened cook with the claws of his Tasmanian tiger.

Suddenly there rose over a bunkboard an immense, compact, livid body, as thickly figured as a tapestry. On the chest was the insignia of the Order of the Garter, with the lion and unicorn rampant, *Honi soit qui mal y pense* in the circle and *Dieu et mon droit* on the bottom scroll; on each shoulder, a red star with violent black rays; round the neck, a bulging snake; under each collarbone, a sprightly robin; on the shoulder blades, butterflies; on the right knee, a skull with crossbones, the skull grinning when he swung his leg; on the left knee, a devil that grinned alternately with the skull. You have before you in the fancy flesh Jimmy Jones, the leading spirit in the four-to-eight.

"Red!" he bellowed, and the chatter ceased. A small, sleepy head, very white, and with a curiously swanlike pose, leered over the opposing bunkboard.

"Are you going to sleep all night and all day too?" inquired Jimmy Jones, who had certainly been doing that himself. "You're an early quick un."

The "early quick un" rolled the china-whites of his eyes, swore sulkily and muffled himself in his blankets again; but as if some importunate duty rested on him, searching his very soul, he wriggled uneasily; and after a few seconds of defiance he jumped out of his bunk and began to slide into his gear.

"Down, down to hell, and say I sent thee thither!" muttered Jimmy Jones sleepily but with some erudition. He relapsed into his bunk and called loudly for his pot of tea. "Bob Shilling, fill my pot."

Bob Shilling filled it; he drank and turned out. Thereupon they all turned out; there was none of them with the temerity to lie on after Jimmy Jones had set foot to the deck.

They dressed rapidly, took each a pot of the fluid called tea and went down to their respective holes. The way led first down two steep flights, past the freezing room, out of which came incongruously a great puff of intolerably hot, moist air; then through the long pass, a narrow gallery presenting a motley of stokehold gear—shirts and dungarees, drying against the yellow ribs of the ship. At the end of this was a low door, which I misjudged, cracking my head in consequence; then a turn to the left and the descent by a long steel ladder into stokehold number one.

This ship contained four double-ended Scotch boilers, and two single boilers aft, next the engine room. This made four stokeholds, the after one the largest, having sixteen fires opening upon it. Each of the double-ended boilers was fired through two boxes at each end and each fireman had four fires—a pass fire, the one next the pass connecting all

the holds and running between the cheeks of the pass boilers; a wing
fire, next the coal bunkers; and two intermediate or low fires, so called
because their fireboxes were set somewhat lower down.

Such is the order of things. Return with me to the chaos of flame,
coal, ashes and hot words wherein I found myself in that first *descensus
Averni*. I wandered into the after hold, coughing, blinking, singed and
useless. I had forgotten to lace my boot; the leather gaped at the top and
a hot cinder tumbled in against my ankle. I yelled, snatched off the boot
and stood on one foot. Evidently this had no bearing on the progress
of the ship.

"Want a job?" said Jimmy Jones. "Take that away. Next hole—to
the left."

He pointed to a steel barrow that stood under his high or pass fire. It
was heaped with the living body of coals he had raked out of the box.
I seized the handles; they were wet with sweat and burning hot. The
malignant coals snapped and spun out against my forearms; the barrow
wobbled—and I dropped it incontinently.

"Throw on some water," said the helpful Jim. I filled a bucket from a
spout in the pass—this water, too, was hot; and I threw it savagely into
the barrow. It returned against me in a blinding cloud of steam. I tore
off my sweatrag, wound it about the hotter of the two handles, and this
time wheeled the barrow into the pass. The forward movement trailed
the steam back full upon me, burning my arms like fire and filling
the pass until I could neither see nor breathe. The ship rolled; I staggered and ground the knuckles of my left hand against the hot side of
the boiler. All at once I came out into the after-center hold; the steam
cleared a little and a chorus went up of: "Haul tight!" But I could not
haul tight. I was hauling very loose indeed, and I trundled grimly into
another barrow and overset it. This barrow had been coming from the
forward hold at great speed, and its skillful operator laid all the blame
on me—and quite right too. In his place I should have done the same.
It was the early quick un; the whites of his eyes now twinkled in a face
gone very gray and hoary. He stood over his barrow, expanding his
really remarkable little chest and tightening his belt.

"Go on!" he shouted.

I went on. Right ahead of me was a huge, molten, snapping mountain of coals, over which hung a thick pall of ashdust, soot and fiery
particles. Here was a vault indeed "fretted with golden fire." Under this

declivity two vague, dusky figures were shoveling like mad into a snuffling bowl-shaped receptacle with barred top. A third stood over this
grating, smashing the larger lumps through it with a steel rod.

"Over there!" shrieked the leaner of these fiends, and directly I had
tilted out that glowing mass he gave an agonizing cry.

"Where's your water?"

Impossible to explain that it had gone up in steam. I backed out,
seized the barrow and fled aft, knocking my heels against the under
part of it in some maddening way. So began the operation known
as cleaning fires. Certain fires were each watch marked in chalk as
burndowns; and the fireman in charge, as the watch drew to its close,
allowed them to die down, leaving a long lane of gray cinders to the left
and saving a patch of fire to the right. The down-coming man cleared
the grate to the left, twisted the live fires over to the empty side, and
pulled out the other and hotter half. Then he spread out his fires again
over the whole, hurling in "cobs"—huge lumps that burn savagely, but
soon crumble and lose heat.

Each fire marked as a burndown yielded, with this foreign coal,
from four to five barrows of ashes. There were five in Jimmy Jones'
little private hell. Five times I lurched through the pass, choked with
steam, toppling—first right, then left—against the glowing surfaces of
steel; and each time I brought down upon myself in some new way the
wrath of those mysterious, catapultic demons, all unrecognizable, who
struggled at the foot of this ever-renewing mountain. When I brought
the empty barrow back for the fifth time the great Jones was lighting a
cigarette. The atmosphere had cleared a little, and he invited me to draw
the pit or ashpan. I swung up the door and seized a rake, or hoe with
a broad blade. The door was hot and the red had only now died out of
the handle of the rake. No matter—"In with it! In with it!" said Jimmy
Jones; and in it went. The shaft rested in a hook. In my left hand, which
was to seize the rake where it smoked, I held a handrag—that is to say,
a square piece of Brussels carpet.

"Make a jolly good dust, whatever you do!" chanted Jones; and so, I
did. He took the rake from me, showed me the more conservative stroke
and how to drag out the back of the pan by using the hook. So, it came
about that somehow or other we cleaned fires—though how, from that
one night's work, I should never have been able to explain.

Hot, dripping, fighting for breath, I got under a ventilator, and at once a cold dagger of air sank into my wet back—enough to kill a dozen men not preserved for worse ends! We were not yet in the hot oceans; it was still possible to draw breath out of the heat. The time was coming shortly when we should cluster in vain under those sooty airholes, with the little spot of yellow sunlight high above.

While I still sat or crouched under the ventilator, regarding a huge raw welt across my gray forearm, I heard from the second stokehold the iron rattle of a shovel on the lid of a mudbox, and the cry: "Fire aft!" The man who rattled this shovel was "on the steam"; it was his duty to watch the steam gauge and give the signal to rake or fire as the pressure fell away from "the red"—two hundred and fifteen pounds. This job was taken in turn; and the less often he found it incumbent upon him to rattle, the more popular was the man on the steam.

Jones began with his wing fire. The trimmer here in the twelve-to-four had luckily left him a good bulk of fuel; for I had not yet begun or thought of beginning to wheel out my heaps. With each shovelful a fierce white blob of flame leaped out of the box with a noise like low thunder; the face of the fireman was strained and distorted; sweat seemed to squirt from the end of his nose, his chin, his neck, his forearms. These last were black and shining, with a high light of yellow on the swollen veins and cleatlike muscles, grown there in the service of these daily agonies. He kept regularly lifting the coal, giving the shovel a vicious thrust far into the box, so as not to heap his coal in front and so block himself off from building up his fire to the rear. No Liverpool fires for him! He threw half a ton of coal into that fire and shut the door. One down! He took the three remaining doors in turn, without stopping, always in the loom of that just tolerable heat—always with the same precision, the same niceness of shovel-play. In his hands a shovel seemed as deft a tool as a lancet or a rapier—never stumbling against the box, yet always, in the upward thrust, faintly lipping it, thus taking the most out of the given angle.

He picked up a slicebar—a tool like a heavy crowbar flattened at one end. This flattened end he coaxed along the bars of the grate under the whole body of the fire. He then pulled it out until he had cleared perhaps four feet of its smoking length from the coals and bore down on it with all his might. I stepped behind him and looked quickly in. Arching over all I saw the heavy crown-sheet, ribbed and frosted, enduring the unendurable; under it the black mound of coal smoldered in jets of white smoke, then suddenly split open from end to end, the whole area leaping up in short, stiff orange flame, driven by the fans below. The orange roared on into a white which is the last white that flame can show; and a rain of hot dust spun down into his face—that black, scorched, unflinching face—while he still clung doggedly to the bar. Twined that way about the hot steel, he was like some writhing gargoyle—grotesque, hideously affected by some constant strain. He drew out the bar, let it fall heavily and clanged to the door. An ugly red began to die out of the tip of the fallen slice. His face was drawn; streams of sweat channeled through those blackly carved features. His giant shoulders drooped—he smiled a gaunt smile; but he was irrepressible.

"Gaw bless us, wot a cheerful blaze!" he said; and the thought of some old gentleman rubbing his hands and drawing up a little nearer to his hearth sent his laughter booming through the long pass. "Trimmer, throw out some coal!" he said.

This was not so bad. We had just coaled at Melbourne, and the bunkers were running, port and starboard. A great fan of coal spread away from the bunker doors, and the coal could be pitched to the fires without the intercession of a barrow. Thus, at the outset, the trimmer's life, in the words of the song, is bold and free. He may roll himself cigarettes, sit about on buckets and tolerate the jeers of those above him. Now, if he chooses, he may learn to be a fireman; he may slice and rake and pitch to his heart's content—and his fireman will beam upon him and take his ease. The trimmer, if he is well-advised, will do nothing of this sort, however, but take his own ease while he may; for his affair is not what it seems at present. Like some malignant fever, it has its phases; and this is but the first of them.

The first watch concluded, I got myself on deck. In a last frenzy of shoveling, I had taken off my shirt and was quite black from the waist up, saving the livid welt across my arm. I saw black, thought black, spit black; the base of my brain was inclosed in a black fog, through which a heavy train of cars was rumbling. The knuckles of my left hand oozed blood and I had twisted my right leg. All things considered, I would do well to ponder my position.

I did ponder it. I discovered by a simple calculation that I had seventy watches to stand; but I have never allowed myself to be alarmed by the merely numerical. Still, I must have spoken my thought aloud, for the man in the bunk next me groaned. I swiveled about wearily.

"That's a long time, mate," said he. His thin body was caved in against the stanchion to his cot. His dirty mustaches were all wild where he had chewed them; his eyes were full of fever. "I'm taking my wife and the kiddies home third class," he whispered.

He got no sympathy for his confessions from the four-to-eight. You will not easily touch the sensibilities of stokers. It fell to me to ask this poor fellow, now and again, how the kiddies were—and the missus. He had special license to go aft and see them. On that first night he despaired. At every movement in the forecastle he would waken.

"What time is it, mate?"

And somebody would say so many bells, and then, seeing that meant nothing to him, translate it into dial time. Then he would sink back in relief and compose his wretched body again to that distressful slumber. The dreaded seven bells had not yet come.

I washed. A stoker in his hours of leisure is a cleanly person—black for four hours, but white like marble the ensuing eight. His ablutions are rigorous and enforced upon him twice a day. A dozen of us were in that washroom, with its slippery deck and its atmosphere of steam, sea-oaths and fragmentary song.

White again, but very sore, I limped into the forecastle. Already that place was too thick to breathe in. The bunks were decorated with wet towels, sweat rags, lurid fiction and articles verging on the nameless. Here and there a glistening arm hung down over a bunkboard. The benches were covered with sooty shoes, slippers, pots of cold tea. A sound of painful breathing filled the place. The heat had come already, and we had jumped out of the frying pan into the fire!

I took my mattress to the fore deck and stretched out on it, intending to light my pipe in a moment or two. There was no wind—or, rather, what there was came up behind the ship and we could not feel it.

"I will light my pipe in a minute," I thought.

Then somebody shook me. I opened my eyes. A black figure was leaning over me.

"Seven bells!" it uttered.

This was incredible. I had only just now lain down. I had still to light my pipe.

"Look here, this is some mistake," I stammered. "I'm in the four-to-eight. I've just come up here!"

This dirty devil was already vanishing. There was no more arguing with him than with time itself.

"It's half past three," he said in a sulky voice. "Suit yourself." He was gone.

PART II

These eight hours off had swept by me in a flood. The four ensuing would show me time in a backwater. I understood now what my bunk-mate had meant by waking up so often. He was husbanding the watch. As I lurched into the pass with my mattress, at one bell I collided with him. He was black again; and he, too, had taken off his shirt. He was painfully thin.

"Mornin', mate!" he said. "Only sixty-eight now." His staring eyes beaconed a kind of grim humor.

"I'd lose count if I were you," I said. The sight of all those shirts hanging about recalled to me that I had not hung out my gear to dry. I found it on the deck, a sodden mass, and crawled into it disconsolately. A tall fellow, immensely wide but all bone, was leaning in the doorway.

"She's beginning to be on the nose," he said.

"What's she turning?" shouted James Irving Jones, referring to the revolutions of the screw a minute.

"Sixty-eight," said the fellow in the door. We began to go down, knotting sweatrags and nursing pots of cold tea. The handrail was hot and slimy with the sweat of the watch just gone off. At the entrance to the long pass a single needlelike drop of hot water fell on my head. At the top of the steel ladder I braised my arm on a dusty joint. I began to wake up.

Then I was plunged again into the blinding business of the burn-downs. The fires were dirtier than overnight—not quite so hot, but more fruitful of ashes. I was beginning to understand a little better the sinuous vagaries of the barrow and I was rapidly growing more canny in the use of water. It was easier to wheel out a white pyramid of coals and stand the abuse of the man who had to shovel it than to struggle through that frightful trailing envelope of steam. Every time I descended on him with my red and sputtering contribution of fire, this hoary-browed figure with sweat-streaked body gesticulated madly and shouted: "Water!" Then I would be gone again, wondering vaguely what he was going to do about it.

At last these fires, too, were drawn, the ashes cleared and the way ready for the coal. The bunkers no longer ran. There was a cleared space of six feet or so inside both doors and I set to work to fill the barrows, following the injunction of the leading man to "make up my 'eaps." At the fourth barrow it occurred to me to lift my lamp and look up. I saw then that I was working under a frowning, dull-black cliff, studded with gleaming cobs or lumps of the round coal. Even as I watched, one of these fell, grazing my shoulder and bringing up in the barrow with a shocking clamor. A little crawling rill of dust stirred— then a rush of larger coal; then, with a roar, the whole bulk of it sank, glacierlike, spreading, cobs bounding viciously down over the slope of it as the slide progressed. A choking dust filled the bunker—the lamp barely shone; but I had jumped out in time.

"Liverpool trimmer getting in his work, eh?" said my fireman, Harry. I thought that Liverpool must have fallen on evil days. A trimmer went through the pass with a can of ice water. I rushed after him and drank cup after cup.

"That's no good," says Harry. "You want to keep away from that. First thing you know you'll be kicking your length on those plates. Cramps!" He placed his hands under his ribs and shook his head. "Rinse your mouth—don't drink!"

"What's it brought in for?" I yelled. That heavy cold against the roof of my mouth was the keenest sensation I had ever known. My mad impulse was to apply it again and again.

"You'll have to get used to that," he said. "Make up your mind to put down the cup after one drink. You'll be tied up in a knot if you don't."

I went back to the coal. Harry stood at the entrance to the bunker, rolling a cigarette.

"You'll tear yourself to pieces that way," he said. Mine was a simple frenzy of shoveling. "Follow your shovel; sink it in; use your knee; lift it carefully. No waste! And see here—don't worry about these fires. Worry is what kills a trimmer. You shovel—that's all. If there's coal out here I'll put it in. If there isn't—no matter. Take your time! Take your time!"

He put his head into the pass.

"Here comes the medicine," he said. "This'll hearten you." The leading man appeared with a black bottle and a tin cup.

"I thought the days of grog were over!" I said.

"No rum, no steam, is the rule in this climate," said Harry grimly, and took his off. I drank mine and went back to the bunker. The heat and the rum turned the whole place into a conjuration of black magic. These were jinnee whipping the lids off burning caldrons; in these puffs of flame and steam, and these ascensions of black dust, I could descry veiled enormities, shapes that dimly threatened me. I was disembodied and could view this puny figure—myself—desperately striving at the bottom of that remote black mountain of coal with a tiny shovel—thrust—thrust—thrust! I seemed to shovel through eons of time!

"Been eating ashes?" said Jimmy Jones when I went into the forecastle. "I'll send you down some jam next time. Ashes and jam work up well."

He twisted a towel about him and went off to wash, singing that song which began: "A trimmer's life is bold and free!"

The man who had a wife among the third-class passengers had caught a cold; he lay in his bunk and coughed until the steel slats rang. A new trimmer had been taken in from the engine room—a shy, small fellow with brown eyes, soft hands, a split singlet. He had already burned one of his hands and the dust was beginning to poison it. He told me in a low voice that he was afraid the work was too hard for him. He could barely lift a barrow. He was a stowaway.

I washed and looked into the messroom; but I could not eat. The three tables there were littered with strange things—fish and sausages in greasy kits; the frames of chickens and turkeys whose substance was already gone; "cobs" or biscuits, imprinted with black thumbs and palms; and here and there cruel blue tins of marmalade with jagged tops. Villainous black coffee stood cold in a dusty kettle on the floor. The men "back on ashes" were entitled to apply to the galley for a "hand rag"—or steak—if they chose to tolerate the impudence of the cook and his remarks on overtime and unionism.

I went, instead, on deck and lay down by the starboard anchor. I was about to go to sleep when a gentleman who had been looking earnestly at this anchor for some minutes suddenly asked me, in a clear, educated, peremptory voice, if they ever cast it. I was about to say that we tied up to one horn or other of the new moon; but, recollecting my duty as servant to the company, I said that when we came to port we cast it in order that the ship might desist from its progress. He then said in businesslike tones that the chain—what appeared of it—had seemed so rusty as to imply disuse; but, of course—

Somebody was prodding me again. I opened my eyes upon the man who called himself the cook, though all he did was to fetch the food out of the galley and submit to the verbal indignities the veritable cook heaped upon him.

"Dinner!" he said. "Spuds, duff and Tasmanian tiger."

On mention of the tiger I turned to again and slept. I could not, in that state, have undergone another passage with this brute.

Then, despite the increasing heat, the watches began to blend a little one with another and to become more a matter of custom. Even my emaciated bunkmate lost his count and would now and then speak of a watch as not too bad. I found after the first week that two hours' sleep sufficed me for the day; and even in the night watch off I took my turn on deck, with a pipe or two, until four bells. Here we gathered, the wits and the blanks, stretched on the deck or the hatches, coughing a good deal, most of us resoundingly—sometimes pacing up and down in carpet slippers, lowly trimmer and masterful fireman alike.

We had a great contempt for the passengers, who were of no use to us except when they were seasick—which put us in chicken. We used to speak of going down and giving 'em a ride. Sometimes there would be a group of us gazing through a certain door with a heavy lattice which stood at the end of the corridor leading into the first-class saloon. This corridor was as incredibly clean and lustrous as a new collar in the hands of a salesman. The dark, shining round of a newel-post was all we could see of the stairway; but there rose here nightly a tide of grandeur and gayety beyond compare—ladies in flashing toilettes; precise gentlemen, bowed in thought, silent of tread, creased and elegant, and delicately holding cigarettes; perhaps smiling at subtleties or proffering civilities to the women with some refined movement of the hand—and, hovering without, those gaunt, white faces, the eyes staring from beneath blackened lids! The comment was mostly cynical—not always decent; but sometimes, too, I have heard a thought simply expressed of how mere flesh and blood could take these widely different roads. One night somebody said it was like looking into a cage; and a bitter voice was heard to ask which side of the door was the inside of the cage—a question, I fancy, difficult to answer. So, we lingered there; and the music of the voices came through the lattice, and the flash of gowns, and fragrance, and the laughter of the women going down into the ballroom.

It was, I think, the morning after we left the port of Colombo, in Ceylon, that the twelve-to-four watch came straggling up with the information that she was unequivocally on the nose at last. There was something wrong with the ventilators aft. Telephoning to the bridge had done no good. Cursing had done no good. We were in for a hot watch.

The ventilators aft—this was my watch aft! It was plain I should not have to rely on hearsay. I was to know soon enough in my own person.

The after stokehold registered 120 degrees Fahrenheit before we opened a fire. Six of the sixteen fires fronting on this hole were burn-downs. Not a breath came out of the ventilators; the steady glow of the place put an instant pressure at the base of the brain. The doors of four burndowns were opened simultaneously and the work began. The heat that poured out of those furnaces had no exit, no allay; we could feel the temperature inexorably mounting. Through gusts of flame I could see those set faces and desperately plunging rakes—pulling out the dead side of the fire, twisting the hottest of the coals over, grappling with the other side. The handles of the barrows seemed red-hot; the cheeks of the boilers as I passed between them shriveled me. My injured leg stabbed me at every step. The noise in my ears grew to a mighty murmur. I passed the tank of ice water, dropped my barrow and drank desperately, cup on cup—in the teeth of what I would have known in a sane moment to be a fatal risk. The ashes seemed to have no end. The men shoveling were walled up in them and worked on, with the red light glowing on their goblin bodies. The rakes plunged endlessly. Now and again a fireman dropped his rake to shovel, first dipping the handle of the shovel in water—for nothing will poison a cracked palm quicker than the sweat of other hands. Then again, the rake, a new outpouring of ashes—and always that insidious and gnawing heat!

This seemed to go on through the whole circle of time and was like one's final establishment in a literal hell! But the fires were cleaned— by sheer persistence and blind shovels they were cleaned; and I found myself, burnt, sodden, with spent lungs, in one of the forward holds, under a ventilator that gave down the faintest possible breath of wind. There were half a dozen of us there from the afterhold, arms upraised, black fists gripping the dusty smokebox chains that hung against the boxhead. Somebody kept yelling monotonously up that sooty aperture. He wanted to tell them to turn the ventilator on the wind, but his lips were dry and the words meaningless.

James Irving Jones was smiling faintly. An ugly red blister had appeared under one of his eyes.

"This is a life for a man—eh, lad?" he said. "Let's get a job as hot-cross-bun-makers—work one day a year, you know! Pull up there, Walt—that's no good. Steady on!" He paused and gazed at me solemnly. "I once knew a trimmer who got squashed between two barrows," he said. "D'ye know what came out of him? Ashes!" It is all in the tradition for a fireman to rag his trimmer.

"Ain't there anybody cries when the little trimmer dies?" said a voice.

"Nobody!" said Jimmy Jones compassionately. "We shovel him in, barrow and all. Gaw bli' me!" he cried, catching sight, apparently for the first time, of the little trimmer with brown eyes, who crouched on a big cob, nursing his poisoned hand. "Is this a trimmer? No? Yes? You don't belong here, son. You come home along of me and I'll get you a job in a tin factory. You can jump through the tin, you know, and make the holes for nutmeg graters."

At this point went the rattle. "Rake aft!" said the iron voice of it, and Jim slung his sweatrag over his shoulder and went aft. As he stooped through the opening to the pass, he seized the little fellow roughly by the shoulder.

"What—swanking?" he shouted. "Wheel out the coal!"

The new trimmer ducked hurriedly into his bunker.

"A bit of sympathy and they're gone!" said Jim to me. "You let one of 'em get to thinkin' himself over and you've got to carry him to the deck."

It was then that Sandy cornered me.

"New job," he said hurriedly. "Coal in the steel decks that's got to be worked out. Get a lamp."

I got a lamp. He preceded me up a burning-hot steel ladder on the port side of the after stokehold and in between the boilerside and the bunker partition. Here he bade me hold up my lamp; and I saw an opening in the steel perhaps a foot square, with three steel steps leading up to it and one over it for the handgrip.

"There's a barrow and a shovel in there," he said. "You're to fill this pocket from the gallery to the left. The pocket is right under this hole on the other side. Look out you don't fall into it. And go through quick—that hole is hot!"

That hole was hot—so were the steps leading to it and everything about it! It was too small for me, besides; and while I stuck there it left a lasting remembrance on my leg. Once through, I straddled the hole and reached my lamp in.

First, I examined the pocket. It was about two and a half feet square and appeared to go down clear to the bilge. By tilting the lamp, however, I saw that it slanted somewhat and was in reality about half full of coal. My barrow, with the shovel in it, stood by, and the gallery to the left was about thirty feet away. When I had drawn my barrow over the sill to it I found it about six feet wide. On one side of it the black ribs of the ship came down—on the other, huge wooden beams laden with dust. Down this unprepossessing gallery I trundled my barrow for perhaps a dozen yards; and there, in that remoteness, was the coal. I hung my lamp and began to shovel.

The first barrow had no effect on the pocket at all—that I could see; its dismal capacity seemed quite unimpaired. A second barrow and a third—still no rise. At the fourth I could see that something had been done; but by now the heat had very nearly conquered me. I filled another barrow. In my eagerness to empty it I ran it into a raised plate and overturned it a yard short of the pocket. I used expressions I had never used before—expressions that it amazed me to find I had by me at all. I banged the shovel against the ribs of the ship and shrieked into the pocket. And even as I leaned into it, I heard a heavy rasp from its depths and a black column of dust rose out of it. They were beginning to undermine me below!

I thrust such coal as I had spilt out of my barrow into that damnable cavity. It was as nothing. I picked up the barrow and stumbled with it back into the bunker. I had barely strength to get it over the slight obstruction the sill afforded.

"This is the last barrow!" I thought to myself. "I've got to get out of this!"

What I breathed seemed to crowd into my lungs like hot lead. Nicely speaking, there was no air in there at all. In proof of this my lamp went out. It did not flicker out! God knows there was no random draft in there to account for its extinguishment. It dwindled, sank and died, though it was full of oil. There was not oxygen enough to feed it! My matches were wet with sweat; I struck twenty before I could get a light—I counted them. Then I pulled out a length of wick, soaked it well and lit it. From counting barrows, I began to count the strokes of my shovel. Suddenly I hit a bolt or rivet in the floor, shattering my wrist against the stopped shovel. I bawled something into the growing blackness and struck into the coal again. Again, a rivet. A third stroke and a fourth. Some bolted trapdoor was evidently laid over the plates at this point.

I began to curse the ship and the maker of it, and the driver of these bolts. I stood perfectly still, and I could feel the sweat rilling all over me. My heart fell against my ribs like a ram and became confused with the huger and steadier hum of the engines. I bent down again and began—putting a kind of furious constraint upon my movements—to work down and tease away small shovelfuls of this reluctant dust. I heaped the barrow high, with an extreme and, as it were, spiteful conscientiousness. I wanted to show my defiance of this hateful conspiracy of things in general. I lifted the full barrow and proceeded toward the pocket. The sill stopped me. I seized the barrow by the guard round the wheel and tugged it over. I resumed the handles, but a mist was coming over things and the light was fading out again. I reached the pocket; but if I had then tilted up my barrow I should not have had strength to keep it out of the chute. I therefore wheeled it broadside on and overturned it.

At this moment the lamp died again. I stood up, plunged my shoulders through that hot, square opening, grasped the hot rail outside, pulled myself out and stumbled somehow down that long scorching steel ladder into the comparative arctic of the afterhold, with its sixteen fires and its 120 degrees Fahrenheit. They had just "pitched"—or fired—down there; and I had perhaps fifteen minutes in which to live again before returning to my bunker.

The reason for the failure of the after ventilators had now somehow got abroad. The first-class passengers had demanded a canvas to be raised—whether or no to screen them from the vulgar, I cannot say.

Suffice it that this canvas, all innocently demanded, served, besides its purpose, to block the wind from those precious openings of ours—at least, when the wind was in this quarter. And so, through those same openings, we sent up our respective and quite frightful opinions of the first-class passengers.

I broke mine off to reinsert myself into that square opening which led into my pocket. I set myself a limit of six barrows; and, with the work so marked out and rid of the deep discouragement of the empty pocket itself, I made it six without a break. Six by six, in that vitiated pocket, with the light failing me every second barrow, I dragged out the watch. The coal roared into the chute and went rasping into the fires, roaring again; and so the steam held to its mark, and the shaft turned, and the ship plowed on—and what more could all those good people up there want?

Yet they did want more. They talked with the younger officers, who would explain how very far below the stokers were and how hot it was down there and generally trying; whereupon several of the bolder ladies would form a hot-and-cold resolve to go down for just one peep, and make up a group; and their particular young sixth or seventh officer— or engineer—would lead them down through the engine room into his boasted inferno; so that all at once a horrified fireman, turning to throw his rake on the plates, would find a lady behind him under a flowery hat. And she would gaze at him with so interested and speculative an air that once, on one of these occasions, James Irving Jones was heard to murmur—though I trust, for his chivalry, not by the lady herself: "Yes, ma'am; we're fed at eight o'clock." Once a clergyman came down very inopportunely. Jimmy Jones was pitching a blower—that is, he was putting coal into a box whose tubes were choked, so that the flame, unable to make any other escape, lunged out viciously through the open door with each shovelful. Jimmy never left shoveling, but he began upon a sea-oath that was as long as his personal history, and even something, I think, more lurid. It was ingeniously, incredibly blasphe-mous; and the turns it took carried him triumphantly to the conclusion of the pitch. The poor cleric had stood through it all, trying to view the scene objectively and painfully desirous of not touching his elbows to the smutty boxhead. He was helped out of the hold perspiring a good deal, sad-eyed and a little smutted after all; and that night—I have it upon good authority—he remarked to the captain that the men in the holds swore terribly. The captain replied that the job was such that well-regulated angels could not be asked to undertake it.

"And you can't threaten these men with hellfire," he continued. "They won't burn—and they know it!"

Somehow I fancy there is more fire in that good preacher's sermons now than once!

Aside from these bold passengers no one ever came into the holds except the boiler-maker, his fat person arrayed in complete khaki; the second engineer, Nobby or Knobby, I cannot say which; and finally that august and self-treasured personality to whom we alluded as "the old chief." The boilermaker was good-natured, appearing to have nothing on his mind at all, though he was the reputed head of the stokehold forces. He repeated his orders many times in a loud, cheery voice, rubbing his hands, moving his lamp about and closing down bunker doors. It was his duty to estimate the coal—to protect it, so to speak, from the unthinking voracity of trimmers, with their brains composed of ashes. He tolerated chaffing, even from the lowliest of the men.

The second engineer was a man with loose-hung arms; a fiery, protruding eye; an incisive tongue; and an inexorable instinct for a Liverpool fire.

"There's why you don't get your steam, you farmer!" he would shout to Sandy, stopping, let us say, opposite the operations of Liverpool Dick. "Put a rake into that!" Sandy would plunge in a rake and disclose woeful hollows to the rear of poor Dick's fires, poor Dick meanwhile standing by, rolling in voluble excuses. Nobby would lean in, the white light gleaming awfully on his projecting eye and thin, tyrannizing nose.

"What's that?" he would explode. "Nothing? It's going out. What have we here? A piece of wood. Throw it on! Throw it on! Keep it going somehow—eh?"

And Liverpool, with a shrug to show how completely he is undone, thrusts in the wood and slams the door sulkily.

Words fail me to describe the visits of the old chief. His appearances were seldom, but of unmeasured significance. He was portly, mild, inquisitive, a good listener. He waxed his mustache. He never lost his temper. Once only I remember him to have offered a suggestion. He requested a fireman not to put in any more of the wet coal. This fireman had not seen him; and, without looking back, he said, "Who the hell are you talking to?" continuing to shovel in the wet coal all the while.

"I'm talking to you," said the old chief composedly. He made every allowance.

He carried with him, in a black cylindrical case, an electric light that came on at the pressure of a button. Armed with this, he made a kind of progress through the holds and bunkers and between the boilers. The second, in close attendance, took up his civil questions and roared them forth again. The old chief would turn his light calmly, without speaking, upon a barrow of ashes, drawing conclusions for himself; and under this moment of illumination these ashes, which had seemed mere dross and formless waste, became all at once typical; characteristic somehow of some precise phase of the infernal process. The trimmers would stop shoveling to stare, at them stupidly. After a time, his square, heavy shoes would go up the ladder in the forward hold; we would see the soles of them put down carefully on the double steel rounds.

"That's the job for you," somebody would say, "pushing that little button!"

"Yes, but he's got a lot on his mind."

"More on his stomach!"

During the whole run from Colombo to Port Said the ship was on the nose. The dreaded afterhold breathed on us like some ancient dragon—and was the worse for the two trimmers here, by their having eight fires to supply apiece instead of four. The holds were, of course, taken in rotation, by both firemen, and; trimmers. After three watches the steel decks, of which I have written, were empty and scraped clean of coal. Every ounce of it was gone. We had pounded it out from behind the steel rungs of side ladders and smashed it down through the sooty slats athwart the ribs—sweeping it all—down to the last black atom of it—into that resounding, dust-spouting, insatiable pocket. There were now three sets of the eights too. The little brown-eyed trimmer's hand was in a sad, snow-white bundle; he was laid up by the doctor and lay in his bunk reading *Oliver Twist* and submitting to be called a passenger by Jimmy Jones. "Give him his tea—tuck him in there, some of you. Give him anything he asks for. Come on; we're going down and give him a ride. Any last requests, Tom, boy?"

A sick man on a ship will always have short shrift. Let him take to his bunk and the cruel suspicion of malingering is alert at once against him, pressing in on him from every side. He must bear not only the physical pain, but a sense of having lost favor in the eyes of his shipmates. He worries and endeavors to put the thing to proof. He must show that he is on his last legs. Failing in this, he will force himself to go reeling down to work when he can scarcely stand, to lighten him of his infamous reputation as a "swanker." He may never lay up at all; may never see the doctor—"go aft to the quack"; may not open his lips upon his trouble, so that his mates are surprised when he comes crashing to the plates some hot watch, the solid barrier of will swept away in physical collapse. Laying up is tolerable to a seaman only when the infirmity is shockingly visible. And for an ill man to go, watch after watch, into those smoking holds is not a pleasant exercise in self-control.

As the firemen become known in the engine room for what they are, through the water they take when operating single boilers, so they become known to trimmers by the amount of coal they shovel. Liverpool Dick was the favorite among them all; for he boasted—and made good his boast—that he pitched but twice a watch. The second stormed at him—but what matter! The second knew what he could do; he—Dick—was only coming back to fetch out his wife to the Colonies and would be done for all time with firing when she tied up at Tilbury.

His firing mate, Walt, differed from him—all calamitously for the trimmer. It was a saying of Jim's that an honest day's work had never yet been done in the holds; that the best of them only wobbled on or off the mark like the indicator on the pressure gauge. Yet Walt, the cockney, never wobbled. He was a tall fellow, with narrow, sloping shoulders, a deep chest—he was in effect cylindrical as to trunk—and a face lined and furrowed like the face of an old man. His chin was underhung in profile, yet massive enough viewed straight on; his lips were always compressed. It was as if a weak character were to be ribbed and bolted by a transforming earnestness. Earnest he certainly was—he had made up his mind individually that the ship should move. His conscientiousness was grim and terrible and rode him like black care, the horseman. He cried out in his high-pitched voice against the slackness of others and confirmed himself momently in his sense of justice toward those devouring fires. Not even in the hottest watches would he omit to slice them after pitching; and when the steam was in his hands his rattle sounded at the least lowering of pressure. I have seen him stoop and snatch out of a passing barrowful of ashes a solitary lump of coal in the interest of the company! What addition this might make to the four thousand tons that would be burned before we docked in Tilbury it was not for him to consider. It was coal—not ashes! Let it go where it should go! He would continue to shovel for a quarter of an hour after the shiftless Liverpool had stopped—Liverpool the while rolling cigarettes and regarding him with that deep disdain which your "swanker" has for men of solid parts. Then Walt would slam the door to his last fire, and those black, sweating mates would glower at each other, each persuaded that his own contempt was the better founded.

"I 'ad a trimmer once," said Walt, mopping himself with his sweat rag, "wot thought I 'ad it in for 'im. Farst as 'e'd wheel it out I'd pop it in. Larst of it was, 'e come at me proper. ''Ere, Gaw bli' me,' 'e says, 'you're doin' this a purpose! You're goin' out of your way to do it! You want to tear me down—that's wot you want!' So I opened the door to the parse fire. ''Ere's the fires,' I says; 'if the coal's 'ere I got to put it in. You fill the fires,' I says, 'and I'll wheel out the coal.' So 'e keeps on," said Walt reflectively. "'E keeps on becos 'e was a game un; by-an'-by 'e does come down proper! 'E was a 'eavy man to get up those ladders"—indeed, in that heat it is not an easy business—"an' w'en I 'ad 'im laid out on deck an' 'e opened his eyes, Gaw bli' me, 'e wanted to fight! 'You're the man!' 'e says. 'Blarst you an' your fires!' . . . We gotter get the steam!" said Walt, as if the recital required a touch of self-justification.

"No trimmer of mine ever 'ad cause to reproach me," said Liverpool, dropping one heavy lid so that I alone might see.

"I guess you ain't ever broke a trimmer's back!" said Walt.

"Too much consideration for the feelin's of others," said Liverpool. He wiped the blade of his shovel clean with his hand rag, drew out a lemon and halved it on that black edge. This lemon the cook had thrown down to the two trimmers in the forward hold, who in return hoisted his coal for him. These trimmers had hastened to lay the offering on Liverpool's altar.

"I 'ave me reward," he said, sucking the blackened acid, "in the gratitoode of me mates."

At this moment, as I remember, there came a prolonged siren from above.

"Boat stations!" grinned Liverpool. "Wot's a pore stoker to do with boat stations, mate? We 'aven't split yet, any'ow."

"Practice, I suppose," I said.

"Maybe—an' maybe not," said Liverpool. "Maybe swimmin' practice—for them on deck! You an' me can watch the little boilers poppifi', mate."

Before now I had not been guilty of thinking too precisely on this event; but, at this whistle and this cheerful comment, it occurred to me to trace out what must ensue down here if "Boat Stations!" should ever sound in earnest. Supposing the strike to be against the side of her, I pictured a wild grapple with the chains of the bunker doors, in the attempt to shut these down and protect the great dusty boilers so long as might be from the fatal touch of the cold sea! I could make out these sweating men, with drawn faces, swaying together there in knots; then failure, perhaps; a savage rush for the long pass, where mayhap the door would have been jammed against however mighty and desperate an effort!

Then the tumultuous recoil down the steel ladder into the forward hold, heels smashing heads; the stirring and buckling and frightful upraising of iron plates; the grinding together of steel barrows; the thunderous roll of coal in the bunkers; some sharp command lost in a shrieking escape of steam from splintered water gauges; then the heavy detonation of exploding boilers in the afterhold; and finally the steam— the steam, in which nothing would live, and in the midst of which these huge receptacles of steel would move from their beds and tumble about in a tangle of chains, platforms and twisted ladders, amid a blackness filled only with steam, fiery soot and the raining out and extinguishment of white fires! Truly, one had better shrug one's shoulders with Liverpool and speak of swimming practice!

The hot run to Port Said began to draw to an end. Once, coming up to "blow," very black and wet, I saw stretching on the starboard side the awful coast of Arabia, gleaming with sand, so withdrawn from human resource that a liner will stop for the smallest boat putting out to plead for water and provisions. Again, I saw the red, cruel, pyramidal entrance to the Red Sea, one point of rock on each coast crowned with its lonely station. One glance round upon this ancient desolation and I must dive below again. The circulation of this monster was impaired. The coal was all gone aft and had to be run out of the forward bunkers. The eight trimmers, very sulky at this affront upon them, went dashing and colliding between the boilers. The screeching barrows had begun to jib; in other words, the wheel pressed against the steel underbody,

moving us to imprecation. There was a swell here, too, which made
even running impossible; and now and again a barrow would run amuck
and bang about the holds with cunning velocity. Such a barrow will put
Hugo's loosened cannon to the blush. We began to doubt whether the
ship would have coal enough to crawl up the canal. "Serve 'em right if
she don't," we muttered, "for driving her this way!"

She did, though, and to spare. I remember shoveling like one gone
mad in the forward bunker toward eight bells to make up my final
heaps. A great bulk of coal had just shifted, sending up a black fog, in
the middle of which I thrust and thrust again, though I could not see the
coal, or the shovel, or my own arm. All at once I became aware of a blur
of light over my shoulder. I stepped back toward it, and as the dust fell,
I saw towering over me, queerly illumined in that gloom, an immense,
black, pockmarked face, surmounted by a blue turban. Then I made out
a gigantic pair of shoulders under a seedy English overcoat; and under
the skirts of this again a red and very dirty drapery.

"This is it!" I thought to myself. "I've gone mad now, right enough!"

Then the figure moved—a knotted fist, glistening with sweat and
dust, held up the lamp to my face; and this apparition plainly asked
me if I had any tobacco! Then I saw we had reached Port Said and
that I had before me an example of the foreign trimmer, who had
come in through a coal port. In another moment the hold was full of
these fantastic figures, uttering weird cries and crowding about me for
tobacco. I leaped back out of the bunker, loosening the chain, which
brought the door down on the run—sealing them up for six hours in a
compartment wherein one not indurated to breathe in dust instead of
air could hardly, I think, have held on for twenty minutes. As I went
through the long pass I heard the coal pouring into the ship from every
side, roaring and rattling into the black pockets; and I knew that inside
were these foreign fiends directing the slide of coal, penned in that
unbreathable blackness—ineluctably. Without, rafts clustered about the
ship; lights burned and flared feebly in curious barred cressets; count-
less lines of figures passed and repassed with tiny baskets, stung into
action by shrill exhortations—Egyptian, Arabian—I know not what the
tongue. A glance at this tiny movement of coal and another at the huge,
black, motionless side of the ship, and you would have thought they
could not have coaled her before the pyramids should crumble! Yet, in
the six hours before midnight, they had poured into her, with these same

baskets, twelve hundred tons! Port Said, archaic though its method, is reputed to be the quickest coaling port in the world.

This coal was the long-anticipated Welsh—a coal dustier than the bulli, if that could be; but it burned with a hotter and steadier fire and kept the steam to the mark with fewer pitches. The Welsh burned, too, with a lesser residue of ashes; and what there was clung to the grate bars in solid masses—"old men"—which came up only to the prod of Jumbo, the giant slice, with two or three straining on his handle. Then, after some teasing and hectoring, a mighty fragment, bleeding red on its underside, glowing in fiery, chaotic scenes, would fall to the plates—to sputter and grow more thickly red. This was fitly called a "trimmer's tombstone," and he must worry it to the winch himself and set it up—for, after Port Said, the Blow-George blew himself no more, but was silent and smug, the deck swept clean round him. A steam winch hauled up the ashes to a little chamber full of dust and steam, where a man with shut eyes and straining lungs overturned the basket of them on a grating that communicated with a chute. This chute spouted them forth into the unregarding sea and they troubled us no more.

Now, too, the forward and forward-center starboard boilers and the single boilers aft were cold and drawn; we were proceeding under twenty-four fires for the city of Naples. It began to be deadly cold. Our backs, blistered but now by burning Arabian suns, were humped under the chill touch of the sunny South. Shivering, I saw the blue, uplifted coast of Crete hang in the sky, while a stray artist, bundled in a thick coat, strode the saloon deck, snapping life into his fingers and trying to sketch. Here were the very waters that had rolled the fair body of Venus toward that charmed coast; yet I must needs slink below, light my pipe and cower against the furnace doors. The baths were now a simple misery of cold, the bunks cheerless, the deck swept by bitter winds. There was but one warm place—the galley; where the cook, full of an enforced accommodativeness, turned his steaks with long black tongs, his hand shaking with rage at this invasion, his tongue full of threats. We hung towels to dry there; toasted bread at his ovens; Reminded him how we daily toiled to keep him in coal—anything to prolong our footing in that steaming, not over-savory place. There was a boiling caldron at one end of it; we yearned to take our baths in that—and spoke of our yearning; whereupon the cook, from the bitterness of his soul, said that he would see us in a warmer place yet! He would have us on his griddle—and he opened and closed his tongs feverishly and raved on.

In the holds there was no more bawling into ventilators. We deliberately closed them and sat on the coal heaps, disconsolate and cold, though we could hear the humming of the fans within and the sound of fires. The grog had stopped; the human engine needs this kind of oil only in the hot oceans and, be assured, will get it nowhere else.

Toulon! The Rock! Now we began to talk of doing things for the last time. We washed clothes for the last time—mustered for the last time—passed our last duff day. It seems necessary to consider this life not as continuous but as broken into voyages—and to think nothing of the next voyage. The mind is bent on finishing the one in hand. One might suppose a new life awaited us in Tilbury—a life of gladness, wherein no seven bells were mingled; a life not of dust and looming fires but of beer, of leisure everlasting. You spoke of getting up at noon to a plate of ham and eggs; of sauntering into the White Hart and ordering a foaming pot. And then more sleep! Out of uninterrupted slumber to awake to ham and eggs, with the prospect of a pint of beer—this is the desideratum of your stoker. In this will he smother unquiet memories of heat, dust and Tasmanian tiger. What reckons he of it that in ten days he will be back to his furnaces, with the rattle in his ears, "Rake aft!" and the clang of bars and rakes on steel plates! For this fortnight he is free as air; free to stroll about and patronize and receive the homage of the fair—conquering in a whirlwind, for his time is short. The next voyage? Ah, in some other life!

One of us had a trade—a tinsmith, he thought, should make a comfortable wage ashore. Another had no trade; but he, too, would forswear this business. He who was leading stoker in the navy had visions of his wife, a competent and sympathetic woman, it would seem—a seamstress, whom he had set up in business at an expense of thirty pounds and who now made a great deal more money than he did himself. A good investment, to his way of thinking! She was a sensible woman too—never failing to lay in a dozen of stout against his homecoming; and once, to keep him by her longer, she had got him "proper drunk," so that he missed his ship. This was playing on his weakness to some purpose, if you liked. No danger of his ever waking up and finding his book of discharges on his plate for breakfast! They had a gray bird, brought from the West Coast—once a very profane creature—which she had broken of sea-habits of speech. Very seldom he burst off now. A great comfort to her. This trip was his last as well. The trip was everybody's last, a statement that served as a buffer to the shocking fact that it was nobody's last!

Back they will come to it—all of them; back to the rakes, and seven bells, and Tasmanian tiger. For this land they cherish, whose solid green so thrills them in the outer anchorage at Plymouth, will, after all, not tolerate them long. The White Hart will soon ingulf their payday; and then, unlike my friend of the gray bird and the incomparably profitable wife, they will find their "books" laid by their plates; and their sea-gear brushed and conspicuously got together for them near the door. So—one more pot on the credit of the next voyage! And perchance a last kiss on the strength of youth alone—this hard youth, moving great ships through trial by fire; full of the giant strivings of the humble—this youth which adventures and profits nothing, unless in the illusion of adventure. And then again, the great cradle of the seas!

Now we are conning our deduction sheets in Tilbury dock—these sheets whereon the dusty god of figures has set down things that will not bear thinking of. Here is little Red, with drooping cigarette, who has been logged ten shillings, partly because he came aboard in drink at Colombo and punched a fat quartermaster in the stomach with a bottle; and partly because, when called into the inquisitorial chart-house, he doffed his black little stoker's cap respectfully in that stern presence and scattered dust over the resplendent floor and the Day's Work column. "A bit thick!" he calls it. Aye, Red, a bit thicker still, I am thinking, and blacker than thine offending cap! Five pound was too magnificent a payday to come to you in all its luster—they must chip it in the interests of discipline, to teach you to take your "'olidays" with less hilarity; but will you be any the less hilarious on four pound ten than on the more colossal five, poor Red?

And Bob Shilling, too, is having trouble with his sheet. Only two pound ten coming to Bob; but this is because he got ashore in Sydney and missed the boat and had to go overland to Melbourne to pick her up, under the company's auspices. Better luck and a plumper payday next voyage, Bob Shilling—and your health too! James Irving Jones is wrongly charged with boots and is in a state to fling the ones he has into the face of the fat storekeeper who has wronged him. Trust Jim to set this matter straight!

Now behold the comically smeared face of Sandy in the after pass! "She's tied up!" says he. "Draw fires!"

And out upon the plates tumble all the blazing heaps, roaring and burning blue and red, subsiding into the wet grays.

"Finish!"

The livid rakes clatter in behind the boilers; barrows go sliding and jumping into bunkers—all abandoned! Another moment and the holes are empty; nothing there—in that soft gray light, amid these dusty chains and pitted boiler fronts and chalk-marked box heads—but a slight steaming and sputtering of drawn fires and the swish of water against the bunker doors! We are tied up!

WITH THE CURRENT

From *The Smart Set* (July 1913)

A moving tale of a young American adventurer crossing through the back country of Australia via his wits, will, and homemade canoe. Drawn from Hallet's own travels with his friend Frank Hyde, with whom he sailed to Sydney in 1912, "the big Yank" encounters harsh weather, menacing wildlife, and a medley of strange characters—a beaten-down old man, a stunning young woman, and a sadistic baron. Part mystery, part romance. Long but engaging tale of the grip of fate and fortune that lies around the next bend of the river.

The man in the boat, stopping his paddle, looked up the leprous trunk of a gray gum overhanging, and presently shook his head.

"No," he said aloud, "you might make a dish to deceive the Queen of Spain, as my old pardner said. But I reckon you're an impeerative dish."

The "impeerative" dish, a gray lizard, moved a little, doubtingly, with a kind of sinuous languor, and a scraping of its scales against the dead wood. A dapper and thoughtful reptile, it plainly never found itself in advance of its occasions.

"Good-bye, gohanna," said the man in the boat good-humoredly. He shifted his mat of wheat bags and shot out again into the current. Trailing his huge paddle, he rolled himself a cigarette, looking keenly ahead through the heat which brimmed out of this deep sun-baked fissure, at the bottom of which a thread of river ran. He knew it all: the mud, the heat, the blue sky, the gray banks, the sly crackings, the slow, tepid current, over a sparkle of sands, over polished pebbles, over green quivering films wavering from the sunk boles of fallen trees. The river, in four weeks, had spoken its heart to him a thousand times, menacing him, for his indifference, with snags, shallows; wooing him in dark pools with possibilities of river cod, luring him, teasing him with dallying bends, teaching him anew the folly of toil, of stress, which was the one folly of his life.

But though he knew it, he had not wearied of it. The heat and silence and emptiness were comforting to him, like a warm blanket on a cold night. Yes, he had known cold nights; he, with his fish's blood. Drifting along here lazily, between steep banks of cracked mud, which revealed the onslaughts of wet seasons past, he thought of those bitter watches in the Southern Ocean; the black deck, like the roof of a barn, of that old bark which he had deserted in Sydney to be his own man again at any cost; the glazed yards, the wind swelling over the break of the poop, droning in the taut rigging. That was his one weakness—cold. It was his policy, when he steered his own course, to traffic in the torrid zone. Not that he always steered his own course. He had been caught up, now and then, certainly. On occasion he had gone end over end, like a leaf of autumn. All his life, indeed, at intervals, he had known the servitude of the seas, but as a means, not an end. Only incidentally was he an able seaman. Almost alone among his kind he had a faculty of "sticking ashore" when he chose.

And now he chose. Dragging his paddle through the sluggish current, he thought of the cool sea with pleasure, as of a mistress for whom his infatuation was not fatal. He bore no chains. He stood alone, momentous, colossally selfish, without aims, without responsibilities. No one, man or woman, had ever thwarted him of the new horizons which he sought; these horizons which his feet might never pass, his eye never penetrated. By the blue distance alone could he be subjugated; into whose depths he projected his visions, and lost them, conquering at a stroke time, space and this humankind, through which his burly figure passed, ever passed. He was of those who are free by being footloose; and free in vain.

Thus, he dreamed and drifted, self-sufficing; a lolling giant with a scarred body and a child's heart, the jaw of a lion, the eye of a gazelle. He had full capacity for wonder. He floated there in a bath of clarifying indolence, without a shadow of the spirit of urgency upon him, following the current, whose gentle movement could alone appease him, satisfying that strange hunger of the heart which drives your wanderer, it may be half against his will, to sudden ends. He stretches out mighty arms to receive all, and receives nothing; and yet, in wondering, recovers somewhat, too.

In remote time—three months, half a year—he might find himself at the port of Adelaide, the sea quivering before him in the heat there, with the rusty liners which he knew so well stolid against the docks. But now, drawing some secret solace from this deep entombment of his being in solitude, he was content to let that lie in prospect, against the hour of his need.

So, he drifted, and presently, yawning, he said, "Holy Mackinaw!" profoundly and without occasion. Then he pushed back the felt hat, with broad brim, which sat close on his black hair, and smiled, a slow companionable smile, like a taunt to the solitudes around him. Talking to himself, eh? He had done that before, and he knew what a weight of isolation it required. There had been a fellow from the back country at a bar in Sydney who had answered his own questions instead of other people's. He pondered the fact.

Suddenly, forging into a green, quiet pool, he snapped a spoonhook out behind him, for it was in these pools that river cod might lurk, and it was certainly true that he must provision before night. With effortless strokes he drove across this pool, turning back to watch his spoon twinkling over the sands of a bar, which wavered up in yellow brilliance through the warm green depths. They held the sparkle of true gold, these sands, not figurative; this gold which lies thinly dusted over all that land, kindling adventure in the heart with its faint promise, everywhere repeated.

Passing the pool without a strike, he drew out the hook, and holding it by the line, twirled it in the yellow sunshine, whose rays fell upon him like hot bars, massive and tangible.

A cockatoo, half immersed, bumped the boat. It had eaten rabbit poison and was dying; in its eyes, over which a film was rising, a look of black immediacy. The man, nipping it by the claws, watched curiously the withdrawal of life from that warm body.

"It's the Grim Destroyer, birdie," he muttered. It was his habit to refer to death in these terms, as to a shabby person, always at his elbow, to whom he played the patron, but who, he knew, would someday take "a fresh twist" out of him, playing him some low trick or other in return.

With a clutter in the throat, and a last ruffle of the wings, the cockatoo fell sidewise, knocking its beak against the boat. The man pondered again, with corrugated brow and drooping cigarette; and presently, plucking the sulphur-colored crest from the head of the dead bird, he arranged the wet feathers artfully around the three barbs of his hook. As ever, the opportunist.

"Tempted to bite at it myself," he said joyously. He dropped the dead cockatoo overboard, and dipping his antediluvian paddle, struck out again into the current. A whole flight of cockatoos, chalk-white, with brilliant yellow crests erected, lit on an aged gum tree, and seemed to set its dead limbs into a clatter with their perverse screeching—this desolate sound, as of a diamond on glass, which made emptiness more empty. They glared down upon him, frowning and ruffling, as if in a spirit of personal anger at his appropriation of those feathers. Again, he smiled, that slow smile from the depths of a contented spirit; the smile of a man without reverses, for whom things visible have no terrors; the smile of a man who has the world all to himself.

At the next bend the sun fell more nearly in his face, and his eyes narrowed. A broad beach of dimpling sands shone on his left; and on his right a solitary black hog was reaming his way deeper into a trembling mire. The long snout worked softly at its end, gleaming; and the bristles on its arc of spine, razor-edged, shivered under this rising ecstasy of mud. The hog, lethargically sinking, expressed the depth and completeness of its experience in a grunt, a wrapt sound, luxurious and gross.

"Damn you," said the man; "wish I could get the hang of that."

He made the sound himself and waited for the hog to correct him. But the hog, sulking in its bed of mud, with poisonous green bubbles rising on its flanks, appeared now content with its efforts, and closed its eyes. The man laughed, and again dipped his paddle.

Ahead of him a teal flapped its wings, dragging half out of water, luring him with its disabled look; but he knew all about that now. The teal was drawing his attention from its young—an exhibition of superfluous cunning, for he couldn't have found them in any case. He knew all about it. He knew all about everything now. Deeply satisfied with his knowledge of the subtler aspects of things, he laid the paddle on his knee and rolled another cigarette. Lighting it, he saw that his supply of matches was running low; and since that, too, afforded an outlet for his surprising acquaintance with shifts, he took the remaining matches, and dipping them in water, to soften the tips, he split each one carefully into fours, and laid these needle-like splinters out to dry. It had been a week since he had passed a house, and on that river a man without fire was a man without hope.

He took another turn now, shutting out the problem in contentment afforded by the hog; and as he swept his new horizon with the old eagerness, conscious of a vague seduction in each turning, though the changes were incredibly minute, an expression of genuine surprise tempered the mellow serenity of that dark face, which seemed to hold the sunshine.

"Holy Mackinaw!" he said again, but this time with a heavier and more justified inflection. For there was a man sitting on the bank.

This man was old and lean and puckered; but his monkey's face, a web of wrinkles, showed his eyes bold and roving, with the same quality in them of quick and searching appraisal which marked the eyes of the man in the boat. He was sitting on a soiled cotton bundle in two parts, joined by a strap; a black can, full of dents and wooden plugs and clay-colored water, was coming to a boil over a fire whose blaze this swagman quickened sparingly with small twigs.

"New chum?" he inquired, with a kind of casualness, as if conversation were a thing of naught. Indeed, since he kept to the road, like a proper swagman, his opportunities to talk came oftener than those of the man in the boat.

"Yes," said the latter. Aware that he was heard, he found his voice a trifle thick, as if clogged or rusted from disuse.

The man on the bank, lifting his can from the blaze, dashed a pinch of tea into it and set it back a moment. Withdrawing it again, he looked thoughtfully at his red lumpish boots, ironclads, these, with the impregnable leather in billows, and the loop of hot nails on the soles shining in the sun. He seemed to argue with himself whether it were worthwhile to go on.

"Yorky or Lanky?" he said presently, turning his tea into a dirty cup.

"Yank," said the man in the boat.

Then they were both silent, while the man on the shore looked at his boots again, as if these dumb oracles had left him doubtful. The silence, whose spell they had broken, closed in again, like a fog, encroaching on thought, burying the faculty and desire of speech deeper and deeper.

The tea stopped boiling in the battered can; the glowing twigs went gray, quivering into impalpability. One of them spurted blue flame, with the sound of a remote siren; and the swagman continued looking at his impenetrable boots. The Yank regarded him with contained amusement, his big forearms flattened against his knees.

"There you 'ave it, then," said the swagman suddenly, with a mighty effort bringing the circles of their experience into tangential relation again. "Needn't 'ave arst."

"Knew all the time?" inquired the Yank gently.

The swagman nodded.

"You go 'ookin' it off on this bloody river, luk this 'ere—in a boat."

He regarded the boat with disdain, and for so long a time that communication was endangered again.

"Easier than the road, and plenty of water. And whole feet," said the Yank, advancing his speckled toes proudly over the side of the boat. The swagman pushed his dirty helmet back.

"I've 'oofed it back an' forth 'ere fifteen years," he said; "an' I'll 'oof it fifteen more afore I tykes to boats. You won't get 'arf a mile beyond 'ere, any road."

"That's what they said a hundred miles back," replied the Yank, his brown eyes sparkling.

"An' wot do you know about stytions?" said the swagman. "'Ow's people goin' to know about yer, if all yer does is to suck yer bloody pipe, luk tha' there, sittin' in a boat? W'ere's yer tucker comin' from, howsever, muckin' along down there?"

"Now you're talking, pardner," said the Yank. "I wouldn't mention it to a living soul but you; but the fact is, I'm out of tucker."

"My precious life's blood!" said the swagman, with a more sympathetic interest. His eye fell on the burlap bag bulging with his own tucker, and he went on half apprehensively.

"'Ere. You go on 'arf a 'undred bends an' you come to Sir Robert Lansing's. 'Im as owns 'arf the pubs between 'ere an' Sydney. 'E's good for a lot, 'e is. Bread, man, an' a flamin' great lump of meat. Sir Robert hisself is a bit of a spoofer; but 'is ward, now—the young lady—an elegant bit o' goods, that. You arst arfter 'er. . . . Skin like a byby."

He ground his heavy boot into the circle of dead fire, and getting up, swung his swag into place over a withered shoulder.

"She won't tyke pay, an' she won't arst yer t'work," he said, moving off. "She's a good plucked 'un, my crimson oath!"

"Try the boat a way," suggested the Yank amiably.

The swagman looked back from under his immense mysterious load, doubled into its covering of dirty cotton.

"The road'll do, me champion," he said. "I 'ad a job in Ballarat at two pun ten once, afore I knew the road. Work, man; often and often till the gray of the mornin'. But I ain't leavin' a good job for no boats. It's the road I 'ungers for."

He moved off, at his painful hobble, bowed under that load; thinking perhaps of the miseries of Ballarat in the days of two pun ten. For now, behold him. He lived as he chose. If he did his five miles a day, he was content, vaguely conscious of having outwitted something that had dogged him. And all unnoticeably subsistence crept into his bag, and he was happy.

"The road, eh?" thought the man in the boat, moving off again on the languid current. "Stiffen up, Mede," he said, addressing his boat, curiously named Medea. He must be getting on himself. And while the river led before him like a challenge, he conceded something to the road, this sturdy preference of the little swagman. A grim, cracked, parching road it might be, truly, yet it would call, twitching at him with a crook in the middle distance, and finally compelling him with a seductive dip against the far horizon. And he might know that he would be never a bit the better for it; that its taverns would deny him, its dusts poison him, its lone infinities oppress him; yet would he move out again upon it, his swag enormous on his shoulder, and the something urgent in his heart appeased.

Feeling the silence and the heat thick upon him, the Yank fell to his dreams again.

"Young lady on ahead, eh?" he reflected. The idea had little to commend itself to him. There had been young ladies a-plenty in Sydney, yet he had not tarried there. His few experiments had convinced him that here lay the sole source of danger to his freedom. He went among them like a cat among crockery.

Now and then, taking his paddle out, he listened profoundly, resolving this confusion of minute sounds into the elements he knew,

and straining for the new notes which should defy his experience. He
heard behind him a melancholy crow, like a lost soul lamenting in those
wastes; and then a prolonged "B-a-a-a" from some distant sheep, with
its suggestion of shivering helplessness, like an abandoned child. Then
he saw the solemn black ears of a rabbit, stock still, crouched behind
a log. Taking out his paddle cautiously, he drifted down upon the log,
hanging over his experiment with bated breath, his eyes beaming with
a sudden hope that the little animal would not perceive him.

"Thinks he's out of sight," he said delightedly; and having come
as near as he could, he yelled, with appalling power. The little rabbit
jumped immoderately and flinging up its hind legs and twinkling tuft
of cotton tail, dived into its hutch.

"Not enough fur to him to make a hummingbird a pair of leggings,"
said the Yank affectionately, with a last sympathizing twinkle.

For the third time since his recent interview the river turned. He
drew the boat to the bank, and driving his paddle deep into the mud,
threw a hitch of his painter around the handle. Then he put on his
boots, and laying his landing board across the mire, struggled up the
bank, gouging his heels deep into the yielding clay. Gaining the top, he
shaded his eyes with one hand and stood motionless. Yellow reaches of
empty land confronted him; dead gums, dead grass, dead sheep, dead
silence. Burnt, level, desolate, the land stretched from the river to the
mountains; and through the haze the mountains smoldered, greenish
purple, as if eaten to the heart by these prevailing fires.

At first, he saw no human touch in all that desolation; but then his
eyes, sweeping the vast prospect again with their passionate desire for
physical detail, sighted a red blot on the yellow ground, perhaps a mile
away. He began to move toward it. He must take every chance now.
As he strode along, a sort of oppression rose about him, weighting his
steps, choking him. He stumbled, for he was already a little faint from
hunger, and the day was reeling hot. He was in the bush now, and no
mistake; as deep in as mortal man could get. Suddenly it seemed to
him as if he were too far into that nameless and characterless solitude
ever to get out. It circled him like a yellow indestructible plaque, struck
with bones, as of sacrifices—a disk of some substance reposing over
an abyss of intolerable heat. Then he smiled, largely. These were the
chances he courted; they stilled in his breast the questions he could not
answer. They were things to be dealt with.

He passed the red hide of a calf, withered over the end of a dead log, and a little beyond the skeleton of a sheep, its dazzling, frightfully white ribs curved regularly, distinct against a grayish ground of rabbit droppings. Everything dead—it was like the end of the world; like the surface of a dead planet.

The red shack was further off than he had thought; and when he came to it he was out of temper, because of the turfy unevenness of the ground and a suspicion, which had been growing on him, that the shack was tenantless. It was as miserable a place as shiftless selector ever turned his hand to. It was blind ended, without windows; its roof of corrugated iron shone blistering silver in the fierce sun; and the door was not hinged but laid against the side of it. The tank was empty and burning to the touch. There was nothing inside but a collection of musty rubbish and an unmade bed. He stood staring at that disgusting litter, with its heavy meaning; and then his jaws settled together, and a savage light grew in his eyes. The perverseness of things was working him up into his fighting temper.

Then he heard a slight cough, which came through the wall of the house with surprising distinctness. This proof of somebody within a few feet of him, coming just as he had resigned himself to being quite alone, unsettled him. In some queer way, he felt it a sinister thing, this cough and nothing more. No movement, no inquiry, apparently, though the fellow must have heard him bungling about in there. Standing in the center of the room, on beaten earth, he fingered the handle of his sheath knife, expecting a shadow to fall across the yellow foreground framed in the warped doorway. And then a narrow shadow did fall there, and hesitate, and lengthen; and presently a dusty guinea hen came into sight, obliviously picking about.

This absurdity roused him out of his waiting trance; and he stepped through the doorway and turned the comer of the hut. There was a man there, sitting on a broken bucket and staring off into the blurred distance.

"Got any mutton?" said the big Yank, moistening his lips.

He saw then that this was a very singular man before him. He was broad and heavily built; his thick legs were encased in leggings of black leather; and his clothes were wrinkled, as if he had slept in them, without knowing how—and on the bare ground, too, by the twigs and dirt across the shoulders. His broad, low forehead was white under the vizor of his cap, but his cheeks and his pointed chin were burned a terrible pink. He looked flabby and ill exercised.

"Any mutton?" said the Yank again.

"No," he answered. He continued to gaze at the distant gums with unmeaning earnestness. His chin rested on the handle of an axe, and the axe head was brilliant with rust, clear to its blunted edge.

It seemed to the big Yank as if the land were billowing away from him. At the edge of the cleared space, he saw a phalanx of ringed gums, with twisted branches, bleached bone in color, flung against the sky like scourges. There was no sound except a sort of muttering, very minute, as if the earth were ready to burst open. The dead gums wavered about in the blue of that filmy distance.

"This isn't your place, I reckon?" said the Yank.

The man shook his head. His pale eyes were fixed on those gums with a ravenous questioning.

"Owner's underground likely," said the Yank. "Smacks of the Grim Destroyer, eh? Well, one of these pleasant little rambles is enough for a morning—I'm going back to the boat."

The man lifted his chin from the handle of the axe.

"You've got a boat?" he said, with his first sign of interest. His voice came harshly, at a queer pitch, with the same difficulty, as of something long disused, and coming into play again, which the Yank had noted in his own voice.

"Yes," said the Yank. "Come along? There's some shade there, and a Sydney Bulletin a few months old."

"Yes," said the man. "I'm looking for a place. I was here a few years ago, and I came by the river. I think I'd remember, there."

"Ah!" said the Yank. "Looking for Sir Robert, like the rest of us?"

A light of pure fear leapt in those unsightly eyes.

"What do you want of him?" he said.

"Tucker," said the Yank. "Flour and mutton. Let's get out of this."

They went stumbling toward the river through deserted paddocks, which smoldered ahead of them like blankets thrown over a fire to stifle it. This man was weak at the knees and staggered over the least obstruction. The Yank, putting out his hand once to support him, felt the big forearm horribly soft to his fingers. The fellow's breath came in grunts, too, and his seared cheeks wobbled. Obedient and helpless, he hastened toward the river, the bronzed Yank urging him along. Yet behind that lax face something lurked, something not at all wobbling—indomitable rather—as if some terrible resolve were to be forced upon a weak man by sorry circumstance, by his fate. What else could have driven this fat, incompetent body so deep into the wilderness?

Coming to the end of those scorching paddocks, with their withered grass and their scattering of hides and white bones, the big Yank lowered his companion down the shaking bank, and settled him in the boat, under the burlap hanging of the cabin.

"I've certainly got to provision before long," he murmured, taking the paddle again. The man in his bunk, leaning back, blinked at the surface of the yellow river, with its imperceptible current, its steep banks and its eternal gray coping of mud, full of sprawling cracks, like webs, starting from innumerable centers.

"He's sure got something on his mind," thought the Yank, watching this man, who would not lay back comfortably, but sat staring at these banks, where landmarks seemed one and all to have toppled down, easing themselves in mud, as if consciously taking the tone of things there.

"This sort of thing won't do for you," said the Yank. "Not the life for you at all. Here you are without any swag—no liquor—money's no good, half the time. You're forty miles from ink or whiskey."

Something in the pose of that man baffled him—the head, hung forward, watching the banks, and the thick shoulders rounded, as if by the tension of some effort. Like everything that lay in that relentless sunshine, thoughts, purposes, the wildest desires smoldered, scarcely enduring, not feeling the passage of time more than this far-flung, inanimate yellow field, interwoven with bones and whole curious patterns of dead animals—like a burial ground of living hopes.

"Not that you need ink, but you might whiskey," said the Yank. His affability fell, stroke by stroke, on deaf ears. The man was consumed by memories, attempted memories.

"It's a black wattle," he said presently. "If you see a black wattle—"

His eye fell on a long knife with a worn blade which stood up in the bottom of the boat, intolerable to the eye—a fierce gleam.

"Not many wattles by the river," said the Yank. "River oaks and gums mostly."

"But there's this one," said the man. "There's this one. I came here once before and saw it."

For the first time he fixed his pale eye definitely on the other; and the tall Yank, looking squarely at him in turn, thought to himself:

"That's it, then. I've seen you before."

This did not surprise him. In the twenty years of his roving, he had seen and retained so many faces that he seemed to know everybody now, intimately; as if they were all crowded into one small shop. As with most people it seems well-nigh incredible that a known face should ever have been strange, so with him, since all were known, by so many being known, none ever had been strange.

"But where?"

This query nagged him, as a lost word might on the tip of the tongue. He plied his paddle, and called to mind a multiplicity of scenes, full of faces. And what faces! Fierce, mild, innocent, designing. He rejected them all. These were queer fish rising from the soundless depths of his experience. But he couldn't recall where he had seen him.

"I'd like to buy that knife," said the man, who had not taken his eyes from it all this while.

"Two shillings," said the Yank promptly.

The man paid, counting sixpences out of a worn, black wallet. Then he jerked the knife out of the bottom of the boat and held it in one pink, freckled hand, testing the edge.

"That's a good beginning," said the Yank. "But you need more than that. You need swag, man—or there's likely to be a strange face in hell for breakfast one of these cold mornings."

"This is all I need," said the man. He leaned over it, and his noisy breathing ceased. He balanced it, held it several ways, and finally, laying it down, scanned the banks again, with their desperate sameness, their fringe of gums slanting out over the river; their in-numerable roots—now hanging straight down, where a freshet had carried away the soil, now writhing into a grisly tangle, with dark openings—like a nest of snakes, and again huge and tenacious, like the tense knuckles of giant hands, thrust deeply in against the insidious encroachments of the river.

They went on in silence, opposing each other, the crude boat creaking along, unhurried, at the will of the dull current, where the thin leaves of the gums twirled idly, and the sun fell with the same withering insistence. It was the sort of place where it might seem as if nothing, by any possibility, could happen; as if life ran too thin for comment, and the inanimate held sway for sheer lack of human material to give it habitable touches. And yet, under the heavy stillness and quiescence of the bush, there grew in the consciousness of the big Yank, as his paddle sank into those yellow depths, endlessly, a sense of something toward; of a resolve, secret, like the solitude, burning always behind the stolid face of this silent passenger, with the dead fixity of his look like a veil between them. But in the bush men ask no pointed questions; they meet, and part, without divulging ends.

And, finally, holding his paddle poised in midair, the man in the sun said colorlessly:

"There's your black wattle."

The man in shadow shifted his gross bulk, with a movement of the lips and quickened breathing.

"Ay, that's it," he said.

In silence they drew abreast of it.

"We don't want to land here," said the Yank. "We'll go on to the cook's shed. That must be on the river somewhere."

"I'll land here," said the man. "You'll find the cook's shed around that turn, I think."

"As you say," returned the Yank, not sorry to part company with him. His fat, lax person hung on a man heavier than the silences.

The black wattle was all in yellow bloom and cast a deep fragrance. The bank beside it had been trampled down into a roadway, ending at the river's edge in a rough pier. The Yank swung into this; and his passenger, after a brief moment of indecision, got up stiffly, and sliding the long blade of the knife into his belt, stepped ashore.

"I'm not coming back," he said then; and the sound of these words, falling on his own ears, seemed to frighten him. He staggered up the bank a little way, and stopped and looked back and went on again, braced as if for an effort beyond his powers.

"Have a drink first," said the Yank impartially, gazing at him with level eyes. The man shook his head, swallowed and began to walk steadily up the roadway. The Yank, without much curiosity, without waiting even to see the end of him, dipped his paddle and moved off on the sluggish current.

"Cook's shed ought to turn up soon," he thought. "I'll give him notice of that fellow. Queer customer to be hanging around here."

He sent the boat along with vigorous, even strokes. Straining against the paddle, he dropped out of his mind the unpleasant image of his recent passenger. But the sight of that roadway, leading in to its sheep station, filled the dry crevice ahead of him with promise. Without a doubt, the cook's shed would be somewhere on the riverbank.

The next bend was an oxbow, and he doubled back, at the mercy of this capricious river. Presently he came upon a line of wheat bags, stiff with mud, drying on a wire netting. He sorted them over, and picking out the cleanest, dropped them calmly into the boat. A fish pole stuck deep in the mud, with the line out, attracted him. In a stroke he was upon it; but the hook was bare even of bait. Rummaging in the bottom of the boat, he found a clam, opened it, and tossed back the hook baited. Then, with his old kindly smile, he rolled a cigarette, and drew on it deeply. These inconsequences, these chance meetings, these idle and amiable moments, were all that would make up his progress to the sea. They were enough.

Then he spied the cook's shed under a gum tree, a lean-to of stringy bark, whitewashed, looking rather like a discarded marshmallow. He was some way above it still, but his eye, measuring the bank, decided for him that here was obviously where he must ascend, and he tied the boat to a root, and slid his feet into the heavy boots again. Picking up his blackened billy-can, and his burlap nosebag, he got out, raised both arms, yawning, and went up the bank. Pest! A hot day.

His eye met these unsteady yellow undulations with disfavor. After all, the river was the better place. There was a kind of madness about these still sheep; these dusty, baggy, unbelievable sheep, posed on wooden legs, and staring at him mistrustfully.

"The bush needs a fairy," he said then, and thought at once of the young lady with skin "like a baby," who wouldn't ask him to work, whatever she did. How about her? . . . Looking round at these charred stumps, at the yellow ground rising in front of him like a blister which the sun had raised on some tawny hide, he failed to bring her among the number of his visions. In that somnolent sunshine, with mud and bones and dead timber all about, it wasn't possible. . . . And, after all, what was a swagman's dream? She would have her shoes unbuttoned at the top, like all those others. She would have lost heart and hope, even if she were there, by some miracle, lurking behind the gums, which mocked the thought, drawn up in stolid ranks. Suns would have withered her; the sorrows of the bush, pressing in relentlessly, would have disfigured her. They crumpled in this heat like a stray paper in a gust of flame.

With a sigh for the passing of romance, which could still cast the blight of its emptiness upon his heart, with its sublime conviction of that emptiness, he broke in upon the reveries of the dolorous cook, who sat on a bench, hungrily inclining his ear to the cracked melody, with a recurrent hiccup in it, which came trembling out of the shining red maelstrom of a blistered horn—a sound smothered and sibilant, the engulfing of mermaids. The cook sat there, engrossed, perspiring, a small fellow with large ears, a large mustache, shaken in his whole person, like a reed, before this tinny blast, lost in vain imaginings; for this was that land of melancholy, where men came to forget and stayed to remember.

"Well, mate?" said the Yank.

"It ain't sundown yet," said the cook satirically, observing the burlap bag. With a movement of his little finger, he stopped the spinning number.

"Correct," said the Yank. "I'm not a sundowner yet. I'll pay for what you give me."

"And that won't be much, then," said the cook. But seeing in the smile of the big Yank nothing but what was companionable, and daunted a little, perhaps, by his proportions, he hastened to add amiably: "What there is you're welcome to, I'm sure of that. No charge for tucker 'ere. If you was to wait, Miss Aury will be coming over with the tomatoes an' maybe a squash or two."

"Ah!" said the Yank. "Miss Aury!" "Yes," said the cook. "And a clipper-built girl, too, I'm bloody well sure of that."

The cook, picking up the bag, went into his shed. The Yank, gazing off across the uneven acreage, with its cropped, barren look, saw the low roofs of the estate glittering in sunlight.

"Miss Aury, eh?" he muttered.

A dog barked distantly; and then a little dog, with a flank as bare as the ground, waddled out of the shed, howled once or twice discreetly in answer, and composed himself again to slumber. The cook, coming out with the bag, looked at the animal with wrath and pity.

"Flash mugs," he said forlornly. "Never knew any good to come of shearing time."

"Sheared the dog for you, did they?" said the Yank gently, full of sympathy, taking his bag.

"Right down to 'is bleedin' lit'le 'ide," said the cook. "Their idea of 'umor. Easier for 'im to get at the hinsects, they said. My oath! I'd 'a' been in Sydney a week gone, if the dawg was right. An' 'ere I am tied up, losin' three quid a week by 'im."

He sat down limply.

"Goin' to wait for them tomatoes?" he asked.

"Why, yes," said the Yank. "Reckon I'll wait for Miss Aury. Got news of her up the line, I guess, from a swaggie."

"Ay," said the cook. "You would then. She feeds them swaggies proper. She'd give 'em the larst thing she 'ad in the 'aouse. They don't bother me now none. Right up to the 'aouse with 'em. 'Please, mum, I got caught short of Ballarat without no salt. A thousand pardings, but could yer spare an honest man goin' to 'is job a pinch of salt?' 'An' 'ow are yer for bread an' mutton?' says she. 'Maybe I can shift along,' says they. An' she says, 'You poor things,' an' empties the 'aouse into their nosebags. It's the likes of 'er as keeps swaggies on th' 'ump, I s'y. But she will 'ave it so, and wot's a bloody cook to s'y?"

Helpless before the problem of the cook, the Yank smiled.

"She in 'er fine feathers, too," said the cook. "She will dress like a lydy, no matter 'ow. 'Igh 'eels, an' a trail to 'er o'nights. An' she's a vixen with Sir Robert, to make up for the kind 'eart she 'as for the swaggies. Not as I blyme 'er there. 'E's an 'arf-faced one, Sir Robert is. There 'e sits an' sits in 'is bloomin' study, with 'is 'ands pluckin' 'is books, and 'is eyes goin' all over. A bit powdery, Sir Robert, I'm takin' it. Not as 'e's out of 'is 'ead, but 'e 'as the 'orrors, like."

The cook shifted his quid, and spat over the body of the shorn dog.

"'E was a bad 'un, they s'y, in the town. They s'y so. I'm a new chum. I can't s'y for meself, but they s'y 'e 'ad a row with the father of that girl, over th' mother, y'know; an' the father went to jile over it. I'm venturin' it 'ad better 'ave been Sir Robert, and me drawin' two quid a week from 'eem, too. 'E 'as 'is thoughts, if you arst me. Larst night, w'en I stepped onto the veranda, with the supper, 'e 'eard me, an' he went out of 'is 'ead proper.

"'Wot's that?' 'e says, jumpin' up an' clappin' 'is 'and to 'is 'ead. 'My God, wot's that?'

"'Supper, sir,' says I, that shaken I nearly dropped it, to look at 'is eyes.

"'Bring it round by the back after this, me man,' says 'e. 'Is fyce was the color o' that dawg. An' while I was settin' the table, 'e says, 'Robson,' 'e says, 'wot's the day of the month?'

"''Ang me if I know, sir,' I says.

"'You'll 'ang, no fear,' says 'e. My crimson word, if the dawg 'ad been right, I'd 'a' snatched 'im there, bald-'eaded! 'If it comes to 'anging,' I'd 'a' said, 'there's morn'n me 'as their fears of tha' there.' So, I would. But you can see for yerself, the dawg ain't fit to travel. Wot I s'y is, wot's 'e want of the day of the month? Wot's any decent man out 'ere want with the day of the month?"

"Or the month itself, or the year?" said the Yank compliantly. "What's the good of time?"

Again, from over the rise they heard the distant howl of a dog, a prolonged ululation, dying and renewing itself, as if smothered under the thick day. The fat little dog who had been sheared got to his legs again, quivering, and howled back, with the same lack of self-confidence he had displayed before.

"Nasty yodel Sir Robert's hound has got," said the Yank. "Guess I won't wait for the young lady after all. Got to be getting on. By the way, I dropped a man over there on the other side. Queer genius. Better scour him up before dark. He might get into the sheep."

"Not 'e," said the cook. "'E knows better. Bloody bad business, cutting up sheep out here."

"Keep a weather eye out, though," said the Yank. "He's no swaggie. Well, much obliged."

He raised the bag, full of unknown obligations.

"It's nothing to me," grinned the cook, quite truly. He was amiable, nothing more. "She'd ought to 'ave come before this."

"I can dream about her," said the Yank, grinning in turn. He strode off in the direction of his boat. He wasn't really in a hurry. It was only that surcease of motion faintly plagued him. Picking his way over fallen gums, he heard the strident note of the phonograph beginning again; and he stopped to listen, smiling. Then he flung a piece of bone, one of those white, jagged, porous bones with which all the bush is paved, at a vanishing rabbit; and in a moment or two he was standing on the bank above his boat. But as he was going down, he saw, with that schooled eye of his, the deep mark of a small heel in the clay.

He stopped, and raising his eyes a little, followed the trail of this new foot quite up to the side of his boat. Musingly deliberate, he went on down the bank, with his head bent, and moved by some whim, like a foreshadowing, he trod out these small depressions, one by one, with his own heavy heel.

Arrived at his landing plank, he saw that the burlap curtains of his bunk had been dropped all round, which gave him further pause. He stood there like something done in bronze, with the pleasurable sense of a thing utterly unforeseen and quite incredible. The silence grew and grew, enforcing itself upon him like a substance in that moment of complete inaction; and suddenly, quavering through it, came the unpleasant howling of Sir Robert's dog, very faint now.

Then he stepped quietly into the boat, sinking that end deeply, and rattling the pans for'ard. He drew in the muddy plank, and after thinking again, rolled down his trousers over his ankles. Then he lifted his paddle, but held it poised in midair, transfixed. His eye was caught by a draggled yellow tassel peeping out from under the coarse fringe of his burlap curtain.

Silently, as if in the presence of some amazing hallucination, which a noise would shatter, he dipped the paddle and the *Medea* shot into mid-stream. Then, while she drifted, he sat, absorbed, twirling his black mustache, given over altogether to minute consideration of this tassel. And by degrees he became conscious of a slight fragrance, and of added weight in the boat; living weight, boasting a yellow tassel.

"Caesar's old jumped-up ghost!" he said aloud meditatively. He settled himself back and looked at his cabin as if it were a new thing altogether, something perpetrated upon him in his absence. The burlap curtains clung to the stanchions unbetrayingly; and the sun fell on the tin roof in a continuous discharge of these rays, smoldering gold, which caused it to snap and buckle from time to time. A smell of blistered varnish came from it.

"Fool notion," he muttered, mulling the thing over in his mind. It was unlikely—rather. Here he was in a country where a man had advance information of all the women within a radius of fifty miles—and then these blessed heelmarks—and that tassel. No. He blinked his eyes again, as if he felt something irritating them and again leveled them on that object. Yes, a tassel. He began to feel a little annoyed; and with this there crept in an obstinate resolution not to make the first move. There was no lack of time. He had all day, all the days, in fact.

"It's that bush fairy."

He formulated this to himself, paddling lazily, content to regard his cabin impassively, with its seamy flaps and its glowing top, which seemed to shift about when he looked at it. It must be almighty hot in there.

The moments drifted by, and with them the cracked banks and the interrupted animals with mud-caked bellies, stolidly belying possibilities. He became unreasonably averse to putting things to proof. This situation, so poignant in the imagining, crumbled with the least motion he made toward that cabin.

"Queer lark, this."

He tormented himself to find his image of the ward of that great man. Vixen. Vixen. The cook's word for it. But would she have this sort of daring, this particular insanity under that sun—jumping into the leaky boat of a runaway sailorman on a cruise for tucker?

He was certainly annoyed. He felt as if something had descended on him, in a cloud, invisible—and with this power to stir his senses, clog his reason, baffle his experience. It worked corruption to his blood, even. He felt an ardor up springing, in a foaming current, smothering his heart; the ardor of youth, of dreams, a swift assault upon him by these impulses which he had overthrown long since, to be lord of the earth and his occasions, untrammeled. It was a thing sudden as a spark, consuming, nourishing itself on nothing, on that yellow tassel. For one instant he renewed himself, deep sunk as he was on that lonely river, drawing upon the magic of solitude, and his thoughts were rapid, a golden flight across the glowing sun. And for that instant he felt his heart shaking him. Pest! The heat was turning his head.

He dipped his paddle and composed himself. Men out here were always fancying women gliding across their trails. Hitherto he had steered clear of that weakness. He was growing old, then, couldn't steel

himself. These soft entangling arms! Looking back, he counted three
good partners snared in them, lost to him, lopped away from him like
limbs, and he was conscious that in fact some share of his life blood
had gone with them. Two of them had died fighting, going out like
men, even in the coils of that last weakness. But the third—he could see
him, now, that fellow, slim, freckled, ardent, as good a mate as ever lay
aloft to stifle and stow a t'ga'ns'l. There he stood, over that campfire,
beaconing now across the years, with a kind of fearful perplexity in his
brown face, with its rough shock of hair; the look of a man shot, after
the first paralyzing moment.

"I'm going back," he had said. "That girl—"

He couldn't understand it himself; he was drawn back, down, in a
current, like a man into a gulf of waters, out. And the big Yank, who
now sat recalling him, staring at that cabin, remembered how he had
pleaded, fought, ridiculed, in vain. That fellow had simply walked off
into the night, without looking back. It was like destruction. He'd never
seen him again. He remembered the set silly smile on his lips; his eyes,
that were like caverns, with a secret glow at the back of them. Plague
take him and his girl! A fine litter they'd have by now.

Again, his eyes came to rest on that tassel. A child's folly. There was
no one in his cabin. That sly vixen—yes, he would take the cook's word
for it—that vixen had looked into it and away again for a lark, leaving
that tassel, like a taunt to him in his complacency. But at that moment
the slight fragrance fell against him again, staggering, like a wave, irre-
futable. And again, he was conscious of an added weight dragging at
his paddle. Battered beyond endurance by these stealthy evidences of
that neighborhood, he stopped paddling, and reaching out a hand to the
starboard stanchion, unhooked the burlap.

He blinked and lowered his head. Ah, so there was someone there, at
all events! A girl—a grown girl, too, thought the Yank, gazing at her
with the same lively interest he might have shown for some deep-sea
fish which had never come to light before. She sat cross-legged in his
bunk, in a kind of precious disorder, with the golden rope of her girdle
running away from her waist and ending in the yellow tassel. Her hair,
too, was yellow and tumbled, and the white dress smirched with mud,
where she had swept the banks in her quick descent. One arm, white
and round and rigid, with the little wrinkle at the elbow deep, was thrust

out to a stanchion for support, and the wide flowing sleeve fell away from it. The big Yank, avid of detail, saw all this before he met her eyes squarely. When he saw that they were blue, but moreover hard with fear, with horror, he said simply:

"Well, by the piper that played before Paul!"

He swore by this musician only on state occasions.

The girl began to breathe rapidly again, as if after long repression, with quivering little intakes, on which her breast rose and fell pitifully. Deep in the shadow of the cabin, she leaned toward him; and he saw then that she had a rusty pistol in her lap.

"Don't stop," she said. "Go on."

"Where's the—party going to be?" said the Yank, impressed. He remembered how, in silently composing her, he had had her shoes gaping at the top; and behold, not shoes, but slippers, white, soft-seeming things, with a pitch down to the soles from towering little heels, clay-covered.

"Just paddle," she retorted in a whisper. "You've got to take me to the town, without it's being known. Something has happened and I—I can't go by the road."

"That town is a week away by this river," said the Yank, whispering in return, as if he were already in possession of these secrets with their charm, their dread, crowding upon him out of the bush.

"I know it."

"We can't very well—"

"We've got to," she said, and then he saw the muscles tighten in the arm which held her away from the stanchion, and she lifted the pistol out of her lap.

"*You've* got to," she said then. With vivid lips and deep eyes, she leaned nearer still, launching those compulsive shafts. The eyes had an evasive depth, like twilight, full of invisible urgencies. This soft, mysterious presence was suddenly wound all about him, forcing him, and he felt that he was going to do whatever she required, without comment. His compliance was more than the humoring of a caprice; it was born of a tyranny from without, before which he fell back, a little grimly.

"Well," he said, "I reckon you've got the drop."

Watching her, he put in the paddle again with a kind of craft, as if he really intended to do something about this, though he might seem to submit. This was the story he had heard about them: that they always had their way. Burying himself always in these remotenesses, he had accustomed himself to going as he pleased, like a conqueror. There was nothing a man couldn't do with men. But women! And now more especially this one, flashing upon him with suddenness, scintillating in a gloom, with the violet suggestion in the eyes, the downright posture, and all these things, white and golden, streaming away from her, like the testimony of things routed to her willfulness. A premonition went through him, like the first tremor of defeat. His vision was clouded; his day full of unaccountabilities. She was indeed a vastly provoking ripple on the smooth surface of the day's blank dream. The boat went faster and faster, and the water smacked against the overhang forward.

Raising her head, she looked squarely at him again; and that look went deeper than the sunshine.

"We must travel by night, too, if we can," she whispered, and shivered slightly, stirring the soft stuff on her bosom.

These minute whisperings made over the very banks of the river into a conspiracy of intentness. The least sounds of the bush were silenced, as if to allow these mysterious syllables to pass over them to the ends of the earth. He remembered how he had frightened the rabbit. He had yelled then, knowing that he could not be heard; now, as he bent closer to her, experiencing that fragrance, the incomparable softness and delicacy of her against the crude stuff of his boat, like a thing encumbering him, he whispered, too, as if he feared the communication of his lightest word to the secret sources of her dread, lurking, as they must, somewhere behind those twisted gum trees.

"You're being followed, then?" he asked.

"Yes."

"And why?"

Obdurate silence grew between them; and presently he drew in the paddle.

"If you're running away from Sir Robert," he said gently, "it's a bad move. You take it from me—"

He stopped at the expression in those eyes, dilated wide.

"Can't you paddle," she cried despairingly, "without wanting to know? You'll not know."

"I could paddle back and find out," he suggested. "That's the proper thing—paddle back."

"Well, then," she said, and he heard her breath drawn through her teeth, "you'll not paddle back."

And for the second time she lifted the pistol into sight. Ah, that was it, then. He had come all this way of his own accord, sought out this river, like a dog making a bed for itself, and now he was to be driven along, willy nilly, with a chit of a girl holding a gun to his nose.

"You've got the drop," he said again, politely. "Yours to command. But that's a nervous-looking gun."

Again, the boat forged ahead under his powerful strokes. He caught himself looking back over his shoulder as he made the bends, following the direction of those glowing eyes, distraught, with their haunted depths. Noting the rigid pose of her body against the stanchion, he said:

"It can't be as bad as all that."

But by now every influence of the bush was stirring him into a kind of reasonless activity. He felt the chase growing upon him momently and put forth all his giant's power. The muscles in his arm leapt and sank tortuously, agony muscles, grown there in many services. The boat quivered to his strokes; his dark face shone with sweat; and the burlap curtains swayed slightly. By the leaves on the water he saw how he was outrunning the current, whose pace was his own pace; and then he understood that the expedition, by this strange chance, had been snatched out of his hands. Something at last was enforced upon him.

But as he worked his mind was busy. The fat, pink cheeks of the passenger he had left behind hung before him, in the heat. Those burnt, wobbling cheeks became all at once portentous. The man had gone in, and she had come out, all within an hour. How was that? The rambling words of the cook, too, came back to him in snatches, like vague lights. Sir Robert's inquiry about the day of the month, the shocking face he made over that step on the veranda. And now something had happened. His mind twisted like a snake through the maze of possibilities. What had happened, then?

He stole a look at the pistol; and another, and another; and decided that it had not been fired recently. Doubtful even if it was loaded. A precautionary pistol. Driving on furiously with his paddle, he recalled the words of the ancient swaggie, that she was a "good plucked 'un; skin like a byby. Wouldn't arst yer t' work." He smiled grimly at that thought. Wouldn't ask him to work? What would you call this, then? In his preoccupation, he sheered the surface of the river in bringing his paddle forward, and sent a warm frayed sheet of water, burning in green diamonds, over that white dress.

"Sorry," he mumbled.

Staring over his shoulder, she made no answer. Moment by moment, she seemed to feel this menace drawing closer, without noise; something which must crush her finally. His big shoulders drew together; he bent forward like a man under the lash, his eyes fixed on the smooth current breaking into foam under his paddle and gently washing the clay banks. He was like a man crouching under a blow deferred, harrowing him. Yet all the while silence hung round them like a curtain; this everlasting muffling silence of the bush, the heavier for the sudden inexplicable crackings, the creaking of dead limbs, the soft flap of wings and the distant bellowing of cattle; that noise, like a blending of rich horns, which rose on a sad vibrant note, an earth muttering, half protest, half resignation. The very animals were ill at ease in that abounding quiet and abandon.

Time passed. He sat glaring at the river, which slid under him, chuckling against the warped bottom of the boat. He came again and again to the end of his few facts, made out nothing. He was half annoyed, harassed with doubts. Here he was blindly paddling a girl on a lost river; a pretty girl, frightened out of her wits, descending on him like a perverse gift of cross-grained gods. They were running away, and a devilish kind of together-ness about it, too. A chill crept up his spine; he felt it unmistakably, for a new experience. The thing looked preconcerted; it put him in a wrong light altogether. What was he to say if—

He looked back and quickened his stroke. Then he cast about for something decisive to say. This childish reticence of hers would have to be broken through. She should talk, or by the Lord Harry, she should leave his boat. Then he looked at her, but no words came. She sat with head averted; a figure strangely soft, affecting him like a slow poison with her beauty. Line by line, look by look, she stole over him, and with no words passing, his quizzical patronage and the slight sense of affront he had cherished at the impertinence of this appeal ebbed. He turned to the river, like a big hulk, high and dry, keeling over. After twenty years of the high seas—in a blow, at a breath, stranded, on an unknown coast.

And suddenly he ran into cool shadow and raised his head in astonishment. Gazing down the river, he seemed to come slowly to himself as out of a surprising dream. He saw a straight reach shining ahead of him, bound in by walls of clay which rose perpendicularly to a great height. As far as his eye could reach, ahead, these cliffs of burnt clay loomed above them, the stark gums leaning out dizzily over the river, high up. The current of time had quickened perceptibly, unlike the languid and sinuous current of the river over which they hung. He felt that hours had been snatched by him.

"No danger here," he said, trailing his paddle. He gazed, rapt, into the fordable violet of those eyes, which were turned wide upon him, as if in terror of that shadow, which fell with sudden stealth about the boat.

"Maybe we'd better camp," he said. "No way they can get at us here, without ropes. The sun's going."

"Ah, no, keep on," she implored him; and again, he dipped his paddle. The walls of clay reared higher; that to the right already frowning in shadow, and the other dying from splotched yellow into rusty red, as the sun fell. Into these surfaces were struck strangely fantastic chance reliefs, caused by the draining of waters from the higher level—towers, friezes, assaulting battalions of fierce creatures streaming downward, as if in an arrested flood of action. And as these surfaces of dim enchantment rose, the sky narrowed, losing its blue virulence, and becoming, low down, a clear green, infinitely graduated. Then across that band of sky, with its fringes of black ruinous gums, there went a plump flight of starlings, black as ink, and then a crow, more swift, on limp, dilapidated wings. The silence on the river, in that gray canyon, was broken only by the rhythmic sound of the paddle, a melancholy protest from the vanished crow; a scarce audible rippling of waters. And these silent walls, darkening, with their nests of bottle birds in rows like little cannon, and their foreshadowing reliefs, seemed to aspire, immeasurably, rising into the sky, and sending down to these two stealthily, in the half dusk that now lay upon the river, assurances of this discretion of nature, which could thus dwarf their odd companionship into a common secrecy, solid as the quiet, in which all things were possible.

Creaking on his seat, he leaned forward, blinking his eyes, half expecting her to have vanished, somehow, into the indefinite bosom of this quiet. But she still sat there, cramped against the stanchion, fingering that golden rope, which seemed to him now like a strand untwisted from her own being, still and yet tempestuously streaming out over the bunkboard, ending in that absurd tassel.

He would have spoken, but through that gloaming she seemed very far, as if his voice could never reach her, without frightening. And again, he was struck by a sense of her extraordinary fineness, the incongruity of her presence here at the bottom of this appalling riverbed. His eye fell like a caress on the yellow of her hair, which he had yet to see struck into gold by that fierce sunshine, and on the slim strength and competence of line lurking under those white folds, which the early gloom caused to glimmer. A little golden locket, slung by a chain around her neck, rose and fell, hovering, by which he might see that she was quieter now.

"She could have dressed more sensibly—" he found himself thinking. It had been flight, wild flight, unpremeditated, beyond a doubt. Something that had flashed and fallen here, and now lay, walled in with him, for good or evil, irrevocably.

He drew a deep breath, and found his tongue for one remark:

"Put the curtains up. There's no air in there."

She fumbled a moment and threw them back. He made no movement to help her, just intuition plucking him back from that approach. But as the sallow green light fell upon her, she shrank into the bunk, and at once dropped the curtain on that side, so that his vision of her was of an instant only, wavering out in all softness to him, with averted face, and shrouded again in the gloom of his cabin.

He paddled on, only his arms moving, his still face massively composed, its grave general scrutiny of things belying the tumult, the rising whispers in his brain, from which he resolutely turned. And as he paddled, darkness, like something overhanging in a dream, reached down into that canyon, deepening, rising in a brown gloom, which swept the clay walls clear of definite illusion, leaving them blank and ponderous, the sides of a crevice running on interminably, as if to show that there could be but one path for these two who were lost and swallowed up in it.

"I think we will beach her here," he said. "I can't see the water now."

The girl in the bunk made no movement, no reply; and as he could see nothing of her now either, it grew upon him again that possibly she was not there at all.

As the *Medea* grated on the soft beach, he stepped into the water, and with a slow, powerful movement brought her on broadside and half clear of the river.

Standing up and stretching his arms, he listened intently. The mere silence of the bush, high above, had given place now to a hush, a more deliberate quietude, as if possible utterances were choked by the impalpable thickness of the falling night. And suddenly through that hush there came a hateful gust of insane laughter, as if someone standing above were rocking back and forth on his heels, under the impulsion of some devilish amusing thought. It was like a comment on the futility of things, on the stopped machinery of this world, on the meaningless wastes, the array of bones and fallen bodies and dead gums ringing them round. This laughter, tailing off at length into an exhausted titter, as if it had reached a point where the intensity of the conception throttled it, was taken up far and wide, by indivisible circles, in spasms, paroxysms of unaccountable prophetic mirth, struggling out of unseen throats, and falling hideously through the gloom, suggesting that even in these depths concealment was of no avail. It was merely the evening chorus of the cuckoo burroughs, those cynical birds with hunched shoulders and wise eyebrows, who deride alike the darkness and the dawn; and yet, to the big Yank, standing on the white sands so far below them, the sound was ugly. It was like the fatuous merriment of blockheads who have stumbled on the truth. He glanced at the still figure of the girl, lax in the bunk; and tilted up his head with something like a shudder, for what was ominous in that familiar sound. He peopled the land above him with dark figures, gliding among the gums, over that black jagged fissure, waiting, following after, with a calm patience like the patience of the bush under withering days. He shook himself awake. There he stood with his sheath knife drawn. "Like an old woman," he muttered, and he slipped it back contemptuously and built his fire.

There was something very piratical about him, with the black crown of derby hat—his evening wear—settled over his forehead, and the red handkerchief knotted about his throat. Under his feet twinkled the smooth sands, with their hint of gold, like the touch of art or myth or poetry to that secret place; and over him the early stars were blazoning.

He went to and fro, with stealthy steps, gathering timber for the fire, which must go all night against the dawn chill; and as the yellow glare increased, the shadow of his big body roved over the beach, like a caprice of darkness whimsically attendant on his chance footsteps. And this sprawling shadow that he cast made him seem mightier in his own person. His was a figure to stand alone, certainly; it appeared in his gait, like a willful child's, in his rocking shoulders, in the grave and humorous acceptance of all things in his brown eyes.

Always he had reached his goal each night, wherever he had unslung his swag and built his fire. If he never got beyond it, what matter, since the night was warm? Life, for him a series of gigantic efforts, coming to nothing, had hitherto engaged him like an idleness, a luxury; all things had reached out to him to be considered. Prolonging his youth, he had gone rioting past the finger posts of staid and stay-at-home wisdoms, trusting that when he came, if indeed he ever came at all, to that gray time toward which all these stolid maxims point, some magic in the genius of the road would raise up protection for him, as his bones grew cold.

And now what trick was the sly spirit playing him? Genius of the road, forsooth. He was trapped, haunted, fleeing before he knew not what, full of vague Terrors. He was no longer his own man. That slow, masterful current of his being, on which he had idled so magnificently, was now a boiling flood, as if some tributary force, mightier than his own, had entered him. Wrath leapt in him; he felt that she was rising all about him like a tide, softly, tyrannically merciless. She was using him for ends she would not disclose.

He swung his arms, making vague gestures toward the outer dark. He would have to get rid of her. He glanced at her covertly. There she sat, on the edge of the boat, with her feet in the sand, gazing through the fire at the dark clay wall beyond, tensely preoccupied with the faint noises of the bush above. In a twinkling the wrath which his old spirit of singleness had kindled in him died; and a fierce necessity sprang up in him to comfort, reassure. He ached with the sudden intensity of this desire to bear part of that burden, whatever it might be; and holding the fork with which he had been turning pancakes, he made a step toward her. But then an invisible armor seemed to be clamped at one stroke on those big limbs, constraining them, and he remained staring through the tines of the fork into the fire.

"It's pretty bad, but a man has got to eat," he reflected then. Aloud he said: "Will you eat something?"

She shook her head.

He ate his pancakes and drank his tea in silence, thinking that tomorrow he would make her eat. He would begin to assert himself presently, when he had got his bearings. He lit his pipe, pinching a hot coal into the bowl of it with a scarred forefinger.

The unearthly chorus of the cuckoo burroughs had died away, and there was no noise in that black and tortuous fissure, with its looming walls and its one red brazier of light, save the slight ripple of the current, nosing its way along into the unknown, going always toward the sea.

Brooding by the fire, he thought of the lights of Sydney, two months back, the star-pointed harbor glittering under cloudless night, the cool deck of that baldheaded old bark under his bare feet, the hilarity of the great port. He had left that port only to make another, some port to the south, which he had never seen, toward which this slow current, rippling past, was imperceptibly making. The promise of life had lain under these innumerable horizons, forever unfulfilled. His prog-ress, blind as that of the current, meant nothing, led him everywhere, nowhere.

His eye fell stealthily again on the figure of the girl in his boat. By the piper that played before Paul! By the long-horned, blue-gilled cattle that went ahead of Moses into the wilderness! She was growing on him! He recurred to her; each of his thoughts took flight, it might have been, from that golden head, bent down, as if she were falling asleep. Ah, falling asleep! His spirit of malice, struggling with pity, moved him.

"Are we going watch and watch?" he inquired, throwing wood on the fire. She started, gasped, threw up her head.

"I had nearly fallen asleep," she said, in a low voice.

"That won't do," he said. "That won't do at all. When you're asleep, I'll steal that nervous-looking gun of yours and paddle back."

Wild terror filled her; she stood up and swayed toward him, with her arms outstretched.

"You wouldn't do that," she cried; "you wouldn't! Can't you trust—only for another day? But not now—you'll not take me back?"

With those mournful eyes pressing him, he said:

"Why, no," utterly abashed. He added incoherently, "Only that gun sort of—"

He stopped ruefully.

Impetuously she ran to the boat and whirled the aged pistol into the river.

"I trust you," she said. "Even to—"

She stood there against the blackness, like a slender shaft, like a
sorrowful caryatid erect under the burden of the black night. The yellow
inconstancy of flame played over her; she stood absolutely still, alone,
as he was alone, imploring, across a chasm. In a flash he understood
that she wasn't afraid of him; that this trust was full and childlike.

"You lie down and—sleep," he said, stumbling over the words.
"You'll feel better in the morning. I reckon we're all right here."

He turned away from her and began throwing more timber toward
the fire. Then he found a great clay-covered trunk and dragged it to the
fire for a back log, his heavy arms cracking under the weight. After that
he stood watching this blaze and running the red handkerchief slowly
over his face.

Yellow devils, he called his fires when alone, and he loved to ponder
them, to mark where the fissures opened, and the red towers tumbled,
and the heart of the wood glowed and fell in ashes. So he thrust back the
night with his villifying flame, which, in leaping up, imputed menace,
ambush, to the wicked gray tangle of the bush above and the great bare
trunks of the gums, stripped of bark, showing pale blue and bone color
and fanglike yellow. Tonight, behind them, he saw vague forms, relentless and pursuing, hovering above and looking down with evil faces on
these sands, with their leaping flames, their inconsequent remoteness.
He sat cross-legged on the sands, smoking his pipe, and as he dreamed,
he felt a dimness about him; the black wall of clay seemed to waver; an
angry horde swarmed over the lip of it with gleaming eyes and vengeful
faces.

A coal snapped, and spun out against his ankle, and he opened his
eyes. The fire had died down; the night was pointed with cold stars; in
that dreaming stillness, which seemed to descend out of the blue night,
as if mysteriously distilled from above, laying soft restraints upon
thought and action, there was no sound but the gentle lapping of the
current, eager, successive little voices breaking in chuckles, and one
other sound, faint and regular . . .

"She's fast asleep," he thought, looking at her.

"She ought to have a blanket," he began to suggest to himself, but for
a long time he made no move. If she should waken . . .

But then, bracing himself, he went over the sands, noiselessly, with
a rolling gait. Bending over the stem of the boat, he reached out two

blankets from the locker there, army blankets, shot and patched and burnt, which had gone through three campaigns. Dropping one, he unfolded the other and waved it back and forth at arm's length. Then, holding his breath, he came quite up to the cabin, and by aching degrees lowered the blanket over her. Leaning toward her, he was more than ever conscious of the fullness of her charm, of the oppressive sweetness. As if he breathed some part of it, his heart was slow and heavy and then fast, like the heart of a man laboring on a great height. The red lips, parted, drew him, like a magnet. In sleep the face had lost its look of strain and terror. He came close, wrestling with a mad impulse. What, then, if he merely touched those lips with his, hidden as he was, deep down there, in the bottom of an unconsidered river? What aspersion was there to be cast, or who to cast it? He felt as if something was due to him for all those years of rigid denial, when houses and people were things for him to strike among and shake off, like a frailty. And here was something marvelously in his keeping, like what he had always imagined to hover behind shut blinds, half proffered to him, out of the dark, out of the unquestioning serenity of the night. Was he to draw back—

He bent lower, until even through the shadow which he cast he seemed to see the very grain and impulse of her. But at that moment he saw her very distinctly flinging the pistol into the dark water; with a swirl of her dress, and that binding gesture of trust: something intuitive, an inner strength. She was right; she should be right. He drew back, though the blood was pounding in him.

Taking the other blanket, he lay down by the fire. Then he looked up at the stars and grinned slightly. There was something about this. . . . He recalled all those emotions which had surged through him thickly, clutching his heart, as he bent over her. That wouldn't do. He knew only the stable earth. And here . . . Out of a clear sky, too; and in this burning bush, where an old shoe wouldn't turn up if you wanted one. Wondering, he fell asleep.

When he awoke, the gray chasm of the river walls was faintly touched with red at its top. It was like a raw wet wound. His fire had fallen, and the air was cold and sharp. Already the cuckoo burroughs were abroad, jeering at this reluctant dawn; and nearer at hand, a magpie, an insolent bird in a black vest and shirtsleeve wings, like a clerk on a hot day, croaked disconsolately, with a sound like a door swung and swung again on a rusted hinge.

He got up, as he had got up these last twenty years mostly, rumpled, disheveled, chilled through and through, with the face of a big baboon, as he put it to himself, leaning over the water. His head dripping, he went back to the fire and kicked it into new life, where it lingered among the ashes.

"Holy Mackinaw!" he said then and looked toward the boat. She lay there awake, muffled in that grim blanket.

"Cold?" he asked.

"Very."

"This chill strikes the river just before daybreak," he went on. "But the sun is coming up now. Stand over the fire."

Throwing aside the blanket, she stood up, stiffly, as he had, and went slowly to the fire. Shivering under the friendly glow, she yawned, and then at once put up both hands to her tumbled hair, more tumbled now than ever. These dawn activities became them, thought the big baboon, feeling his rough chin ruefully. She rose out of the trampled vicinity of the fire, like a white flame, in the softness and indefiniteness of her awakening. There was a red mark on the rounded arm as she held it up, where it had fallen over the edge of the boat in her sleep. But her eyes were on that glittering green reach of river behind them, closed in by the cold scarred walls of yellow clay.

They ate hastily of the cook's mutton, while the sun, rising, reached down its first warm beams, livening the surface of the river, dispelling mists, provoking long shadows from above.

Looking at her, with his cup of tea raised, he murmured, "A fine morning, Miss Aury," and felt uncommonly satisfied with himself.

The sun fell on her, singling her out from the gray white of that beach, with its-feebler glint of gold. She shimmered there like the radiance on closed lashes. But from the checked look on her face, he saw that there was something wrong with the rapidity of that advance; and he set about putting things back into the boat, dumb and baffled. When she came to step in, she turned her head suddenly, showing him, frantically near, the deep violet of her eyes. That swift movement was a deliberate surprisal of him.

"How do you come to know my name, like that?" she said.

"From the cook," he whispered secretly. She turned away.

She seemed to recede from him again. It was as if the sun, in casting down these other shadows, included the shadow of that dread. She turned her eyes past him, to the gaunt surfaces of clay rising so high, with their wet reliefs, their heavy secrecy, their leaning stillness, and the morning sky flaming above them in one long ragged slip. Beyond them she could not look, and she crept back into the bunk and lowered her head.

And for hours they said nothing, while the boat ran on, now gathering speed and grumbling over rapids, and again silently borne on the current, driven by the smooth strokes of that paddle with its vast yellow blade. In a trance he watched his brown fist, swollen over the handle, pass before his eyes, gleaming, and repass and pass again, like something foreign to him, with the darting regularity of a piece of a machine, willing, without will. He felt constrained, lumbering, ineffective—unfinished. He would have to shave when it came night.

Suddenly conscious of a lack of bearings, a remoteness in his attitude, he promised himself that in a moment he would look at her again, say something. He would do it at the next bend. He made the bend, silent, and continued so, with a rising astonishment at himself. He was glib ordinarily, free and easy, a man of genial parts. Who was she to become thus an unwitting licenser of his speech, to provoke him into this nice examination of words, which he fished out of chaos, and flung back again, dumb, disgruntled? She was too fine, altogether. He began to believe that a man would have to piece together prayers, or something, to address her. In vain he exhorted himself; and after a time he was afraid even to look at her, because he felt that blue eye on him, fathoming his incompetence.

Slowly the clay precipices lowered, and by the time the banks were at their old level, the sun was sinking, too, and the rabbits, lured by the shadows, began to come out of their hutches, watching the strange boat, to the last possible moment, with bright, unwinking eyes, and stock still, bolt upright ears. The day passed, like all these somnolent days, in a blur, in a bluish yellow mist of pitiless heat, through which consciousness ran like a prolonged musing.

It was in the late afternoon that, sweeping the boat around a bend, he held the paddle suspended.

"Draw down that curtain," he said guardedly. "There's a man ahead."

He heard her breathe sharply, saw the fright in her eyes turned toward him, as if to draw promises from him, all in one moment, lingeringly eloquent. Then the heavy burlap fell between them.

Just ahead of him, a big pipe ran down into the water; he heard the hum of an engine, unseen, on the bank above, and beside the pipe stood a sallow man in shirt sleeves, smoking.

"Come far?" asked the man, as he drew down on him.

"Quite a patch," said the Yank, holding the boat against the bank.

"Know anything about the trouble in Lansing's station?"

"No; what's that?"

"Sir Robert's dead; stabbed, 'bout noon yesterday. Stabbed sitting in his chair."

The big Yank's fingers closed about the handle of his paddle in a terrible grip; and he felt his heart stop and then rack itself to pieces in his breast. Sweat rilled all over him.

"No," he forced himself to say.

"Fact," said the man. "An' there don't seem to be but one answer. That bit of a ward of his is gone. They hadn't got on too well together, after she'd got a taste of the town, y' know. She's like the rest of 'em, fond of the fine feathers; an' he wouldn't have it, old Sir Robert wouldn't. They say he was pretty much of a buck in his day. That's the way with these toffs, once they get out here in the back country. No nonsense for 'em then. She was a fine spirited girl, that Aurelia Darnley; but you can't tell what the best of 'em will do, out here. They go mad, with the sun shearing off their pretty complexions. But, my God, to come on him, and stab him! That's not in nature."

The man went on talking comfortably about the event, and brushing mud from the rusted pipe with the flat of his hand.

"If it was a man as done it now, he might get clear," he said. "The bush is a mighty disappearin' sort of a place, as Ned Kelly said. But a woman, man, she's no chance at all."

"You say they're out after her already," said the Yank in a dull tone, looking at his paddle.

"A few of 'em went by this mornin'. She can't be far. She'll have to come out on the roads or die of starvation."

"Yes," said the Yank. "Of course. So long."

He took his paddle out of the bank, and the *Medea* began to move slowly on the current.

"Traveling alone?" said the man.

The Yank looked at his burlap cabin.

"Yes," he said. "I'm not much of a hand for company."

"No more am I," said the man, growing distant. Another bend snatched him out of sight, and still while the dusk grew stealthily the Yank sat staring at the cabin. A great ominous bank of clouds was rising to the south, giving promise of rain and hastening the night. In the minute stillness he heard occasional droppings of dead branches above him.

"All right," he heard himself saying after a time. He kept looking ahead into the rising gloom, at the sharp needlelike silver streaks on the brown water. Then he heard the burlap tear sharply.

"So, you—"

He stopped short, feeling her white face intent upon him steadfast in the shadow.

"If you believed it," she said, her voice of breaking pitch, "why did you say you were alone? Why didn't you—"

"Don't ask me those questions," he said stridently. "If you think—"

He stopped again, horribly, his head hung back, staring up with wide eyes, full of a terror like her own. High above, in the fading sky, an ugly bird hovered, with jagged wings, black as ink, outspread, motionless. The big Yank sat transfixed, glaring, the force of all the superstitions he had beating upon him like surf. He felt her lean out of the cabin, following his eyes; and as the meaning of his pause broke upon her, and she saw his dreadful thought fully, she trembled, and he felt the thrill of that trembling through and through him. But in a moment, recovering, she crowded herself against a stanchion, and thrusting her long, slim arm through the gloom, with the palm out, rigid, and the white film of her sleeve falling away from it, she cried despairingly:

"The sheep. It's the sheep he's watching."

Only the head of the mired sheep was out of water, that stolid head with fixed eyes and liberal, patient, acquiescing lips. It made no outcry. It had the look of having waited several days, a week even, without turning its head. The river, which had risen slightly, just failed its nostrils.

Turning, the Yank met those calm, trustful eyes through the gathering dusk. It was a Cots', an aristocrat among sheep, with a smooth, noble forehead, a resignation and sublimity of manner, a dumb expectancy . . .

He drew his sheath knife, and reaching over, seized the sheep by the nostrils and tilted up its head.

"We'll have to take our food as we can get it, now," he muttered.

Then he was aware of her, close beside him, tremulous, breathing still that heavy breath of enchantment on him; and immediately he felt her hand, tense and hot, on his forearm.

"No!" she cried, "not that. No, no, no!"

The silence following was like a weight. With her hand detaining him he said aloud:

"No, by God, it's not true. It's not true."

There was no echo; the bush smothered the cry as it smothered day and all things. With a powerful snap, he drew the sheep clear of the mud and tossed it to the bank.

For an instant the creature stood there, uncertain, its body a disgusting black, its flanks quivering. Then, pointing its benign white forehead toward them through the gloom, it compressed its soft, amiable lips and scrambled up the bank. At the top it hesitated, then baa'd loudly and disappeared.

"Well, what now?" he thought to himself. Night was fast falling, the pink clouds in the south were turned a frowning purple, and reaching higher; giant ramparts, behind which were crouched the forces of heaven, which he knew and feared now for the first time. A drop of rain, blown at a long slant, fell in his face.

And suddenly the banks of this river swarmed out at him, through gloom; he caught again the sparkle of watching eyes, of shadowy figures gliding there, with dark faces, prying out the secret fastness of this wretched girl, with her sweet odors, her languors and mysteries, which had risen about him imperceptibly—like a tide—until now he was bound, smitten by these terrors streaming through the dark. Like a woman.

He dipped his paddle savagely, and the *Medea* shot along at random, though now he could scarcely see the forward part of the boat at all. No matter. Some merciful snag might spring through the blackness and club them out of thought, send them together into these warm depths, with the sands of gold to hide them. With a bursting heart, he felt that he must come to a solution, sharply, as by awakening out of the hideous situation of a dream. Yet he knew, too, that there would be no such awakening. And he felt that the old freedom was gone, that this knowledge of her crime put before him another knowledge—of these bonds, tight about his heart, which bound him to her—like iron. Under cover of thickening night, floating between these grim banks, with their twisting roots, their snakelike drapings, their dim suggestions of horror which only the nature of his present thought could force upon him, he found himself an accessory, bound over to the consummation of crime. Well, he would get her away, since he had begun; and tear himself clear of her vicinity as he might.

He drove on through the dark, following the slight glitter of ripples which the night wind spread across the shallow stream. After a time, he held out his paddle, and then there came the horrible volleying laughter of those birds again, rocking on their dead limbs, invisible, like the involuntary comment of nature on the folly of hope in such a place. Listening, he thought: "What's the end? What's the end of this?" This was what came of wandering, this sudden entanglement, after twenty years, coiling about in folds without texture, impalpable, final. There was nothing he could reach with his hands, those mighty hands, driving the paddle, which had so far solved all of life for him. This thing rose within him, poisoning his resolves. He was whirled, apathetic, a deadly force without power of his own, through the strange deadliness of that night.

They stole on without noise, in a black void, without vibration, as if suspended in some formless element, disembodied, very speech crushed out of them. He was conscious of thinking: "Why doesn't the woman say something, cry out, sob?"

She was beyond that. She lay huddled in the bunk, motionless, and her soft whiteness, shimmering through the dark, was one with that hushed unreality. But then she shifted in her place slightly and he heard the boards of the bunk creak under her, and at once, in a flood of remembrance, reconstructing her out on the dark, he understood that she was precious, not so poisonous as precious. He remembered how she had looked pitifully at the mired sheep and stopped the knife with her soft strong fingers, deep in his arm. He could feel them still, plucking him back, back—from what? And now he whispered, as he had called out then in agony: "It's not true." But he dared not question her.

Instead, his mind turned to that evil bird, prospecting on spread wings, following aft, with the leisure of certainty; the black beak, with its cruel curve against the sunset, the humped back, as if ready for a pounce, the ragged wing, disheveled, unkempt, speaking to that hideous outlawry of the skies. His blood ran cold, and since by then the quavering, unearthly chorus of the cuckoo burroughs had died out, he dipped his paddle again and the boat moved on, protesting.

Suddenly forked lightning split the black hold of this abhorrent night to the south; he had a prospect of voluminous cloud, black, turgescent, overhanging all this: these river banks, ghastly gray, with deep sprawling lines and numberless bared roots writhing down, forever failing the water; the leaning gums, with smooth ashen trunks, naked of bark, ringed and mottled, at the dead point before a plunge, and all their twisted branches blunt, where the ends had snapped off. There was a sapped, dead look to them, with the frightful certainty and the frightful impossibility of outlines in a dream. He saw it in one flash, like a deathly composition, with the oily river running through it in a thick imperceptible current, scummed at its edges. It vanished, and he had a sense of something vast and menacing, which had sprung at him once out of the vague, and now crouched meditating, foreshadowing an end.

In that brief moment of illumination he had seen a white beach, curving to his left, where the river turned; and in the succeeding blackness he drove the boat toward it, and in a moment heard the soft hiss of sand under him and felt the *Medea* conceding everything to the slope of the beach.

Silently he stepped out and dragged the boat higher. Groping through the heavy gloom, he found twigs and branches and built his fire. Now he had a light, and might look at her if he chose; but he was afraid of the expression which might be in those eyes, and he looked instead at the beach, sliding into shadow, and now and then heaped timber on his fire. But if he had looked, he would have found something there, in those tragic depths, which had not been there before, a fierce yearning, a heavy wistfulness, without hope. As she lay in the coarse bunk with her golden rope tangled about her, she seemed to strain toward him, beseeching, her eyes woefully on the heavy back, black between her and the firelight. But she made no sound.

Then there came another fearful flash of lightning, this time followed by thunder; and then a soft, inexorable tapping among the leaves, a rilling sound in the stilled water, a drumming on the tin roof of the cabin. The fire hissed and spluttered, dying into a dull glow; and turning from it suddenly, he stepped to the forepart of the *Medea* and pulled out of it a heavy yellow oilskin coat.

"Let me put this about you," he said thickly, bending over her. "It will rain in there."

She leaned forward, obedient, and as he settled it about her shoulders, a strand of hair brushed his cheek, seeming to linger. He paused, still holding the coat, rigid; and a pure gust of tenderness passed over him, rising through him like a torrent and washing him clean of those more terrible impulses which not even his sense of horror had rid him of, in deadening all else.

"Move further in," he said.

She receded from him, docile and imploring; a warmth came from her, kindling in his big body an imperishable fire of response and yearning, against which the rain beat vainly.

And suddenly there came out of the black south, from beyond the bend in the river, a prolonged roaring like the noise of an appalling surf gathering from afar. They waited, muffled in thick silence like profuse nothingness, through which the warm rain fell in its own direction. It seemed as if this coming wind must sweep everything before it, whirling up all the bush into the black heart of its destructive flight. Still they waited, everything forgotten in the common strain of this expectation of the storm. And that terrible, murmurous sound came nearer, nearer, and then, in one moment, with a rending of limbs, a groaning, a rising hiss of tormented waters on the black stream, it was upon them, like a vast rout of all the elements, lashing open the curtains to the boat, pouring about them with a warm voracity, seeming to increase, incredibly; un-breathable, like something fluid, and as if ever renewing, merging all minor noise in one dread overtone. It was like the visible passage of an inexorable spirit through the black spaces above them. The rain disintegrated under it and sank into their faces in a stinging spray. Stray bits of vegetation bruised their flesh. Turning, they bowed before it, mute, enduring.

Then there came a flash of lightning more vivid than any yet, striking out of this roaring blackness all those thousands of gray trunks rocking in black shadow, bitterly distorted, like sentient beings under the lash, crouching, driven all one way in hordes. And in that moment, held over to the black one following, he saw, with a thrill of questioning horror, a lumbering body running madly without reason amid those reeling trees, plunging forward with head sunk at a blind, groping gait.

But he saw, too, all in the same flash, something which concerned him nearer: a huge dead gum, stripped of branches, swaying on the opposite bank and sinking toward him, like a livid finger marking him out as the victim of the storm. He saw the naked roots draw clear of the soil with terrible reluctance, writhing and alive, seeming to claw for holds. And in that moment it was dark again.

With a flash of the physical decision which years of that life had built up in him, he stooped, snatched up that soft figure under him and staggered along the beach, plunging his body fiercely into the solid fury of wind and rain. Holding her close, he felt her lie unquestioningly there, her heart frightening him. He felt her being like a living factor of light in that deep void against the rushing of invisible winds; something warm and tangible, which his shoulders crowded over, protectingly. He awaited in blackness the fall of that tree, which to his baffled imagination seemed to hang there into infinity.

Then it fell, clear of the boat, he thought, though it was hard to judge, for his ears were full of the savage droning of the wind, which showed no sign of abating. Hearing the faint splash of the fallen gum, he strained her closer in a mood of overpowering thankfulness.

"On a shoestring, that," he muttered. For the first time he wanted his life, singly, ardently. The rain fell against him in sheets, and he bent his head into it and raised her a little in his arms. Then he felt her wet cheek against his; he bent lower still, kissed her. He felt her lips cling to his, as if in the spasm of some shock, and in that warm, unremitting contact, which gave him warning of this return upon him of outpouring passion, he seemed to be swung aloft, as on a crest of meeting waves, fortified against all else. Into that moment he crowded all his intensity of yearning; as if he might not know the next. It was indeed like a last moment, in which both snatched willfully at something beyond dreams, forever denied them while life had been a commonplace. All his life he had been holding her so, in prospect, as all her life she had been held. Wanderings, strivings, wounds, fevers, all the ills he had heaped upon himself in his restless march; each delay, each tardy moment, each whimsical embarkment, all had tended, with a staggering intricacy of unrevealed intent, to this. And he felt the wind, choked with rain, streaming between their wet faces, powerless in its rush against the rush of this passion, irrevocable, insurgent, unsatisfied, whirling them up out of that crashing desolation, while yet he held her close in the sticky oils, his legs braced, his body leaning forward into the pitch of the wind.

At length he turned, and stumbling back to the boat, lowered her into the bunk, and stood up his spare planks against the cabin forward to avert the mighty tug of the wind from that frail body. But when she felt his arms leave her, and his presence lost to her by that, for nothing could be seen now, she began to sob—uncontrollably. And this sound of her sobbing, coming to him faintly as if from a long way off, was intolerably sad to him, and the ugly phrases of the storm were all at once appalling portents of this black doom overhanging her; this doom cried abroad to all nature, in a smothered chorus of damned voices, hurried through space on the wings of wrecking winds.

"She can't stand that," he thought, and crept closer. Yet he wanted this racket to go on forever. It put a physical strain upon him which made the other endurable. When it should die away again, that silent blackness would face him with his own thoughts.

"It won't last," he shouted, but the words were dashed from his lips. Then his hand fell against her wet arm, with that filmy sleeve molded on it. She made a pitiful movement of approach, cowed out of all reserve, and he put his arm about her under the heavy oilskins and drew her close.

And presently he felt a pressure on his shoulder, which was her head fallen against it; and after more time a faint glow, at which he shivered, penetrating his sodden clothing; which was the warmth of her shoulder against him.

"Suppose it true even," he thought, "she shall live. Better that than—"

He sat staring into the blackness, torn by that thought; a thousand wild resolves leapt in his brain. She must be got to the coast. He would war upon them all, single-handed. He would find peace for both of them; and she should forget—somewhere.

By imperceptible degrees the storm was going; the thick dark lost its oppressive weight, lifted a trifle; the hiss on the water was less shrill; he saw outlines, a glittering of running water over a black surface; and he heard the wind overhead at a more lingering gait, snuffling and subsiding.

"Who am I, to judge?" he thought. "I have killed—"

Mad scenes of war rioted in him. He had seen red himself. He knew the irresistible onslaught of that wish to kill, to blot out hated faces.

Motionless, he tried to think it inevitable, a thing forced upon a wild nature by circumstance, by the awful monotony of these yellow wastes, with their stark trees, like the fangs of dead animals stuck everywhere.

She drew a little staggering breath, which touched him out of immobility; he bent his head, to catch the sound of her breathing, but not daring to move, as if this position of theirs were final; he held his arm rigid, and felt her soft in the hollow of it.

Then his mind turned to grapple with that horrible figure he had seen, whipped about like a top, running through the night as the gum fell. He knew that it was the man who had bought his knife, and stopped him at the blade wattle; and he felt that he was at the bottom of this . . . And hard upon the heels of that came a sharp vision of that great ragged bird circling above them in the sunset. Impossible to rid himself of that thought. He knew that it was still there, invisible, in that furious dark sky, tottering, sliding down the wind, but forever beating back in its wheelings, not to be thwarted—watching, watching.

Then he felt against his side a softly recurrent pressure; and by this he knew that she slept, exhausted; and that knowledge checked the wild impulse he had to plunge into the bush, fleeing from her and from the evil shadow and dread omen of that bird, high above, or so he thought, in the night, veering on rumpled wings.

He sat there all night, without sleeping, without moving almost, holding her in one aching arm. The rain stopped; the wind died; minute, languid droppings made the renewed silence of the bush heavier and more oppressive. He saw himself stopped in what now seemed a gray mire over a black pool; with the one dead limb of the livid old gum tree which had fallen dimly twisted out over him.

Numbed, enduring, he sat there with his thoughts; and the night was like eternal night. He couldn't imagine the reappearance of that fierce sun which had looked down on him yesterday. Impossible that this black, formless hole should glow green again and the black sky dissolve in burning blue. All that world of vivid color had been snuffed out—the heavens pinched clean together.

With torturing slowness, as if near the end of time, the limb of that dead gum became more strictly visible. It seemed to grow again, to model itself out of chaos, to struggle forth from the mass of a ruined world.

When at last it was distinct, and hung dark and shining over him, with crystal drops trembling from it in the morning wind, the sun came up, startlingly rapid, like something desperately overdue, reddening that murky crevice in the land with brilliant promise, sanctioning the mud, even, and the dead trees; and the poor sodden *Medea*, and for a last touch sending a solid javelin of light into the yellow mouth of a small lizard that crept out upon the limb, his heart beating visibly under his pursy throat.

Looking up at the cold sky, overarching like a thin film of fresh blue, rent in the east by a great sheaf of glowing yellows rising into it, dispersing it, he saw no moving speck anywhere about, and breathed deeply; then lowered his gaze to that still face against his shoulder, with its beauty, its pallor, its confounding innocence, overshadowed by unutterable guilt. Suddenly she seemed to waver, receding, like a white thing sinking through clear waters, lost, twinkling down, down. There were actually tears in his eyes. He shook his head, but they came again, blinding him. Lost! Lost!

And as this cold light grew, yellowing and sharpening the dead waste through which that idle river ran, it fell with intolerable poignancy on this face, fallen back in sleep, on the thin lips with their divining bow, a trifle pale; on the cold cheek, turned away, as she lay, so that this soft curve, in which he lost himself with wonder, was not completed. And thinking, as men will, that upon a time she had not been, it came to him, like an argument for a just God, that now she was, in all that felicity, line by line, woven out of inmost dreams. . . .

But then there came beating upon him again and again with ravening force that hideous fact which she had not denied. Up the river a man lay in his study dead with a knife in him. The mournful howl of that dog came back to him with terrible significance. It had been then; just before that—

Looking down at that fineness, at the sweet sleep which the dawn light grew upon, his soul cried "No" and again "No" mightily to this thought that she must be torn from him, out of his very arms. And from that instant it was he, not she, who was pursued. He felt in himself a fierce antagonism to this retribution in the hands of the few who might organize, hanging over them as surely as the sun, more deadly for hovering invisible. They would search the river last, for there were no boats there save his, and it was therefore an unlikely place to look; but they would search it and come upon them in a day, two days, a week perhaps. And then—

"It's man against man out here," he thought, filled with a resolution born in the black night. He knew the full force of that old argument of anarchy, older than Ned Kelly, that man cannot carry his law into the bush but only his gun and his ready hand, no more.

He looked again cautiously into the sky, where in its far hollows, incomparably delicate, flocks of cloud drifted, soft and palpitating with reflected color, gold, rose, saffron. Nothing more tangible. And at the green current, polished, smooth, surging forward, silent, with a surface of mirrored blue and silver, wherein he could see reflected plumes of a celestial pillaging. This current was going to the sea; and he, too, must go to the sea.

Sudden panic seized him; he turned his set face stiffly over his shoulder, looking back with smoldering eyes. Then in a fever of action he lifted her in the rustling oilskins and laid her in the bunk. But as he did so something fell out of the deep folds of her dress, rapping the side of the boat and falling on the sand. It was the knife he had given that fellow of the black wattle, and a stain, like a corrosion of the metal, ran halfway up the worn blade.

He stood there rubbing it in a dull reverie; and then he stooped and put it beside her again, and going to the locker aft, drew out his gun. He went over it carefully, blowing on the lock and grinding the blue barrel over and over in his rough palm. Then he laid it noiselessly on his seat and swung the boat easily into the river.

Well out on the current, he darted his eyes ahead, behind; penetrating with burning intentness the wet debris on the banks, the huge fallen trunks, covered with slime and insects. Ambush! At the least sound he stopped, lowering his hand to the gun and then reconsidering. Between silent strokes he thought, monotonously: "Not alone—not alone, I reckon," his eyes on that still form with the draggled girdle wound about it.

The rift which had been dawn widened into day, and the sun, falling on her in her fresh disorder, touched her into a livingness of youth and charm, awakening her outwardly, while still she slept, with one arm across her breast and the other by her side, not quite in contact with the black handle of that crooked knife.

Above the river the birds were already softly voluble; the long dapper leaves of the gums which were yet alive hung languid and shining, glowing green after long drought. The deep morning quiet had in it peace, freshness, innocence, unmolested slow awakening to the torment of day. Impossible not to hope.

But as he passed a snag in mid-stream, he saw, gleaming half the length of it a black snake, immaculate, inert, with a thing very like a red jewel fixed in the wicked head, a jewel lapped by seven black and shining shields. He made a rapid pass at it with the cumbrous paddle, but the snake slipped into the water like a darting shadow.

"Have to be careful of these banks now," he reflected. "The river's rising—driving them out."

Then he shivered with consuming black disgust of the place; and the deadliness of things now, when he sought life so ardently, assailed him for the first time, cramping his heart with that nameless dread which falls so surely, unseen, when the soul aspires, and is bound, as if withering before the leaping progress and unfathomable hopeless end of all desire.

The day passed, and the pursuit had not disclosed itself. All through those burning yellow hours, with their poisonous burden of time, unrolling hopes, despairs, in slow succession, he had sat on his creaking seat, dipping his paddle with a murderous energy, as if unlimbering himself for a last stand. And now, as day again faded from the hot sky, he felt a grim satisfaction in that dying light, and in the uninterrupted serenity of the bush, darkening above, with promise of concealing night.

"It is nearly night now," he heard her say.

"Yes," he answered heavily. Their only words since morning had been to mark the progress of the day. But when their eyes met, there had been a quickening, had passed a remembrance, like a solace, of the wild heart of the storm, of that swift uprising and interlocking of souls under its thunderous, discordant fury.

As he spoke now, he trailed his paddle, listening, and they floated silently over a deep pool, still and black as the ink in a magician's hand. On the banks all forms of trees and animals were dark and tortuous against a green-gold west. He saw a wagtail busy on the forehead of a sheep, pecking about amongst the fleece; two cows, regarding him with woeful, curious, uplifted noses, with wrinkles of disapprobation for this strange invader of their pool. A fish—perhaps the mythical and

wily river cod, which he had never caught—leapt in some black border
of this pool, and the wide ripples stole out invitingly in silver arcs. In
the contrasted light, the clotted foliage of the gums seemed strangely
foreign; a fantastic eerie, nowhere. And the quiet deepened and deepened, with the growing dimness, haunting him; a rich shadow invested
all the bush, a brown which darkened imperceptibly as a dying fire, a
color warm and rich, out of which came now and again the mad laughter
of the cuckoo burroughs and the wrathful screeching of cockatoos.

"We may as well stop," he said. "These snags—"

Suddenly he made out, on a pebbly peninsula, a coal-black rabbit,
bolt upright beside a log.

"Supper," he said in a whisper. He picked a stone out of the bottom
of the boat, and with his arm hanging lax, drifted down upon the rabbit.
He felt her lean out of the cabin so that she might see ahead. So silently
they went, and so precisely headed for that little ball of fur, that there
was nothing to suggest the altering of distance, unless the growing of
the rabbit in the eye. And suddenly the chase sat up, straight as a major,
his ears erected high, his little forelegs hanging. There he held himself,
as if for vespers, with not even the twitch of a suspicious whisker. So
intimately near him in his guilelessness they drew, and so hung upon
his attitude, and the little quiver in his jet-black ears, that they forgot
all else. The water was only a darker shade of the brown dusk through
which they floated. It might have been a charmed river, a dream rabbit,
an enchanted boat. . . . He raised his arm.

Then, without warning, they heard the trampling of a heavy foot in
the bush above them. The brown eyes of the big Yank turned from the
rabbit with a savage twinkle.

"At last!" he cried; and with one mighty stroke he drove the boat into
the beach and snatched up his gun.

Then he felt her slim body, in its woeful finery, passionately about
him in a fierce resistance to his going; but he shook her off and ran
stumbling across the beach to the beginning of the steep bank. Naked
roots, crusted with mud, reached down to him, and grasping his gun by
its barrel, he swung himself madly up. But at the very moment when he
came level with the upper ground, he felt a sharp stab in his arm; and
at once a deadly current of ice and flame leapt through all his big body,
stopping his heart. Holding himself by one hand, he shook off something dark and writhing from his free arm; and then, his head falling

back, he was conscious of a dreadful face, flabby, wobbling, pallid with fear, hanging over him out of the bush, and instantly receding. It was the man of the black wattle.

Then he fell, striking first on some cruelly jagged surface and crumpling up on the soft sand below. But in an instant, he was on his feet, full of an overwhelming desire to live. He groped his way toward the boat, unable now to feel his feet, as if, in some shocking manner, he ran upon stumps of his legs alone. He saw her coming swiftly toward him through the gloom; the image of her like the last picture of vivid life his fading brain would ever know. He held out his arm, staring at her with dim eyes.

"The whiskey—forward," he whispered, with bursting tongue, "and the razor—at the head of the bunk."

He sank to his knees; but she was back to him on the instant. There was about a minute and a half to scarify, he knew. Opening the razor, he slashed himself deeply half a dozen times, and would have bent forward to put his lips to the flowing wounds, but she dashed her hand to his face.

"Your lip is cracked," she screamed. Her voice came to him, terribly insistent, remote, tiny, as if something had descended smothering the universe. Then he heard her saying, "Drink, drink," very far off, and felt the glass neck of a bottle knocking his teeth. He put out his hand, swaying over a yawning chasm of blackness, into which everything was sinking, and seized the bottle. Tilting it up, he drank, choking, as if he were to do nothing but that until he died. The bottle seemed coated with some soft substance, like fur; the sands were furry, to his knees. His sense of touch was going, then. He tried to rouse himself, to will something, to persist, even among these damnable shadows wavering upon him; but then an extraordinary sense of wellbeing invaded him, all torment was stilled. He ceased to struggle, sinking back into nothingness like a feather through space, and knew only of a dim weight, a soft straining at the arm where blood must be flowing still. She had her lips to the wound, sucking the poison. A good plucked 'un—skin like a baby. . . . His throat burned faintly, like a foretaste. . . . He would assuredly go to hell, having taken no precautions. . . . Therefore . . .

He opened his eyes stupidly. He had picked up again the thread of himself, somehow, out of that blackness, but it was as if he had lain there forever first. He was conscious only of an immense passage of time.

Bringing his eyes to rest above him, he was aware of blue letters on a yellow ground. "Maltby's White Horse Whiskey." That was the stray tin sign he had bent over his cabin for a roof. He discovered that he lay in his own boat, and his dry hands closed on the wheat bags lining the bunk under him. His right arm was swollen and ached savagely as he came more awake. Then he saw, still without moving, an enormous system of iron girders, like a lattice work, thrown from bank to bank ahead of him, and through the bars of this a red sun smoldering. Night or morning? Night, he decided, by the warmth. Then he heard the snapping of a fire to his left, and with that sound, so comforting and so familiar, he regained all his personality at once.

Suddenly with a grinding roar a black streak shot among those girders and vanished.

"It's a railroad bridge," he thought, surprised. How had he come—

And at that moment he heard a voice, her voice, very near him.

"You had better go before the sun falls," she said. This voice was cold, insistent; and there was no answer. Pivoting on his elbow, the big Yank rolled himself half out of the boat and brushed his eyes. She had been kneeling on the beach beside a tiny fire, but she turned swiftly toward him as he rose in the bunk, and cried out, "Your arm," in caution.

He looked at it stupidly, and found it wrapped in a stained bandage; and directly, sending his eyes in quest, he saw the jagged tear out of the bottom of her dress. He felt somehow as if this were a part of her binding him.

"You cut too deep," she said, and then, seeing that his eyes had traveled beyond her, she turned to the fire again and stood drooping, over it. He was looking steadily at the gross figure of that man, who seemed fixed at the very center of all this madness. He was sitting on a log, inert, like a stuffed thing. His black leggings were scratched and fouled, his cheeks scored, his pale eyes blank and motionless under the shiny vizor of his cap. He sat all slumped together, as if his will had quite deserted him, as if a crushing weight hung from either shoulder.

"So, it's you," said the Yank, twisting slightly, and looking over the bulge of his shoulder. "Well, you certainly play in luck, stranger. If it hadn't been for that snake—"

Wrath overcoming weakness, he swayed to his feet. The hopeless apathy of that fellow infuriated him.

"Why, you pusillanimous—"

Something plucked at him unseen, and he shut his mouth on a favorite oath.

"You come dogging along like this, saying nothing—I tell you, I'd have shot you down," he muttered.

The man stirred, shook, rippled all over like the flank of an irritated animal. Then he spoke a few words and repeated them a little louder.

"I wish you had," he mumbled. "My God, I wish you had!"

The Yank, disgusted, speechless with rage at his weakness, at the spectacle of this man with his fat face and his sodden body, moved his swollen arm, and it came against the crooked knife. He closed his fingers round the handle and held it up.

"How's this?" he shouted. The man seemed like a dead symbol, an unresponsive, ghastly figure in a dream not to be moved, not to be assailed by any mortal voice. "I sell you a knife, and then I find it on this girl. What's the answer?"

The girl shivered over the glow of the fire. The man looked at the knife and came horribly alive.

"Oh, yes, that knife," he said. He made a motion as if beseeching the big Yank to lay it down. "I killed him!" he shrieked suddenly. His eyes rolled in his head, like the eyes of an inverted doll. He brushed a hand across them and peered stealthily at the knife again.

"That's it," he said. "I could see the sun on his bald head, over the chair—shining—eh? He was asleep, but his arm moved. I crept up on him, from behind, and drove it into him, while he slept. He went—like that—"

He jerked himself forward, and a grunt came from him. He sat there, rigid, staring at the black girders of the bridge. The sun had set.

His fat, indecisive face twisted with sudden passion, with a lingering brutality of reminiscence.

"He was gone," he said in a hollow voice, with a kind of astonishment as if even now he could not believe in that consummation. "I killed him." These words rang clear through his mumblings with a note of finality, of triumph even. "I said I would, and I did. I said it every day for sixteen years, and I couldn't back out then. I say I couldn't back out."

He shouted; his eyes were terrible.

"I was afraid, that's true; but it had to be done."

"That's it, then," said the Yank. "I saw you in jail—in Melbourne. I don't forget faces."

"So, you did," said the man. "They all saw me; they came and saw me sitting there, behind those bars, waiting. I was waiting, and they didn't know. He came and saw me, and he didn't know. He knows now—"

He rocked on the dead trunk in a horrible satisfaction, shot with a more horrible fear. He went on again.

"He swore me into that place. God witness it, I was innocent. He perjured his black soul that's gone to dance in hell now. Dance in hell. I was a man then; I had a wife, a baby—that girl, Aurelia. He never forgave . . . And when she died, he took the child. It was like the mother, it seems, like the mother he coveted. And what was I to do? I waited. I broke stone and sat in that cell and waited. Sixteen years. And then I came out. A month ago—like this."

The Yank leaned toward him.

"That may be so," he said. "But you ought to have made a clean job with that knife. No use leaving rag ends. What do you calculate to do now?"

"I don't know," said the man dully. "I don't know; that God's truth. I was afraid, afraid when I struck him, afraid. I could hear him breathing—that cursed sun on his head—and I struck . . . Sixteen years—I'd sworn it. It won't be sixteen years this time. Not that. They're closing in. Death this time. That's something . . . I crawled to her, my child. She didn't know me, her father; but she believed. She took the knife and told me to go. Nobody had seen; I could get away and nobody know. My God, I wanted to get away! I wanted time; I wanted to remember—"

He twined his soft hands together and gasped. He had wanted to remember.

"And how about the girl?" said the big Yank in fierce disgust. "You wanted them to think—"

"Ah, that's it," said the man. "When I could think—I could see. Why not? The daughter of a convict. No, no . . . So I followed along those banks, watching her. She's a pretty thing. Look at her. She might have come to me once—her father. But not now—I'm nothing to her now."

The girl stood tall and motionless by the fire, her torn dress falling in long folds.

"It's this—it's the nights. I can't stand 'em . . . That damned bald head bobbing around."

The man's head fell; he breathed heavily. Without turning, the girl said again:

"You had better go."

"Yes, I'll go," he said; "there's nothing else."

The tall Yank, swaying, made a step toward him.

"Not much," he said. "You're the man they're looking for and they don't know it. It's high time they knew. Are you going to let them take your own daughter?"

"Why, no, that's it," said the man. "I'm going—into the town. I'm going—"

He stopped, as if in that moment he had died.

"Let him go," said the girl apathetically. "Let him go."

The Yank fell back weakly into his boat, and the man went stumbling across the beach. When he came to the bank, he half turned and went on again blindly, shielding his face with his arms, as he had done running before the storm. The faint yellow in the west seemed to be draining away into the heart of remoteness. For an instant they saw his bulky shoulders ragged against it and he was gone.

Then the Yank began to speak.

"This is all true?" he questioned. "You ran away to shield this man, your father; to give him time?"

She nodded faintly.

"But, my God, if he had got away for good, don't you see that you wouldn't have come clear?"

"Yes," she whispered. "But I didn't then. He came crawling to me, as he said—and I thought of those sixteen years; and it seemed the only thing."

He sank away from her, folding himself back into the bunk with one sinuous movement, and looking empty-eyed at the roof of his cabin.

"You didn't know, of course," he muttered, "while you lived with Sir Robert—"

"I knew my father was in prison. Only that."

He looked at her steadily, lying there inert, the roll of his bared arm huge in shadow, with some blurred tattooing on it. And he saw that he was only a big baboon, after all; a crude, gigantic plaything, tossed from sea to land, land to sea, in unavailing alternation. The very fact of him was incongruous, against that slim delicacy, that golden strength, with its crown of gold dim under the early stars. They were like the ends of two stubborn destinies, bent almost together by the might of some ungovernable malice, trembling on the release, which should snap them back—forever.

There seemed to be no current to his thought now, no impulsion. With a kind of idleness, an impersonal curiosity, he asked:

"How did I come to get in the boat?"

"I dragged you there," she said. "The dew was falling."

"You are strong," he said, wistfully admiring. "Very strong—very beautiful."

He mumbled this truth over to himself, unheeding, like a man who can neither hurt nor further himself by candid speech.

All at once the sight of her was more than he could stand.

"You've no more need of me," he said, bitterly abrupt. "You don't need anybody to go killing off people chasing you. That's over . . . Oh, yes. I'd have shot him. I'd have shot him down like a dog, if the snake hadn't struck. I'd have shot them all down. I meant to make a red track of them clear to the coast, if it had to be. I meant to get you clear. . . ."

His voice was nothing now but a fierce whisper.

"I thought you did it. That's the man I am."

His head fell forward; he lost himself in the rising gloom.

"There was another girl once a nurse in Akron, Ohio—Medea—you'll see her name on the boat. I had a wrong idea about her once, and she turned me out. Been going ever since."

He felt that she stood there with her cold eyes sending down withering judgment on him. For the first time there seemed to be just meaning in that mad laughter of the birds echoing round, as if through emptiness.

"How did we get down here?" he asked idly, unable to bear that silence.

"The river rose," she said. She was very close; her voice trembled. "Three or four feet. I couldn't hold the boat, so I steered. You slept all night and all day. And he followed—along the banks. I could hear him."

He heard her breathing faster.

"I've done what you asked," he said. "Here you are at the town. I'm all right now. A little rest. You might push me out into the current; I think . . . I'll drift along a bit."

She made no move, but stood there in that torturing proximity, robed in shadow. And suddenly these wastes, these desert spaces, the whole idle wild, rose to confront him with their emptiness, their frightening emptiness. He was afraid, like a child again, softened, as if she had drained away his strength, his singleness, with those soft lips, in sucking out the poison. He was afraid to go on, leaving her there, shimmering, growing fainter, vanishing for all time. He was accustomed to conquest; and now he felt ultimately beaten, bound by a million thongs. Getting on had lost its meaning, had become abhorrent at the very moment when it had become most necessary.

Suddenly a crow flew over the river, a dark shadow, with the speed of thought. It came close; they heard the siffle of its wings.

"That's bad," he thought. "These cursed birds."

Then she spoke, in little sobbing breaths.

"Do you suppose I care what you thought? Who wouldn't think? You wouldn't give me up. You'd have seen me through to the coast. I know it. Why—ah, why?"

He half rose again, straining toward her. Why? He had a question he could answer now. All these other questions that had baffled him, drawing him on; questions that had plagued him as he lay out on rocking yards, in storms, with the black oaths of struggling men in his ears, the bourdon of wild canvas; questions that had leapt out at him under burning suns, over blinding snows, lashing him on, on to the end, the end of youth, of hope, of life, they had their answer here.

"I—wanted—you," he breathed, with parched lips. "But I'm telling you—I thought—"

"What do you think now?" she said. "You've seen him. What do you think?"

She was close beside him now, not daring to look up, vague, tremulous, despairing of him.

"With that blood in me," she added, in a spirit of passionate precaution.

"That blood?" he said stupidly. "There's no accounting for where a flower—"

He stopped. She seemed to be nodding toward him through the dark, swaying, sinking—toward him. He saw her arms, white in the dark, those slim, strong arms that had lifted him, in all his worthless bulk, outstretched, forbidding, opposing him, entreating him—prisoning him.

"If you went," she whispered, warm and riotous against him, "I should die. I'm afraid . . . afraid to be alone."

"That's it," he said eagerly, holding her close with a great wonder. "That's the trouble with me. I'm afraid to go on alone. Queer thing, too; I never was before."

It was quite dark now; the bush hung over them like a rich tapestry, dimly wrought with figures, a great, silent pageant of the wild, assembling its moods, its yellow inconsequences, its prone spirit hovering in silence, defeated. And the unseen current, rippling against the boat, went its way, unchecked, unhurried, toward the port that he would never see. He had dropped his eyes from all horizons.

THE RAZOR OF PEDRO DUTEL

Published as one of *The Grim Thirteen* (1917)

Hallet's story was selected for a collection of short stories whose unhappy endings led editors to reject them—the clever idea of Frederick Stuart Greene, editor at Dodd, Mead and Co. Like "With the Current," this lively story also draws on Hallet's hair-raising travels with his former shipmate Hyde "on the wallaby"—through the unsettled wilds of Australia in 1912–1913.

At the time the man, Pedro Dutel, discovered that my partner, Frank Hyde, was a competent barber, we were cracking granite on top of a blazing mountain, in whose purple shadow Dutel had built his house, close by the riverbed. I can still feel the cold air of that wide, shining hall of his, the yield of those wicker chairs to my sore ribs; I can still see the great prospect of plain and mountain to the north, as we sat, all three of us, on the veranda. And I can still see my partner, pausing, with the razor held away from the chin of our host, to glance somewhat wistfully at the river.

"You think it will rise?"

"It has a frog in its throat," murmured Dutel, again submitting his cheek to that resplendent leaf of steel which stroked the skin lightly as a feather fallen from the wings of sleep.

Our boat was moored just around the bend; but although we knew that our host, in this suave opinion of his, had an eye to his shaves, we knew also, that somewhere back among those dim, round-shouldered mountains lay a sack of rain. Yet the river, only half asleep in its bed, enticed, haunted us with its many-voiced dream-tale of the south, lying under twilight haze, like a mistress too languorous to rise, but willing to be won. It lay still, with scarcely a ripple, between its mysteriously figured walls of half-baked clay.

"It is too early to pick grapes there," Dutel let fall, waving his arm southward.

"I and Dick have got money," said old Frank. He wiped the razor on a clean towel, and added: "We have heard about a lady a day's run down the creek. And we are drawn that way. We are ladies' men."

At these words our immaculate Dutel came upright in his chair with a light in his dark eyes.

"Ah, you have heard," he said. "The wife of Amberg. My friends, yes, a devoted lady. But it is a bad family."

Lying back in his long chair, with eyes half shut again, he burst into the liquid speech characteristic of him. Amberg, he said, was a queer man, certainly a queer man, coming of a bad family, one of these bad families made bad by solitude and hard luck. Mad, poor devils, rather than bad. Their badness had a necessary quality in it, like the inexorable processes of indifferent nature. These people were numbed by their sequestering fate, indifferent to toil, as to the mournful fact of life itself, conducted in the thick of an unforgiving wilderness. They struck as the blind lightning strikes, from the pressure of invisible tormenting forces.

For his part, Pedro Dutel knew nothing authentic of Amberg; and in the bush one never inquired. Never inquired. One assumed, one understood. Nevertheless, it was said that Amberg had brought his wife from the towns, from Melbourne probably, where she had been a barmaid. He had retreated here to discuss her, like a dog with a bone.

But rumors here were of little account. Men came and went, shadows, lean brown shadows, shepherding spectral sheep, or knocking white bones together to startle rabbits from under cover. They were disappointed men, these selectors; men driven out of the fat, fertile margins by the shouldering in of capital, money from home in vast blocks. They were dour spirits driven to conceal from all but God the exasperating fact of their continuing poverty. Yes, and they cursed God as well, whose awful benediction, cast upon them from the starry softness of those deep skies, they could neither fathom nor escape. This ironic and velvety splendor could only plunge them deeper into blasphemy.

"They work to no purpose," said our host Dutel.

Few men, he said, would have, in the face of such incredible obstacles, this dark spirit of patience with the land, this iron courage, standing up unmoved and scornful of results out of a tangle of roots: of roots planted in a baked land fallen into cracks and strewn with bones, with stumps, innumerable stumps. A day's work to a stump.

Pedro Dutel, over whose dark face had flashed an appearance of grim mirth, warned us that there were stumps now on his own estate, which would account for a dozen bad families. Land-clearing machinery was known to exist, but it was not at the beck of these selectors.

"They worry them out."

In an interval between these worryings Amberg had brought into this back-block a wife who could be called—yes, a beautiful woman. Mr. Dutel had once been fortified in his own soul by a sight of her at the edge of his estate. A sulky and magnificent figure of a woman, tall as the fabled goose, with a neck as white, after all these suns. A barmaid, had he said?

He rubbed his hands, as if this description had set her before him in a new light; as if he half wondered why he had sat here all this time, idle, with that neighbor down the river.

But this miracle of a wife had given an odd turn to Amberg's badness. He was said to be jealous, insanely jealous; and this jealousy had as good as buried her in that solitude. No one would go near the place. Amberg was a very powerful fellow, and people feared some outburst of his jealousy.

Dutel stopped speaking, and in the silence, night fell, swift as a net over the fluttering wings of day. That round fragment of a granite mountain hung over us, like the black bag out of which night had been poured since time began. A servant brought a candle to the elbow of our host, who pouted his lips to the flame, lighting a cigarette.

Yes, there seemed to be no doubt that the man Amberg was jealous of his wife. He had as good as told him, Dutel, to keep away, at the same time that he had accepted a bottle of very good whiskey at his hands.

The eyes of our host beamed. Could we sympathize with her? She was alone, cut off from her kind; destined to confound nobody with a display of that bewildering beauty.

"A beautiful woman is nobody's possession," said our host smoothly. "She is reflected into many hearts, as the sun shines on many waters."

It was beyond analysis; a strange thing. Showing perhaps that to meet with a sane mind the oppressive immensity of all this—here he waved his arm at the bush—the something unmoved, impassive; men must live together, they must run the risk of their wives' affections being stolen away. That was the price. Of what use the retaining of a wife, however beautiful, at the cost of reason, at the cost of life itself?

"She will kill him ultimately, of course," said Pedro Dutel.

Our host exerted himself cheerfully in the role of philosopher. His pleasant voice, speaking without rancor, was strangely at odds with the dark magnificence, or even majesty of his face, with its full lips, its bold eyes, in the corners of which seemed to lie shadows of rapacious dreams. In his rumpled suit of yellow linen, he seemed immense of body, as an ape; and his arm hung by his side like an ape's. When he moved it, as in a gesture, there was an inclusive crook in it; he would hold the hand outstretched, until the smoke from his cigarette settled into a vague spire, a tiny motionless column, delicately tremulous at the top, as if magically issuing into fragrant wreaths, evoked to fall upon the head of this reasonable man with warlike eyes. An immense chain of wrought gold extended along the hollow under his ribs, a chain of gold glittering in the blue night, like some mute and all-powerful bond between the man and his philosophy. He was rich, so we had heard; this station of his was an experiment, a mere nothing, outlying here as if to give him a chance to air his thoughts. Comfortable people, as old Frank had said, were in a position to say dog-gone-d comfortable things.

Something in all this had silenced even my partner's tongue; but now he said:

"This here Amberg has been breaking stone up there, along with I and Dick. She had all her chance then."

Dutel's eye flashed a sudden special intelligence at him. Uttering the single word "Yes," he crushed out his cigarette in the candlestick; and stood listening profoundly, as if attuning himself to the night, to the music of the spheres. Yawning, he stretched his thick arms out, perhaps in a prayer for the freedom of the earth. The yellow light of the candle, streaming upward against his swarthy face, which was slightly pitted, gave it the strength of its dark hollows.

"He stopped in here to-night, on the way to his selection," he said slowly after a time. "He has worked enough. I let him have what he wanted."

Dutel spoke contemptuously, as of an animal he had indulged; and shortly after we turned in. We were sleeping in an abandoned dairy;

sleeping hard, too, desperately hard, with the ring of that healthy granite in our ears; and our very heart shaken by the repeated impact of mauls, swung in racking half-circles.

In the morning we felt actually sodden; our hands were cracked; the ribs seemed wrenched away from the spine. As it was, we had stayed longer than most navvies would have found it convenient. We were not professional rock-men; and we had had enough.

Dutel, with a regretful sigh, that arched his vast chest, said at breakfast: "You are going, then?"

"We reckon so."

"And down the river?"

"We will take tea of that lady of yourn."

Dutel hesitated, and suddenly brought out of his pocket a razor, not the one which Frank had used in shaving him. This was a larger blade, held between two slats of yellow ivory, inlaid with silver points. The name of our host was delicately painted in black on one of these slips of ivory. This instrument had a look at once of murder, antiquity and art.

"It is a good piece of steel, but it needs to be honed," he said. "Our friend Amberg has a bluestone which will do the business. I gave it to him, and afterward lost mine."

Looking at us soberly he added in a quiet tone:

"That razor has a history. It has cut many throats. It is yours! I imagine it will sweat blood on warm nights."

As he expected, my partner received this hint with a consummate twinkle of appreciation. Hah. It would sweat blood. He pondered the hideous and pleasing attribute, sitting cross-legged in the boat, which creaked over the imperceptible current. Do you think this propensity of a slip of steel to sweat blood was nothing to a man of imagination? It was in all, I tell you. He believed it. That razor was dear and necessitous to his heart. Its sudden presentation had deflected him from an original intention of steering clear of Amberg's selection altogether. The chance of a bluestone overbore the risk that might be run by breaking the lady's seclusion. Dutel had certainly made us a careful estimate of her. I seemed to see again the dark figure of our host, just as he stood on the bank above us, in loose linen, with a friendly and speculative gleam in his fierce eyes, which possessed, appropriated, whatever they fell on.

Although we were to be a day's journey by the river, it was nevertheless true that the selector Amberg's land adjoined Dutel's estate.

The river ran five miles to the road's one.

Toward night, the river turned, bringing our backs to the sun.

"Another one of them red-roaring oxbows," said my partner. "This here river is limp enough for a stock whip."

The sun was just over the trees, a forest of tea-trees on the left, where we came abreast of Amberg's selection. There was a shack of stringy bark on the riverbank, but seeing a flash of a roof inland, we turned our steps at once that way. It was a sad place, a gloomy prospect for a couple of swagmen. Lying all about on the hot turf were the charred and rifled trunks of ringed gums, yawning, with black mouths, like giant overturned mortars. They were invested with rabbits, and showed here and there, through cracks, tufts of fur.

In the short grass white bones glimmered in links and crosses and odd broken patterns of a past mortality. The bush, crowding this withered patch, shone sallow green, dense and mute. The sun behind us hung over the tea-trees like a hot copper boiler. There was not a sound.

The house was blind-ended, unkempt, smeared with whitewash. Against the rear of it hung, pegged out, the skins of half a dozen black snakes, with beautiful crimson bellies. We eyed our bare feet doubtfully but turned the corner of the house.

The wife of Amberg, whom the magic of Dutel's tongue had touched already, was on the porch, washing her bare arms in a tin basin. We were at first shocked to see those arms brilliantly sprayed with blood above the elbow, until we saw just beyond her, the bodies of three opened sheep hanging from the roof of the porch by loops of harness. They were like glittering red caverns; her extraordinary brooding face seemed pale as death against them.

She became aware of us as she was drying her arms, and said calmly, without the least start or confusion:

"Are you travelling from Sydney?"

"That same port, ma'am."

We unconsciously drew together in our wonder at the flashing perfection of this creature whom the bush had swallowed up. Not all the cunning of Dutel's tongue could have invested her with half her charm of the wild. There was something dream-like and smooth in her reception of us. In a calm voice she told us there was water in the dam. She would lay out mutton for us. Tea. Did we care for tea?

Her eyes were blue as a tropical sea, a blue too deep for any sun to fade. They swam by us, they were fixed on middle distance, conveying, through their unwinking regard, the terrifying stillness in that woman's soul. For days, for years, it may be, she had given ear to a whole countryside. It seemed to us as if she had confused our voices with the voices of the bush, which had for so long held her in its smothering trap. Was she mad?

If so, she had taken the tone of her unreason from that universal hush, which was like wool in the ears. She gave the whole vicinity, merging as it was in night, a touch of dream, the rare beauty and pathetically fleeting emotion of a dream. She stood before us, half remembered, or like something we had been destined to see. In the limp droop of those magnificent arms, still moist, glowing pink in the face of a rayless sun, there was something unreserved and abstracted. She was listening, eternally listening. Her very movements were lingering, stealthy, as if ever so light a noise might intercept some scarcely audible message.

She went into the house, gliding like the ghost of some bright substance.

In filling our basin with fresh water from the dam, we stumbled upon a bit of wire fencing, sunk into the ground as the preliminary to a wheat field. There was no wheat but caught in one of the lower meshes of the wire was a small, gray lizard, dead many moons, its mouth of yellow satin wide open, minutely horrifying.

"King Dick," said my partner, stopping short, "that little reptile has starved to death. It wedged itself in there and—"

He looked back at that silent house with the three disemboweled sheep hanging from its roof.

"This is a dead-end of a place," he muttered. "Where is Amberg, I wonder?"

We saw no trace of him; and yet something in her attitude proclaimed his presence, the haunting presence of a fourth person throwing his shadow across that place.

A glance sufficed to reveal that he was not in the house itself. An inner room, not quite dark, contained only a rumpled bed, and a chair on the seat of which was stuck a bit of melted candle. The ceiling over us consisted of two bulging folds of burlap with a black split in the center, leading into the gloom of rafters. As with all these back-block hovels, the chimney was the main thing, a huge maw, in whose blackness hung a round kettle by six or seven sooty links. A narrow door stood in the wall to the left of this chimney.

"Have you lived long in these parts, ma'am?" asked Frank. His voice was thick.

"Four years," she said.

She walked past us to the chimney, and her bare feet made less noise on the red dirt than the feet of the geese.

"Awful quiet," he rumbled over his mutton. "Awful quiet here."

"Yes," she said. She seemed a little fluttered as if meditating some impulsive move from the gloom of the chimney. Her hands were softly crossed at her throat; she swung poised, as if she might have taken flight. And all the time we felt the unconscious power of some other personality lurking in that rapid dusk.

"I and King Dick was working with your husband up at Bald Top," Frank went on. This forbearance of hers to produce a husband had worked a nameless uneasiness in him. He felt that the presence of this man, even with his explosive instinct of jealousy, would relieve a situation already growing tense.

In answer she only dropped her eyelids and leaned back against the chimney.

"Has he—has he showed up?" My partner insisted on accounting for this husband.

And these words were sufficient, for she made a gesture toward the shack by the river's edge, and in a deep ringing tone, which for the first time rendered the music in her voice, she cried:

"He is out there. Drunk."

That, then, was what he had wanted of Dutel; something with which to combat the solitude, or the tearing insistence of this jealousy, provoked in him simply by the appalling beauty of a woman whom he had dared to put beyond the approaches of men, only to find that she turned a deaf ear to him as well. He may have felt himself the desperate illusoriness of that beauty. She was no more than a rebellious wraith, shimmering in the midst of this forlorn clearing.

"He came back in drink," she whispered. "Pig."

"Doggone his measly hide," said old Frank in hollow tones. "That is no way to treat a lady, ma'am."

He stood up, scratching his chin.

Suddenly her bosom heaved, she seemed to be let loose in redoubled beauty from that shadowy chimney corner; and her fiery blue eyes were fixed resolutely on my partner's apprehensive face. Yes, it was so they had come at him in the past. Her shoulders narrowed until little soft ridges of pliant muscle rose over them at the neck. Her few whispered words hissed in our ears like arrows.

"You have a boat. Take me. Take me away. O, dear God, take me to the town."

Imperious and adroit, she flung out both arms to my partner as if to melt him within the full circle of them, while she overwhelmed him with the mad urgency of her astonishing eyes. She coaxed him with the sudden unreserve of a child, sinking slowly to her knees, letting fall her head, backward, to display the longest line of her throat.

"The river may rise," she whispered passionately, "but what of that? I hope he may die in there. He will never know—need never know. Come—be quick."

She mumbled disjointed words, sobbing, with her arms laid across his knee. She could assume no position that had not a strong beauty, a persuading charm of wildness. Her leg, bare to knee, lay on the earthen floor in a thick shadow which was rising all round as night fell. Rapt and astonished, we gazed down at her prone body. Our eyes met, for one second. We looked different ways, not able to speak, or even think in terms of solid reason. We stared at that magnificent goose, coming weightily out of the chimney corner. Its undiscerning gravity gave it a singular look of command in the midst of this madness. The pallor of its neck was not more striking than that of hers against the curling tendrils of tawny hair into which the sun, falling through a chink in the western wall of the hut, struck uncertain fire.

We remained as if turned to stone, striving for some adequate sign, some word to utter, strong and yet civil, something that would detach us, once and for all, from this woman. The moment called for discretion, almost for a kind of understanding tenderness. We were wordless men.

Clearing his throat old Frank manages to eject the single word, "Lonesome," crouching over her, massive and sorrowful. For a moment he looked down in amazement, as if some bright weapon had pierced his heart already. With a vague stroking gesture of his hand toward her hair, he mumbled:

"Turn in. You will feel different about this in the morning."

"Then you will not take me?" she cried fiercely.

"No, ma'am," said my partner. He began to be fierce too. An immense resolution was there, in the cant of his nose. He was being asked to run away with another man's wife and by the wife herself. No, sir, he had a proper regard for property in wives. It was not the same thing, at all, as if he had asked her to run away.

"Nobody will take me," she said with deep bitterness. "Are you going to leave me? Will you leave me alone here? What is my life to him?"

"You have got a man," said old Frank dubiously. Men had got drunk in his experience, without parting from their wives.

In this confusion he went fumbling in his pockets, and drew out the razor Pedro Dutel had given him. The last rays of the sun, coming through a knot hole, sparkled faintly on its silver points, and clearly illuminated the name, Pedro Dutel, which he read intently, holding the razor still. As if meaning to soothe her, he said:

"Now, there is a razor that sweats blood. Yes, ma'am, it has cut so many throats it will sweat blood on warm nights. It was given I and Dick by a duke."

She leaned forward, half-forgetful of the plea she had been making, her lips parted. And then the red spot of sun fled, and darkness fell, like the black shadow of a squall, blotting out the expression of her face.

"Have you got a bluestone," he inquired, trying little by little to turn the talk into a safe channel. I heard him lay the razor on the table with a deliberate click, like a signal; and then the dull voice of the girl, which had a peculiar flatness except when she exerted it strongly:

"I will see," she said.

Old Frank, noiseless in bare feet, joined me in the doorway, and we felt rather than saw her rise from her crouching position, and pass through the door by the chimney. We looked out into the night.

The silence surrounding that unlucky place was so great that you could have heard the stars knocking together in the sky. Through the door, the trunks of the dead gums rose glimmering, in groups, festooned by tangled ribbons of bark. They made strange shapes of sorrow, like leaning crosses, age-encrusted monoliths. In their scarred and bone-like rounds, they suggested all kinds of livid terrors—terrors of madness. A neighborhood like that will very quickly take the tinge of a sick brain.

"We will mosey out of here, to-night," muttered my partner.

There was not a trace of wind or sound. There seemed literally nothing between us and high heaven to dim the burning scrutiny of those southern stars which, little by little, dissolved the brown of dusk into an incredible solution of crystal blue, rayed by fixed lights. The dark line of the bush haunted us. It was as if we had been shut in on some black bottom, alone with one pitiful girl, through whose mad eyes we were receiving this odd distortion of the landscape. We abhorred the earth we stood on, swung there in that illusory cold round of space, so devilishly pierced by sharp stars. I tell you, we were baffled by the wonder of that inconsiderate illumination, which shone over this horror so deadly wide on that deep round of velvet.

We were roused from this ghastly reverie by a creak of the door by the chimney. At the same time, we heard the soft thud of that girl's feet. She dropped something on the now invisible table, panting, and sprang back forcibly.

"Holy Mackinaw," said Frank.

He took several steps into the room and banged into the table. As his hand slid across that surface, it touched the razor he had laid there. The blade was open, and he picked it up.

"King Dick," he whispered, "it's wet. The dog-goned thing is wet!"

He had slapped it against the palm of his hand.

"Light a match," he said.

I lit one. Under the steadily burning flame, we saw a broad smear of blood across the palm of his hand.

"You've cut it," I said hoarsely.

He plunged his fist in the bucket of water under the table. We lit another match and stared again. There was no sign of a cut.

And then that girl came between us, fierce, hoarse-breathing. Her foot fell on mine, giving me the sense of that solid body, quivering all over from the receding impulse of an abhorrent crime. That warm dusty sole, like living velvet, horrified me, and I thrust her back. Suddenly she laughed, not a laugh that can be talked about, a banshee scream, torn out of her by the powers of black silence, of those twin brooding infinities of sky and bush.

"It—has—sweat—blood," she stated then. The devil had touched her with his own humour.

For half a second, I believe old Frank actually considered the astounding possibility. It had become part of his life to believe that lurid myth. Recovering his reason, he seized the girl by her shoulders and swayed her back and forth.

"What have you done now?" he cried hoarsely. He got no answer; but in struggling she brought down the fishpoles out of their corner.

We heard their tips rip across the sagging burlap and immediately there came several distinct, horrible raps on the beaten dirt, the noise of plump things falling.

"Let go!" Her voice was smothered.

Directly, something cold and sinuous touched my ankle in the blackness. That burlap had been alive.

I stood bolt upright, frozen, without words to voice my horror. By the grotesque, statue-like stillness which had overtaken the body of my partner, I knew that one of the coiling things had touched his own flesh as well. He dropped his arms, or rather lowered them with extreme slowness. The faintest blue light possible shone through the door, and after an appalling interval, we crept toward it, sliding our feet forward by inchmeal, never raising them from the dirt.

Standing in the door we looked back, heavily and strangely; and again, I tell you that mocking blackness held the twisted shapes of dreams. We heard her breathe, hard and fast, as if she had been running after us, full tilt. We saw her arms held out to us, as if fixed in a despairing appeal.

"You had nested them snakes!" old Frank muttered.

A cold chill swarmed up my spine. Was it so that she had safeguarded her appeal?

Suddenly our one raging desire was to withdraw from that house. That we should drag her to some remote justice of men, dealt her by a fellow whose life had not indurated him to making a choice of evils, this thought never came to us. We were half-glad she had killed that man who had buried her alive. But at the same time—strange fact—the woman had become a virulent poison to us. With a shudder I recalled her warm foot crushed against mine, the hot breath shrieking out of her. She had the self-sufficiency, then, of an ancient fury. We became accessories after the fact, and our one thought was to rid her of the fatal menace of our testimony. Without us nothing would be proved; for months, it might be, nothing would be known. The words of Dutel reverberated in my head; that when they struck, out here, it was like the inexorable process of indifferent nature. Equally with love, or with the softest tenderness, this violent death had the sanction of the stars. What had he called them? The inviolate stars. We found ourselves going toward the river—fast.

Heavy clouds had obscured all stars in the north; rain hung about; and we heard the voice of the river, hoarse, menacing. It was getting ready to clear itself of the frog in its throat.

We spoke no words. Plunging down the bank—a runway of hot slime—we made no question of the profound importance of getting beyond the sphere of that malign beauty, whatever the cost, on the instant. She had shown us, in one fearful glimpse, how the logic of the dead wild ended the combat of souls.

We jumped into the boat, and my partner stroked her into the stream, with a convulsive movement of his arms. When we were well on the current, a faint crackling above caused us to lift our eyes.

"Holy old crow!" he cried despairingly.

That indomitable woman stood there above us, faintly illuminated by the starshine. A rising wind shook her skirts, making the rigid determination of her body more conspicuous. With the strength of a strong man, she had raised on end one of those rifled gumtrees, a leprous trunk with a hideous bell-mouth. She had torn her dress; there was a dark line as of blood, on her bare shoulder, and the arm joining it was white and massive, the arm of an Amazon, broad with the strain of lifting.

My thick brain began to understand, in flashes of amazed calculation, that she meant to dash us in pieces. We were being whirled by the current directly under that part of the bank where she hung poised. This maenadic spirit, black as an iron maiden, except for a gleam of light on her shoulders, wrestling with that tree trunk like some woman Cyclops, blindly bent on hurling us to destruction. Fascinated, we beheld the tree rise, with her arms solid under it as bars. She would never fail . . .

The boat could not be stopped; its flat bottom took no purchase on the current: but the whole business was over in a second, during which we saw that great tree slide over the clay bank with the sluggish and formidable ease of a ship launching. It fell short by two feet!

We had no time to be grateful for that mercy of chance. We were beset with watery terrors now. The river was suddenly rising in its bed and shrieking, like a man struggling with a nightmare. The stump she had hurled rose after us, gleaming and twirling, its roots rising like Medusa's locks. I heard my partner roar out to me to capture that tree. It was fairly dogging us, rolling over and over, seeming to nose the stern of the boat lovingly. I thrust it ahead. Handing me the paddle, my partner knelt, and lashed the thing to the side, the heavy end projecting, for a ram.

Then we fled on the current, through a night that had no end. We hardly spoke to one another; but with each moment, our satisfaction increased to think of the distance we were putting between us and that uncompromising woman. All or nothing. She had not been grateful to us for simply running away.

When day came, we felt we had come into a new land, which had only a soothing ignorance of the night's work. That was like a dream. The razor might have sweat blood, for all we knew now. We were well out of it at least. Miles away. A good thirty miles away, at the rate the current had driven us. The riverbed was already half full and sending down to us odd lots from the backcountry: rabbits, submerged sheep, capsized crows and cockatoos.

All these things we made out through a thick mist, almost a fog, which had blown in from the coast. I speared at them with the paddle, thinking to improve the state of my mind by a little activity of that sort. I was an accessory, you understand; an accessory after the fact.

At length old Frank grunted at me from his position forward, where he had been opening a mess of freshwater clams. In a moment he raised the burlap to let me look through the cabin.

"King Dick," he said, "they is a tarnation crew of rabbits in that log."

He spoke jocularly; and then, shifting his eyes, fixed them on two draggled tufts of some substance like fur. These tufts protruded through a crack in our ram, which the continual battering of the night had widened.

"Yes, rabbits," he continued, in a ghastly voice. The impossible twinkle died out of his eye.

"What would you say if we let that log go about its business, partner?"

"Let it go, in God's name."

I could not drag myself from contemplation of those two iron gray tufts. I saw his fingers stumble among the lashings, I caught a glimmer from his sick eyes as they rolled in his head with aversion to that task. His hands hung over the reluctant knots, gleaming.

As he crouched, I made a turn of the river with a broad sweep of the paddle; and at once I had occasion to shout to him:

"Hold on."

Directly in our path, stretching fatally across the narrow waterway was the trunk of a huge gum, thick and straight as the body of a python. The water rushed against it; poured over it. That log had a look of something alive, stubborn, reptilian. The river here began to run rapidly, as its bed tilted downward. With the momentum gathered by our ram, we surged forward unavoidably.

"Leave it—to take up the shock," I howled. He desisted doubtfully, watching our terrific advance against that barricading gum. I was just able, by sinking the paddle deep, to maintain a head-on course, the boat shaking like a jelly under the strain.

Old Frank, looking at our ram, said twice, with horrible doubtfulness: "It will split."

He was undeniably right. When that great bell-mouthed log, rotten through and through, came against the submerged gum, the impact threw us forward on our faces. But nothing could prevent our seeing that log open, like a brand in the heart of a fire, disclosing the body of the man Amberg dressed in black leather, as we had last seen him. He looked like a shriveled beetle. We had only time to see his eyes, and the two diabolical tufts of his forked beard, when with the evenness of some ceremony, like a baptism, he plunged under the log. It was in vain that we watched for him to reappear.

After a while we became convinced that we had better land. On high ground we stamped our feet and breathed the gratifying strangeness of that countryside. It was like all we had seen, except that we saw it now subdued or etherealised, softened by this unusual mist. We swung inland like two madmen. Perhaps we fancied we were going to arrange something, to take the edge off the casualness of that death. I think we wanted to make patent and formal acknowledgment to men that, after all, it was a man that had died, whatever his faults. Not a beetle. Not a black beetle.

We took our way over a random scattering of skeletons, ribs, hoofs, dung. The continual glare of these bleached bones, eloquent of death, seemed to work a mocking corruption of our own bodies. We remembered that living hearts had only now hung in those peculiar spaces, had throbbed, stopped, rotted, blown away, while the stars shone— these inviolate stars—and the bush gave no sign. Our lives hung upon a thread, transient as a spark. We breathed thickly; while the spongy ground sent up hot little puffs of dust at our heels.

"There's a shack," said my partner.

It loomed close upon us in the mist, a house like all the other houses of the bush. And yet, happening to glance down at the ground, I saw that this was not precisely as other houses. I cried hoarsely to my partner to look down.

We were gaping into the yellow mouth of that dead lizard caught in his wire mesh!

I tell you, I felt then as if we were the center of a mad vortex, at the place where infinities meet. This recurrence of the lizard was exasperating and fiendishly ill-timed, like the bizarre duplication in the train of nightmares. Choked with a feeling like wrath, as if this dead reptile had contrived to put himself maliciously in my way again, I glared down—and then my partner with a low oath lifted his bare heel and ground that mummified little atom deep into the scaly soil.

"The river's turned," he mumbled. "Dratted oxbow."

We were back again!

As if to force us to look at last into the secret heart of the bush, the river had turned on itself and re-conveyed us to that accursed spot.

We stared ahead, and as the mist slowly lifted, we saw the house more plainly; and the three gutted sheep, still hanging red and cavernous from the porch.

We came upon the house, rocking from side to side, with discreet and noiseless steps, as if our lives depended upon utter stealth. And as we reached the narrow door at the side of the chimney—which stood open a little way; we heard a voice speaking in strong and liquid tones. It was Dutel.

When he heard the thud of our bare heels, and saw us standing in the doorway, he looked up pleasantly. Amberg's wife had flung herself across his knees, and with one ape-like arm extended, he toyed with her hair, raising and letting it fall musingly. And in his warlike eyes was reared the full flame of that remote spark which had kindled there as he told us in gentle tones that a beautiful woman belongs to no man. How had he said it? "The sun shines on many waters."

"Ah, gentlemen," he said, still in his pleasant voice, "I see you have returned for your razor."

ON A CALM SEA

From *American Magazine* (September 1913)

Engaging tale of suspense, jealousy, and death aboard a ship becalmed at sea. Tensions flare between a cagey old captain, a beautiful young woman, and a brooding crew member who shares an unhappy, unclear past relationship with the woman.

"A bark," said Colonel Anson, from his steamer chair; "and pretty deep t'ga'ns'ls, too. Those are old sails, I fancy. It was a good thing for sailormen when ships began to carry double t'ga'ns'ls, I can tell you. It makes a howling difference in heavy weather. Many a new t'ga'ns'l I've had to make after a blow, because some fool lost his temper aloft and put a knife into the old one. A single t'ga'ns'l is a deep sail for three men to pull up."

"You've been a sailmaker too, then," said the man charged with making up a list of the things the colonel had been.

"Yes," said the colonel. "I was only a boy then; I've gone through life now, and I've seen nothing worse than that first voyage of mine as sailmaker. . . . It's this calm sea that brings it back; the burnish on it, and the look of that old bark yonder.

"A calm doesn't mean much on a steamship; the mind is satisfied by the movement, appeased. You get on in all weathers. But take that bark now. I venture to say she's made nothing but driftway the last two days or more. There isn't half a knot a watch in her sails. That's a strain; even on a dull mind, a strain. Not everybody's inward eye, you know, can be called the bliss of solitude. It's a poisoned eye mostly, a baleful eye. You force a man to think, and he'll think evil. The calm forces a man to think. Bear that in mind."

As he pulled on his cigarette, he seemed to look at that bark with yearning, as all men must who have known the sea actively.

"On a calm sea. There's where you'll meet with trouble. It was so with that first ship of mine, certainly. I was nearly a man grown at that time; nineteen, tall and heavy; but a stiff, without any knowledge of the sea. My father had a big sail loft in Melbourne, and I'd learned to use a palm and needle rather young in life. I knew a good bit about sail, but not a thing about ships. And because my father knew the sea as well as he knew sail, I had to run away from home to ship.

"I began badly by stowing away in the forepeak of a bark—the *Amos W. Fuller*, an American ship, I believe. That was a grim place, that forepeak, for a lad that hadn't been away from home. It was black as the pit with the hatch on, hot, and full of barrels of sand and salt pork and lime. I could hear that pork soughing and chuckling inside the staves, which wasn't good for me. A lot of gin-carries and blocks were strung up on wires over my head, and I got some cruel bumps from them. One of the barrels had overridden its chocks and kept charging about there. Every time she rolled, I thought I was gone.

"I was glad enough when they took the hatch off and found me. One of the men was a good-hearted chap.

"'Stay where you are,' he whispered. He saw my case at once. 'I think she touches at Sydney. I guess we can feed you up till then.'

"'No,' I said, 'I want to come up. I'm going to sea.'

"'We've got a terrible old man aft, on stiffs,' he said.

"I didn't care by then. Nothing could be worse than that black hole of blocks and barrels. So, they took me aft to the old man.

"He was a tough one, no mistake. As I look back on him, I see points about him that didn't impress me then. He'd strike a man at first as a scholar. He was tall and thin, with stooping shoulders and a rather delicate face, when it was shaved. Aboard ship he let it come out to a heavy stubble, deliberately giving himself the look of an intelligent criminal. He had the most terrible eye I ever saw in a human face. The line of the lower lid was straight, straight as a horizon; and when he drew open his eye, it was like an ugly gray dawn.

"'So this is the fifth ace we had up our sleeve,' he said, and I felt a chill through me. I wished I had stayed in the forepeak. He looked capable of making me walk a plank, or of hanging me at a yardarm. But my trade saved me.

"'They say you can use your palm and needle,' he said. 'Well, go into the sailmaker's locker; and jump out of it handy when there's a pull on the braces.'

"It was in Montevideo that things began to happen. The crew left while we lay there; we lost time getting another. The old man was ashore a good deal, and then when we put to sea he began cracking on like mad. He hung red lights port and starboard, signaling 'Not under command,' and then he swept the seas before him.

"She splintered two top gallant-yards the first night of it, and we hauled her round and put back into Montevideo. It wasn't safe to get within range of the poop.

"Back in Montevideo, this crew left too; swam ashore, most of 'em. Wouldn't wait to man a boat. It was a week before we weighed anchor. The old man had been ashore all that week. By the look of him when he came back, he'd been drinking pretty steadily. I thought there was a queer look about him too, as if he were pulling against something. He stood on the poop that night, talking to the pilot, with his hair ruffled and his eyes on Montevideo. He seemed shaken, undecided; and that made him more of a bull than ever.

"But those two cracked yards hadn't taught him anything; for he held on that night in the teeth of a head wind, and a head sea, that smothered her fore and aft. And about two bells in the morning watch the fore top gallant mast carried away. That big stick came down hard, I can tell you. And some way or other it fell forward instead of aft and carried most of the jib boom along with it. The little port bo's'n, standing there with his legs braced, and looking up at the ruin, spied me in the door of the sailmaker's locker.

"'Go aft to the old man,' he roared, 'and tell 'im the foret'gallan'mast has carried away?'

"It wasn't a job I cared about, but I went aft, jumping some, I warrant you. The ship was making hard work of that sea with her head sails gone to smash.

"The skipper was sitting under the mess-room skylight, dressed, and taking a cup of coffee. He was a sallow enough figure in that light, with a dirty cap on his head and a shiny briar in his long, bony fingers. The old mate was sitting on the medicine chest.

"'Foret'gallan'mast carried away, sir,' I reported. 'And the jib-boom along with it?'

"The old man put down his coffee with a mighty odd look on his face. He was actually relieved at something or other.

"'No good running away,' he said.

"The ship went over heavily, rumbling on her plates, in a way she had. You could feel her shiver as she put her nose under. The old man rescued his coffee and sat nursing his black chin.

"'I say, it's no good running away from trouble, Mister,' he roared. The old mate jumped off the medicine chest.

"'Quite right, sir,' he said. He was an old dog to put his tail between his legs.

"The skipper sat there rubbing his pipe with a skinny finger, and rolling his lips in. What had he been running away from?

"'When the sea goes down, square the crojjuk,' he said to the mate. 'We're putting back into Montevideo.' He smiled then.

"Back in Montevideo we sent up a new top gallant mast, fixed a new jib-boom for'ard, and shipped our third crew. And this trip in, even the fat sailmaker had had enough. We lay out some way from the piers, but he greased himself and slid off the fore chains with his bag. I hung over the jib boom, watching his big white shoulder mooning along through the dark. All at once I felt like a great man, a tradesman proper. If only the old man wouldn't bother to ship another sailmaker, I was made. And I was fairly competent, too; good for any sail but the foretopmast-staysail. Any sailmaker breathes a prayer when he lays out his bolts for that sail.

"As a tradesman, working by the day, I had all night in; and I was fast asleep when we towed out of Montevideo for the third time. The cook—he was a new cook, a man from Philadelphia, in North America—had to tell me the important things taking place in that middle watch.

"The cook said there could hardly be any doubt of that, for the new steward had been one of the witnesses to the formal part of the ceremony ashore. The old man had gone out of his head altogether; shaved himself, for one thing, and put a flower in his coat, and behaved generally like a madman, all for this chit of a woman.

"'He's a fine figger ashore,' I remember the cook's saying. I hadn't seen him ashore; my picture of him was in that brown, evil-smelling mess-room with the dirty skullcap, and the villainous stubble chin. But I believe there might have been a kind of distinction in his bearing. He was above the average of seafaring men in learning; had some books in his cabin that I thought then were tough books to crack. He had the seaman's love of 'Oliver Twist' too. Used to read it chapter by chapter, and tell it over to one of the apprentices, in the middle watch, to frighten him. But that old man could frighten a boy by reading him a verse out of the Bible. He frightened the whole lot of us, finally, reading out of the Bible.

"'She's a looker too,' said the cook, of this lady aft. She had come over the rail as if she had wings to her heels. Didn't stretch out her arms in that helpless way women have in getting in and out of boats.

"And there was another queer thing too, by the cook's account. She appeared to know one of the men in the starboard watch. This was a big black-headed gorilla who had come aboard only the night before, and he was leaning on the starboard capstan aft when she came over. She stopped short at sight of him and laughed a light little scornful laugh. (The cook was a careful fellow in his descriptions. He read Bulwer Lytton a good deal.) She looked around to make sure that the old man was still over the side, it appeared, and then she laughed again, and trailed a bit of the stuff she wore on her shoulders over the big forearm of the man leaning on the capstan. The fellow didn't move, didn't shrink, but his look was beyond the cook's power of analysis. It boded no good, that was sure.

"What was of more immediate concern to me, they hadn't shipped a sailmaker, and that left me in charge of my locker. I was a full-fledged tradesman then, and no mistake."

The colonel's shoulders shook a little with amusement as he thought of the figure he cut then. Mighty few men can look back on their youth with that sort of amusement.

"It was easy going for a week or more, a six-knot breeze on the quarter, good and dry, from the southwest. The old man was quiet as a lamb with the fine new golden toy he had. He let the mate run the ship. He was in his cabin a good deal. He took his love, or whatever it was, temperately.

"But she preferred the poop and kept out of that stuffy cabin all she could. She liked to sun herself and watch the men aloft and spin out that gold hair of hers for them. She was one of those creatures who flirt with any honest man. She had no mercy on the poor dumb animals at all.

"It amused her to set the whole ship into a fever, by stretching out a foot, or laying a strand of that yellow hair against her cheek. She charged those listless watches like batteries, thrilled them with possibilities which weren't possibilities, except as anything is a possibility on board a ship.

"There was a kind of mad competition for the secret enthralling favors she shot at us from the serenity of that poop with those deep eyes of hers that had a green tinge. The young fellows were at their monkey tricks aloft, engaging her with their recklessness. They couldn't even go up to overhaul a buntline in the regular manner. They began to see, in the light of her admiration, that they were stupendous fellows.

"And whenever there was a pull on the crossjack braces, there she'd be, leaning down, with her elbows on the rail, mocking that big, black-headed fellow. He was the best seaman in his watch, and he led on the braces; and whenever he'd sing out she'd mimic him.

"'Yu hoh ho. Ah dhu,' she'd say. He was like a big sulky dog. Wouldn't look at her even. And he wouldn't talk, not even with the men in the watch. They called him Big Anton. No one in that crew knew anything about him; but it began to be known that his coming aboard had something to do with her.

"She wasn't afraid of any of them; wasn't afraid of the old man himself even. I think the truth was that she had not the slightest idea what a burning focus of emotions was on her, what a power she was in that place of blank horizons. She was one of those who can't look beneath the calm sea.

"Every man on the ship watched her, talked about her, tried to drag something out of Big Anton, who knew. But they didn't succeed there. And then, one calm dog watch, somebody said something he shouldn't have said about her. It was bound to come.

"I looked at Big Anton. He was working one hand around on the wrist, not looking much upset. He meditated a moment, loosened his arm and shot it out. He seemed to make hardly any effort, but the fellow crumpled up like a split sail and went to the deck, twitching all over, blind to the world.

"'Anymore?' says Big Anton. There weren't any more. Big Anton himself stood there brooding and trifling with his sheath-knife, while they were throwing water over the body of the man who had misdemeaned himself. Suddenly, shielding his eyes, he said:

"'It's a flat calm falling. A flat calm.' He knew the danger of that.

"And the calm came on, as he said; beat the water out into a hot blue disk, like something solid, with tawny patches on it. That calm emptied sail, set the pitch rising in the seams, and the blood thickening in the body. The iron bulwarks of the ship seemed to glow and quiver with the heat. The pork rotted in the barrels, the water rotted, tempers rotted. At the end of a week of that, there wasn't a bit of sound moral fiber on the ship. The mate got out the holystones, which were invented to deal with a situation like this; but the men made heavy work of it. They lost interest in the poop then.

"But the captain's wife lost interest in nothing. The calm was made for her. She loved to bask in that yellow heat, stiffen herself, lying back in the canvas chair, as if to accentuate her slenderness before going lax again . . . with her toes pointing to the lost horizon. Her eye-shafts were poignant as ever. There was something feline about her; that stealthy finish to her least movement, the lazy complacency, the veiled regard. And almost always she was playing with that yellow hair, plaiting it, drawing it under her chin, lowering her lids. She was the spirit of the calm incarnate.

"I used to put a slit in my awning so that I could spy her when she came on deck. Finally, I had a slit for all possible positions of that deck chair.

"The men were holystoning the afterdeck for a good while; and she gave Big Anton full measure of deviltry. Once, leaning far down over the rail, she murmured, 'Are you glad you came? Are you glad you came?' in that voice of hers, like a tumult of sweet voices. Out of a depth of calm, it came strangely. Big Anton went on sliding his stone across the deck in silence. There she was, hovering above him with her hair spun out like a sunset cloud, glowing, the lips parted, those elfin eyes half-closed, languorous even in that mood. And the heavy stone went 'rasp, rasp' and he didn't look up. But from underneath my awning I could see the shirt tighten over that heavy bent back.

"It was surprising how long it was before the old man became aware that she knew that black-headed fellow. He was utterly unlike his

former self. He was secretive, cautious, lulled. He shaved daily, dressed
like a naval commander, and paraded the poop with glasses under his
arm. He was lord of his ship still, dread of him was as lively as ever;
but he took a quieter satisfaction in it. And when he looked at her, those
ugly clouded eyes of his would soften; he would draw down the lids
and smile, and lower that grim chin to hear what she was saying.

"They played cribbage together, up there, under their awning; and
she beat him, and he laughed softly to himself. The old man had found
a way to make the sea tolerable, that was certain. Everybody for'ard,
including Big Anton, knew it was the only way to make the sea tolerable. And yet we lay ail that while smothered under a burning calm.
It was the sort of weather that meant broken heads with that old man,
once. But now he never came off the poop.

"I used to figure and figure on the possible things that might happen
to Big Anton if the skipper ever found out what was going on, or what
had gone on, for that matter. Anton was big, as strong as any three
men on the ship, and as quick as a snake; but the skipper, I knew, went
armed.

"Then it seemed that Big Anton knew this too. One day he stood in
my locker door, smiling at me and pulling down that glossy imperial
of his.

"'Sails,' says Anton, 'the men tell me you've got a gun.'

"'But no bullets,' I said; and I was almighty glad I had no bullets.

"'No bullets,' says Anton. 'Ah!'

"He hooked his big toe into a bight of canvas, and focused his eyes
on that blurred sea, with its burning points of light.

"'There's some lead for'ard,' he said after a time, 'but no powder.
No powder.'

"Muttering to himself and pulling his black beard, he moved away.
That eternal silence and heat and lack of movement seemed to germi-
nate evil within him. On the braces his voice was a bellow; now it was
a purr, minute, hard to catch, the thick note of repressed power in it. All
at once a blinding admiration for the man filled me. I felt that he was
bigger every way than the skipper. His calm was deadly. I understood
that Big Anton had already set his life aside, dedicated it to something
or other. It had been in the back of his head all the time; but when the
wind died, he gave himself up to it altogether.

"And one watch Big Anton got a job putting a long splice in the crossjack-sheet, and because the devil was in it she was on the poop. The old man was in the chart house, I think. Anyhow, I heard that deck chair of hers scraping across the poop gently; and pretty soon she put her foot through the railing. Only the foot, and a bit of ankle in a black silk stocking. Big Anton stopped twisting his strands, and suddenly dug his spike into the deck, determining something with the movement. He rolled half over, with the palm of his hand on that blistering deck, meaning to get up, and then he stopped again. She was cautiously putting her hand through the rail, holding a bit of white paper, and she let that drop.

"Big Anton snatched at it and read it. He squatted there, the paper crumpled in his fist, glaring into the scuppers, his big scarred leg showing a bulge of muscle along the calf. There was a burning point of light on the tip of her shoe above him, and she held it motionless. Then he got up, wrenching the spike out of the deck, and went for'ard, tossing it up and down in his hand. The sun had got into the steel and the spike was blistering, like everything else. It was nearly eight bells—noon.

"The old man, coming out with his sextant, began pacing up and down, now and again adjusting his instrument and looking up at the mizzent'ga'ns'l. He had a fixed smile on his face, the sort of involuntary smile a young man will carry around for an hour after he's stolen a kiss. It was extraordinary to see it on that hard face. He stopped once and raised the skylight over the mess-room and murmured something. She was down there with a little book, I figured, waiting to take the observations he called out to her.

"Then I saw something that gave me a chill. This ship was an uncommon type, with a raised section amidships, and a bridge running fore and aft, between the poop and the section head. The fo'c'stle companionway came out on this section head; and now I saw Big Anton thrust his shoulders out, look steadily at the poop, and begin to walk along that yellow bridge. He had the fo'c'stle biscuit barge under his left arm, and his sheath-knife palmed in his right hand, fixed there in the way known to knife-throwers. He wanted biscuits worse than I ever have.

"The old man, behind the chart house, couldn't see him, which was lucky for the old man, for I think Big Anton had meant to end him there.

But when he found he could get down into the cabin unmolested he changed his mind and standing in the chart-house door on the lee side sank his knife slowly back into its worn leather sheath.

"Then Big Anton disappeared into the cabin, and at the same time the old man called out his reading.

"I heard him say, 'Let her go off a little' to the man at the wheel, and then the chart-house hid him.

"I was in a kind of trance. I cut a strip of canvas and went up on the poop on the lee side, where there was a split in the awning. I got up on the pin-rail for the mizzen top gallant-braces, and began to put on my patch, watching the old man like a cat. He never had bothered his head to look down into the cabin at such times; always spoke with his eyes on the horizon; but there was the chance that he might.

"And he did. He looked squarely down. He set his sextant on the top of the binnacle, put his bony hands on the frame of the skylight, and glared down. He didn't say a word; but his ugly eyes came open wider and wider, and I could see his long back straining into a kind of a hump, as a bird's will before it dives. I thought he would go through glass and all.

"There was something comic in that attitude which made it dreadful. I couldn't see what he saw, never knew what he saw, indeed. It was brief enough. The whole thing was a matter of seconds. I was so close, swaying over him on those braces, that I could see that granite chin of his reflected in the hot glass. But I couldn't see through the glass.

"First his hand went to his hip-pocket, and his long fingers writhed around something there. Then he stopped. I held my breath, waiting, with my needle half through the patch. Then I saw that if he didn't do something at once I should cry out, break under the strain completely.

"But he didn't shoot. He drew back carefully and dropped his arm to his side.

"'Strike eight bells, Mister,' he said to the mate. He walked away a few paces, revolving his lips, looking off through the glare of that burnished sea. Not a sign of wind anywhere.

"And then Big Anton came out of the cabin, with his barge full of biscuits, and went for'ard. When he reached the section he set the barge on the donkey-house and flashed his knife into the rail around the mainmast. It went as true as a bullet. Big Anton walked over to the rail and drew it out slowly; and then the old mate struck eight bells, and he went below. The old man was standing on the poop, turning the screws to his sextant.

"It wasn't the usual thing, of course; not mutiny, nor anything like it. Big Anton kept his own counsel. He made no effort to stir up the men against the old man. He had nothing to say to them at all. But they all knew that death hung over that ship. They were as much afraid of Big Anton as if he had already done what he intended. They gave him elbow room, and that was all. But he knew how he stood. He meant to make this his last ship, now. You could see that life had left him just this to do, and no more. It's hard to believe that of some men, but it was true of him. And the odds were terribly against him.

"That was the longest afternoon I ever passed.

"The night was even harder to bear than day. The moon was like this moon now, dissolving in a sky full of stars. The watch on deck was stretched about on the section. Looking out of my port, I could see the sails waver up the mizzen as that long swell rolled her over.

"I had rigged my hammock in the sail locker, to get the privacy proper to a tradesman. It was. a musty little place, reeking hot, stuffed with bolts of canvas, skeins of yarn, fids, forcers, frames of one kind or another. This was the price I paid for exclusiveness.

"I lay there that night a long time, twitching about in my musty hammock, surmising, dwelling with the shameless insistence of youth on the points which commended her to me.

"All at once I felt a clutch at my shoulder, and even in my sleep I had a conviction that it was the old man. He wove himself into the dream he cut short. I sat up, and he put a clammy hand over my mouth and forced me back. The moonlight, falling through the port on his face, warned me to hold my tongue. Those terrible gray eyes of his, burning over the straight lower lids, held me like a vise. He had no need to hold my mouth.

"'No noise,' he said. 'Take a bolt of canvas and your palm and needle and come aft with me.'

"Then I knew for certain what he had done. I never had a darker moment than that, when I was fumbling around there for canvas, with those eyes sinking into me, and that thin ghastly figure of his bent over, waiting, in the moonlight.

"He said something like 'Keep your nerve,' in a contemptuous way, and preceded me up the companionway. I followed him, dragging that

bolt of canvas after me, and I began to wonder if we should meet Big
Anton on the way. It was his watch on deck. It seemed hardly possible
that the significance of my going aft with a bolt of canvas should escape
him. We went up into that heat, that silence, without speaking.

"Big Anton was leaning on the starboard capstan, in shadow, motionless, pondering. The old man led the way toward the port ladder;
and when he was abreast of the starboard capstan, Big Anton leaned
forward with a sudden, fierce, constraining movement, and a knife
flashed out of the dark. But the old man had sprung for the ladder,
nimble as a spider, and the knife went into the sea. Big Anton came out
squarely into the moonlight, inviting death. But the old man, who had
taken out his pistol, put it back in his pocket.

"'Time enough,' he mumbled, and seized me by the arm and thrust
me in through the chart-house door. Then he locked both doors, port
and starboard, picked up a dark lantern from the deck.

"'Go on,' he said. 'Starboard cabin.'

"At that moment six bells went hurriedly, the cracked bell on the
fo'c'stle head jangled its answer back, and I heard the deep cry of the
lookout throbbing from end to end of that stagnant ship, 'A—a—a-l-l's
well.'

"It died without echo, prolonged and cut sharply off like something
smothered.

"Then we went into that cabin. He'd stuffed a magazine into the
port; and for the awful moment it took him to come in and shut and
lock the door, there was no light in there. Then I heard him draw his
breath through his teeth in one slow, agonizing intake, and settle the
dark lantern on the bunk there.

"She lay there with her eyes open, and her right arm hanging down
bare over the bunkboard. Her hair was loose, too; that yellow hair that
she used to play with on the poop. She lay there long and orderly and
languorous, almost as I'd seen her, time and again, in that canvas chair.
Almost, but not quite. She was dead. I don't know what he'd done to
her, but she was quite dead. I felt that at once. I stood there staring,
not making a move, perfectly rigid, my eyes resting in a trance on the
white arm flattened against the bunk board, on the nose with its little
tilt upwards, on those great eyes opened wide on nothing. It was incredible to me then. I couldn't fathom it, or stomach it. I wasn't afraid. I
felt a sort of fierceness of pity clutch at my aching throat. I stood there

swallowing. All at once I felt as if she had been mine, mine—as if all the heavy force of this emotion disclosed me to her, even in death.

"'Get to work,' said the old man. He took my elbow in a grip of iron and shoved me for'ard.

"'I've not done this before,' I said in a whisper. I burnt all over with strange emotions. I couldn't regard her as dead.

"Then I came out of that, feeling his fingers sinking into my arm again; and made a spasmodic movement or two, unrolling a length of canvas, adjusting my palm.

"But before I could touch her, the old man had swept me aside and stooped over her himself. It seemed to me that I caught the flutter of her eyelashes, but it was his breath that stirred them. He stood there, breathing heavily, sweat shining on him, hanging from the black stubble that was coming out on his chin already. He held the lantern steadily to her face, and the light fell so strongly there that I thought her bloom had not quite gone, and that I saw it fading—calm sinking into calm. But his features were granite. They forbade him a display of his agony, his remorse. Could he have looked at her without remorse?

"He lifted her up, almost gently, and I wound the canvas about her.

"I don't know how long it was before we laid that gray bundle back into the bunk, nor can I say what thoughts I had while I was stitching. They were homeward-bounders, everyone, those stitches. I had no mind to linger over it. And when I had done, the old man said:

"'Now go back to your locker.'

"He didn't ask me not to talk, he didn't threaten me.

"I stumbled up the companionway. Nothing had changed. It was all the same; the same madness of slack sail and chafing gear; the same unbreathable tropic night. It was like prolonging an interim to infinity. That calm was responsible—for the whole pitiful business. The blackest mind wouldn't have had time in heavy weather . . . not time for that.

"The next day, at noon, she went over the side, with the ship aback, or as much aback as she could be in that calm. The old man had borrowed a Bible from the steward, and he stood over her and read a few verses in a voice as even as the ship's keel. He was the lord of his horizons—jury, judge, executioner. And he stood there reading those verses. There was nobody on that ship that didn't know—even while he was reading, turning out those phrases, without emotion. They knew he had killed her, as certainly as I knew it; and yet we all stood with bared heads while he read, as if this service were like any other.

"'As the cloud is consumed and vanisheth away, so he that goeth down to the grave shall come up no more.'

"He came upon these passages by chance, and chance dealt heavily and justly with him. But he went on without a break. It wasn't hypocrisy; he had no need to cover anything. There was nothing he could cover. It was the thing to do; the incomprehensible procedure given to all men, and seamen with them, for this mortal end. The men's eyes were fixed upon that gray canvas roll, inert on its frightful yellow plank, poised. Only the man holding the plank had turned away from it, and his arms shook as if under an intolerable weight.

"'Oh, remember that my life is wind; mine eye shall no more see good.'

"There was a hush, a persistent stertorous breathing, shame-facedness, that heavy note of dumb sympathy, of wonder at the lonely flight of a soul out of those blank spaces. The old man went on reading in a heavy voice, intoning, like a preacher, and every time he came to the end of a verse, he raised his eyes and looked at Big Anton, as if he were reading for his benefit too. Big Anton was slouched over against the mizzen stay sail halyards. He seemed fumbling aimlessly with the rope, and yet I wondered. I thought it strange if it should prove that he had shot his bolt. And he hadn't—quite.

"As the body went over the side, I saw him crouch, lifting the halyards from their pin; and the next moment a great sprawling loop settled over the old man's shoulders, and slipped down, pinioning his arms. Jerking the loop tight, Big Anton began to come up hand over hand, a blazing madness of energy, a black look of hope in his face. But the old man, with his hand doubled in his pocket, could still shoot. Leaning back strongly on the rope, he shot twice. His coat began to burn, but at the second shot Big Anton faltered, pitching forward on his face, and sending the old man into the scuppers.

"And that was all. The old man had given us a taste of his omnipotence, shown us the quality of his calm, the deadliness of it. And the sea gave back calm for calm; but more, it gave back calm, impenetrable oily calm, for violence and death.

"That was the flat end of the whole business; that shot, and Big Anton falling on his face, thwarted. But there's one thing more—the touch of irony. They got the old man clear of the rope, and he stood up and leaned on the starboard pin-rail. He'd been a terrible man to look in the eye, all his life; but now the thing wasn't to be done at all. I had in the corner of my eye the image of that gaunt figure stooping there, glaring at the horizon, the coat still smoldering a trifle where the two shots had come through it. It was as hot and silent as ever off there; above, the same flat sluggish sound of dead sail slatting, clews fretting, and wire sheets rasping the side of the ship when she rolled.

"Suddenly, through that mass of heat, piercing the yellow curtain of that calm, my eye caught something—a darkening and freshening, as yet immensely distant. The skipper had already seen it. Drawing back his shoulders stiffly, he rubbed those cruel white talons of his together and spoke to the mate in his old voice, a voice falling through that awful stillness like a hammer on hot steel:

"'Square in the crojjuk, Mister. The wind's coming . . . over the quarter.'"

MAKING PORT

From *Every Week* (March 20, 1916)

Very readable tale of shipboard life and the cruel twists of fate that overwhelm duty and honor. The focus is on a curmudgeonly English sailor who pursues a Sisyphean quest to return to his home port, Liverpool.

As soon as old Tom was hoisted aboard the bark *Forensic*, he sat down on a hatch and inquired, "Whar to?" in an awed voice.

The new crew of that old hooker was lying about in the scuppers, after the manner of new crews: but one among us, Spike Moran by name, sat up and answered him:

"Where to? Why, you was there when the articles were signed, old feller. Sydney, New South Wales. Where was you hoping to go?"

"Liverpool," said that strange old man.

"Oho, I remember," said Spike. "You are the old one I was talking to on the tug, ain't you?"

"Ay."

With grave despondency he confessed to us that he had been trying to ship for Liverpool any time the last twelve years. Is there anything more uncertain than a seafaring life? As we looked closely at him, the old fellow turned his bleached eyes toward the Battery, and scratched his hide of a rhinoceros through the old yellow unwashed singlet he wore—scratched his ribs with a slow motion, as if numbed by the contrarieties of fate.

"What part of Liverpool?"

"Christian Street," said old Tom.

Christian Street—of all streets in the world of sailormen, the most unchristian and the most unholy!

"You keep away from Christian Street," said Spike, "if you want to keep your claws on a pay-day."

Then old Tom, without moving his head, said, in a voice of feigned contempt, that he had a wife in Christian Street.

"Three years older than what I am," he said sorrowfully.

"How old are you, Tom?"

"Sixty-four," answered that melancholy old man.

Spike laughed.

"You would have more cause to complain if you was young, old feller," he said. "It don't make no real difference to you now, having a wife, unless you need nursing. But supposing you was young, and a girl was waiting for you in Sydney, New South Wales, and then you was shipped on the wrong ship, you'd have a right to complain, hey?"

Old Tom's eyes flashed with a light of scorn for youth, and he inquired:

"What girl is this?"

"The mission girl," said Spike proudly, gladly; "the one that comes out to the ship with the organ."

"Ay," said old Tom.

"You know her?"

"Ay," said old Tom.

Closing his eyes, he affected to remember that girl. No sailor can afford to be ignorant of any port or any ship or any woman mentioned in the narrative of a shipmate.

"She wears rough pearls," said Spike, "in a chain round her neck. She is the daughter of a pearl-diver."

"Looking out for her beauty," said old Tom. "I know her. Yes, I have seen her. Black hair."

"No. Brown," said Spike.

"Oh, ay," said old Tom. "Yes; I remember her."

He was an old man going the wrong way again, and he looked at Spike with a kind of hatred.

It appeared that Spike's prospect of happiness, whispered about the ship, had set the whole crew against him—all save little Jewdler, the apprentice, and me. You do not know how strong can be the attack on a man's soul by a combined ship's crew. He could do nothing to please them. He shaved them, he cooked special dishes for that watch, he lanced wire-poisoned fingers which the Old Man wouldn't touch, he stood for hours as policeman to the watch, in the tropics. You have heard of these nights wherein deep skies and soft trades induce the watch on deck to sleep in odd corners, out of the light of the moon? He was unwearied in serving those men. In vain. His good nature was like oil on this fiery resentment. It blazed up against him everywhere, until at last the starboard bo'sun, a battered, rough-handed sea-devil, found courage to strike him to the deck.

Later, still smiling, with his head bound in a bloody rag, he talked to old Tom.

"You are an old man, Tom," he said; "you had ought to know. Ain't a girl worth being kicked about a little to get? Ain't there some consolation to a beaten man in the thought that she is there?"

With the red rag fluttering at his brows, he pointed east, whispering: "There is a woman for you."

All this was lost on old Tom and shattered against his stony ill will. What he knew he would not impart. Well, why should he? This world of water was just the dazzling blue ruin of his hopes.

"Whar to?" he had said feebly; and the mocking fates would only echo him. His voice came up to us as hollow as the echo in a tomb.

Twelve years already of plowing the seas, in an effort to set foot again on the stones of Christian Street. In vain. The malign fates had conspired with the gray gods of the deep to over set the plans of that unlucky old Ulysses. Ships had floundered under him. He had crawled up out of the sea to wander on inhospitable coasts. He had drunk fatal beers and had waked in the fo'c'sles of ill-starred packets—forsaken old sea-wagons that had borne him protesting to Calcutta or Bangkok or the mythical island of Yap, when he wanted to get to Liverpool.

Now, after these mighty agonies, he sat, bound for New South Wales, on that glittering sea-track that led fourteen thousand miles away from Christian Street. Poor old Tom!

Old Tom never softened his animosity toward Spike. He seemed to know from the first that his destiny would link with that big sailor's. It was in vain that we reminded him that he was the oldest man on the ship and would be made night watchman in Sydney and have it soft; and that possibly this very ship would go to Liverpool.

"I'm done," said old Tom. "This is my last ship."

In a ghastly whisper he told us he could no longer swarm up a rope. Had tried and failed. The sap was out of him. This was his last ship.

Moving heavily in his oilskins, he whispered to us:

"We will all have to leave this ship, too, I am thinking. I saw a blue light off the foreyard-arm the other night."

"When was that, Tom?" asked little Jewdler. "What wheel was that?"

"The gravy-eyed wheel," said old Tom sadly.

"Must've been a star," said little Jewdler, mystified.

"No, it wasn't no star," said old Tom, in the unruffled tones of a man sure of his ground. "Ain't you never heard of death lights? There's going to be death on this ship."

"How is that, Tom?" we whispered, terrified.

But old Tom was careful not to let fall too much wisdom. He wouldn't tell us how it came that a blue light meant death.

But he was right—old Tom was right.

The starboard bo'sun was a hound—a military hound: one of these ill-conditioned rats who had come out of the Boer War with a scar or two and a yearning to demonstrate authority. He hounded Spike, on account of that girl in Sydney, until Spike knocked him down with his bare fist. Then the bo'sun came with his knife—two men saw it in his hand—and Spike knocked him down again, with a belaying pin. And this time the bo'sun did not get up.

He had sea burial, and Spike they chained in the sail locker. The Old Man was tearing mad, too, because the death of that man had made the ship shorthanded—as if there were not already enough farmers in the crew. It was like spearing him to make his ship shorthanded, and he told the mate he intended to see justice done. We knew what that meant; and we looked upon our shipmate thenceforth as a dead man.

The Old Man, as it happened, hadn't the least confidence in his two mates, and he had had a row with the port bo'sun over the proper way of sending down a yard. Therefore, he intrusted the keys of that locker to old Tom—who venerated the skipper, and also cursed him through the seven cycles of time.

Strange to think of Spike, the gentle-hearted, tied to a ring in an iron wall. We were afraid to creep there by night and speak to him through the port. Was he to die? A man who was in love to die? To exchange the torment of the seas for the black void of death? It was hard: but very likely. The word of the skipper would be law in that foreign court.

My heart filled with hatred of that old man who held the keys of Spike's prison. He was sitting on the after-hatch forcing the strands of a great yellow hawser with his teakwood fiddle. He was making ready the bowline. His big, crusty fingers moved with care. Many voyages he had terminated thus, not counting them in his life, since they did not lead to Liverpool.

In the hands of that old man the suggestion of this huge rope was hideous. My eye fell on him again and again as I played the ship through those giant seas. That yellow shard of a man held the keys, held the destiny of Spike in the hollow of his hand.

Ordinarily it's a calm and holy business, furling the wings of the ship as she is going into harbor. There is a touch of awe in what you do to her then; as if you were stroking your good angel. There's the exhilaration of relief, and certain wild anticipations too, awakened by land odors. It is a lazy moment of hush and speculation, and of unconscious religion; and the ship bears you away into the dark heart of the unknown.

But this time we were struck with horror to see that dark coast rising before us. The ship was a funeral ship, straddled by death and the black vengeance that old Tom bore in his heart for Spike, our ship-mate. Even now we could hardly credit the gloomy significance of this incarceration.

Little Jewdler and I, as we lay on the upper topsail-yard, gazed hard at that beacon throbbing through the dark gloom of the night—this night so still, so vast, so full of space. Once we had felt like storm-ridden vikings: now we quailed—the black water swarmed and seethed in coils and flickerings of phosphorescence; a silver band of light streamed by unendingly at the waterline, throwing up a light of magic on the ship's gray hull, making her under-body soft and unsubstantial.

All the while we heard the quiet voices of the watch aft floating up to us, we saw the coals in their pipes gleam and fade, like tiny beacons. We knew that they were leaning about, asking one another in throaty whispers who would stick to a ship where murder had been done.

Then we saw old Tom, sitting apart, in his yellow singlet, nursing memories of Liverpool in his heart of leather! We heard him say to the mate, in calm tones:

"There's a heavy dew falling. That means a shift of wind in this latitude."

We were filled with hate of his calm voice. Lying with our chins on the round of that wide hanging yard, we recreated that starboard bo'sun only to do him to death again.

And high over the Southern Cross we saw swinging the red star that Spike had given that mission girl for her own. As if it had been a spark from the fire in his heart, it glowed deep.

"Must be eight bells," said the apprentice.

He clamored down and struck it. As we met again on the deck, the bo'sun said, "Watch is aft, sir," in the chastened voice of a man without enmities.

The voice of the mate came down in a tolerant undertone:

"Relieve the wheel and look-out."

The watch dissolved. Rolling men in shore-going shirts brushed past us. We heard a terrifying whisper from a big Yank:

"I tell you I'm not going to see an American citizen done to death."

At once that black ship seemed to be alive with the mutterings of conspiracy. Our hearts thumped. Would they attempt a rescue at the eleventh hour? We crept after the Yank, and heard him say to a silent Dane:

"Sharks are nothing. He could splash when he got away from the ship. Better than swinging."

"Swinging!" We writhed on the latch, little Jewdler and I. That word hissed like a snake; it whistled through the air like a bullet.

Suddenly we saw the Yank padding after Tom in his bare feet, and we rolled into the shadow of the hatch. They stopped within five feet of us. We saw the teeth of that Yank shining against his terrifying beard. He had a deep, abrupt voice; his bold nose seemed to forge at you like a ram. But old Tom was turned half away from him.

"Are you going to see a man done to death? You give us the key, and we will see the man over the side all right, all right."

Old Tom hung his two fists at his side and looked round him.

"You ought to be ashamed of yourself—tempting an old man to desert his duty."

"Duty!" cried the Yank bitterly. "Why, dam it, there isn't no such word. I would shed my blood to save that boy from the rope."

"No," said old Tom.

He sat down on the hatch, weighty and incorruptible, puffing out a cloud of smoke. He seemed to be possessed by some rigorous ideal of conduct, and to peer down on us from some impregnable rampart.

The Yank raised his shadowy white arms and cursed. We saw his face glisten with sweat as he lashed past us. Then Jewdler rose up from the deck in front of old Tom, and whispered to him:

"Don't you want to save a man's life? What difference does it make whether you stay by this hooker or not? You could pretend you lost the key."

Old Tom leaned forward and said huskily: "I'm watchman of the ship."

"Well, what of it if you are? Ain't there no other ships?"

"She's going to Liverpool," said old Tom. "Ain't you heard the news? This ship goes to Liverpool, and where she goes, I goes."

Liverpool! What hope was there of shaking the resolution of that old man whose withered heart was set on Liverpool? He sat mooning at us, very stiff, as if swathed in bandages—the old mummy! What earthly difference did it make where he was? His wife in Liverpool had probably deserted him. We thought there was something exasperating and inopportune in that old man's yearning to see his wife again. Was it likely that he had anything in common with that ardent lover in the sail-locker?

"Tom, have you fed him to-night?" whispered Jewdler.

"Ay," said Tom.

There he was close up in the dark; he went through the motion of scratching his ribs.

"How is he?"

"Why, comfortable," said Tom; "comfortable as an old shoe."

It was too much to believe.

A puff of wind came in our faces with that piercing land odor on it, and a spice, as it seemed, of sandalwood and sunbaked earth. Little Jewdler sighed desperately.

"He was going to get married, Tom," he said regretfully.

"Ay, that's right," said old Tom densely. "Let him marry."

"He can't now," wailed Jewdler. "They'll string him up."

"Well, that's certain, too," said old Tom.

He had the habit, exasperating to youth, of accepting all statements without amendment and without rebellion. He never reconciled conflicts. Experience had shown him they were irreconcilable. He had learned to submit himself austerely to the fates and bow his head beneath the yoke of time the oppressor.

Still, he was one of the finest sailormen under the canopy of heaven. He was watchman of the ship. He knew his duty.

"What are we going to say to this mission girl, when she comes aboard?" asked little Jewdler.

"She will have to sorrow," said old Tom harshly. "This will be her cross. We all have our cross, and this will be hers."

Was he bent on making all destinies as cruel as his own?

"He did kill the bo'sun, sure enough," said old Tom. "And there ain't enough of us is positive the bo'sun had a knife in his hand at the time."

"The Dane saw it," said Jewdler eagerly.

Old Tom gloomed at us reproachfully. We wanted to cast him into the sea, but we remembered in time that he was one of the finest sailormen under the canopy of heaven.

"Weren't you ever in love?" we whispered to him mournfully.

"Love—ha!" said old Tom. He squirmed in his singlet. The vast blue night grew deeper over us, bearing musky smells.

"Love—ha!"

We should loathe the memory of this which should have been a magic time for sailors—to be under tow in such a night of stars. But this time the savor of coming to land was lost. The yellow lights were like eyes—the eyes of those hounds of the law that were so soon to be set on the great body of Spike and bring it down.

The ship was like a dream ship stealing into an enchanted harbor, betraying life only in the watchful coals of those pipes along the topgallant rail.

And now all was over. The town lay fully revealed, shimmering, striking animated golden points into the surface of the harbor. We heard the roar of the anchor-chain tumbling up out of its iron locker—a voice from the tug:

"Let go. Give her forty fathom."

The immense black masts of the ship moved slowly against the stars as she swayed back on her chain.

There we were at last—quieted, after four months. The very deck under us seemed to have lost its spring. It was ponderous, like a rock-ledge to the soles of our feet. Had those hatches ever resounded to the thump of weather seas? Had Spike killed the bo'sun? Had we actually seen that ill-omened man tilted overside with the shackles at his ankles?

Driven to it by sheer disbelief, we approached the sail-locker. That ghastly white iron wall intimidated us. The wraith of Spike seemed to extend itself out of that port with its poison-green brass rim. We laid our cheeks against the iron, whispering: "Spike, Spike."

Then we heard the noise of his chains. He was manacled at the wrists—tied to a ring in the wall.

Suddenly his face filled the port. We were shocked to see it. His eyes burned on us, luminous, like an animal's in the dark. We shrank back, as if the chains had sunk through to the soul and made a strange creature of him—less than man. We were desperately ashamed of this feeling, which in no way shook our loyalty.

"We've dropped anchor, Spike," said Jewdler.

"Ay," said Spike.

His voice was as still as the ship. Had he actually spoken? We could hear water dripping somewhere, and a link or two falling in Spike's chain.

Suddenly he murmured:

"I have filed this chain. Can you get the key to the locker? In God's name—"

We had to confess that we had failed. Staring in, we heard him fall back and say, in profound melancholy:

"I am a dead man."

It was actually like a voice from the tomb. We crowded up close to the port, looking into the glazed eyes of that doomed man whose soul was sinking in him like a fire dying down.

"I had rather be et by a shark," he whispered. "I would rather have my heart snapped out by a gray-nurse than swing."

"Swing!" He had spoken the word aloud. With his own lips that intrepid sailorman had framed the abhorrent syllable that spelled the end.

We found no words deep enough to be a consolation to a man so far removed from the good offices of mere benevolence.

Then, in turning away to get a full breath, we saw that old Tom was coming off the section-head—coming down slowly and weightily, with the deliberation of an incorruptible man whom nothing can hasten and nothing can retard. Yes, we had a mournful conviction that nothing was to be hoped from that detestable old fellow with his mind bent on Liverpool. His heart had withered with his body. He was as far from the tremors of youth as if he had been born old.

What did he portend? Of course, if he allowed the prisoner to escape, he must escape with him, since there would be no more peace on that ship. Well, what of it? Couldn't the queer old codger get another ship bound for Liverpool? Well, could he? For twelve years he had been trying to do just that. Now, at last, the way was plain. But if he let the prisoner escape—

No, he would never do it. We felt that he was as obdurate as the iron wall we were leaning against.

We were interrupted by the voice of Spike floating through the port: "Listen. That's the oars of the mission boat!"

We heard the sound of oars approaching the ship.

"It may be the harbor-master," mumbled Jewdler.

"No," said Spike. "She is coming."

His voice died.

At this moment across the quiet decks we heard the amused voice of the Old Man calling over to the mate:

"It's the mission boat. Lower away the accommodation steps."

Affrighted, we fled away from that port. The weight of tragedy was too heavy for us. Yet nothing could prevent us from pausing at the accommodation steps as the mission folk came over with their portable organ.

We saw the girl spring to the deck, laughing, without assistance, and look round her quickly. She knew the ship. We shrank behind the rack of capstan bars to avoid her questioning eye.

At this moment a slight wind sprang across the harbor, lifting the gray awning on the poop, and bringing a land fragrance with it, which forever fixed the scene in memory: the girl looking for her lover, in vain.

It was terrible to see her standing expectant in the waist of that great ship, which seemed to be running over with four whispers of crime.

She sighed, twisted her hands together, and followed the organ.

Jewdler and I muttered together, seeing that they had set down the organ within a dozen feet of Spike's port. We crept over the hatch, wriggling on our bellies, and were in time to see her hang her hat on an iron belaying pin—the second from the brace-pins.

The hair crawled on our necks. This was the pin Spike had used to crush in the skull of that bo'sun! We thought we heard his chains clank again. Certainly, he must now be staring at her. The girl stood with her hands folded, while the organist offered prayer. Bitterly that ship stood in need of prayer.

It was quiet. The crew of that old *Forensic* were looming out of shadow. Their heavy arms hung down, they twisted spun yarn in their fists. Then she sang.

All was calm; you could fancy you were dreaming. The brine crystals were still sparkling in ridges on the deck, where the seas had been falling down into that corner not twenty hours back. Yes, at that very spot we had struggled on the braces with foam at our necks, and that dead bo'sun bellowing in our ears. How could we believe in the actuality of that slim girl singing there beside an organ? Yet she was there. The pure line of her cheek was sweetly drawn against the great crooked rail of the starboard fence, which gleamed red with blistered paint. Had we, in truth, ever seen that huge iron bulwark sinking in foam?

She ended her song.

Then, as the organist stood up to speak, she descried Jewdler and me lying on the hatch, and came toward us with a look of smiling indifference. But the moment she had glided into the shadow of the bridge, she whispered:

"Where is Jake Moran?"

She caught her breath with eagerness.

"He's on board, isn't he?"

We nodded and swallowed hard.

"Where is he?"

I felt her moist hand about my wrist. I was choking. I had never had anything soft like that wrap itself about me before.

"Where is he?" she said again.

We stared at her like two little penguins that have just swallowed something. You have seen them hump their shoulders and look baffled and secret, haven't you?

"He's in the sail-locker," said Jewdler. He pointed at that black port, which looked so grim against the white wall of the section-head.

"Why—why isn't he on deck?"

"Chains," said Jewdler, gulping. "Locked in."

Suddenly we both blurted out in agonized tones:

"He killed the starboard bo'sun."

She seemed to slack and riffle like a sail when you luff ship.

"All fair and square," we whispered. "He had to. The bo'sun was coming at him with a knife."

She was stunned. Something she had held shut in her hand dropped to the deck. We never knew what it was.

Still, we felt a strange solace in the sorrow of that woman. To linger near her, even as bearers of tragedy, was to experience something of the stimulation of romance. We saw in her eyes the light of some desperate protective instinct.

"Take me to him," she whispered.

Could we?

Glaring down the deck, we saw the sallow missioner talking to the crew in kindly tones. Those gentle precepts of his, falling on the ears of shaggy men, seemed to be numbered among the things that are drowned in storm, and overmatched by the sea's wickedness. The men were looking at him with rapt attention, with strange amusement, knowing that Spike the murderer was just behind him.

Old Tom was on the outermost edge of the circle. When we touched him, he turned slowly, with his head solid on his huge shrunken shoulders. As soon as he spied the girl, he knew what was wanted of him.

"Come on, Tom," we urged him; "let her see him. You can come yourself."

The girl came toward us, trying to appear calm. A damp strand of bronze hair clung to her cheek; and the eye glittered woefully in the shadow of this. In another second she had stumbled over a ring bolt, and this flung her suddenly against him. Old Tom, taking her by the shoulders, put her away from him slowly.

As if he knew his danger, his smoky eyes rested forbiddingly a moment on the desperate face of that girl. He swallowed, scratched his ribs, shook his head stiffly, as if bewildered by the nature of this attack.

Suddenly the mission girl made a swift gesture, laying one hand on her bosom, as if abandoning her heart to that old man without words. Her other hand touched my arm. She was trembling from head to foot.

"Come," said old Tom harshly.

We glared at him. Was it possible? He was actually shuffling toward the alley way on which the iron door of the locker opened. We floated after him, rustling against pegged oilskins.

We heard the girl's quivering breath drawn as the key turned in the lock. The iron door swung open, and we were in a position to see Spike leaning out from the wall where he was chained.

Suddenly I recollected that he had filed his chain. Would he try to escape? No; he made no movement, save to move a little way behind a heap of musty canvas.

The girl uttered a faint cry, as if her heart were broken. Stumbling past us, she fell at his feet, putting her arms about him with that protective gesture which seemed to assert that he might rest content, for she would never let him go. Had she a power to reverse the malign decrees of men simply by fierce rebellion in the heart?

"You are not afraid of me?" said Spike in harsh tones. "You are not afraid of me?"

He looked down at her fiercely, strangely, as if at something lost to him, whose mist-like soft shadow still clung, deceiving him.

She shook her head, trembling against him. Lowering his arms about her, he let the chains slip, and stood up unshackled, holding her where the light, streaming through the port, fell on her face.

"You came too late," he said.

"No—no!" she cried. "Not too late. If you could not help it, you will not be punished."

Spike fixed her mournfully with a look of his old gentleness.

"I must die," he said distinctly. "Make up your mind to this."

For an instant he laid his cheek against hers. Then his eye fell on the figure of Tom, lingering in the door with distaste expressed in every line of his decrepit old body.

"They will take the skipper's word for it," he said. "The word of an able seaman is nothing."

Lying in his arms, she reached up her hands to his face and suddenly whispered:

"If you could come away now—in the mission boat—while he is talking. There is a freighter about to weigh anchor. You could escape and come to me again."

Spike's eye gleamed; but he looked at old Tom almost with amusement.

"No chance," he said. "You can't bribe the jailer."

"Yes, come," she whispered, with the same strange insistence. She drew him unresisting over the heap of canvas; and, turning on old Tom, cried in a moment of concentrated passion:

"Who are you, to part us? I love him. Do you understand, old man? Let him go with me."

"Hah," said that old man surrounded by mysteries. "And what becomes of me?"

"Let him go," she said again, with hypnotic force. "He shall not die!"

"Hah," said old Tom.

He opened his mouth, as if to hurl at her one of those contemptuous phrases of an old-fashioned sailor holding on to his duty like grim death. Perhaps in that moment the vision of Christian Street was strongly present to him. He had only to hold the key firm, turn it in the lock again, to attain Liverpool at last. The satisfaction of his twelve years' quest was near.

But the irony of the sea is eternal. It is said that the sea is salt with the tears of women who have sorrowed over its disasters. And yet, none but able seamen can know properly the atrocities of which it is guilty in its devilish unrest.

Old Tom suddenly uttered the amazing syllables:

"Take him."

He had betrayed himself in two words.

Without more, we crept aft in the shadow of the hatches. Would he repent and cry out, after all? Would the lure of Christian Street defeat him in the midst of his intended sacrifice?

We trembled and swallowed our hearts, seeing those red stars stream across the sky again. Looking back at the crew still clustered about the organ, we fixed our eyes on the little red hat hanging on the belaying-pin that had done the mischief.

"Goodbye, *Forensic*" murmured Spike Moran.

One by one, we dropped into that mission boat.

When old Tom came last of all with his concertina, he sat on it, and squeezed out a little sound, a little sob. Horror-struck, we leaned against the gray side of the ship, waiting. The black water came up to those scored and dented iron plates without a ripple.

What hugeness, what torment, what impregnability expressed in a ship's side! And what uncertainty. There was no movement over our heads, and we drifted away.

Spike rowed. The girl, taking the tiller ropes, leaned forward with a dawn of hope on her face, which we saw glimmering through darkness like a shell sinking in clear water.

Not a word was spoken. Holding our breath, we approached the red side of a tramp.

"Take in your oars," said the girl.

Drifting against that ship, we heard the ring of feet running on her iron decks and the sound of the chain going through the hawse-pipe. She was already weighing anchor.

At this moment old Tom's hand rasped on the plates and caught a trailing end of rope. He pulled: it came taut.

Staring aloft with wrinkled brow, he muttered, "There's a coal port just overhead."

Spike had already seen it. He rose from his oars, taking the girl in his arms and murmuring to her, "I will come again."

But at these words it seemed to me that old Tom shook his head, slowly, sadly. What was the promise of an able seaman to come again? The winds blow where they list.

The two who were young stood up together, silent, desperate: and, as her hands met behind his neck, she cried earnestly:

"You will come again? Jake, you will come?"

He kissed her. This was what pay he had for six months of soaking in the misery of five oceans. He went away in his skin it may be said. And some phantom of promise seemed to whisper along the black side of the ship, as he ascended the rope. She was still standing, her arms lifted, even after he had left them. He slipped through the port.

And there was old Tom, looking around for a place to sit down. You see how age had betrayed him. He could no longer swarm up a rope.

Yes, he had lost his chance. Wasn't it bitterness to have been betrayed by some memory, some softening recollection of the wild justice of early love? I affirm to you that this was heroism. It's unlikely he ever got to Liverpool you know. Too old. And he couldn't go back to the *Forensic*. This last memory of his life was a memory of dereliction.

With a shamed face, he mumbled: "Another dollar for Gertie," sitting back in the stern-sheets, bewildered, scratching his ribs, with that slow motion of his, through the yellow singlet that had no buttons on the chest.

Just then the great tramp began to move. We heard the jar of the engines, and the clang of an iron lever, dropping from the winch, I suppose.

The woman was still staring at that black opening in the unknown ship that had swallowed up her lover; but old Tom, with mystery on every hand, stood up, bracing himself against the thwarts of the mission boat. Turning up his old face, full of grave despondency and puzzlement, he cried out in a rusty voice:

"Whar to?"

And, seeming to come out of the very skies, a harsh voice, rolling along the iron decks:

"Liverpool."

FASHIONING THE HOLLOW OAK

From *The Century* (June 1917)

Lively, meticulously detailed account of the building of a fully rigged sailing ship by a colorful old salt, both builder and captain. From its loft-molding to launch, the story offers a marvelous and insightful description of the strength, majesty, and fateful fragility of these "white wings" of the sea as the age of sail is being pushed into history by steam and iron.

Not long ago we had stopped building ships in our town. No keels were being laid, the chips were gray in the yards, and the very bed-logs on which the hulls of some of the fleetest and most famous ships in all the world had first been pitched now rotted away. Even while reminiscence of seamanship had grown dim, and of the old builders there remained nothing but their shells, decayed old mansions on the river-front, with woeful portholes staring from under shaggy eaves in the direction of departed ships. Things had come to such a pass that old Judson was heard to say mournfully that never again in this life would he see a raft of Eastern mixed timbers floating down the river.

The pale monster Steam had gobbled all, it seemed. White wings had vanished from the seas like cot cobwebs from old rafters. A great pity and a crying shame, Judson averred, he would not concede himself to be afloat in steam. The hollow oak his mansion was, with Eastern mixed substituted in the place of nobler woods, it must be added. Oak, the king of woods, has come to be scarcer than hen's teeth in our neck of the woods.

Then came delectable evidence that the Golden Fleece may still serve to reward the quest of wooden argosies. Glittering tales were told of ships in the African mahogany trade paying for themselves out of the profits of a single voyage. And then overnight we shook of the "Giant Lethargy" and began to build ships again. One morning I found old Judson in a dusty mold-loft "fairly down on his marrow-bones again," as he confessed, and laying down the lines of a new vessel. There was a wonderful tangle of lines on that smooth floor. A great number of vessels long since broken up, or left to rot in Hospital Cove, stared up at him there. They came up one by one to the tender tracing of his thumb, and towered before him, redolent of tar, invincibly hewn and halted. Or so it had seemed; but for the most part they were only wraith ships now, dismantled, dead, and gone, early loves, old charges, some of which he had built, some of which he had sailed, at least one of which had foundered under him in an open seaway.

"I whittled them out first," he said softly, and hummed a little tune. He had whittled them out. It was even so. Men of this day speak reverently of the powers of that mighty sculptor who had held great ships, like infants, in the hollow of his hand; projected them entire from a block of wood, and pronounced them seaworthy while they were still no more than trees "up north." He launched them first on invisible ways.

Halcyon days! A good many men might have been found then to whittle out a model of a ship, but they have passed, and old Judson is alone in his proficiency. His knowledge and his cunning are unique. He bears himself a trifle austerely in consequence. There are no more like him. Do you see what that may mean in an age when human parts, no less than iron, are now well standardized?

"Here's the *James K. Whitehead*, now," murmured Judson, as who should say, "Alas! poor Yorick!" "She went down here last winter off Falmouth with a load of paving-stone. I was well out of her, however. I had only a sixty-fourth in her. There's the floor timbers of the *Sally Hooper*. One of the last vessels I had a hand in. Burned at sea."

He stared sorrowfully, picking them up from memory, proud ships, swift ships, showing the East Indian fleet a clean pair of heels. Strong ships, too, as strong as wit of man and weight of oak could make them; but yet, these myriad blurred lines were all that remained of them, and even these indistinguishable to all but Judson.

"They don't much outlive a dog," he told me in sad tones. "Fifteen years' insurance at the most."

And now he was sending men into the north woods to cut the frames for still another, which is to say, the ribs according to the molds, and the molds according to the lines traced on the loft floor. Nature is generous and variable. A grain will be found somewhere among her knotty roots to flow precisely as these molds require. Planking may be steamed, but the ribs of the ship must grow to their destiny unforced, even from the dreaming heart of the acorn.

But long before these frames were floated down the river a keel had been square-hewn, shod, hair-jointed, painted red, and left on the keel-blocks to await the imposition of the ship itself. The keel comes first; and it must hear and suffer all.

And now the yard was growing yellow and spongy as of old; stinging fragrance of pine mingled with sourness of oak; and chips flourished like wavelets in a wooden ocean. Faces were seen hovering over the keel-blocks strange to the new generation—faces of ancient ship-carpenters derelict these many years, outcast, forgotten.

But the art still smoldered in them. In these finger-ends and shoulder-joints ax-cunning still persisted. The knowledge of the workman, as of the master workman, is learned in a hard school, handed down to him by word of mouth or ushered into him by salutation of foot while he is young. I asked old Judson if there was not a book on building wooden ships, and he said he thought there was. It seemed to him that he had heard tell of one. Well, he had built ships enough to know for certain if hooks had been necessary to the building. Knowledge had seeped into him, rather. Very possibly all his life he had been porous to the fluid solicitations of this science.

A shipyard makes a wonderful loafing-ground. What better place to "bask and dream" on summer mornings, listening to the snarl of the mill, the tramp of great horses on the spongy soil, the multitudinous knocking, tumult of woods, clink of chains, creak and whine of tackle, and the stutter of the riveters? The blue river rushes past, foaming among the bed logs aft; and there, just out of reach, the fat, yellow bones of the new sea adventurer hang glistening. Beginning aft, they haul them into place, eight ribs a day on each side. To articulate the skeleton of a ship seems as easy as to weave a basket. Indeed, with the frame "hung up," as the expression goes, she looks much like some great yellow market-basket of the gods, ready for wattling.

And now they swing the stem-piece into place, the very nose of her, of oak decidedly, and painted robin's-egg blue. The stem is held at the proper slant by giant shears, taking heavy purchase, until the frames can be brought forward to fill the gap. This single stick of wood rough-hewn though it still is, has cost the builder close to three hundred dollars in the labor of axes.

At this stage there is to be noted the terrific provisional character of the ship. In her frames alone she is without strength, a very eggshell; then day by day, plank by plank, bolt by bolt, seam by seam, she stiffens and catches the support of her spine. Her strength, like the strength of man, perhaps, is only the sum total of blows dealt her from without. The treenail-drivers alone hit her, on a sober calculation, half a million times.

"She hasn't a leg to stand on yet," Judson said at a time when she had yet to feel the constraint of planking. With an inviting gesture he shouldered his way between two of her ribs on the port bow. "But she has the spine of a sperm-whale already."

He pointed to the great keelson atop the keel, and the sister keelsons bedded deep on each side.

"Strong as mortal man can make them," he rumbled, "and still not strong enough. There's a last straw waiting somewhere out yonder to break the back of this camel, and never you forget it."

Still, acknowledging her weakness, he surveyed her with pride, and found her worthy of a birth-certificate at least.

"Planking will bring out her lines," he assured me. "I want you to watch for the out-plank gang."

He was right. The subtilies of the ship-builder's craft are perhaps best displayed in the mid-planking, for this is the true skin and much-enduring cuticle of the ship and must be veritably soaked in oil in such wise that it will stand sea grief.

One balmy morning I saw steam spurting from the rusted corners of the steam box and noted a line of coffee cans warming at the tap against the noon hour. Down in the shadow of the ship the broad-ax men were hewing mightily to the time and not a hair over, all with that easy and disregarding motion learned in the good old days. The good old days, as Judson might say, when air-driven augers were unheard of, when twenty men were in requisition in place of eight, and when men carried beams into the ship on their own shoulders, and shirts not infrequently stuck before nightfall to the over-driven flesh. Efficiency was never heard of then, and yet ships staggered somehow into being, notwithstanding.

"I hate to be cramped the way I am for axmen," said Judson in my ear.

"I have heard talk of using a band-saw on those planks to get the bevel, in place of axmen," I said. "I should think that would be faster business."

Judson tweaked his hairy nose and looked at me with a bleak eye.

"What kind of consideration is that showing to broadax-men?" he inquired.

I answered nothing, and to clench me he threw out this:

"Then, again, if I let those axmen go, who is going to carry the plank to the side of the ship, I wonder?"

Who indeed? Do you suggest a tackle of some sort? A hoist? It is not so that it was done of old. Did not the Egyptians carry plank to the ship on their shoulders? The patriarchs of the yard would view with grave mistrust a ship which had been treated to too liberal a dose of the bandsaw. Rats might not go aboard such a ship, and in that case, it would be more than the devil and Tom Walker could do together to ship a crew.

As it to verify Judson in his argument, a plank that had been steaming half an hour was drawn out of the steam-box.

A horse dragged it smoking at the end of hook and chain to the port bow, and there a cry of "hot plank!" went up from the leader of the axmen. Those eight robust reasons why plank should not be sawed, but axed, rather, dropped their axes, girded their loins, took up the plank, walked it to the side of the ship, and dapped it into place.

"This is the first plank of the upper garboard-strake," said Judson. "Watch it curl. Did ever you see the like? Five inches through, and by heaven! it lays down like butter in a tub. I tell you what, ability to make a wagon spoke is no sign that you can build a ship. There isn't a straight line here. The bevel of that plank changes every foot or so. Halt, hear it sing! They'll have it sprung in a jiffy."

The broadax-men, seemingly beyond fear of superannuation, sang all together on the plank:

"Ye ho! Come to you a trifle! Now, hold hard!"

The planking boss applied a self-holding screw, like an iron latch, to the forward end of the plank. But could it then be sprung in against the ribs all its length, seeing that here, on a fairway of twenty feet, the surface of the oak must be twisted until it was at right angles with itself? Ring bolts hung above and below the beleaguered plank, and through these giant rings they thrust battered, sledge-bitten logs; "ring staffs," they are called. These in place, they drove in oak wedges between the staffs and the outer surface of the plank; and as they sledged, the plank began to sink to its seam, creaking. Creak, creak.

"Every time. Dry welt her home! Oh, spring her in!"

They tortured the plank with an application of pressure every way, top side and bottom side, butt, bevel, and face. The prying genius of oaken wedges forced the plant until it seemed as if the wood itself must disintegrate, so huge its unwillingness to be wrung, so grievous the urgency of the wringing. The self-holding screw forward bit deep into the grain, and the oak bulged and protested. A vessel surely is born with agony to her timbers.

"Look there," said Judson, "she must be sprung in close; she must be snugged in all she will hold once and for all. All the spikes and trunnels in the world won't draw her closer than she can be wedged. They have all they can do to hold what the wedges win."

"Wood to wood," sang the axmen, jocularly.

The grizzled planker shoved his rule into the seam. The outer edges of it were quite a quarter of an inch apart. Was it, then, wood to wood, inch for inch, on the inner scant?

"Wood to wood is the theory of planking," said Judson; "but there is room enough for theory inside the ship. It goes better in the cargo than in the seams, heh? Look here, I have had men here daft enough to say that the plank ought to come down until you can't shove so much as the point of a case-knife through that inner seam. Well, consider. Those planks, in the nature of things, are going to soak and swell; and then, sir, if they haven't a trifle of elbow room or the warn, they will draw their butt-baits to get it. I don't know anything more wilful than an underwater plank when it don't lay comfortable. A sick boy won't thrash around anymore."

What was to be avoided, he said, was a hollow seam; and that was where the planks were farther apart on the inner seam than on the outer.

"A ship with hollow seams will spew her oakum, no matter how you hoss it into her."

He fastened his eye upon the ship's dubber, away up forward. That man was snapping chalked twine, like a spar-maker getting his "eights." He had nailed the ends of it, and now he picked it up like a harp string and twanged it against the crude and unfair ribs. A chalk-line resulted, jumping from-rib to rib, for the space of eight or ten ribs. The dubber lifted his adz, and began to hew away shavings of the thickness of rice-paper. He was responsible for the true sculpturing of the ship; the planks can no more than bend themselves to his lines.

"In the old days before the fairing process they used to fair them up by the naked eye," said Judson. "Stand at the stem and squint your eye down port and starboard and decide to take off a leetle mite here and a leetle mite there. And that was why those old ships were sometimes crabs on the port tack, while they would nestle down to starboard like a lady, and contrariwise."

Now came the treenail-gang to fasten the plank. First, men with augers, who bored through the plank, two holes at each rib, the upper one going clear through the skin of the ship; and then the treenail-drivers.

What, then, are treenails, or "trunnels," as they are called? What but wooden spikes—*tree* nails in good truth—by means of which chiefly the vessel is pegged together. Wood makes a stronger fastener than iron for a wooden ship. Fiber engages fiber; wood has a better "cling" than metal; and once fairly lodged in the frame, these wooden pegs become incorporated with the ship, as much so as if it had grown one skin. Treenails play with the ship, yield as the planks yield, and return as they do; whereas iron, if it should draw or move with some wrenching of the ship's side, holds its new angle intractably, and never subordinates itself to the personality of the hull.

Treenails above the waterline are made of locust, the fiber of which does not shrink: under water, chiefly of greenheart oak.

The treenail-drivers, ranging themselves along the plank, dipped the treenail ends in grease, and stepped them in the holes appointed. Next, they went at them with silver-nosed mauls, and pelted them smartly in. "*Tick, tock; tick, tock.*" The handle of the maul slid loosely in the web of the right thumb. The wielder thereof never closed his right hand tight; indeed, did not appear even to watch the treenail-head, but the maul traveled irresistibly, as if in an air groove appointed to it. The pitch of the treenail music goes ringing higher and higher with each stroke; there is no sound more heartening; it is, in fact, the most musical of all the ship's noises. I should suppose the xylophone might have been invented by a treenail-driver.

The alternated strokes of the treenail drivers have an automatism like the movement of a clock; and, as with the clock a strong beat is followed by a weak one, so with the treenail strokes where an old man and a young one work together. The treenails speak sweetly, and with a frosty tang in the utterance, while the treenailers sway and sledge, sway and sledge, in a fine-spun reverie, and with a languid, dream-like, yet powerful motion. It seems as if they might be set to driving treenails in their sleep and never get enough of it. It has, in fact, a medicinal value, it appears. It is in the tradition of one yard that a rich young man cured himself of sleeping lethargy by driving treenails. It is further averred that this same young man became so clever with his tools that he could set a treenail-end on a kid glove and bring the wood to a point with his ax, and yet not so much as graze the leather. Very little of this wizardry of the craft is left now.

"There, now," said Judson, "that plank is on for keeps."

"You think it will hang on?"

"Like grim death to a rusty nigger," he replied.

When the ship was only partly planked, the spar-maker began to fashion her four lower masts. Day by day he shaped those ninety-foot-octagonal-butted sticks into miraculous roundness where they lay in the shadow of the ship. In the late afternoon their satiny surfaces were all one blinding yellow glare from the slanted rays of the sun.

"Smooth as a girl's cheek, I guess," said the spar-maker.

His stooped and ape-like old body swayed fore and aft to accompany his plane. His body had a chronic concavity in its length which suggested the merciless convexity of the mast.

"What thickness, Mr. Spar-maker?"

"Thirty inches at the heel."

"Something better than a toothpick, I believe."

"A bean-pole. I've seen 'em go as high as thirty-six."

Resinous shavings writhed upward through the body of his fascinating plane. Great shavings and small shavings and very meticulous shavings and shavings that were no shavings, all to the crisp tune of well-conditioned steel engaging wood. That old fellow was evidently intent on outdoing smoothness itself. Each shaving was a deep and perfumed satisfaction to the heart.

As a boy I used to stand by the hour, slack-witted, tranced, to behold planes and drawing-knives slither over and back, over and back, on that yellow, gleaming round. Smooth, smoother, smoothest. Now, now at last the thing is smooth; and then, when it seems as if the very desideratum of smoothness has been reached, yet another shaving. A haunting mystery is spar-making.

On pleasant evenings critics collected in the shadow of the ship, sitting on the dewy spars, prowling through her ribs, or, at a later stage, peering thoughtfully down her hatches. They came through the dusk and shook their heads sadly over what they saw. The old order changeth. The ship had no lines, they said, for one thing. There was no sharpness in her bow, and no sweetness in her stern. She was a very moonfish in design, a century old while still lying in her cradle. The deck houses were too high; they should have been saddled, and not framed. Oh, the bitter workmanship of these degenerate days!

But the vessel, the thing, in itself, defied them, shriveled them with her monstrous bulk, and made criticism a thing of naught in the presence of her invincible strength.

Was she, then, so invincible? From her deck the blackened bones of ships in Hospital Cove rose up in serried ranks to confute so proud a claim. What had old Judson sorrowfully said? She would not much outlast a dog.

"She looks as if she would never break up in this world," I said one afternoon to the boss of the deck-planking gang.

"Look you there," he answered, with a gesture into the gigantic oak-and-pine abysm at our feet. Mysterious bellowings and rumblings proceeded out of it, as if Victor Hugo's mad cannon were let loose down there, or a consignment of wild bulls.

"Come now below."

We swung ourselves down to her floor timbers.

There, running the length of the ship, were the timbers making up keelson and sister keelsons, bedded together, thick-set and enormous, lock-scarfed, strapped with iron, bolted, a huge fagot of timbers, each timber fourteen inches square at the butt, a fagot two hundred feet long and nearly four feet square—the backbone of the ship, no less. It staggered the imagination to peer into the gloomy recesses of that echoing cavern, so full and bold in the jowl. The place seemed to have been hewn and hollowed out of one primeval log, a dugout of incredible proportions. I took note of the massive hanging knees which support the deck beams—knees as thick as knees of elephants. Frail and withered the hand of the builder as it rested on the vertebrae of that tremendous spine. He was a midge engulfed in the bowels of that leviathan, no more to look at than Jonah in the belly of the whale.

Yet he had bodied forth and launched into the services of men many such. Some were living yet, and some were sunk in the mudflat at Hospital Cove, eaten to the heart with the slow fires which burn the old iron out of them. A sad contrast with these fat, yellow bones, their mottled surfaces newly axed. And yet, as for the new ship, with her nose now pointed so disdainfully heavenward for ease of launching, "let her paint an inch thick, to this favor she must come."

"Maybe, if she was to batter on a reef, she would break up in course of time, but never in an open seaway," affirmed the deck-planking boss.

"They will crack in a seaway," said a sad voice behind us, the voice of Judson.

"Well, maybe some ships, but not those they used to put what you could call workmanship into. Why, man alive, I have been away from here a good many years, but I remember in the old days one ship where the keelsons were built up to a height of nearly five feet above the floor timbers. Do you suppose that ever that would crack? It ain't in reason."

"It would crack, yes," reaffirmed old Judson. "It would crack if it was plagued."

He was seaman no less than builder. He knew the power of ships, but he knew the power of the sea as well.

"Never that ship," returned the carpenter. "You should have seen the knees of her. The ceiling was nine inches deep over her floor timbers, with a thick streak of twelve inches at the bilge. She was oak all through. White oak, man, even the hanging-knees. Why, I remember going to the old man and saying, 'Hack is better than oak for hanging-knees,' and he drew off and says, 'Jim,' he says, 'if there is anything grown better than white oak, I don't want to see it coming aboard at my time of life.'"

"What was the name of that ship, Jim?"

"The bark *Paragon*."

Judson took out of his pocket a black plug, and bit into it with a slow and wise motion.

"The *Paragon*. By the merciful! old stager, you have been away from the coast these late years, I reckon."

"True enough."

"Now, what would you say if I was to tell you that that selfsame ship, the *Paragon*, was lost like you say she couldn't have been lost, in an open seaway?"

"If it was any other living man telling me, I would say he lied," mumbled the carpenter. "Of course, if you tell me—"

"Exactly so."

"Ain't you thinking of some other ship, Mister? That *Paragon* was just indestructible, if a ship ever was."

"Was she so?" returned old Judson. "Well for me I'm indestructible myself, then, for I'm here to tell the tale, and I was boson of her when she broke in two like a stick of candy."

"Broke in two!" muttered the carpenter. "There was her backbone piled as high as my chin. I could just reach up to it with my dinner-pail when I was dubbing her floor timbers."

"No matter, it went like that," said Judson, snapping a splinter between thumb and finger. "We were coming from New Caledonia loaded with nickel ore, and one minute she was a solid ship, and next she hung out over a wave. Lord God, the devil, and Tom Walker couldn't have held her together then. She foundered, and that's matter of record."

"Where did she go?" inquired the ship's carpenter, more subdued.

"Just for'ard of the beam. The watch below had come on deck to take in topsails; there was I whooping like mad on the yard-arm when there come a shudder through her like as if she had stumbled; down went the yard I was on, cockbilled to port, and there she was, opened just for'ard of the beam, as I say."

"You don't say!" said the shipman, sorrowfully. "Opened."

"Stood open like a grave. And next I knew the masts were going past my ears like tall shadows."

"Thirty-two inches at the butt they were," murmured the carpenter, plaintively, twitching out a shaving from his belt. "I can hear them now, as if it was yesterday, entering the step. Just before the mainmast was hard down the old man slipped a five-dollar gold piece under the heel of it for luck."

"Ship's luck is in the wind," retorted Judson. "Those masts were jolted out of her, I tell you, like quills out of a porcupine. Snapped off short, and down they came, and next a ring of foam around the ship where she squatted down, and a roaring over the fo'c'sle-head; and then it was lights out, and no more noise, and plump I went in the water like a kitten into a wash-boiler."

"In the open sea, too!" repeated the carpenter. "She was hung up as solid as a fort, to all appearances."

"Here you are building ships, and you don't know nothing about the power of water," said the seaman, with the age-old contempt of his tribe for the land where he had brought his bones to rest at length. "It staggers a man like all the powers of hell rushing to the south. What's a ship amount to in a wind? Her weight is what brings her to grief."

"That is mortal truth," replied the shipwright. "If only she had the strength there is in the bolted frame, and the weight of an eggshell along with it, no God's legion of pounding would break her up. She could stand any sickening quantity of grief then. But, sure enough, her weight stands in her way when it comes to rocks and coral-reefs and the like o' that."

"The best of 'em will come to grief," said Judson.

"You're a lucky man to be alive, in my opinion."

"The sea will never cheat the gallows, I reckon."

The old builder went off to see to the salting of his charge. For just as men are salted in the blood stream, so, too, the ship must be salted. From fifty to three hundred hogsheads of salt are usually shaken down between her ribs before the last few streaks of planking are put on. This invisible cargo of salt, never unloaded, but sometimes renewed by their salacious majesties, forms, with the inevitable leak through the planking, a brine which trickles down and keeps her timbers sound, shiver though they may. At the line between wind and water, which is the line of lightest load, there should be a wooden salt-stop wedged in between the ribs before the planking covers them.

Inside, air streaks are left in her ceiling—the planking on the inner surfaces of the ribs, that is—both for the renewing of salt and to let in air upon her bones. A ship is an organism very imperfectly protected at best from the ravages of decay. She is weather-beaten even lying in her cradle. Now, a ship's skin, like man's, must breathe; or, like the gilded boy who headed the pope's procession, she will make a quick end by suffocation. Man, therefore, in constructing this organism, clumsily adopts the perfected devices of nature, and lets in air and brine in goodly measure to play upon her vitals. So, it is also that the leakiest boat which will still float is the longest-lived and least subject to dry rot. Old barges hove together like baskets for coal-carriers are sound and sweet after the dear knows how long a service; and a packet that was put together tighter than a miser's dream of heaven begins to stink between the wind and water in six or seven years. Then when the insurance men open her flanks fore and aft, port and starboard, above water and below, the rot can be scooped out with a shovel. The poet truly says:

Lilies that fester smell far worse than weeds.

At length the ship was planked, planed over all, the mellow clack of caulking hammers resounded, and the time had come to pick up those afore-mentioned bean-poles; in short, to step the masts.

They raised up mighty shear-poles on the deck over the foremast-hole. These were crossed high in air a few feet from their tips, and bound there with a great, yellow shear-head lashing of twenty turns or more of rope. These giant shears were guyed fore and aft; their heels were stepped port and starboard in movable wooden sockets, which could be sledged over a greased deck when it became necessary to walk the shears from one mast hole to another.

From the head of the shears hung the mast purchase, a block, or pulley, in which was set an iron ring. This ring they lowered overside, and took twenty turns of rope through it, and around the mast, nearer the truck than the heel—that is, nearer the top than the bottom. The rope led from this lashing to a block at the top of the shears, thence to the stem of the vessel, thence to a monstrous block on the ground, and last of all seven turns around the shining barrel of a horse-crab, or windlass with a perpendicular drum. Even as I watched, two heavy horses began to plow a black circle round the crab in the spongy dirt, the truck of the mast up reared, and a man stationed on the lashing itself began to shout out to his subordinates: "Slack the guy! Snug in the heel there! Get that gant-line higher up! There! Hold that!"

He went on from this to a volley of unintelligible, ringing yells, and the horses revolving about the lustrous barrel of the weather-beaten crab arched their necks and seemed proud to exert their strength in so tremendous an employment.

Higher and higher the truck erected itself with a stealthy motion, as if meaning to surprise the ship and slink aboard unobserved. At length the heel itself was swung inboard; the greasy, yellow stick reeled against the sky; the shears quivered.

With a handy billy, they drew the heel over the destined spot. And now a man took the mast squarely between two huge and leathery palms. An instant he stood so, wrapt, considering, poised like a woman threading a needle with bated breath. The sun flashed from the brass rim of a horn grease-pot at his hip. Unless you raised your eyes to the purchase and the crossed shears, you beheld him holding the mast balanced by his own might. The heel, notched half a foot deep across its diameter, moved an inch or two over and back.

"Lower away!"

They slacked the fall, and the mast sank like a serpent through the hole.

I ran down into the hold. The yellow butt was sliding through the 'tween-decks with the same suggestion of noiseless stealth—the more noiseless for the boomings on every hand caused by the fall of mauls and caulking-hammers on the outer skin of the ship.

Next appeared the boss rigger's chief assistant, seething with objurgation.

"Slack away on the fall!" he yelled.

The notched heel of the mast, continuing its miraculous progress into the bowels of the ship, had come to within a few inches of the step appointed to receive it.

"Lower a little inch! Hold!"

This wild shriek was reechoed from the deck above, borne aloft in muffled accents until it rebounded from the vault of heaven. And now the mast mysteriously twirled, so as to bring the notch in the heel precisely fore and aft; but it was not quite over the step.

"Wedge her forward!"

Heavy blows fell; the heel crept over its socket.

"Hold! Slack away on the fall!"

A faint voice called:

"Fall all gone."

"What's wrong, then? She's entered the step. She's clear all round."

He peered delicately all round that orifice, brushed it with his finger-tips, as if a grain of dust had checked the mast in its descent. Next, he began to swear and lash out at a wedge simultaneously. The invisible man above picked up this red refrain like a torch, whirled it round once or twice to fan it into flame, and cast it up out of the pit he was in.

"Ease away the wedges for'ard, then!" cried my ship's carpenter.

He hit the mast once more, and now with an invincible *pung*, that shook the ship all round, as if a battering-ram had found its mark, the mast fell into place. That heavy heel tramped on the keelson like the foot of an elephant on a matchbox.

"Hard down!"

And in that moment the monstrous round of the mast assumed a look of immobility, as if it had not moved since time began, as if not all the machinations of man could ever coax it to give even the fraction of an inch again; hard down, and guaranteed to stand without hitching, wind and weather permitting, for the space of twenty years. And yet a moment back it had twirled like a watch-charm at the end of its chain.

"This is a quiet crew," said the carpenter, mildly. He dusted his palms together. "In the old days they used to pick up these sticks and step them with their mouths, as you might say."

The good old days—days of the clipper ships, days of the vinegar ships! Marvelous rigs, marvelous men, too. They had a stomach for anything then. In that golden morning tide of life, it seemed, a skipper would think nothing of slipping a five-dollar gold piece under the heel of the mast as it was going into place. He valued his ship; and besides, it was a day of faith. Later the gold dwindled to a bright penny. Men were losing confidence in their ships then, maybe; but it was a fact that the trade-winds had never been the same since. Was it likely that, if there was any demon of sailor's luck prowling the seven seas, he would be fooled by a bright penny?

Truly the old order changeth.

A day came when she was ready for the plunge. Her sticks were in, her paint was on, she was copper painted below water, because that paint continually scales off, and disposes of borers before they can get a foothold. Her stores were slung aboard, a fire kindled in the galley, a cook installed to watch it, and still no movement in all the length and breadth of her.

Now comes her destined hour. A hush has fallen on the yard for once. The sawmill no longer puffs forth its yellow cloud over the rushing river; neither clink of chain nor cluck of broadax falls on the ear; a touch of frost is in the air. The ship lies rotund and gleaming in her cradle, her jib boom pointing to the skies. So slowly has she come into being here that she now seems part and parcel of the landscape, one with all our hopes and fears; wedged and blocked and bill-shored here as if for all eternity.

And yet even now all hangs by a hair. The ways have been built up to her bilges; the bilges rest on boards, the under faces of which are smeared with beef tallow or the like. These boards in turn rest on the top of the ways, similarly greased. Nothing remains but to split out the keel blocks and let the great new foundling of the seas slide into her element.

A flag-draped platform has been built against her nose; the daughter of the new owner stands there with a bottle of spring water.

Judson, strolling out from a critical inspection of the forward keel-blocks, turns his bleak eyes toward that platform, tweaks his hairy nose again, and mutters:

"There's two of the handsomest women in town brought face to face and rubbing noses."

And touching one of these same handsome women, the sincerity of his compliment is not to be questioned for a moment. The grim builder has faith in the lines of his ship.

The giant enterprise is near an end. It remains to be seen if so huge and long calculated a pile will veritably start, move, plunge away, all of a piece as she is, making her final bow to the reedy marshland of her birth; the sea adventurer, coming out of that first dip with a personality all her own, something stately and steadfast, but something rebellious, stubborn, too, it may be, or even antagonistic to her builder. After all this time she is to roll out of her cradle, this baby of a million love-taps, go her own gait, take her destiny out of these pygmy hands forever. There is a strain of Frankenstein's monster in the thought. These men have mysteriously endowed the ship with a certain nature, good or ill, stiff or cranky or easy; she will sail better or worse according as the shavings shall decree which old Judson dropped from his model six months back. Were they well and truly taken? A single shaving there, more or less, might make the difference between a swift and a slow ship. By all means, these should be well-meditated shavings.

And what of Judson himself while all hangs in the balance? He saunters fore and aft as the sound of the axes biting into the after blocks comes to his ears. Will the ways hold? They are built up of keel timbers, and are calculated to withstand the mightiest lateral thrust, but the ship's bulk transcends mathematics a little in its unrelenting and ponderous reality. Nothing, then, can be certainly predicated of it.

A powerful draft, always moving along the ship's bottom, through openings between the keel-blocks, ruffles the old fellow's gray hair. He picks at a blob of grease on the ways, stretches up an arm to the garboard-strake, touches a joint in the shoe—hair-joints everyone—and another coat of paint would lick them out of sight. His eye kindled with admiration of a good job.

Men were coming nearer with the axes. Behind the axmen came a boy carrying a pot of paint with which he painted in desperate strokes the uncovered portions of the shoe as the keel-blocks dropped away. The ship, almost released, hung on his very shoulders, and he was in a hurry.

"She will snap out twenty or thirty blocks in all likelihood," said Judson.

The ship hung over us with every hallmark of an immovable body still. Then did it seem as if she had moved a grain, the thousandth part of an inch? I fastened my eye on a knot in the shoe but could not verify that movement. That the ship should actually move seemed as unlikely as a fable. The axmen, however, came faster and faster. They saw nothing of the fable in it. Besides, they had a certain distaste for work of this description.

"She's on a shoe-string now," they whispered.

Thirty blocks to go. The last ship from these ways had snapped twenty-five. The youth whose sacred duty it was to paint the bottom of the keel braced himself and lashed out with flying strokes. Surely the time of this leviathan was at hand.

On a shoestring. The mighty structure now clung to twenty blocks of pine as lightly as a withered oak leaf to its twig. It needed nothing but an inspiration, perhaps, to start it—a shout, a breath of wind, a yielding joint, perhaps a child's finger laid on the immense prow. The song of a bird will shiver a glacier into action.

All this while we stood about, kicking at chips and waiting—waiting for her "to take a fancy to it." But it seemed as if she could not ever break out of bounds as long as that habit of stock-stillness was fastened on her. Perhaps if only the imaginations of men, to say nothing of their axes, would credit her with the possibility of movement she would move. For if the men who put all but the breath of life into her falter at this moment, on whom is she to lean? She has not yet come into her own.

"The grease may have stuck," said Judson, calmly, standing a little aside.

There had been times, he said, in hot weather when the ship's launching company had had to jump up and down fore and aft to start her. Judson had met his first wife while jumping up and down at a moonlight launching.

Suddenly his eyes gleamed.

"She is gone."

She had moved as imperceptibly as a swan drifting—

A thrill of life along her keel.

The phrase of the poet is worn thin, is ancient coinage; but the moment is the most tremendous to which the labor of man can give rise. Came a cracking, a splintering; twenty blocks were mashed and rolled end for end, and the youth with the paint-pot jumped like a hare to escape squirting splinters. The ship settled on the ways, and with the magic smoothness of a dream wherein vast solids seem to float like feathers, the hull withdrew into the river.

I was aware of the draft that blew under the ship, of a harsh burr and whisper from the ways as the giant shoe moved overhead; then she was gone, like a gray cloud rolling away. The draft was no more, and I was confronted by a long laneway of sheer space, that the bulwarks of the ship had seemed to fill invincibly a moment back.

The good ship *Little Turk* was in the river, with three tugs straining to check her from fetching the other bank. A faint cheer was wafted from her bow.

Judson stared at her wonderingly. He picked his way among yellow shards of keel-blocks, going toward the river's-edge; and now I saw that he was tossing up and down in his hand the model of the ship—the little block of wood to which she owed all she had of seaworthiness and all the graces of her being.

"She is a good ship," I said.

"She's a good ship if she will sail," said Judson.

In these words, he confessed that she was strange to him. He held the model horizontal between his thumbs and raised his eyes slowly, slowly.

"She went in easy, I'll say that much. Well, she's all ready for the rats to come aboard, and—I reckon we can still build ships."

BLUE-WATER LAW

From the *Saturday Evening Post* (May 3, 1919)

In one of only two articles in this collection, Hallet examines the new Merchant Seaman's Act, passed by Congress in March 1915 to protect seamen's rights. He focuses on the abusive practice of "shanghaiing" and use of "crimps" (runners hired by shipping companies and captains to staff their ships). Prospective sailors were routinely bribed with drink and women and often found themselves conscripted onto vessels with all their wages already committed.

"Whoever . . . shall procure . . . another, by force or threats or by representations which he knows to be untrue, or while the person so procured is intoxicated . . . to go on board of any such vessel, or to sign or in any wise enter into any agreement to go on board . . . shall be fined not more than one thousand dollars."

"If, within twenty-four hours after the arrival of any vessel at any port in the United States, any person, then being on board such vessel, solicits any seaman to become a lodger at the house of any person letting lodgings for hire . . . he shall . . . be punishable . . ."

Perhaps I can partly bring out the meaning of these two provisions of our navigation laws by relating my first experience at breaking into any merchant marine. And first, as I thought, I had to find my ship. I could think of no simpler way of doing this than walking along the Brooklyn piers until I saw what looked to me a likely ship; and then to go aboard and make known my wish to ship aboard that ship. Well, I did precisely that; and they laughed at me. The captain, the sailmaker and the ship's cat all joined in a laugh at my expense. I had given myself away by merely asking for a job.

What should a man do, then, who wanted to put to sea? I sought out the company that owned this vessel or at least chaptered her. The marine superintendent was courteous, but he gave me to understand that to ask that right worshipful company for this sort of job was, to say the least of it, irregular.

THE CRIMP AND HIS MEN

"Where do you get your crews, then?" He said that to the best of his belief they sharked them up somehow, as they were needed; but then, he said, sailors were what was needed, and not greenhorns. And indeed, it was implied in his speech that there was no way of beginning to be a sailor. You either were a sailor or you were not. If you were you would know well enough how to go about getting a job; and if you were not you had better stay ashore, because you would not amount to Hannah Cook on a ship.

In the end it appeared that the most likely and only approved way of joining a ship was to get drunk in the right quarter and wake up on the ship. The trail had led me deviously from the highly polished counters of the aforesaid company to a villainous little waterside den, where I verily believe were sharked up and bound together by the bond of pennilessness the worst roomful of ruffians the world could show. Not one of them would ever be hanged for his good looks. There were Long John Silvers there, I will stake my bottom dollar on it; there were three-fingered men and one-armed men and one-eyed men and men whose noses had been bashed in level with their faces. There were men whose speech was like a clap of thunder and more men who spoke in beery whispers. Every tongue in Europe and Asia was represented there, and a bond between them was their common servitude to salt water and to the shifty-eyed individual who was known as the crimp, or boarding master.

He it was who had raked them together like so many winnings as fast as they disembarked; or even coming alongside as soon as the hook was dropped to solicit their patronage of his house. No man who came to his house had ever complained of a lack of creature comforts. And who else met them and offered them a roof over their heads as this man did? They went with him and he fed them beef and cabbage and fig pudding and rotgut whisky until if they wanted to move their heads they must move their trunks, too, because they were "all of a piece," as one of them affirmed to me.

The crimp was now able to say to those wanting seamen that he and he only held that commodity and would part with it—at a price. As a matter of fact, he got two prices—one from the shipmaster to whom he sold his commodity, the other from the men themselves. On signing the articles, the men were allowed to draw three months' advance pay; and this the boarding master saw that they drew and handed to him in exchange for past benefits conferred. There was seldom any saying in what these benefits consisted, but his claims were not contested. Sick of themselves, the men by that time wanted nothing in the wide world but to be put back on a ship again. Money was nothing to them; they wrote it away with an oath.

Though I was neither drunk nor subject to his whims I slipped the boarding master a certain fee to run me in with the crew of the ship about which I had made inquiries. It was as easily done as that, when once a man had got the hang of it. I loafed many hours in that waterside hole, where the moldering walls were covered with tobacco juice and the stairs looked ripe for some sort of Dickens murder any hour of the twenty-four. Not a very inviting beginning, you will say.

When the shipmaster was ready for his crew the man master stepped out and read a list of those present who were to get their gear and appear before the consul. The poor creatures crowded about, panting and swearing in their eagerness to be among the elect. Shortly a swaying, stumbling gang was on its way to the consul's office, and there the articles were read to them.

As to the articles of the contract which they signed, most seamen knew nothing to the end of their days. If they were in shape to listen at all they listened much as they might listen to a hymn being chanted in Latin, or a chapter of the Koran being read. On this occasion few were in shape to listen at all. Some of them did lean forward blearily when wages were mentioned. Able seamen were set down in those articles against a sum of four pound ten a month—twenty-two dollars. They didn't even come up to the terms of that old chantey which moans that a dollar a day is a white man's pay. A description of the voyage contemplated was read, but in so low a voice that not a man in the lot could tell afterward within fifteen thousand miles of where he was bound. It was an interesting speculation for weeks after we had put to sea.

Certain fines and penalties were read more loudly. I remember one fine of five shillings for bringing "knuckle dusters," or brass knuckles, aboard.

ONCE ABOARD THE *LUGGER*

And then those men went up and signed or made their mark. The captain of the ship was there, watching them. He may have had a nominal right to protest them, but he did not speak a word. The crimp was the sole source of his supply, and he must stand or fall by that selection. And it was a wonderful selection.

A tug lay at the battery. It was a warm summer's night. I well recall how weird the whole proceeding seemed to me to be one of that maudlin group staggering toward the pier, each man bowed over his bag and mattress, for this was an English ship, and a man must bring his own furniture aboard. Bags, mattresses and men cascaded to the deck of the tug. When we sided with the ship, which was berthed at Constable's Hook, my amiable sailmaker passed down a bowline, a running bowline, and one by one hauled up the members of the crew and dumped them down on deck, with a face as solemn as if he were cod fishing.

The crimp came aboard with a last bottle of whisky for them to sober up on enough to stick out a line to the tug and get the ship down to her anchorage off Staten Island. They swore that he was a good crimp, their brother; he was never the man to ship them and leave them in the lurch. You could depend on that man to keep you in drink till the last possible minute. Still it proved to be not enough; and several, including the boson, got into the boson's locker and drank the top off some shellac that was there. There were sick men on that old hooker. She lay at anchor three days, with every man aboard her drunk, from the captain down.

Such was the process; like it or not, that was the one way to put to sea. I don't mean to say that men were out-and-out shanghaied as an everyday matter; most of them were only too glad to get out of the clutches of the thing that had them, whatever it was. But if a young fellow wanted to go to sea he was met at the outset by this evil and questionable atmosphere, this topsy-turvy madness which communicated its taint to the whole seafaring life.

I do not know how to be forcible enough in saying that a revolution has taken place in that scheme of things. American ships—millions of tons of them—are in the water now; and bred-in-the-bone Americans are manning them and being put in training to man them. None of this business of going to a foreign consul and hearing strange talk about knuckle dusters. That is not one of our national institutions. And you do not have that sense of taking a plunge, of isolating yourself from your kind, that once you could not be without. There are plenty of your own kind in with you now. We want and we intend to have a merchant marine that shall have the traits of a national institution. As one step in this process the Shipping Board has made sure that the business of putting to sea shall no longer have that questionable taint about it, as of the barter and sale of slaves.

Everybody must know by this time that the Shipping Board has set apart schools and ships for the training of officers and crews. That was a wartime measure, but it has not come to an end with the war. The second annual report of the Shipping Board states that it has seven training ships in the Atlantic Squadron and four in the Pacific Squadron, besides a ship at New Orleans and one at Cleveland. These ships have a total capacity of more than 4,500 apprentices.

The idea is to give these apprentices in a short time what they might be a long time getting under old conditions. If you want to know what an exasperating mystery an old-line sailor can make of his trade, ask him to make a bowline for you. He will turn it out in a twinkling and grin at you, and you are none the wiser. You will have to lope round and camp on his trail for weeks, and still be none the wiser. On ships of private companies, the greenhorn will be given very little rope and wire to spoil. Now on these training ships there is an instructor to each ten apprentices, and the men do actually twist up the rope in their own hands, and learn the rudiments as fast as their own ability permits. This training goes on for a month or six weeks, and the men, though not then able seamen by any means, are ready to be brigaded with regular crews of merchant ships.

And the recruiting service does not let go of the men here. It has established a sea-service bureau, whose job is to place these men and in general to find crews for the merchant marine. This bureau has now branch offices in all the leading ports, and these offices have decent and comfortable quarters for the men, and are the places where the American sailor transacts his shore-going business, the logical and only place to look for a ship, and the logical and only place to look for a crew.

A NEW CLASS OF SEAMEN

The boarding master was hit a hard blow by the provisions of the statute, but he is doomed by this new arrangement. I have been in several of these offices and comparing them with the dens of old I can say that it is a case of complete substitution of one thing for another. What we have got now is an American office; self-respecting young men coming there, with a definite purpose, knowing what they want, and knowing in advance the terms upon which it will be granted them. It is not an adventure only it is a business.

These are the men who when they sign a ship's articles want to know and they do know what is in those articles. They do not intend to put their necks in a noose with the willful obtuseness of sailors of former times. They are the new marine in the making.

Clause after clause in the older sections of the statute show the legislator in the act of trying to protect the seaman against his own childish ignorance. He could not sign away his lien on the ship for wages, he could not sign away his salvage rights; his signature, even if he set it down, would be null and void, like the signature of a minor. We are getting together a set of men who will not need that sort of protection.

One of the finest bits of evidence that our statutes were got up to apply to foreign seamen and not to native Americans may be seen in the clause which says: "No seaman in the merchant service shall wear any sheath knife on shipboard." That does not mean that the sheath knife is outworn; it can never be outworn. It means that the men who were being shipped were that sort of men who use knives in quarrels. Now since the death of Colonel Bowie and his adherents I think it is demonstrable that we are not a knife-wielding people in this sense. The worst products of our blended stock do not resort by instinct to cold steel when their blood is up. And I think that as soon as we can show that we are manning our ships with our own men we should, out of respect for them, if nothing more, scratch this law off our books.

Indeed, I do not well see how a man is to get along without a sheath knife if he ships on a windjammer. My own sheath knife hangs on the wall before me, a beautifully brutal dirk, I confess. It has a fine dark brass-riveted handle, marked with three right crosses; and the very pirate of whom I bought it knew not himself the meaning of those crosses. They went back of him. Its long and strong blade is thrust into a leather sheath with a fancy fringe, this sheath of my own laborious making. Many the night aloft I have had occasion to whip that thing out of its sheath. A jackknife has not the backbone and the instant avail- ability. We can restore the sheath knife into favor if our crews are to be truly American.

If men want to fight, even knife-using men, weapons will not be lacking. I have seen a man's nose and right ear sliced off in one and the same twinkling—and in a workmanlike manner, too—with a bread knife; and a ship must carry that. With a belt, and a sheath knife hanging from that same, the whole figure of the sailor was rounded out, and he appeared like what he was, a foursquare man, capable of dealing with any emergency in a self-respecting fashion.

It may be profitable to dip into the statutes a little further. We observe under crew accommodations, for example, that on new ships each seaman shall have one hundred and twenty cubic feet all to himself. Much may be done with one hundred and twenty feet. There is also a provision insisting on a washing place. No one ever seemed to want to wash when I first went to sea. There were many strange growls, but a growl because a ship didn't have a shower bath would have been a growl beyond the wildest of those salty imaginations. They brought along salt-water soap to wash their clothes with, and there they thought the duty ended. It was still possible in those days to resort to a German proverb to the effect that clothes make people. Therefore, if you washed clothes you in some sort washed people.

Only as a fireman was I privileged to wash without being thought finical. I used to come up striped like a zebra, draw a pail of hot suds, and face a quarter of an hour's agony scrouging dust out of my eyelids, and digging out the sooty caverns of my ears, and grooming and mopping off divers muscular backs, and having my own duly mopped off in turn.

But a shower bath! That we wotted not of. And shower baths are now the rule.

CONDITIONS IMPROVING

The trade of firing is improved in many particulars since oil burners have come in. I have seen firemen going down on watch with novels under their arms. Peep at the combustion once in a while, and for the rest you are free to read Milton's *Paradise Lost*. Indeed, firemen are no longer worth a write-up, because if you can't tell people that theirs is a miserable job you had better tell people nothing. "The poor stoker" has been so long commiserated that it will never do to suggest that he lives a life of riotous ease. Yet such is getting to be the true case on all documented vessels of the oil-burning kind, and if the oil burners prevail, as seems likely, this ease of the stoker will become universal.

Note again that forecastles are to be fumigated, at such intervals as the surgeon general shall suggest, and I hope he will suggest that that be with fair frequency. I know our men think British ships the most unkempt in the world, but I know also of my own knowledge that the British are clever in their treatment of fo'c'stles. I shipped once on a lime-juicer—a mail packet plying between London and the colonies—and I had forgotten to bring my bed, my donkey's breakfast, aboard. English sailors are supposed to travel with mattresses on their backs, stuffed with chopped straw—enough to make a breakfast for one healthy donkey. This makes the business of joining a ship more interesting. Well, they gave me a naked bunk with a pipe frame and four steel slats and told me to take what comfort I could. I couldn't sleep in the bunk, and so I curled up on the cement deck. And very soon I saw that that deck had been marvelously treated. It had been swabbed up in a strong solution of carbolic acid.

Still I am all for hygiene on a ship.

Let me say in passing that every meal I had on that ship I had to go begging for a plate and a knife and fork and a cup; squat beside a better man until he was through with his own; all this because I had brought none of these things aboard and nobody had taken thought for such a poor beggar as I. I lost caste fearfully there; I was looked upon as a beach comber, an inferior bloke lost to all self-respect, because I did not have a mattress and a quilt, a knife and fork. Does that seem strange to you? It is operative in our own country, however. A friend of mine trying to get a job—through an agency—in some borax mills found that it all depended on whether or not he could produce a quilt. If he had a quilt, he was a citizen and a man of substance; if he had it not, he was a tramp.

Such of our new ships as I have been privileged to see have every facility for keeping quarters clean. The forecastle is a man's house; it is literally his castle, and if he cannot find himself at home there, he loses heart. I remember with loathing one leaky foreign fo'c'stle of which I was a denizen, where coal dust mingled with brine and made a black ooze two inches deep which squelched up between my toes every time I got out of my bunk. That sort of thing will make any kind of sailorman quote Scripture.

THE RAVAGES OF AFRICAN GOLF

On our new ships such conditions will not be tolerated. As to bunks, these cannot, according to the law, be more than two deep. The merchant-mariner sleeps on springs of the latest mesh type, fastened to a pipe frame, without those open joints which might harbor recluses. There have been fo'c'stles, I grant you, where a man might feel, as soon as he had doused the glim, as if a prairie fire were creeping up his flank. But I do not think any man will say of our modern ships—such as those built and manned by the Shipping Board—that they are dirty or verminous or rat-infested; or likely to become so.

The law on the subject of seamen's wages is remarkably full. I cannot here examine it in detail, but it is notable among other things that a man while in a foreign port may demand half his wages earned up to that time, but he must not ask oftener than every five days. This is a great advance over the old days, when all advances were at the pleasure of the old man.

As a matter of fact, the less chance a man has to get at his pay day en route the better off he is in the end. If he will accept this fact and let his money lie, he will find that he is actually making a great deal more money than men ashore who nominally draw more than he does. First, because for so long he is at sea and can spend nothing; and second, because bed and board are provided him. He is "found."

This assumes, of course, that our friend does not indulge in that disastrous game known as craps, or African golf, which, from my observation as a waster of time and money, is second to none. Nothing gets done on a ship where the disease of craps has made inroads. Everything is drawn toward that charmed circle. It may be and perhaps has been carried so far as to endanger the ship. A crap watch below means a sleepy lookout on deck. Still, it is fair to say for our present merchant marine that this is specifically a Navy disease. It is well known that skillful golfers enlist for the sole purpose of cleaning up at this backlots abomination. It is time these miserable land sharks—they are not sailors—who batten on the wages of better men were rounded up.

Let a man use horse sense, then, and he will save money at a rate that will astound him. The mate on my last ship told me that he had saved half of all the wages he had ever earned at sea. Who ashore could say as much? And yet ashore this mate was not afraid to spend money in reasonable amounts. The gain comes from being for such long periods beyond the seductions of that lick-pocket, a great city.

It is now unlawful to pay any seaman wages in advance of the time when he has actually earned the same or to pay such advance wages to any other person for the shipment of seamen. This again is directed against the activities of crimps. It does not prevent a seaman from allotting a portion of the wages he may earn to be paid to those dependent upon him ashore, but these allotments are not paid until they are actually earned by the absent sailor.

People often say: "What do you do if you are sick at sea?" The best procedure is to get into your bunk and think of home. The truth is that more humorous than tragic things occur to me in connection with sickness at sea. In the first place there used to be a practice of soldiering or playing off sick; that was one of the childlike attributes of the oldschool sailor. As soon as he had got well down into the rolling or the roaring forties, when furling sail was nasty business and the watch on deck was long and cold, he was likely to take to his bunk with some mysterious pain or other and call for medicine. Nobody could decide whether his agony was real or not. You remember that poor nigger in *The Nigger of the Narcissus* who kept them all guessing so long, and who died just as they had finally decided that there was nothing the matter with him. The real malingerer would go to mad lengths in his search for verisimilitude.

I recall one shipmate, a soldier, who had got a bullet in his leg at the siege of some Chinese city or other. The slug had not been taken out for fear of stiffening his leg. By exerting pressure against this slug, he could shift it in such wise as to clog the blood stream; and in half an hour his upper leg would be swelled fearfully, and the man incapacitated. But the torture to which he subjected himself was real. This man was a great sea humorist.

Real cases of soldiering developed on long cruises, when some mean-spirited men deliberately took advantage of the fact that they must be fed whether they worked or not. I have seen no pronounced cases of it in steam, and do not think much is known of it there. In any case such men can be got rid of quickly.

HEALTH IN SALT AIR

For some reason or other you don't seem to fall sick at sea in any bona fide fashion. Sluice enough salt over it and the body of man would, I think, take on immortality. There is more in the pickling process than that process is commonly given credit for. Even when the conditions were ever so bad my health, for some contrary reason, was ever so good. I was made of whipcord. So long as there was food of some kind any kind would do. Any fuel would serve to stoke me; I had fires in me then that would consume anything. I could turn in soaking wet, lie there steaming for hours, turn out as wet as ever, into my cod oils again and out on deck in tart weather, and yet take no cold. Is it the salt that does it, the free current of the air, the absence of poison-laden dust? A germ would have to have the wings of an albatross to follow you on some of these foreign voyages.

However, it is a statutory provision that on all merchant vessels that make voyages of more than three days' duration between ports and carry a crew of more than twelve seamen there shall be constructed a compartment for hospital purposes. In connection with the blithe use to which a hospital may be put I cannot refrain from mentioning the case of Jumbo Smith, who was along last trip to learn to be an engineer. This

Jumbo was the most downright willing man I ever saw come aboard a ship. All the powers of darkness couldn't hold him back from work, you would have said. Not content with tinkering the engine, if he happened to be off watch when the ship docked or undocked, he would jump in like mad with the sailors and heave away and yell as good as four men. He was as good as four men for just a week, and after that it took the services of four men to see that he wanted nothing. He had the influenza, and had it bad, but he was one of these iron-sided sorts whom salt water had pickled, and he weathered the flu and got so that he could sit up and have what the gunners called his "chow" brought to him.

The weather was perfect, and Jumbo sat there day after day with a happy smile; and sometimes he looked wistful, too, as if he would give ten years of his life to be down there working and knowing the joy of work. And after a time, it began to look as if Jumbo would have his wish gratified before long, because his appetite was picking up and color was coming back into his cheeks. He may have thought so himself, though nobody suggested it to him. At any rate he picked a dark night for his first effort at walking and fell off the roof of a motor truck to the foredeck and broke his leg in three places.

We were in the war zone then; the cruiser had left us, as her habit was on arriving at a mathematical line of longitude, regardless of whether the destroyers had picked us up or no; and it was in this gap that a good many of us were bagged. On this occasion we found the destroyers all about us in the morning; but they were French destroyers and had no surgeon on board. Later in the day we found an American patrol boat with a surgeon on board, dropped out of convoy and took on the surgeon.

He set Jumbo's leg with the aid of three men, two pints of ether and a block and tackle.

"Go ahead, regardless of me, gentlemen," Jumbo told them. He was ghastly pale, but he had lost nothing of that invincible cheerfulness. He was one of these fellows who fairly radiate unluckiness. Incidentally he gave me a bad watch picking up that convoy again toward dark, when I could no longer make out which leg of the zigzag they were on, or how I was going to ease in there, precisely. A bunch of ships like that will turn and dart like a school of minnows up a salt creek if just the shadow of trouble falls over them.

As soon as we docked, Jumbo Smith was taken ashore with his leg in a cast, and we began to get accounts of the wonderful time he was having, somewhere, surrounded with pretty nurses who were just fighting each other off over this hero who had bravely got his leg broken while sneaking through the war zone. Jumbo lay there looking like the original viking, and he told them it was nothing, nothing at all; any other man would have done the same.

One of his officers, who overheard this, told us that that was true, any other fool man would have done the same that took it into his lunkhead to go walking on the tops of automobiles on a dark night with a head sea driving into her. It was all hair for Jumbo. His gifted ears heard nothing but condolence. And after two weeks of that dream of fair women tender hands lifted him up and bore him back to his flagship, where he reclined on the boat deck in front of the hospital with a "Kiss me, Hardy" look depicted on his pale face.

THE LUCK OF JUMBO SMITH

But the sea air revived him, and he picked up wonderfully, made friends with the wireless, had the daily press shoved under his door or into his bunk each morning and conferred with his colleagues about the running of the ship during the morning hours. Cheerful. Always cheerful. But still with that old wistfulness in his eye when he would see good men going about their work on the decks below. Still, no man bore the burden of disappointed hopes better than he. Calm afternoons he spent getting the hang of his new crutches. And so, the old wagon purred and pounded across the North Atlantic, and Jumbo was lifted up again and put into a taxi and went nobody knew whither.

About a week later, when we had just got the rocks out of the ship and the wops were still swabbing up her limbers, we saw a man coming over the side whom we mistook for a rear admiral at the least. It was Jumbo Smith. He wore a uniform with beautiful golden propeller blades on the collar; he wore a cap with a great golden eagle perched just over the visor; he wore that golden smile which seemed to say, "What cheer, workmen?" He was tapping a British-looking cane against his one good knee, and—he boasted a wound stripe.

"Well," he said, "of course I told 'em it was nothing."

He had to be sheepish with that crowd. And there all those shirt-sleeved merchant-mariners—sea democrats, blood brothers to the kitchen democrats; those men who affected to abhor and spit upon uniforms but who secretly hankered after them as the hairy bee hankers after the lady flower, in Whitman's phrase; those men who had borne with him and propped him up and carried him on litters, and to whom he had been a burden like that which Christian bore on his way to the Eternal City, glared and glowered, and one of them said:

"Why, you bunch of sweet-smelling nothing, you long-drawn-out pinch of misery, is this what we get for being kind to you? Where was you wounded, at the Battle of Mobile Bay? Hey? Get off the burning deck! Did you tell them all about that time when the shrapnel was raining down on you? Did you tell them about being torpedoed and throwed up on the mahogany coast?"

"No, sir," said Jumbo Smith, with that same dogged cheerfulness, and the air of a man making the best of a bad business; "I hung to it that it was nothing; but shucks, they thought I was lying to them!"

I tell Jumbo's experience to show how pleasant life in a ship's hospital may be.

To return to the statutes: The seaman has certain rights of protest, but now that voyages are short I think his best remedy is to leave the ship if he has a grievance against it. I will state briefly some of his privileges, however. "If any member of the crew considers himself aggrieved . . . he shall represent the same to the master . . . in a quiet and orderly manner."

Brothers, I have seen ships where that took doing. Instance the case of old Patty Lee, a seaman who had been beating to windward for so many years that his beard streamed all one way. His brow had five permanent disapproval wrinkles bitten in by time and treatment. He made oath that the pea soup was nothing but rocks and gravel, and in his lion's voice he roared—in the fo'c'stle—that it was an outrage that able seamen should be forced to take it into their gizzards.

PICKINGS FOR SEA LAWYERS

Now be it said here, pea soup is the test of the sea cook, and no such soup is fairly in the great tradition unless it is soup of such sort that if you stand a spoon up in the middle of it the said spoon will continue to maintain the perpendicular after all adventitious aids have been withdrawn, like a pole sticking in a mud bank. That is the only sort of soup that will stick to the ribs. And that was emphatically not the sort of soup that old Patty in a quiet and orderly manner took aft one stormy noon, with a spoon supine in it, for the old man to try it with.

"I want to ask you, sir, if you think that is the sort of soup, sir, that ought to be put before a sailor, sir," said old Patty.

"Give it to the fishes, then," said the autocrat, and lifted his boot against it and kicked it, plate and all, into the sea; all in a quiet and orderly manner.

The sea lawyer still finds pickings. If he can get a majority of the crew in a foreign port to sign a paper that that ship is leaking dangerously or that she is "insufficiently supplied with sails, rigging, anchors," and so on, or that she is undermanned or that the provisions are rank or low, he can get the consul to appoint a committee of three to make a survey or look into the cause of the complaint.

As to sails, I think a good many steamships give cause of complaint by failing to carry them. If they once get out of coal or oil, as they very well may, or if their engines break down and they have no sails, they are in a bad way at once. There cannot well be conceived a more helpless object than a big steamship with nothing more to propel her than a couple of bridge awnings and a spare tarpaulin. It seems absurd that such should be the case, but I have known quite a few such ships to be lacking in sails altogether.

There is a wise provision against shipping seamen to work alternately in the fireroom and on deck. Men shipped for deck service cannot be put in the fireroom. I went decking on the Lakes once, but when I wasn't lifting hatches on and off, I was down below cleaning fires. One of my associates there after forty-eight hours of continuous service got word that he would be allowed to turn in at the end of a certain watch. Just as the watch, an eternity in itself, was about to end, the ship went off Eastern time, and we had to do the last hour over again. My associate came upon the mate in the act of twirling the minute hand of a clock back in a complete circle. At his last gasp he ventured to protest.

The mate, a hard case, ground out: "What's the matter? No sleep? You people make me sick! You can sleep all winter, can't you? Can't you even keep your eyes open summers?"

Here is another curious provision effective on American vessels, antiquated now that we are getting American crews for those vessels; and that is, that no vessel shall be permitted to depart from any port of the United States unless she has on board a crew not less than seventy-five per cent of whom are able to understand any order given by the officers of such a vessel. This will show as nothing else could the lamentable condition we were in. What would you say to a business conducted on shore wherein only seventy-five percent of the personnel knew what was being said to them? And how much more necessary to the safe voyaging of a great ship was it that her officers should be immediately understood, not by some proportion of the crew, but by every last man jack of them?

I once knew an old captain who said that born sailors knew well enough what wanted to be done by some kind of instinct; and he preferred to hire one or two sailors of each race, because such sailors couldn't plot or mutiny or foment trouble, conspiracy having as one of its first requirements that those conspiring shall be able to talk among themselves. As for myself I shall be glad to bid adieu forever to the sign language.

Every ship must carry a medicine chest, and every ship not a whaler must carry a slop chest. The medicine chest may indeed be sometimes what its name implies, a brass-bound chest, which gives out a pharmaceutical whiff whenever its lid is raised. The slop chest, however, is invariably a locker or seagoing shop full of things necessary to the sailorman. It was much maligned formerly as a sort of robber's den, and the captain was supposed to take three or four separate profits out of it and retire from the sea for the rest of his natural days.

THE SLOP-CHEST CEREMONY

To give a landlubber some notion of the look and function of the thing I will describe slop-chest night on the old *Juteopolis*. Saturday night was set apart for this ceremony. The sailmaker, who kept store, soaped and oiled his hair and even perfumed himself to make himself more worthy, and one of the apprentices sat at the end of the cabin with a great black book open in which he jotted down the articles taken away by the crew. A fine smell of tar, tobacco and oilskins came out of the place. The tobacco came in giant black plugs, so steeped in glycerin that no man could smoke it until he had first shaved it fine with an ax and tossed it up and down in a paper over the fo'c'stle lamp to dry it out. Besides tobacco, Sails would sell you stockings, shirts, underwear, pipes, sea boots, sheath knives. There was nothing resembling a ban on sheath knives on that ship. A man without one was a lame duck indeed.

Everybody talked in whispers, in guttural monosyllables, because the old man was felt to be not far away. He glowed through the partitions of sycamore and bird's-eye maple like some red-hot object slowly cooling there. Everybody felt queer to be in those intimate quarters and to be actually viewing the preserve dish on the sideboard out of which the great man ate. Therefore no one failed to be of that glum company. Let them rail all the rest of the week at the slop chest, Saturday night would find them there again listening to the scratching of the high and mighty apprentice's pen.

No, there was nothing like slop-chest night to break the back of the sea's monotony. No night was too wild and no sea too heavy to prevent the watch below from mustering aft in anticipation of that majestic ceremony. Robbery it might be; but unholy fascinating work too. My recent experience has been that you can buy cheaper and better onboard ship than ashore. I have not bought shoes ashore for nearly two years.

A further clause is to the effect that if a foreign voyage is to exceed fourteen days the ship must carry in the slop chest at least one suit of woolen clothing for each seaman. The statute looked out for them, since experience showed that they did not look out for themselves.

There used to be, of course, hard cases who would stick out against the seductions of the slop chest. I remember that little whiskery boson with the dread voice and the silvery spotted forearms, who preferred paddling his feet about in the bitter waters of the Antarctic Ocean, when washing down mornings, to buying sea boots out of the slop chest. He would have climbed out on an iceberg barefooted sooner than have resorted to that robber's cave. Blue-footed, black-hearted, red-rimmed, he toughed his watches through. And then, when he jumped the ship in Sydney, he stole the captain's overcoat and carried it on his shoulders sixty miles through blistering heat, only to have it stolen from him in turn when he got to Newcastle. He told me the sad story later in Melbourne.

THE OLD TRIBE AND THE NEW

There was a fine example of old-school seaman, by the way. A small body; terrible hands—invincible hands if once they closed on your throat, squirm how you would; a voice as deep as a horn; and a knowledge of the wiles of seamanship as wide as the sea itself. He was like a raw breath down the backs of the watch on deck. He had come out of a prison ship on the Mersey; no man had seen more horrors; he held everybody on that ship under the leash of his rugged physical experience. I would have trusted more to the instant judgment of that ignorant little cockney, with his eyes of a wild boar about to charge, than to the captain of the ship. He could sense things better. He had more seamanship. I seem to feel the heel of that iron hand nipping my fingers as we sway together on the braces, the black foresail bellowing overhead, water falling over the weather fence with a roar, the wild cries of the watch on desk making confusion worse confounded. All my five senses kicked out naked in the lap of things; but I felt obscurely that bos' could see through that snarl. That little man could be guaranteed to function as a seaman in all weathers. Like a well-jeweled watch, he could run true in any one of five positions. Yet when ashore he was a poor outcast who begged for pennies at street corners, helping his cause by a trick he had of throwing his wrists out of joint and glaring at you with rum-dumb eyes.

I do not hope to make our new tribe of seamen out of such as he. I rely rather on the many young men whom the Army and Navy will discharge, men who have looked into the bright face of danger and can never again quite get the dazzle out of their eyes. I think a good many of them will reject the prosaic terms of their old life if they can lay hold of a trade or profession which will satisfy their craving for adventure and yet be a solid achievement too.

Well, here it lies, ready to their hand. They are the men for it. Here is one, a flight commander, aghast at the somber thought of a return to civil life, who writes me: "My Fitness Report classifies me as an expert pilot, calm, forceful, overbold, with excellent initiative."

These are the men for our money if they can be induced to take seamen's wages while they are learning the sea, with a good prospect of advancement. Time and tide will sever the "over" from the "bold"; and for the rest these are the very men whom the tall water delights to fashion and make her own. I am convinced that we have unlimited resources in them.

THE HARBOR MASTER

From *Harper's Monthly* (June/July 1921)

A marvelous tale of a shy, reclusive man, the harbor master, and his seduction by the New England town's most mysterious, willful, and sexy woman, Caddie Sills. The plot twists its way to a dark ending, turning on the sale of a string of pearls sold by Caddie to reclaim the bankrupted ship of a former lover.

Coming ashore one summer's night from Meteor Island, Jethro Rackby was met by Peter Loud—Deepwater Peter he was called, because even so early he had gone one foreign voyage. Peter was going round with a paper containing the subscription to a dance.

"Come, Harbor Master," he said; "put your thumb mark in the corner along with the rest of us."

Rackby drew back. "Why should I dance?" he muttered.

He was town clerk as well as harbor master—a scholarly man with visionary, pale eyes, and a great solitary, as Peter knew.

"Why? I'll tell you why," said Peter. "To bring joy to Caddie Sills's heart, if nothing more. The girl would throw all the rest of us in a heap to-morrow for a firm hold of you, Rackby."

He winked at Zinie Shadd, who swayed on his heels soberly.

Rackby turned his eyes toward the black mound of Meteor Island, which lay like a shaggy stone Cerberus at the harbor's mouth.

The star-pointed harbor was quiet at his feet. Shadows in the water were deep and languid, betokening an early fall of rain through the still air. But from the rim of the sea, where the surf was seen only as a white glow waxing and waning, a constant drone was borne in to them—a thunder of the white horses' hoofs trampling on Pull-an'-be-Damned; the vindictive sound of seas falling down one after another on wasted rocks, on shifting sand bars—a powerful monotone seeming to increase in the ear with fuller attention. The contrast was marked between the heavy-lying peace of the inner harbor and that hungry reverberation from without of waters seeking fresh holds along a mutilated coast. On damp nights when the wind hauled to the southeast, men stood still in their tracks, and said, simply, "There's the Old Roke," as if it was the Old Man of the Sea himself. The sound was a living personality in their ears. . . . Women whom the sea had widowed shivered and rattled irons when the Old Roke came close to their windows; but the men listened, as if they had been called—each by his own name.

"What's the ringle jingle of feet by the side of that?" Rackby said, his mystified face turned toward the water. "I'm a man for slow tunes, Peter. No, no, no; put your paper up again."

"No? You're a denying sort of a crab, and no mistake. Always seeing how fast you can crawl backward out of pleasure."

"I mistrust women."

"You cleave to the spirit and turn from the flesh, that I know. But here's a woman with a voice to waken the dead."

"That's the voice on the seaward side of Meteor," answered Rackby.

"Cad Sills is flesh and blood of the Old Roke, I'm agreed," said Deepwater Peter. "She's a seafaring woman, that's certain. Next door to ending in a fish's tail, too, sometimes I think, when I see her carrying on. . . . Maybe you've seen her sporting with the horseshoe crabs and all o' that at Pull-an'-be-Damned?"

"No, I can't say that."

"No, it wasn't to be expected, you with your head and shoulders walking around in a barrel of jam."

The harbor master smiled wistfully.

"More I don't require," he said.

"Ah, so you say now. . . . Well, marry the sea, then. It's a slippery embrace, take the word of a man who has gone foreign voyages."

"I mistrust the sea," said Jethro.

"So you do. . . . You mistrust the sea and the like o' that, and you mistrust women and the like o' that. There's too much heaving and tossing in such waters for a harbor master, hey?"

"I'm at home here, that's a fact," said Jethro. "I know the tides and the buoys. I can find my way in the dark, where another man would be at a total loss. I'm never suffering for landmarks."

"Landmarks!" roared Deepwater Peter. "What's a landmark good for but to take a new departure?"

To the sea-goers, tilted on a bench in the shadow of the Customs House, he added, "What life must be without a touch of lady fever is more than I can tell."

A red-bearded viking at the end of the bench rose and took Peter's shoulders in a fearful grip.

"What's all this talk of lady fever?"

"Let be, Cap'n Dreed!" cried Peter. His boisterousness failed him like wind going out of a sail. He twisted out of the big seaman's grip and from a distance shouted, "If you weren't so cussed bashful, you might have had something more than a libel pinned to your mainmast by now, with all this time in port."

There was a general shifting along the bench, to make room for possible fray. It was a sore point with Sam Dreed that the ship chandler had that day effected a lien for labor on his ship, and the libel was nailed to the mast.

"Now they'll scandalize each other," murmured Zinie Shadd.

They were turned from that purpose only by the sudden passing at their backs of the woman in question, Caddie Sills.

Quiet reigned. The older men crossed their legs, sat far down on their spines, and narrowed their eyes. The brick wall of the Customs House, held from collapsing by a row of rusty iron stairs, seemed to bulge more than its wont for the moment—its upper window, a ship's deadlight, round and expressionless as the eye of a codfish.

Cad Sills ran her eye over them deftly, as if they were the separate strings of an instrument which could afford gratification to her only when swept lightly all at one time by her tingling finger tips, or, more likely, by the intangible plectrum in her black eye.

The man she selected for her nod was Sam Dreed, however.

Peter Loud felt the walls of his heart pinch together with jealousy.

It was all in a second's dreaming. "Gape and swallow," as Zinie Shadd said, from his end of the bench. The woman passed with a supercilious turn of her head away from them.

"That's a footloose woman if ever there was one."

With all her gift of badinage, she was a solitary soul. The men feared
no less than they admired her. They were shy of that wild courage,
fearful to put so dark a mystery to the solution. The women hated her,
backbit, and would not make friends, because of the fatal instantaneous
power she wielded to spin men's blood and pitch their souls derelict on
that impassioned current. Who shall put his finger on the source of this
power? There were girls upon girls with eyes as black, cheeks as like
hers as fruit ripened on the same bough, hair as thick and lustrous . . .
yet at the sound of Caddie Sills's bare footfall eyes shifted and glowed,
and in the imaginations of these men the women of their choice grew
pale as the ashes that fringe a fallen fire.

"She's a perilous woman," muttered the collector of the port. "Sticks
in the slant of a man's eye like the shadow of sin. Ah! there he goes,
like the leaves of autumn."

Samuel Dreed trod the dust of the road with a wonderful swaying of
his body, denominated the Western Ocean roll. He was a mighty man,
all were agreed; not a nose of wax, even for Cad Sills to twist.

"Plump she'll go in his canvas bag, along with his sea boots and his
palm and needle, if she's not precious careful, with her shillyshallying,"
said Zinie Shadd. "I know the character of the man, from long acquaintance, and I know that what he says he'll do he'll do, and no holding off
at arm's length, either, for any considerable period of time."

Such was the situation of Cad Sills. A dark, lush, ignorant, entrancing
woman, for whose sake decent men stood ready to drop their principles
like rags—yes, at a mere secret sign manifested in her eye, where the
warmth of her blood was sometimes seen as a crimson spark alighted
on black velvet. She went against the good government of souls.

Even Rackby had taken note of her once, deep as his head was in
the clouds by preference and custom. It was a day in late November.
No snow had fallen, and she floated past him like a cloud shadow as
he plodded in the yellow road which turned east at the Preaching Tree.
She passed, looked back, slashed a piece of dripping kelp through the
air so close that salt drops stung his pale eyes, laughed aloud, and at
the top of her laugh, broke into a wild, sweet song unfamiliar to him.
It was a voice unlike the flat voices of women thereabouts—strong,
sweet, sustained, throbbing with a personal sense of the passion which
lurked in the warm notes.

Her foot was bare, and more shapely in consequence than if she had had a habit of wearing shoes. Its shape was the delicate shape of strength native to such a foot, and each toe left its print distinct and even in the dust. With his eye for queer details, he remembered that print and associated with it the yellow rutted road, the rusty alders in the meadow beyond, and the pale spire of the church thrust into a November sky.

He called this to mind when on the night of the dance information came to his ear that she had sold her pearls to lift the lien on Cap'n Sam Dreed's ship, with her own hands tearing down the libel from the mast and grinding it under her heel.

No man whom she had once passed and silently interrogated could quite forget her, not even Jethro Rackby. The harbor master swayed on his oars, collected himself, and looked forward across the dimpled floor of his harbor, which in its quietude was like a lump of massy silver or rich ore, displaying here and there a spur of light, a surface sparkle. The serenity of his own soul was in part a reflection of this nightly calm, when the spruce on the bank could not be known from its fellow in the water by a man standing on his head. Moreover, to maintain this calm was the plain duty of the harbor master. For five years he had held that office by an annual vote of the town meeting. With his title went authority to say where were the harbor lines, to order the removal of hulks, to provide for keeping open a channel through winter ice—in a word, to keep the peace. This peace was of his own substance.

It was rudely shattered. On the night following the dance Cad Sills put herself in his path for the second time and this time she gave him short shrift. He was pushing forward, near sundown, to take the impulse of an eddy at the edge of Pull-an'-be-Damned when he saw that predatory, songful woman balanced knee-deep in rushing water, her arms tossing.

"She's drowning herself after her quarrel with Sam Dreed," was his first thought. He had just heard a fine tale of that quarrel. The truth was not quite so bold. She had been caught by the tide, which, first peering over the rim of that extended flat, had then shot forth a frothy tongue, and in a twinkling lapped her up.

Jethro presently brought up the webs of his two thumbs hard at her armpits, and took her into his boat, dripping.

"She's not so plump as she was ashore," he said to himself with a vague astonishment. She was as lean as a man at the hips, and finned away like a mermaid, as became a daughter of the Old Roke.

"Steady now, my girl. . . . Heave and away."

There they stood confronting each other. Enraptured, life given into her hand again, Cad Sills flung her arms about his neck and kissed him—a moist, full-budded, passionate, and salty kiss. Even on the edge of doom, it was plain, she would not be able to modulate, tone, or contain these kisses, each of which launched a fiery barb into the recipient's bosom.

The little fisherman had not known what elemental thing was in a kiss before. He bit his lip and fell back slowly. Then, after a second's vain reflection, he seized the butts of his oars, which had begun to knock together. Caddie Sills sank across a thwart and shivered a little to mark the crowding together of white horses at the very place where she had stood. Contrary currents caused the tide to horse in strongly over Pull-an'-be-Damned.

"What a ninny!" she whispered. "Was I sick with love, I wonder?"

The harbor master answered with the motion of his oars.

She glanced at him shrewdly, then struck her hands together at her breast, which she caused to rise and fall stormily. She was, in fact, a storm petrel in the guise of woman.

"You have saved my life," she cried out, "when not another man in all this world would have lifted so much as his little finger. Do what you will with me after this. Let me be your slave, your dog. . . . I am a lost woman if you will not take pity on me."

Rackby's heart came into his throat with the slow surge of a sculpin on a hook.

"Nothing. . . . Nothing at all. Nothing in the world. I happened along. . . . Just a happen so."

The girl stood up, looked at him long and long, cried, "Thank you for nothing, then, Mr. Happen-so," and from the humility of gratitude she went to the extreme of impudence, and laughed in his face—a ringing, brazen laugh, with the wild sweetness in it which he had noted in the song she sang on that November hillside.

"You're a caution, little man, you're a caution," she said, slanting her lashes. "You certainly are. I've heard of you. Yes, I have, only this morning. I'm a solitary like yourself. See here. You and I could set the world on fire if we joined hands. Do you know that?"

The little man was struck dumb at his oars for very fear of the boldness of her advance. He recognized this for an original and fearsome, not to say delectable, vein of talk. She came on like the sea itself, impetuous and all-embracing. Unfathomed, too. Could fancy itself construct a woman so, pat to his hand?

"Is it true that you despise women as they say?" she whispered. She breathed close and electrified the tip of his ear with a tendril of hair. He saw that she wore coral now, in place of the pearls. But her lips were redder than the coral. He raised his head.

"Yesterday morning you sold pearls for the benefit of Sam Dreed," he said, in dull tones. "And here you are with your brimstone fairly in my boat."

He looked at her as if the Old Roke himself had clambered into the boat, with his spell of doom.

"I am not afraid of helping honest men in trouble that I know of," said Cad Sills, sucking in her lower lip. "But do you throw that up to me?"

Jethro felt the wickedness of his position like a breath of fire fanning his cheek. Perilously tempted, he sagged back on the oars without a word.

"Soho! you're setting me ashore," said that dark woman, laughing. "I don't wear very well in the eye and that's a plain conclusion."

She laid a finger to her breast, and her eye mocked him. This brazen hardness put him from his half-formed purpose. He addressed himself to the oars, and the dory grated on the shore.

"Good-by, then, little man," she said, springing past him.

But even now she lingered and looked back, biting the coral and letting it fall, intimating that a word, a whispered syllable, might lay her low.

He sat like a man crushed to earth. When he raised his head, she was gone.

Was this the voice from the seaward side of Meteor? True, the sea had yielded this wild being up, but did she speak with the sea's voice? She had at least the sea's inconstancy, the sea's abandonment.

Her words were hot and heavy in little Rackby's heart. Serene harbor master that he was, the unearthly quiet of his harbor was an affront upon him in his present mood. Now that she was lost to him, he could not, by any make-shift of reason, be rid of the impulse that had come upon him to jump fairly out of his own skin in an effort to recapture that tormenting woman. . . .

He drifted down upon Meteor Island, bowed and self-reproachful, like a spirit approaching the confines of the dead. He stepped ashore and passed the painter of his dory through its ring.

On the crest of the island, at the very spot where, scientists averred, a meteorite had fallen in some prehistoric age, there stood a thick grove, chiefly of hemlock trees. Here on this night he paused. A strange inertness filled all nature. Not a whisper from the branches overhead, not a rustle from the dark mold underfoot. Moonlight in one place flecked the motionless leaves of an alder. Trunk and twigs were quite dissolved in darkness—nothing but the silver pattern of the leaves was shown in random sprays. He felt for an instant disembodied, like these leaves— as if, taking one step too many, he had floated out of his own body and might not return.

"Bear and forbear," he thought. "You wouldn't have stirred, let her say what she would," his heart whispered to the silver leaves.

But he could not forget that wild glance, the wet hand clinging to his wrist, the laugh repeated like an echo from the symphony of that November hillside. He reproached himself withal. What was known of Cad Sills? Little known, and nothing cared to be known. A waif, pursuing him invisibly with a twinkle or flare from her passionate eyes. She was the daughter of a sea captain by his fifth wife. He had escaped the other four. They had died or been deserted in foreign ports, but this one he could not escape. Tradition had it that he lost the figure-head from his ship on the nuptial voyage, attributed this disaster to his bride, and so left her at Rosario, only to find her, after all sail was set, in the forechains, at the very stem of his ship, half drowned, her arms outstretched, a living figurehead. She had swum after him. She outlived him, too, and died in giving birth to Cad Sills, whose blood had thus a trace of sea water. . . .

He entered his house. In his domestic arrangements he was the very figure of a bachelor. His slimsy silver spoon, dented with toothmarks of an ancestor who had died in a delirium, was laid evenly by his plate. The hand lamps on the shelf wore speckled brown-paper bags inverted over their chimneys. A portrait of a man playing the violin hung out, in massive gilt, over the table, like a ship's figurehead projecting over a wharf's end. His red couch bore northeast and southwest, so that he might not lose good sleep by opposing his body to the flow of magnetic currents.

On this night he drew out from a hole in the upholstery of the couch a bag of stenciled canvas, which chinked. It was full of money, in gold and silver pieces. He counted it, and sat thoughtful. Later he went out of the house and stood looking at the sea as if for a sign. But the sea gave him no sign; and on that night at least had no voice.

It was three days before he came up with Cad Sills again. Then he spied her at nightfall, reclining under the crabapple tree at Hannan's Landing.

The little man came close enough to tread on her shadows, cleared his throat, and almost shouted:

"Did you mean what you said? Did you mean what you said, girl?"

She laughed and threw the core of an apple in his direction.

"I did when I said it, Mr. Happen-so. I did when I said it."

"I'm ready. . . . I'm ready now. We'll be married tomorrows if you don't mind."

"But will I sell my cabbages twice, I wonder? I've had a change of heart since, if I must tell you."

"Surely not in this short space of time," Rackby gasped, dismayed.

A light throbbed in her eye. "Well, perhaps I haven't."

The storm petrel hovered high, swooped close, her lips parted. Her teeth shone with a native luster, as if she had lived on roots and tough things all her life. Again, little Rackby felt that glow of health and hardness in her person, as if one of the cynical and beautiful immortals of the Greeks confronted him. He was heartily afraid of her mystifying power of enchantment, which seemed to betray him to greater lengths than he had dreamed. Even now perhaps all was lost.

"I will meet you tonight, then . . . at the top of the hill. See? By the Preaching Tree."

She nodded her head toward the church corner. "At eight, sharp, by the west face of the clock. And, mind you, Mr. Man, not one jot late or early."

Although he heard the quick fall of her feet in the dust grow fainter, it pleased him not to turn. There was a prickling above his heart and at the cords of his throat. The harbor was as blue as a map suddenly unrolled at his feet. Clouds with a purple warp were massing in the east.

The harbor master stared hard at the low ridge of an outlying island where a cow had been put to pasture. The hillocky back of that lone ruminant grew black as ink in the glow of sunset. The creature exhibited a strange fixity of outline, as if it had been a chance configuration of rocks. Rackby in due time felt a flaming impatience shoot upward from his heels. Water soughed and chuckled at the foot of the crabapple tree, but these eager little voices could no longer soothe or even detain him with their familiar assurances.

He jumped up and stared hard at the west face of the clock, whose gilt hands were still discernible in the fading light. It was five minutes of eight.

When he slipped into the shadow of the Preaching Tree it had grown dark. Fitful lightning flashed. In the meadow fireflies were thick. They made him think of the eager beating of many fiery little hearts, exposed by gloom, lost again in that opalescent glare on the horizon against which the ragged leaves of elm and maple were hung like blobs of ink or swarms of bees.

He breathed fast; he heard mysterious fluted calls. A victim of torturing uncertainty, he strained his ear for that swift footfall. Suddenly he felt her come upon him from behind, buoyant, like a warm wave, and press firm hands over his eyelids. Her hair stung his cheek like ware.

"Guess three times."

Rackby felt the strong beat of that adventurous heart like drums of conquest. He crushed her in his arms until she all but cried out. There was nothing he could say. Her breath carried the keen scent of crushed checkerberry plums. She had been nibbling at tender pippins by the way, like a wild thing.

The harbor master remembered later that he seemed to have twice the number of senses appointed to mortals in that hour. A heavy fragrance fell through the dusk out of the thick of the horse-chestnut tree. A load of hay went by, the rack creaking, the driver sunk well out of sight. He heard the dreaming note of the tree toad; frogs croaked in the lush meadow, water babbled under the crazy wooden sidewalk. . . . The meadow was one vast pulse of fireflies. He felt this industrious flame enter his own wrists.

Then the birches over the way threshed about in a gust of wind. Almost at once rain fell in heavy drops; blinds banged to and fro, a strong smell of dust was in his nostrils, beat up from the road by driving rain.

The girl first put the palm of her hand hard against his cheek, then yielded, with a pliant and surprising motion of the whole body. Her eyes were full of a strange, bright wickedness. Like torches they seemed to cast a crimson light on the already glowing cheek.

Fascinated by this thought, Rackby bent closer. The tented leaves of the horse-chestnut did not stir. Surely the dusky cheek had actually a touch of crimson in the gloom.

This effect, far from being an illusion was produced by a lantern in the fist of a man swinging toward them with vast strides. And now the clock, obeying its north face, struck eight.

Before the last stroke had sounded the girl was made aware of the betraying light. She whirled out of Rackby's arms and ran toward Sam Dreed. The big viking stood with his feet planted well apart, and a mistrustful finger in his beard.

"Touch and go!" cried Caddie Sills, falling on his neck. "Do we go at the top of the tide, mister?"

"What hellion is that under the trees?" he boomed at her, striking the arm down savagely.

"You will laugh when you see," said Cad Sills, wrung with pain, but returning to him on the instant.

"On the wrong side of my face, maybe."

"Can't you see? It's the little harbor master."

"Ah! and standing in the same piece of dark with you, my girl."

Cad Sills laughed wildly. "Did ever I look for more thanks than this from any mortal man? Then I'm not disappointed. But let me ask you, have you taken your ship inside the island to catch the tide?"

"Yes."

"Oh, you have. And would you have done that with the harbor master looking on? Hauled short across the harbor lines? Maybe you think I have a whole chest of pearls at your beck and call, Sam Dreed. Oh, what vexation! Here I hold the little man blindfolded by my wiles . . . and this is my thanks!"

The voice was tearful with self-pity.

"Is that so, my puss?" roared the seaman, melted in a flash. He swung the girl by the waist with his free arm. "You *have* got just enough natural impudence for the tall water and no mistake. Come along."

"Wait!" cried Jethro Rackby. He stepped forward. He felt the first of many wild pangs in thus subjecting himself to last insult. "Where are you going?"

The words had the pitiful vacuity of a detaining question. For what should it matter to Jethro where she went, if she went in company with Sam Dreed?

"How can I tell you that, little man?" Cad Sills flung over her shoulder at him. "The sea is wide and uncertain."

Her full cheek, with its emphatic curve, was almost gaunt in the moment when she fixed her eyes on the wolfish face of that tousle-headed giant who encircled her. Her shoulder blades were pinched back; the line of the marvelous full throat lengthened; she devoured the man with a vehemence of love, brief and fierce as the summer lightning which played below the dark horizon.

She was gone, planting that aerial foot willfully in the dust. Rain-drops ticked from one to another of the broad, green leaves over the harbor master's head. Water might be heard frothing in a nearby cistern.

Suddenly the moon glittered on the parson's birch-wood pile and slanted a beam under the Preaching Tree. Sunk in the thick dust which the rain had slightly stippled in slow droppings, he saw the tender prints of a bare foot, and the cruel tracks of the seaman's great, square-toed boots pointing together toward the sea.

He raised his eyes only with a profound effort. They encountered a blackboard affixed to the fat trunk of the Preaching Tree, on which from day to day the parson wrote the text for its preachments in colored chalk. The moon was full upon it, and Rackby saw in crimson lettering the words, "Woman, hath no man damned thee?" The rest of the text he had rubbed out with his own shoulders in turning to take the girl into his arms.

"I damn ye!" he cried, raising his arms wildly. "Yes, by the Lord, I damn ye up and down. May you burn as I burn, where the worm dieth not, and the fires are not quenched."

So saying, he set his foot down deliberately on the first of the light footprints she had made in springing from his side—as if he might as easily as that blot out the memory of his enslavement.

Thereafter the Customs House twitted him, as if it knew the full extent of his shame. Zinie Shadd called after him to know if he had heard that voice from the sea yet, in his comings and goings.

"Peter Loud was not so easy hung by the heels," that aged loiterer affirmed, "shipping as he did along with the lady herself, as bo's'n for Cap'n Sam Dreed."

Jethro Rackby took to drink somewhat, to drown these utterances, or perhaps to quench some stinging thirst within him which he knew not to be of the soul.

When certain of the elders asked him why he did not cut the drink and take a decent wife, he laughed like a demon, and cried out:

"What's that but to swap the devil for a witch?"

Others he met with a counter question:

"Do you think I will tie a knot with my tongue that I can't untie with my teeth?"

So he sat by himself at the back windows of a water-front saloon, and when he caught a glimpse of the water shining there low in its channels he would shut his lips tight. . . . Who could have thought that it would be the sea itself to throw in his path the woman who had set this blistering agony in his soul? There it lay like rolled glass; the black piles under the footbridge were prolonged to twice their length by their own shadows, so that the bridge seemed lifted enormously high out of water. Beyond the bridge the seine pockets of the mackerel men hung on the shrouds like black cobwebs, and the ships had a blighting look of funeral ships. . . .

He had mistrusted the sea. It was life; it was death; flows slack, and ebb—and his pulse followed it.

Officials of the Customs House could testify that for better than a year, if he mentioned women at all, it was in a tone to convey that his fingers had been sorely burned in that flame and smarted still.

The second autumn from that moment under the Preaching Tree, found him of the same opinion still. He trod the dust a very phantom, while little leaves of cardinal red spun past his nose like the ebbing heart's blood of full-bodied summer. The long leaves of the sumach, too, were like guilty fingers dipped in blood. But the little man paid no heed to the analogies which the seasons presented to his conscience in their dying. Though he thought often of his curse, he had not lifted it. But when he saw a cluster of checkerberry plums in spring gleam withered red against gray moss, on some stony upland, he stood still and pondered.

Then, on a night when the fall wind was at its mightiest and shook the house on Meteor Island as if clods of turf had been hurled against it, he took down his Bible from its stand. At the first page to which he turned, his eye rested on the words, "Woman, hath no man damned thee?"

He bent close, his hand shook, and his blunt finger traced the remainder of that text which he and Cad Sills together had unwittingly erased from the Preaching Tree.

"No man, Lord." . . . "Neither do I damn thee: go, and sin no more."

He left the Bible standing open and ran out-of-doors.

The hemlock grove confronted him a mass of solid green. Night was coming on, as if with an ague, in a succession of coppery cold squalls which had not yet overtaken the dying west. In that quarter the sky was like a vast porch of crimson woodbine.

When this had sunk, night gave a forlorn and indistinguishable look to everything. A spark of ruddy light glowed deep in the valley. The rocking outlines of the hills were lost in rushing darkness. At his back sounded the pathetic clatter of a dead spruce against its living neighbor, bespeaking the deviltry of woodland demons. . . . It was the hour which makes all that man can do seem as nothing in the mournful darkness, causing his works to vanish and be as if they had not been.

At this hour the heart of man may be powerfully stirred, by an anguish, a prayer, or perhaps—a fragrance.

The harbor master, uttering a brief cry, dropped to his knees and remained mute, his arms extended toward the sea in a gesture of reconcilement.

On that night the *Sally Lunn*, Cap'n Sam Dreed, was wrecked on the sands of Pull-an'-be-Damned.

Rackby, who had fallen into a deep sleep, lying northeast and southwest, was awakened by a hand smiting his door in, and a wailing outside of the Old Roke busy with his agonies. In a second his room was full of crowding seamen, at their head Peter Loud, bearing in his arms the dripping form of Caddie Sills. He laid her gently on the couch.

"Where did you break up?" whispered Rackby. He trembled like a leaf.

"Pull-an'-be-Damned," said Deepwater Peter. "The Cap'n's gone. He didn't come away. Men can say what they like of Sam Dreed; he wouldn't come into the boat. I'll tell all the world that."

The crew of the wrecked ship stood heaving and glittering in their oils, plucking their beards with a sense of trespass, hearing the steeple clock tick, and water drum on the worn floor.

"All you men clear out," said Caddie Sills, faintly. "Leave me here with Jethro Rackby."

They set themselves in motion, pushing one against the other with a rasp and shriek of oilskins—and Peter Loud last of all.

The harbor master, not knowing what to say, took a step away from her, came back, and, looking into her pale face, cried out, horror struck, "I damned ye." He dropped on his knees. "Poor girl! I damned ye out and out."

"Hold your horses, Mr. Happen-so," said Cad Sills. "There's no harm in that. I was damned and basted good and brown before you ever took me across your little checkered apron."

She looked at him almost wistfully, as if she had need of him. With her wet hair uncoiling to the floor, she looked as if she had served, herself, for a fateful living figurehead, like her mother before her. The bit of coral was still slung round her throat. The harbor master recalled with what a world of meaning she had caught it between her teeth, on the night of his rescue—the eyes with a half-wistful light as now.

"Come," she said, "Harbor Master. I wasn't good to you, that's true; but still you have done me a wrong in your turn, you say?"

"I hope God will forgive me," said the harbor master.

"No doubt of that, little man. But maybe you would feel none the worse for doing me a favor, feeling as you do."

"Yes, yes."

Her hand sought his. "You see me—how I am. I shall not survive my child, for my mother did not before me. Listen. You are town clerk. You write the names of the newborn on a sheet of ruled paper and that is their name?"

Rackby nodded.

"So much I knew. . . . Come. How would it be if you gave my child your name . . . Rackby? Don't say no to me. Say you will. Just the scratching of a pen, and what a deal of hardship she'll be saved not to be known as Cad Sills over again."

Her hand tightened on his wrist. Recollecting how they had watched the tide horse over Pull-an'-be-Damned thus, he said, eagerly, "Yes, yes, if so be 'tis a she," thinking nothing of the consequences of his promise.

"Now I can go happy," murmured Cad Sills.

"Where will you go?" said the harbor master, timorously, feeling that she was whirled out of his grasp a second time.

"How should I know?" lisped Caddie Sills, with a remembering smile. "The sea is wide and uncertain, little man."

The door opened again. A woman appeared and little Rackby was thrust out among the able seamen.

Three hours later he came and looked down on Cad Sills again. Rain still beat on the black windows. Her lips were parted, as if she were only weary and asleep. But in one glance he saw that she had no need to lie northeast and southwest to make certain of unbroken sleep.

To the child born at the height of the storm the harbor master gave a name, his own—Rackby. He was town clerk, and he gave her this name when he came to register her birth on the broad paper furnished by the government. And for a first name, Day, as coming after that long night of his soul, perhaps.

When this was known, he was fined by the government two hundred dollars. Such is the provision in the statutes, in order that there may be no compromise with the effects of sin.

The harbor master did not regret. He reckoned his life anew from that night when he sat in the dusk with the broad paper before him containing the names of those newly born.

So the years passed, and Day Rackby lived ashore with her adoptive father. When she got big enough, they went by themselves and reopened the house on Meteor Island.

The man was still master of the harbor, but he could not pretend that his authority extended to the sea beyond. There he lost himself in speculation, sometimes wondering if Deepwater Peter had found a thing answering his quest. But Peter did not return to satisfy him on this point.

The harbor master was content to believe that he had erred on the side of the flesh, and that the sea, a jealous mistress, had swept him into the hearing of the gods, who were laughing at him.

As for the child of Cad Sills, people who did not know her often said that her eyes were speaking eyes. Well if it were so, since this voice in the eyes was all the voice she had. She could neither speak nor hear from birth. It was as if kind nature had sealed her ears against those seductive whisperings which—so the gossips said—had been the ruination of her mother.

As she grew older, they said behind their hands that blood would tell, in spite of all. Then, when they saw the girl skipping along the shore with kelp in her hands they said, mistrustfully, that she was "marked" for the sea, beyond the shadow of a doubt.

"She hears well enough, when the sea speaks," Zinie Shadd averred. He had caught her listening in a shell with an intent expression.

"She will turn out to be a chip of the old block," said Zinie Shadd's wife, "or I shall never live to see the back of my neck."

Jethro Rackby heard nothing of such prophecy. He lived at home. Here in his estimation was a being without guile, in whose innocence he might rejoice. His forethought was great and pathetic. He took care that she should learn to caress him with her fingertips alone. He remembered the fatal touch of Cad Sills's kiss at Pull-an'-be-Damned, which had as good as drawn the soul out of his body in a silver thread and tied it in a knot.

Once, too, he had dreamed of waking cold in the middle of the night and finding just a spark on the ashes of his hearth. This lie nursed to flame; the flame sprang up waist-high, hot and yellow. Fearful, he beat it down to a spark again. But then again, he was cold. He puffed at this spark, shivering; the flame grew, and this time, with all he could do, it shot up into the rafters of his house and devoured it. . . .

So it was that the passion of Cad Sills lived with him still.

He taught the child her letters with blue shells, and later to take the motion of his lips for words. She waylaid him everywhere—on the rocks, on the sands, in the depths of the hemlock grove, on tiny antlers of gray caribou moss, with straggling little messages and admonishings of love. Her apron pocket was never without its quota of these tiny shells of brightest peacock blue. They trailed everywhere. He ground them under heel at the threshold of his house. From long association they came to stand for so many inquisitive little voices in themselves, beseeching, questioning, defying.

But for his part, he grew to have a curious belief, even when her head was well above his shoulder, that the strong arch of her bosom must ring out with wild sweet song one day, like that which he had heard on the November hillside, when Caddie Sills had run past him at the Preaching Tree. This voice of Day's was like the voice sleeping in the great bronze horn hanging in a rack, which his father had used to call the hands to dinner, A little wind meant no sound, but a great effort, summoning all the breath in the body, made the brazen throat ring out like a viking's horn, wild and sweet.

So with Day, if an occasion might be great enough to call it forth.

"He always was a notional little man," the women said, on hearing this. The old bachelor was losing his wits. Such doctrine as he held made him out not one whit better off than Zinie Shadd, who averred that the heart of man was but a pendulum swaying in his bosom—though how it still moved when he stood on his head was more than even Zinie Shadd could fathom, to be sure.

"It's the voice of conscience he's thinking of, to my judgment," said one. "That girl is deefer than a haddock and dumb as the stone."

Untouched by gossip, the harbor master felt with pride that his jewel among women was safe, and that here, within four humble walls, he treasured up a being literally without guile, one who grew straight and white as a birch sapling. "Pavilioned in splendor" were the words descriptive of her which he had heard thunderously hymned in church. The hair heavy on her brow was of the red gold of October.

If they might be said to be shipmates sailing the same waters, they yet differed in the direction of their gaze. The harbor master fixed his eyes upon the harbor; but little Day turned hers oftenest upon the blue sea itself, whose mysterious inquietude he had turned from in dismay.

True, the harbor was not without its fascination for her. Leaning over the side of his dory, the sea girl would shiver with delight to descry those dismal forests over which they sailed, dark and dizzying masses full of wavering black holes, through which sometimes a blunt-nosed bronze fish sank like a bolt, and again where sting ray darted, and jelly-fish palpitated with that wavering of fringe which produced the faintest of turmoil at the surface of the water.

This would be at the twilight hour when warm airs alternated with cold, like hopes with despairs. Sparbuoys of silver gray were duplicated in the water, wrinkled like a snout at the least ripple from the oars.

Boats at anchor seemed twice their real size by reason of their dark shadows made one with them. One by one the yellow riding lights were hung, far in. They shone like new-minted coins; the harbor was itself a purse of black velvet, to which the harbor master held the strings. The quiet—the immortal quiet—operated to restore his soul. But at such times Day would put the tips of her fingers mysteriously to her incarnadined dumb lips and appear to hearken on the seaward side. If a willful light came sometimes in her eyes, he did not see it.

But even on the seaward side there would not be heard, on such nights, the slightest sound to break the quiet, unless that of little fish jumping playfully in the violet light and sending out great circles to shimmer toward the horizon.

So, it drew on toward Day Rackby's eighteenth birthday.

One morning in October they set out from Meteor for the village. A cool wind surged through the sparkling brown oak leaves of the oaks at Hannan's Landing.

"They die as the old die," reflected Jethro Rackby, "gnarled, withered, still hanging on when they are all but sapless."

Despite the melancholy thought, his vision was gladdened by a magic clarity extending over all the heavens, and even to the source of the reviving winds. The sea was blown clear of ships. In the harbor a few still sat like seabirds drying plumage. Against the explosive whiteness of wind clouds, their sails looked like wrinkled parchment, or yellowing Egyptian cloth; the patches were mysterious hieroglyphs.

Day sat sleepily in the stern of the dory, her shoulders pinched back, her heavy braid overside and just failing the water, her eyes on the sway of cockles in the bottom of the boat.

Rackby puckered his face, when the square bell tower of the church, white as chalk, came into view, dazzling against the somber green upland. The red crown of a maple showed as if a great spoke of the rising sun had passed across that field and touched the tree to fire with its brilliant heat.

So he had stood—so he had been touched. His heart beat fast, and now he stood under the Preaching Tree again, and drew a whiff of warm hay, clover-spiced, as it went creaking past, a square-topped load, swishing and dropping fragrant tufts. . . . This odor haunted him, as if delights forgotten, only dreamed, or enjoyed in other lives, had drifted past him. . . . Then the vivid touch of Cad Sills's lips.

He glanced up, and at once his oars stumbled, and he nearly dropped them in his fright. For the fraction of a second, he had, it seemed, surprised Cad Sills herself looking at him steadily out of those blue, half-shut lazy eyes of his scrupulously guarded foster child. The flesh cringed on his body. Was she lurking there still? Certainly, he had felt again, in that flash, the kiss, the warm tumult of her body, the fingers dovetailed across his eyes; and even seen the scented hay draw past him, toppling and quivering.

He stared more closely at the girl. She looked nothing like the wild mother. There was no hint of Cad Sills in that golden beauty unless, perhaps, in a certain charming bluntness of sculpturing at the very tip of her nose, a deft touch. Nevertheless, some invisible fury had beat him about the head with her wings there in the bright sunshine.

Disquieted, he resumed the oars. They had drifted close to the bank, and a shower of maple leaves, waxen red, all but fell into the boat.

"These die as the young die," thought the harbor master, sadly. "They delight to go, these adventurers, swooping down at a breath. They are not afraid of the mystery of mold."

His glance returned to the wand-like form of his daughter whose eyes now opened upon his archly.

"So, she would adventure death," he reflected. Almost at as light a whisper from the powers of darkness, too.

They were no sooner ashore than the girl tugged at his hand to stay him. The jeweler's glass front had intrigued her eye, for there, displayed against canary plush, was a string of pearls, like winter moons for size and luster. Her speaking eye flashed on them and her slim fingers twisted and untwisted at her back. She lifted her head and with her forefinger traced a pleading circle round her throat.

A dark cloud came over Rackby's features. These were the pearls, he knew at once, which Caddie Sills had sold in the interest of Cap'n Dreed so long ago. They were a luckless purchase on the part of the jeweler. All the women were agreed that such pearls had bad luck somewhere on the string, and no one had been found to buy.

"Why does he display them at this time of all times, in the face and eyes of everybody?" thought the harbor master.

A laugh sounded behind him. It was Deepwater Peter, holding a gun in one hand, and a dead sheldrake in the other. The red wall of the Customs House bulged over him.

"Ah, there, Jethro!" he said. "Have you married the sea at last and taken a mermaid home to live?"

"This is my daughter, if you please," said Jethro Rackby. An ugly glint was in his usually gentle eye, but he did not refuse the outstretched hand. "You have prospered seemingly."

"Oh, I have enough to carry me through," said Peter. "I picked up a trifle here, and a trifle there, and a leetle pinch from nowhere, just to salt it down. And so, all this time you've been harbor master here?"

His tone was between contempt and tolerance, as befitted the character formed in a harder school, and the harbor master was bitterly silent.

Day had turned from the jewels and was coming toward her father. When she saw the strange man beside him, she stopped short and averted her face, not before observing that Rackby might have passed for Peter's father.

"Not so shy . . . not so shy," murmured Deepwater Peter, as if she had been a wild filly coming up to his hand.

"She cannot hear you," Rackby interposed. The gleam of triumph in his eye was plain.

"Can't hear?"

"Neither speak nor hear."

Peter Loud turned toward the girl again—and this time her blue eye met his, and a spark was struck, not dying out instantly, such a spark as might linger on the surface of a flint struck by steel.

Was it a certain trick of movement, or only the quickened current of his blood that made Deepwater Peter know the truth?

"This is strange," he said.

That wind-blown voice of his, with its deep-water melodiousness, had dropped to a whisper.

"Even providential," the harbor master returned, and his eye glittered.

Peter would have said something to that, but Rackby, with a stern hand at his daughter's elbow, passed out of hearing.

Peter Loud was promptly taken in the coils of that voiceless beauty whose speaking eye had met his so squarely. The mother had played him false, as she had Jethro . . . but with Peter these affairs were easier forgotten.

Within the week, as he was striding over the bare flats of Pull-an'-be-Damned, he saw the flash of something white inside a weir. The sun was low and dazzled him. He came close and saw that this was Rackby's daughter. She had slipped into the weir to tantalize a crab with the sight of her wriggling toes and so had stepped on a sharp shell and cut her foot to the bone.

Peter cried amazedly. The shadow of the weir net on her face and body trembled, but she uttered no slightest sound. It was as if some wild swan had fallen from the azure.

In falling she had hurt her leg and could not walk, Peter tore the sleeves from her arms and bound the foot, then bent eagerly and lifted her out of the weir.

Immediately she hid her cheek in his coat, shivered, set her damp lips with their flavor of sweet salt, full against his.

Deepwater Peter held her tighter yet. How could he know that here, on Pull-an'-be-Damned, within a biscuit's toss of the weirs, Cad Sills had served the same fare to Rackby. He turned and ran, holding her close, and the tide hissed at his heels like a serpent.

The harbor master, lately returned from evening inspection of the harbor, heard the rattle of oars under his wharf, and in no great while he saw Peter advancing with Day limp in his arms.

The sailor brushed past him into the kitchen, and laid the girl down, as he had laid her mother, northeast and southwest. Rackby at his side muttered:

"How come you here like this? How come you?"

A fearful misgiving caused him to drop to his knees. The girl opened her eyes; a new brilliance danced there. With a shiver, the harbor master perceived those signs of a fire got beyond control which had consumed the mother.

"She has cut her foot, friend Rackby," said Peter. "I took the liberty to bring her here . . . so."

Wrath seized the little man. "Thank you for nothing, Peter Loud!" he cried, and these again were the very words Cad Sills had hurled at him when he had saved her life at Pull-an'-be-Damned.

"That's as you say," said Deepwater Peter.

"You have done your worst now," said Jethro. "If I find you here again, I will shoot you down like a dog."

Peter laughed very bitterly. "You have got what is yours, Harbor Master," he said, "and it takes two to make a quarrel."

But as he was going through the door he looked back. The girl unclosed her eyes, and a light played out of them that followed him into the dark and streamed across the heavens like the meteorite that had once fallen on Meteor Island.

Peter had taken a wreath of fire to his heart. The girl attended him like something in the corner of his eye. Times past count, he plied his oars among the cross currents to the westward of that island, hoping to catch a glimpse of his siren on the crags.

Sometimes for long moments he lay on his oars, hearing the blue tide with a ceaseless motion heave and swirl and gutter all round its rocky border, and the serpents' hiss come from some Medusa's head of trailing weed uttered in venomous warning. Under flying moons, the shaggy hemlock grove was like a bearskin thrown over the white and leprous nakedness of stony flanks. At the approach of storm, the shadows stealing forth from that sullen, bowbacked ridge were blue-filmed, like the languid veil which may be seen to hang before blue, tear-dimmed eyes.

Deepwater Peter felt from the first that he could not dwell for long on the mysteries of that island without meeting little Rackby's mad challenge. Insensibly he drew near . . . and at last set foot on its shores again. Late on a clear afternoon he landed in the very lee of the island, at a point where the stone rampart was fifty feet in height, white as a bone, and pitted like a mass of grout. This cliff was split from top to bottom, perhaps by frosts, perhaps by the fall of the buried meteor. A little cove lay at the base of this crevasse, and here a bed of whitest sand had sifted in, rimmed by a great heap of well-sanded, bright-blue shells of every size and shape. This was the storehouse from which Day Rackby drew her speaking shells.

He looped the painter of his dory under a stone and ascended the rock. His heart was in his throat. All the world hitherto had not prof-fered him such choice adventure, if he had read the signs aright. As if directed by the intuition of his heart, he slipped into the shadows of the grove. Fragrance was broadcast there, the clean fragrance of nature at her most alone. Crows whirred overhead; their hoarse plaint, with its hint of desolation, made a kind of emptiness in the wood, and he went on, step by step, as in a dream, wrapt, expectant. Was she here? Could Rackby's will detain her here, a presence so swift, mischievous, and aerial? Such a spirit could not be held in the hollow of a man's hand. He remembered how in his youth a man had tried to keep wild foxes on this same island, for breeding purposes, but they had whisked their brushes in his face and swum ashore.

The green dusk was multiplied many times now by tiny spruces, no thicker than a man's thumb, which grew up in racks and created a dense blackness, its edges pierced by quivering shafts of the sun, some of which, as if by special providence, fell between all the outer saplings, and struck far in. A certain dream sallowness was manifested in that sunlit glimpse. The air was quiet. Minutest things seemed to marshal themselves as if alone and unobserved, so that it was strange to spy them out.

"She is not here," he thought. His footfall was nothing on the soft mold. Portly trunks of the hemlocks began to bar his way. The thick shade entreated secrecy; he stood still, and saw his dryad, a green apparition, kneeling at the foot of a beech tree, and looking down. In the stillness, which absorbed all but the beating of his heart, he heard the dry tick, tick of a beech leaf falling. Those that still clung to the sleek upper boughs were no more than a delicate yellow cloud or glowing autumnal atmosphere suffusing the black bole of the tree with a light of pure enchantment. He was surprised that anything so vaporous and colorful should come from the same sap that circulated through the bark and body of the thick tree itself. But then he reflected that, after all, the crown and flame of Sam Dreed's life was Day Rackby.

Had she, perhaps, descended from that yellow cloud above her? Deepwater Peter had a moment of that speechless joy which comes when all the doors in the house of vision are flung open at one time.

His feet sank unheeded in a patch of mold. He saw now that her eye was on the silent welling of a spring into a sunken barrel. She had one hand curled about the rim. The arm was of touching whiteness against that cold, black round, which faithfully reflected the silver sheen of the flesh on its under parts. Red and yellow leaves, crimped and curled, sat or drifted to her breath in the pool, as if they had been gaudy little swans.

Suddenly the sun sent a pale shaft, tinctured with lustrous green, through the hemlock shades. This shaft of light moved over the forest floor, grew ruddy, spied out a secret sparkle hidden in a fallen leaf, shone on twisting threads of gossamer-like lines of running silver on which the gloom was threaded, and, last of all, blazing in the face of that fascinating dryad, caused her to draw back.

Peter, as mute as she, stretched out his arms. She darted past him in a flash, putting her finger to her lips and looking back. The light through the tiny spruces dappled her body; she stopped as if shot; he came forward, humble and adoring, thinking to crush into this moment, within these arms, all that mortal beauty, the ignis fatuus of romance.

His lips were parted. He seemed now to have her with her back against a solid wall of rock outcropping, green-starred; but next instant she had slipped into a cleft where his big shoulders would not go. Her eyes shone like crystals in that inviting darkness.

"What can I do for you?" said Peter, voicelessly.

Day Rackby pinched her shoulders back, leaned forward, and drew a mischievous finger round her throat.

On that night Jethro stole more than one look at the girl while she was getting supper. Of late, when she came near him, she adopted a beloved-old-fool style of treatment which was new to him.

She was more a woman than formerly, perhaps. He did not understand her whimsies. But still they had talked kindly to each other with their eyes. They communed in mysterious ways—by looks, by slight pressures, by the innumerable intuitions which had grown up, coral-wise, from the depths of silence.

But this intercourse was founded upon sympathy. That once gone, she became unfathomable and lost to him, as much so as if visible bonds had been severed. . . .

A certain terror possessed him at the waywardness she manifested. Evidently some concession must be made.

"Come," he said, turning her face toward him with a tremulous hand. "I will make you a little gift for your birthday. What shall it be?"

She stood still . . . then made the very gesture to her bosom and around her neck, which had already sent Peter scurrying landward.

The movement evoked a deadly dull in Rackby's heart. Was the past, then, to rise against him, and stretch out its bloodless hands to link with living ones? That sinister co-tenant he had seen peering at him through the blue eyes would get the better of him yet.

Conscious of his mood, she leaped away from him like a fawn. A guilty light was in her eye, and she ran out of the house.

Rackby followed her in terror, not knowing which way to go in the
lonely darkness to come up with her. In his turn he remembered the man
who had tried to keep wild foxes on Meteor.

The harbor was calm, wondrous calm, with that blackness in the
water which always precedes the *rigor mortis* of winter itself. All calm,
all in order . . . not a ship of all those ships displaying riding lights to
transgress the harbor lines he had decreed. How, then, should his own
house not be in order?

But this was just what he had thought when Caddie Sills first darted
the affliction of love into his bosom. Somewhere beyond the harbor
mouth were the whispers of the tide's unrest, never to be quite shut out.
Let him turn his back on that prospect as he would, the Old Roke would
scandalize him still.

A man overtaken by deadly sickness, he resolved upon any sacrifice
to effect a cure. On the morrow he presented himself at the jeweler's
and asked to be shown the necklace.

"It is sold at last," said the jeweler, going through the motions of
washing his hands.

"Sold? Who to?"

"To Peter Loud," said the jeweler.

Jethro Rackby pressed the glass case hard with his finger ends. What
should Deepwater Peter be doing with a string of pearls? He must go at
once. Yet he must not return empty handed. He bought a small pendant,
saw it folded into its case, and dropped the case into his pocket.

When he came to the harbor's edge, he found a fleecy fog had stolen
in. The horn at the harbor's mouth groaned like a sick horse. As he
pulled toward Meteor the fog by degrees stole into his very brain until
he could not rightly distinguish the present from the past, and Caddie
Sills, lean-hipped and dripping, seemed to hover in the stern.

At one stroke he pulled out of the fog. Then he saw a strong, thick
rainbow burning at the edge of the fog, a jewel laid in cotton wool. Its
arch just reached the top of the bank, and one brilliant foot was planted
on Meteor Island.

"That signifies that I shall soon be out of my trouble," he thought,
joyfully.

The fog lifted; the green shore stood out again mistily, then more
vividly, like a creation of the brain. He saw the black piles of the

herring wharf, and next the west face of the church clock, the hands and numerals glittering like gold.

The harbor was now as calm as a pond, except for the pink and dove color running vaporously on the back of a long swell from the south. A white light played on the threshold of the sea, and the dark bank of seaward-rolling fog presently revealed that trembling silver line in all its length, broken only where the sullen dome of Meteor rose into it.

High above, two wondrous knotty silver clouds floated, whose image perfectly appeared in the water.

"Glory be!" said Jethro Rackby, aloud. He hastened his stroke.

Rackby, returning to the gray house with his purchase, peered past its stone rampart before going in. His eye softened in anticipation of welcome. Surely no angel half so lovely was ever hidden at the heart of night.

The kitchen was empty. So were all the rooms of the house, he soon enough found out. Not a sound but that of the steeple clock on the kitchen shelf, waddling on at its imperfect gait, loud for a few seconds, and then low.

Jethro went outside. The stillness rising through the blue dusk was marvelous, perfect. But an icy misgiving raced through his frame. He began to walk faster, scanning the ground. At first in his search he did not call aloud, perhaps because all his intercourse with her had been silent, as if she were indeed only the voice of conscience in a radiant guise. And when at length he did cry out, it was only as agony may wring from the lips a cry to God.

He called on her in broken phrases to come back. Let her only come, she might be sure of forgiveness. He was an old man now and asked for nothing but a corner in her house. Then again, he had here a little surprise for her. Ah! Had she thought of that? Come; he would not open the package without a kiss from her finger ends.

He hurried forward, hoarse breathing. A note of terrible joy cracked his voice when the thought came to him that she was hiding mischievously. That was it—she was hiding . . . just fooling her old father. Come; it wouldn't do to be far from his side on these dark nights. The sea was wide and uncertain . . . wide and uncertain.

But he remembered that ominous purchase of the pearls by Deepwater Peter and shivered. His voice passed into a wail. Little by little he stumbled through the hemlock grove, beseeching each tree to yield

up out of obdurate shadow that beloved form, to vouchsafe him the lisp
of flying feet over dead beech leaves. But the trees stood mournfully
apart, unanswering, and rooted deep.

Now he was out upon the pitted crags, calling madly. She should
have all his possessions, and the man into the bargain. Yes, his books,
his silver spoons, that portrait of a man playing on the violin which she
had loved.

With a new hope, he pleaded with her to speak to him, if only once,
to cry out. Had he not said she would, one day? Yes, yes, one little cry
of love, to show that she was not so voiceless as people said. . . .

He stood with awful expectation, a thick hand bending the lobe of his
ear forward. Then through silver silences a muttering was borne to him,
a great lingering roar made and augmented by a million little whispers.
. . . The Old Roke himself, taking toll at the edge of his dominions.

Nothing could approach the lonely terror of that utterance. He ran
forward and threw himself on his knees at the very brink of that cracked
and mauled sea cliff.

It was true that Peter, in his absence, had disembarked a second time
on Meteor . . . a fit habitation for such a woman as Day Rackby. But did
that old madman think that he could coop her up here forever? How far
must he be taken seriously in his threat?

Peter advanced gingerly. Blue water heaved eternally all round that
craggy island, clucked and jabbered in long corridors of faulted stone,
while in its lacy edge winked and sparkled new shells of peacock blue,
coming from the infinite treasury of the sea to join those already on
deposit here.

What, then, was he about? He loved her. What was love? What, in
this case, but an early and late sweetness, a wordless gift, a silent form
floating soft by his side—something seeking and not saying, hoping
and not proving, burning and as yet scarce daring . . . and so, perhaps,
dying.

Then he saw her.

She lay in an angle of the cove, habited in that swimming suit she had
plagued Jethro into buying, for she could swim like a dog. There, for
minutes or hours, she had lain prone upon the sands, nostrils wide, legs
and arms covered with grains of sand in black and gold glints. Staring
at the transfigured flesh, she delighted in this conversion of herself into
a beautiful monster. . . .

Suddenly the sea spoke in her blood, as the gossips had long prophesied, or something very like it. Lying with her golden head in her arms, the splendid shoulders lax, she felt a strong impulse toward the water shoot through her form from head to heel at this wet contact with the naked earth. She felt that she could vanish in the tide and swim forever.

At that moment she heard Peter's step and sprang to her feet. She could not be mistaken. Marvelous man, in whose arms she had lain; fatal trespasser, whom her father had sworn to kill for some vileness in his nature. What could that be? Surely, there was no other man like Peter. She interpreted his motions no less eagerly than his lips.

The sun sank while they stared at each other. Flakes of purple darkness seemed to scale away from the side of the crag whose crest still glowed faintly red. It would be night here shortly. Deepwater Peter gave a great sigh, fumbled with his package, and next the string of pearls swayed from his finger.

"Yours," he uttered, holding them toward her.

Silence intervened. A slate cloud raised its head in the east, and against that her siren's face was pale. Her blue eyes burned on the gems with a strange and haunted light. There was wickedness here, she mistrusted, but how could it touch her?

Peter came toward her, bent over her softly as that shadow in whose violet folds they were wrapped deeper moment by moment. His fingers trembled at the back of her neck and could not find the clasp. Her damp body held motionless as stone under his attempt.

"It is done," he cried, hoarsely.

She sprang free of him on the instant.

"Is this all my thanks?" Peter muttered.

She stooped mischievously and dropped a handful of shells deftly on the sand, one by one. Peter, stooping, read what was written there; he cried for joy, and crushed her in his arms, as little Rackby had crushed her mother, once, under the Preaching Tree.

A strong shudder went through her. The yellow hair whipped about her neck. Then for one instant he saw her eyes go past him and fix themselves high up at the top of that crag. Peter loosened his hold with a cry almost of terror at the light in those eyes. He thought he had seen Cad Sills staring at him.

There was no time to verify such notions. Day Rackby had seen Jethro on his knees, imploring her, voicelessly, with his mysterious right reason, which said, plainer than words, that the touch of Peter's lips was poison to her soul. It seemed to Jethro in that moment that a ringing cry burst from those dumb lips, but perhaps it was one of the voices of the surf. The girl's arms were lifted toward him; she whirled, thrust Peter back, and fled over soft and treacherous hassocks of the purple weed. In another instant she flashed into the dying light on the sea beyond the headland, poised.

The weed lifted and fell, seething, but the cry, even if the old man had heard it once, was not repeated.

THE GULF STREAM

From the *Saturday Evening Post* (April 5, 1924)

A sweet, romantic story of two antagonistic, star-crossed people. Spiced by lively dialogue between a young, introspective man who returns from twelve years away—at sea or in jail is never clear—and an outgoing young woman, the story was included in Edward O'Brien's critically acclaimed Best Short Stories of 1924.

When he came in sight of the old Traill place Charles Gayley felt a touch of the old bitterness in his heart. Time had made few changes in that neighborhood. The road, deep in yellow dust, ran past the house with that same windswept, water-channeled, hoof-pounded ledge in it as of yore, and the house itself, gray and broken-backed, peered at him over a field of uncut hay. The L, angling away from the main house, still had that familiar sag in its ridge where his Grandfather Hiram's pigs had rooted away the underpinning.

In the woodshed door a girl in a white cap was shelling peas into a big tin basin. When she saw that brooding giant of a man with a corncob pipe upside down in his mouth, and his hands bulging in his coat pockets, she stood up abruptly, dusting her hands.

"Hello, Charles Gayley," she cried in her deep, rather husky voice. "So, they've let you out at last."

"They've let me out at last," he said somberly. He had a way of repeating other people's phrases with an ironical twist.

"You look a little pale about the gills still."

"I am shaky," the man confessed. "I feel feathery around the knees all right."

"You've got a right to. I wish you could have seen yourself when they brought you in. I was just leaving the hospital to come on this case. You looked like something the cat brought in. You did for a fact. Burnt to a crisp. Your eyelashes have grown out again. They tell me now you went back aboard that ship just to unchain a dog. Is that so?"

"If I did, I was too late," the man said. "The dog was blown to bits."

"So I understand. It's a wonder anything was left of you. Crazy. You must have known the fire had got near the oil. Maybe it'll teach you a lesson, though. Funny you had to get that kind of a reception home after all this time away. It must be twelve years."

"All of twelve." The man surveyed her. "I see you're the same Mabel Upham."

"If you can trust to appearances, I am, yes. I've got fat and practical, though."

"Yes, you've fleshed up," Charles Gayley said seriously. He looked into the woodshed.

"By Godfrey, time is nothing," he muttered. "I can see you there sitting on a bucket, and smoking sweet-fern cigarettes, as if it was yesterday."

"We rolled the paper round a lead pencil," the girl caught him up excitedly, "and glued them with flour paste." She wrinkled her nose. "Personally, I've given up the habit. I guess I was afraid it would dry up my blood, the way you told me rattan would, if I smoked that. I took a lot of stock in what you said those days."

"That was where you showed your inexperience then," the man said, mooning, and looking as if he had lost interest in the conversation.

"And then again, at that time you hadn't become the full-fledged woman hater you have since," Mabel Upham said, lowering her eyes discreetly and touching a ruffle at her throat with thumb and finger. "You couldn't be hired, probably, to sit smoking sweet fern with a lady nowadays."

"Sweet fern," muttered Charles Gayley. His eyes deepened and ranged. He was quite blind to the mischief under Mabel Upham's skill-fully slanted lashes. "Yes," he muttered. "That was certainly the proper quill. It beat tobacco all hollow. Hanged if I don't take a sack of that sweet fern away to sea."

"I must have had a fearful crush on you at that time," Mabel confided. "Actually, when I heard that you had gone away to sea, I was crazy mad to follow," she went on, wrapping her arms tight about her body, and leaning back against the door. "I was half a mind to change my sex and wear men's clothes."

"Yes, you were."

"I was, really. But then, I was always wanting to do things that any ordinary woman-mortal wouldn't dream of doing."

Charles Gayley discreetly changed the subject, and asked after his Aunt Hitty, who was sick abed upstairs. "She's bad enough. She can't move anything on the left side, I suppose you know."

Doctor Stone had told him that, he said. And he went on at once to ask cumbrously if he might sleep in the barn chamber for a night or two. It was a fancy of his, and the doctor had said that he ought to get his strength back before going aboard ship again.

"I can make you up a bed there as well as not," Mabel Upham said.

"I don't want to make work for you. You let me fix myself up on the floor," he muttered.

Mabel Upham laughed, and shouldered him with her soft shoulder.

"Aren't we considerate?" she breathed, dipping past him. "You haven't changed, have you? I should think going to sea and running in with those queer characters every day would have made a difference in that particular. But you've got that same trick of underestimating your own importance I remember as a child. Don't you think for one minute that I'm not tickled pink to have some human being of the opposite sex on the premises. I've been blue as a whetstone all soul alone in this great ark of a house with that cross-grained old lady pouring her complaints into my ear. Come along."

He saw that her eyes, brown, like her thick hair, and with their vivid, warm, scrutinizing lights, held the well-remembered audacity. It had been no part of his plan to have Upham get his meals for him, but he found himself again coerced—at least to the extent of having supper with her.

"It isn't likely that a man as careful as you are not to make a noise will disturb anybody," she said, arranging the knives and forks with the alacrity of a hospitable woman. "Just turn that fish over in the pan, will you, sailorman, while I'm setting the table."

The faint rattle of a bell in that upper chamber brought back the patient to her mind, and she waltzed out of the kitchen gayly. She came back more thoughtful and shut the door with a deliberate click.

"How she clings to life," she whispered. "It's a Traill characteristic, I guess. Any other man than you would have been blown to bits, like that dog. Seriously, I don't see what she's got to live for. Where there's baby crocodiles on the windowsill, and red devils in the drinking water, why should she want to go on and on and on, one day just like another? Three parts ceiling, from her present position."

"Well, isn't one day pretty much like another for the best of us?" the man questioned, leaning forward, and tracking a moth over the red-and-white-checked tablecloth with his fork. "Don't you find a good deal of sameness to it, taking one thing with another? I notice myself nowadays that yesterday and today and tomorrow all kind of run in together without any distinguishing mark. Half the time I don't know what day of the week it is, and I wouldn't know what to do with the knowledge if I did."

"Half the time you look as if you didn't know what year it was, anno Domini. It must be a family trait," Mabel Upham said, looking at him with close interest. "Let me help you to a little more fish."

Gayley shook his head, but she deposited another fragment on his plate, with a sweep of the arm that wouldn't say no, and he obediently applied his fork to it. He felt as if he had got into a favorable current, while still out of sight of land. He took sly peeps about him at the walls of the kitchen, at the yellow doors that had been planed to a new shape as the house settled. Yesterday and today and tomorrow. They knew all about this habitation, where the very ticking of the clock on the mantel-piece had a kind of reluctant hitch in it. He had been born here, and now he came here a stranger to the place. Yet even now not quite a stranger. His life had at its foundation only the sliding sands of an intrigue, a piece of folly, like a shadow dance, and this shadow dance had taken place here within these walls.

His father, a circus performer, had sat here, in this very stocky wooden chair with the red robin painted on its back—a mere boy in a flashy coat, as Hitty Traill had told the son bitterly. A juggler and knife thrower, a transient who had pierced Ann Traill's heart, as if in a slip of practice, when he had meant to miss her by a hair and only send the shivers through her.

Ann Traill had loved him. Her son felt sure of that, mysteriously sure. These yellow walls seemed impregnated with her impassioned whispers, the shivering fears of her poor heart. But he had been a transient.

He had passed on, evaporated, taking his knives with him; and Ann Traill had died at the birth of her son.

Queer, the man reflected. All the materials remained the same—the little clock cocked up there, with its yellow dial, pretending that time was so precious; the knives and forks lying on the cloth; the limp silver spoons ready to be manipulated. And a girl across the table who might be mistaken at a careless glance for Ann Traill herself. What did it all go to prove? It was a sort of hoax, or like an attempt made by an invisible presence, frustrated, and then set on foot again with a kind of devilish patience. It seemed to him that he could feel Ann Traill's presence at his elbow, behind his chair, with that apprehensive light in her eyes which he had noted in an old photograph of her.

Wind outside took the house in a trembling grip, and he felt the touch of his mother's fingers at his temples. "Good Lord, you're dead with sleep," Mabel Upham said, seeing his head tumble on his chest. "Come this way, and don't make any more noise than you can help with those great boots of yours."

He slept in a bed painted in broad stripes of brown and yellow to imitate a grain that was never grown in mortal forest. Mabel's last whispered injunction to him had been not to smoke his pipe. The smell would filter through the walls, and the old lady's sense of smell was as keen as ever.

"You can't expect to find her reconciled to the name of Gayley," she explained. "I guess she's got a bone to pick with you still on account of your running away and giving the impression that she hadn't been as good to you as she might have been. Your father went against her grain, too, they tell me. He let his hair grow wild over his ears like an ape, Hitty says. Funny, that's the way yours grows."

In the morning, when she referred to that condition of his hair again, he said with a total lack of interest, "Is it? Yes, I guess it is. I never saw much place for barbers in the scheme of things."

"You're not such a woman-killer as he was, at all events," Mabel said composedly, bringing him his eggs. "You don't throw knives, by any chance, do you?"

"Throw knives, no."

"He used to throw knives. For a living, I mean. Hitty says there's one or two marks in the woodwork in the dining room where he stuck one in when he was being playful with your mother. Between you and me and the bedpost, that's not my idea of a frolic."

"Well, no."

Gayley, folded in upon himself, breakfasted ruminantly. When he had finished, he sat sprawled in a chair, his felt storm cap drawn over his eyes, his yellow corncob empty and twirled upside down. Mabel Upham, coming down from the upper regions, as she called them, with a tray, closed the kitchen door very softly.

"You talk about second sight," she whispered. "I think she half suspects already. I had to make up some cock-and-bull story of a man coming to the back door to sell vegetables. If it wasn't for my faculty of telling lies without turning a hair I don't know where I'd be."

"You won't have to tell another one," Charles Gayley said, with his elbows on the table.

"I guess I've got my fill of sentiment. Well, thank you for your trouble. You've sure been good to me."

"So it's 'Hello' and 'Goodbye' with you, is it?" Mabel said, stepping between him and the door. "Eat and run, in other words. I guess you are your father's man, all right. You wait, Mister Man. You haven't heard me say my little say yet. I don't deny it's open to you to walk off and wash your hands of it, but still and all, Hitty's a blood relative of yours, for all her bad opinion of you."

"That's not likely to lead me to inherit," said Gayley with a grim smile.

"Inherit? What under the sun do you think there is left here to inherit? Sea water? Wind? She hasn't got a red cent, Charl. Hiram couldn't have taken very good care of his money, I guess. At all events it's a plain charity case, the way it stands, and if something isn't done, they'll have to take her to the hospital in a day or two. I'm not made of money. I can't work indefinitely for nothing. No, sirree. If I'm going on making one day look just like another to her, the wherewithal has got to be forthcoming."

"If I had a cent of capital" the man began.

"Who said a word about capital?" Mabel cut him short. "I know you haven't much in the way of this world's goods. You don't need capital on a job like this. There's still fish in the sea, I hope. And Hiram did have the grace to leave his dory behind him, and a little fish tackle. I was sorting it over only yesterday and thinking that if the right man would only come and put his shoulder to the wheel the old lady could go on dying at her own pleasure. And then you drop like a bolt out of the blue. Charl, you've got to."

The man tapped his pipestem against his teeth. His jaw slacked. Who could say the proposition was not tempting? He felt as a man might who knew that gold was hidden somewhere in the walls of the house, without knowing precisely where. He still had the aspect of a gloomy man, but he felt back of that a compelling touch, as if something, some charm or power, had got underneath him and was lifting him bodily where he sagged.

"Well, of course, if you feel that way about it there's no help for it," he said.

Hiram Traill's dory was not the staunchest thing afloat, they found; but it would do for that season of the year. Mabel made a contract with a friend of hers, Allen Winter, to look in and take the fish off their hands, in his lobster smack, since it would be a long row round to the inner harbor in the dory. Then, when the situation was explained to him, he suggested that as the market for fish would not pick up for a week or two, it might be best for Gayley to go mackereling in the interval.

"That's easy labor," he said, with the contempt of an old banks fisherman for the seiners.

Gayley followed his advice and shipped out for a week on a seiner. Perhaps that was the best solution of the difficulty, he told Mabel Upham. It was bound to make talk, their living away off in that neck of the woods, like members of one family, with only a paralyzed old woman for a chaperone.

She had tossed her head scornfully. Let it make talk. Gossip was a good thing for people who had just so much talk they had to get out of their systems, first or last.

The man recognized, not for the first time, that flare of wild generosity in her nature. She thought nothing of herself, nothing, apparently, as to what she might or might not get out of this world in her mixed course of dealings with it. She made him ashamed of those days when weights, like clock weights, hung in his chest. He would look at her, and feel the heat coming back into his blood, bringing a queer buoyancy with it, as if he were idling in the middle of a warm current that streamed across the harsh face of the world and made its own pleasant atmosphere. That would be the Gulf Stream, no doubt; that river of a dream which holds its own against the bitter ocean of what passes for real.

He was still cruising in that river when Mabel Upham picked him up in the dory homeward bound and took him off the seiner. The frowzy old schooner, velvet black against a sudden strong white show of light from the moon sliding out of that purple storm head in the east, flapped along like an old reprobate in a dirty dressing gown. Phosphorescent waters swarmed in her wake in silver sparks and coils; away to starboard was a chalk-white lighthouse, burning periodically, like a red coal waxing and waning on that riven granite ledge; and there, broad on the beam, was Mabel Upham standing up to the oars, hailing the ship in that deep voice of hers.

When he dropped into the dory with his bag, she said, "Welcome home," and let him take the oars because he could row faster and she had left the old lady alone too long already.

"Does she keep about the same, or does she seem to fail?" he asked.

"She keeps about the same," Mabel answered, trailing her hands in the water.

In the early days of his going to sea he had had nightmares, terrible dreams of dangling by his eyelids from ships' yards, or more often dreams of being crushed by falling masts or smothered in wet sail; and he had schooled himself to ridicule his own deluded sleeping self, and successfully accuse the nightmare of its true nature, even while he could not shake off its grip definitely enough to come awake. He had said to himself "This is another nightmare" and gone on dreaming it. He thought now that such a method might well enough be applicable to a pleasant dream, such as this, and he did so apply it. It was the easier to take it as a dream because of the unearthly quiet which Mabel enjoined upon him as soon as they had got near the house again.

Neither of them must speak above a whisper, she reminded him, because sound went through these old walls just the same as if they hadn't been there. Mabel was inclined to think the nitroglycerin pills accounted for the sensibility of Aunt Hitty's eardrums.

Whenever Gayley crossed the kitchen floor he went on tiptoe. If he so much as cracked a joint, he looked at Mabel with a panic-stricken eye. It was decidedly dreamlike. Mabel's domestic ardors were tinged, as usual, with her audacious impulses.

She had found sweet fern in his absence and made cigarettes over a lead pencil. He took one, grinning. Mabel, after lighting hers, came round to his side of the table, and blew a puff of hot sweet smoke roguishly in his ear. To his intense surprise he found himself retaliating in kind.

"What luck?" she inquired lightly in her most secret whisper.

He reached into his pocket and laid forty dollars on the table in crumpled bills with fish scales clinging to them. "It's a young fortune, Brother Neptune," she cried, sweeping the money into her apron pocket gayly. "I've got hot biscuits and honey for you, as reward of merit. Well, what's the matter now, old Thunder Ugly? You look as if you had been drawn through seven knot holes, now I can look at you in the light. Don't you like the treatment at this hotel?" "It's this coming and going on tiptoe I can't stomach," he grumbled. "Anybody would think I was a ghost. I feel like reaching out my arms to the walls all the time. What of it if she does know I'm in the house? Let her see me and get it over with. Anybody to hear us whispering together would think something criminal was up." "No, I don't dare risk it," said Mabel shortly, stepping away from him. "She's had a heart attack in your absence, and all that keeps her going really is the nitroglycerin. I know these cases. She may outlive both of us." Mabel Upham breathed on a silver teapot slowly, dimmed her image there, brought it back lustrous with a sweep of her arm, and suddenly put the thing down with a complete absence of sound. "If she does," she whispered, "then we haven't much, either of us, in the way of a lifeline. Let me see your hand."

She snatched it up and spread the fingers. Chin on breast, she explored the rough tracts of that strong hand minutely. "That lifeline doesn't look especially diminutive to me," she said. "Another thing, the line of love is marked clear as anything," she declared, looking at him full. "For all your stand-offishness there's more in you than meets the eye in the way of heart interest, I know. Who is she, Charl?"

"I guess that is something that was left out of my composition when I came into this world." "Ah, Mister Cocksure." "Well, I came into the world by that line, don't forget," he added in a lower voice and with a painful flush. "I'm not likely to," Mabel Upham replied with a sudden fixity of gaze. "Well, children there must be." "Must? Where's the necessity?" he said, fixing his eyes on hers with fierce intentness. "So that's where the shoe pinches, Mister Fastidious," she said thoughtfully. "I tell you flat," Gayley resumed, "if I had my own life to live or not, and the choice was there for me to make, I wouldn't have it. If it was at arm's length, and for me to take as a gift, I wouldn't lift a finger to it. Well, I wasn't consulted." With her hands at her back, Mabel, backed against the door to the right of the stove which opened on the back-stairs, muttered,

"That's perfectly maudlin." Suddenly the old lady's bell jangled on the upper landing. Mabel put a finger to her lips and fled upstairs. Gayley retired at once to his barn chamber. In the morning it was raining, and he went hand lining in the rain. The fish were not biting; and after getting only two fairsized specimens he rowed ashore and went back to the house. He put the two fish on the fish board and split and cleaned them. Then he cleaned and dried his knives and stuck them into the board with a deft twist of the wrist. Suddenly this act, so neat, so unerring, sent a cold chill through him. He sank into a chair without making a motion to take off his wet things. In his absorption he pulled at his almost extinct pipe and produced such clouds of smoke that nothing short of Mabel's choking gasp could rouse him. She was tugging at his coat, he found, after having lifted his cap and laid it on the windowsill. She withdrew the pipe from his mouth, and deliberately ran her cool fingers through his hair and under his chin. They were damp with that fragrant mixture of glycerin and rose water she used to soften them. "Where are you now?" she asked faintly. It was like a question addressed pathetically to some vanished soul. "I was chasing an idea," he replied. He found himself patting her arm. Or perhaps another man inside his body did so. "You were a thousand miles away," the girl laughed a little fearfully. "Half the time you just get my conversation as a kind of echo from the other world, I verily believe. I was wondering whether anything in this world could rouse you out of it. Look here, you're it." She brought the flat of her hand down hard on his shoulder and dodged through the open doorway. It had stopped raining, but water still dripped from the eaves, ticked from leaf to leaf, gurgled in some hidden cistern. The man, feeling as if a crazy enchantment had been cast about him, ran after her through a patch of shining wet witch grass, which slashed at her knees and impeded her. She ran tittering under her breath into one of those wild old wind-driven trees with a scaly low crotch. Gayley took the tip of her shoe in his fingers. She kicked spasmodically. "I will. I'll let you have it full chisel," she cried, blazing.

"Maybe your bark is louder than your bite," he whispered. With a smothered cry Mabel all at once yielded her whole weight and came tumbling anyhow into his arms, her loosened hair, full of lichen scrubbed off the tree's bark, dragging in all its warm scented tangle across his face. "Well, who began it?" she stormed breathlessly, twisting in his arms. "I don't care. Any man that tells me one day is like another has got to have it put to proof. Look at that length of ear you've got. That's a sign of long life, if you did but know it. Look at that lifeline too. Long life again. Long life all along the line. My sorrows, what are you going to do with it all? Moon about and smoke that corncob? It's upside down half the time and you're chewing on the stem. Lord, if you just got a haircut it might help some. Bushed out the way it is over your ears, it looks like wilderness creeping in again. It looks as if all the combing it gets is just what you give it running through the bushes." Mabel's rapid voice died away to nothing, her eyelids fluttered, she turned her head and laid her cheek to his breast hard. He said nothing. Like a man who has tossed off a deep draught recklessly, he had as yet hardly begun to feel the glow within, and yet he recognized that it must follow. He was preoccupied with an odd belief—it amounted to conviction—that this scene was, to all intents and purposes, a repeated one. Life had returned to the attack, minting new bodies, putting on strange disguises, but striking the same note.

Surely, he, Charles Gayley, or another in his shoes, had lived this thing before. Time was nothing. It had only come round again, that dark deception, painted up gorgeously, as ever, with that same pale glitter of rain drops in the apple trees, the same shining turf, that identical crooked little house, black with rain and heavy with portent, leaning there like a conspirator. The gusty blowing of the Forges, forging liquid chains for consciousness, was like a sharp reminder of the hoary antiquity of his fate, since they at least could not have changed their note at all, and even these sly whispers in the wet corn seemed to have been resurrected to torment him with hinting at that unfathomable secret. He found himself whispering tenderly, "What's this? What's this?" Her thin sleeve had ripped in their struggle, and the bare arm beneath quivered with one of those impulses which palpitated through that round shaft of a body like the flame impulses in a glowing ember. Bending her arm to thrust away from him, she brought it out of the torn sleeve, and he noted a series of cruel scars running from shoulder to elbow. They looked recent. "How came you to get that?" he said, frowning at it. She had seemed without a blemish physically.

"That?" She made a wry face, twisting her head sharply and withdrawing her chin, following the line of his gaze. "Oh, that. Vaccination maybe."

"Vaccination, nothing."

"Well, if you know so much—"

"I know better than that," he said severely. "Tell me the truth," he whispered.

"Well, if you must know, it was knifed off," she said briefly, after a second's hesitation.

"Knifed off?"

"Just the way you go to work to peel an apple, yes. The doctor happed to want skin, and want it bad, and nobody else was handy. The man's relatives, if he had any, weren't near enough to supply it from their own carcasses, even if they had been a mind to, so don't you see?"

"I see. He was burned."

"Worse than you were. Much worse. Yes, it was a wicked burn, all right. It came of a horse kicking over a lantern in a barn out Back Narrows way. Well, he got the skin of my arm now, marching it around to suit himself. I guess," she added with her soaring laugh, "that fellow and I have got something in common now. What do you think, Charl?"

Gayley had a strange prickling his throat. What a woman! She would let them tear the living heart from her breast probably, if some poor devil needed it in his extremity. And she tossed off this intelligence without the faintest accent of regret, as if the ruin to her beauty had never given her a second thought. Gayley passed his hand gently over the scars and closed his fingers on the round of the disfigured arm.

"Take ether?" he inquired forlornly.

"Ether, no," the girl retorted. "What do you think I am—a baby? I stood up there with my arm stripped to the shoulder and he sloughed off the skin with his knife and the blood just ran down off my finger ends into a basin."

"By Godfrey," muttered Gayley worshipfully, with a strange stinging flash at his heart, "you couldn't do that without being—You must have been dead in love with that fellow."

Mabel Upham twisting up her hair and standing clear of him laughed shortly.

"Hold your horses, now," she said cooly. "It just so happens that he was as good as an entire stranger to me. There may be more than love back of operations in a hospital, Mister Cocksure. Still and all," she went off, as if inspired to be altogether candid, "it did have that effect on him, it seems."

"That effect? What effect?"

Gayley felt every muscle in his big body tauten.

"Oh, well, the usual effect. People say now he worships me," the girl whispered. "It's that drop of my blood circulating through his body that's done the mischief if you want the science of it. They say he skulks round the house, and shadows me, and won't let me out of his sight if he can help it."

"You see anything of him?" Gayley asked in the tone of an accuser.

"Am I on the witness stand or what?" said Mabel Upham. "When I do see him, I can't refuse to make the usual inquiries after his health, can I, where we are one flesh, so to speak? But as a matter of fact, I haven't caught sight of him for several days. I did find a place yesterday in that angle of the stone wall—you can see it from the front of the house—where somebody had knocked a pipe out two or three times as if he had been sitting there watching and keeping out of sight."

"That? Right there by those two cedars?" Gayley laughed contemptuously. "You see what your imagination can do for you. I was sitting there myself smoking, as it chances."

"Oh. Well, that puts a different complexion on it," the girl said. "Nobody could ever accuse you of watching and waiting for a woman to put in appearance." Gayley, sitting gloomily on the circular stone well cover, said nothing. Mabel, at his back, uttered a deep tremulous sigh, and muttered that it was time for the old's lady's nitroglycerin.

She came back into the kitchen from upstairs looking pale and took a remnant of sweet-fern cigarette off the mantelpiece and lighted it. Gayley made the usual inquiry after his Aunt Hitty's state of health.

"What do you think she'd got in her head now?" Mabel breathed. "And you can't argue her out of it either. She will have it that your father is back mousing round the house. She's seen him passing between her and the door. She's all haired up about it. It makes the flesh creep on my body to hear anyone run on like that. Here, look at the gooseflesh on my forearm."

She thrust it at him, and the queer sweet-smelling smoke from her cigarette wavered into his face. She was breathing fast.

"Maybe he is, for all you know," the man said.

He tore out of the house with a feeling in his breast as if a red barb had hooked him.

For several days the relations between him and Mabel Upham were extremely formal. No allusion was made to that secret lover of hers, whose name, Gayley had come to know, was Bartlett—Jim Bartlett.

The girl made no further effort to rouse him from the depths of his abstraction. Indeed, her behavior was conciliating, half guilty, as if she acknowledged herself to be the cause of their estrangement. She was actually timid with him.

Every night, around sundown, Allen Winter came plowing across the mouth of the harbor in his smack and stopped her while Gayley pitchforked the fish out of his dory to her deck. Winter was a little pinched man with an enormous red mustache.

"How's the old lady?" he would inquire stealthily, turning his head toward the house, which could be seen easily enough from almost any point along the shore.

And when Gayley would answer perfunctorily, "She keeps about the same," a queer light would come into the little man's eyes, and he would turn away hurriedly and pitch the fish farther inboard.

One windy night, when he looked like a sketchy black imp against an angry-colored sky, he suddenly said, "And how's the young lady?" after they had made the usual exchanges.

"She's caught cold, I believe," Gayley said.

This indisposition was actually to be attributed to the pair of wet feet she had got jumping about in wet witch grass, but he said nothing about that.

Winter retreated toward the hatch of the smack with a giant red cod, which he pitched below.

Coming back, he leaned his elbows on the stout rail and inquired, "She set a good table?"

"I can't complain," Gayley said.

"Saving?"

"I don't see any evidence of waste."

"No. Comes of saving stock. Not hard to look at, is she?"

"No."

"No. Elegant-looking woman, I call her. No nonsense about her. Make you a good wife," Winter dropped out.

"She's got a man," Gayley said, with an increasing oppression at his heart.

"Told you so?"

Another limp cod went sailing between them.

"Yes," said Gayley.

"In so many words, though?"

"In so many words, yes. It don't take too many words."

"What's his name?"

"Bartlett."

"Bartlett. That hardware runner. How come he to get a hold on her to that extent? Always looked to me as if she was a little lukewarm toward him. Always looked so."

"Looks. Women look one way, and jump another, don't they?"

Allen Winter laughed like an idiot. "You're learning," he said, wiping away tears.

"She liked this Bartlett well enough to give him the flesh from her body," Gayley said severely.

Allen Winter stared. "Did she now?" he muttered. "And you know, because she told you herself, hey? She's a deep one."

He slapped both his hands on his yellow oilskin apron. Gayley felt his knees suddenly weaken under him. He sat down and seized the oars. The dory whirled away from the smack, shivering and buckling.

"I guess you still got a chance, if nothing splits off more than what's cracked already," Winter yelled after him in a kind of hysterical bellow.

Gayley pulled ashore like a madman. Winter's enigmatic questions had filled him with a devil of insight. What were men's lives? Like these waves, running up each other's backs, yielding to an invisible breath, breaking and crumbling at last against an invincible barrier. It was queer. And there was a crazy invitation in it all.

These stable landmarks—the brimming sea, the wide sky, the sweet Wine Hills purple in the distance—were all waiting on some piece of mischief, some sly look, some vagrant indiscretion, for the privilege of being seen by mortal eyes.

He went charging across the green upland, breathing hard. He knew now what had happened to him. He had been made a fool of. And a woman's hand was in it. A woman's blood likewise. He was a changed man, and the change was definitely for the worse. The little house stood there coyly, with the high grass growing all round it, and seemed to be laughing at him secretly. Very likely it had witnessed resolutions like his before and it had seen them shattered. It had solid knowledge of such imposters as he. He had an impulse to take to his heels, for good and all.

Instead he shouldered open the kitchen door. Mabel, with knit brows, was just inserting a pan of biscuit into the oven. She smiled at him over her shoulder and put a finger to her lip as if to reprove him for his boisterous entrance.

When she saw his expression, she stood in a flash, and he gripped her shoulders in his hands. "I'm the man," he muttered. "Don't try to deny it. I'm the man."

"You're the man?" Mabel repeated with pale lips. "What kind of a conundrum is that, please?"

"You let them cut you up for me. You've been lying to me and laying it off on another man. I tell you I felt the difference. Something's come over me. Why did you do it, girl?"

"Why?" Mabel had grown a little sullen. "Because I'm a kind of human chopping block, I suppose. Maybe it goes with working in a hospital."

"It's made a change in me," the man whispered huskily. "I'm not the man I was."

He struck himself over the heart.

"Not the man you were? No, I guess not. I guess not, Mister man. You wouldn't have been a man at all if it hadn't been for me. Do you know that? I forgot, though," she went on with quivering breath, "a man who is sick of this life wouldn't be grateful to anyone for saving it. That's why I lied to you, if you must know it. Did you think I was going to admit that I was responsible for keeping you on earth, when all you wanted was to lay down and die? Well, hardly! And if you truly want to know why I did it, it was in the interests of science."

"Science," the man whispered. "Yes, I thought there would be science at the back of it. It's softened my brain."

"It wouldn't have far to go," snapped Mabel Upham.

"I don't even get the slant at things I did before."

"I wouldn't attribute that to science," the girl uttered and gave him a marvelously understanding look. "Last year I gave a quart of blood to the old man that drives the mails, and I haven't heard any reproaches from him on the score of science. When I ask him how he's coming on he simply says 'Giddap' to his horse."

"I'll just clear out," Gayley said abruptly, taking his pipe off the mantelpiece.

"And just say 'Thank you for nothing,' will you, before you go?" Mabel cried, very white. "That would be a suitable finish touch to all your tender mercies."

"Don't think I don't appreciate—" the man mumbled. "Don't think—"

"Oh, no, not for a minute. I see your position. And as a matter of fact, I was going to put a flea in your ear anyway tonight, that you had better decamp."

"You were?"

"Yes. I have my troubles with Jim Bartlett, if you want to know. My life nothing but one long wrangle with men. It appears as if when he heard what I had done, and saw my arm, he was frantic. Naturally he hastened to put a wrong interpretation on it. He's perfectly sick over it with jealousy. What is it, as soon as a woman does anything for a man, it's got to be supposed she's in love with him? Well, it's come to a showdown, and Jim's ultimatum is that you have got to go."

"Oh, so that's Jim's ultimatum?"

"It's something like solid ground under my feet, anyway," the girl said. With her back laid flat against the dingy wall. "We either go forward or back in this world, don't we? Jim will either marry me or murder me, one of the other of the two things; and I'm not tired of life enough yet to resist him. I suppose that's the long and short of it."

"What makes you think he will?" Gayley whispered, taking a step toward her. He was rigid as a manikin.

"Oh, well, straws show which way the wind blows, as the man said when the roof fell in on him," the girl answered with a weary motion of her head. "He will, all right." She coughed pathetically and put a hand to her breast. Since Gayley said nothing she added faintly, "I expect him here any minute now. Maybe it would be just as well if he didn't find you here. He's not accountable. Not really."

"Oh, he isn't? You want to tell me I've got to make allowances for a man in his frame of mind, I suppose. Well, what if I'm not accountable myself?"

"Don't you give me these piratical looks," Mabel said in her full-throated voice. "I won't have it. I'm not accustomed to being shouted down by any man living."

In point of fact he hadn't opened his mouth. He simply stood staring, and telling himself that she had willfully fanned this torturing flame in him from the spark dropped in the ashes; fanned it cruelly with her own breath, bringing her lips close, smiling, thinking of the fire that would presently destroy him. Science, was it?

He knew a better name for it. She had made a monkey of him. He could hear her laughing with this Jim Bartlett, telling that pale desperate character that she had taken some of the say-so out of that man Gayley.

She would know how to make it right with Jim. Necessarily, all these tender looks of hers had been only the brimming of her love for another man. It was experimental science and had its relation to the dropping of her own blood insidiously into his veins, when he was lying helpless under her hand.

Suddenly his old notion of the thing dropped over the man's head like a bag. Repetition. Here it was, the very house of love, its walls still standing and supporting that cracked ceiling full of vague smoky continents and lost islands. This was the center of the world, undoubtedly. But walls have ears, tongues, shapes and shadows.

In that second when nothing was to be heard but Mabel's quick breathing, twice to every waddling beat of the kitchen clock, there grew before him the image of that father he had never seen; the youth with yellow hair tumbling over his ears—that gayly caparisoned juggler and knife thrower. He felt that disastrous and romantic man stand up inside him, and take possession of his blood, his eyes, his finger ends.

"Look here, Mabel, what's the matter with my staying where I am?" he whispered hoarsely.

"Ah, you know then," she whispered unexpectedly. "You've found out. Well, I guess opportunity never knocked but just that once."

"I guess you'll have to make yourself a little plainer, Mabel."

"You pick up your traps and go. That's plain enough, I hope."

"Let me stay. There isn't anything I wouldn't do. Let me stay."

"Not if you were the last man living, I wouldn't, now," Mabel uttered strangely.

"I'm a changed man, I tell you."

"I'm a changed woman, then, you'll find, from what people have told you."

"Told me? What under heaven have they told me?"

"Oh, don't I know? Can't I see the difference? They have told you."

Nothing but her flintlike obduracy in the face of his pleading could persuade the man that such a scene was real, and that he was begging at last for the privileges he had scorned and being denied. He felt as if that ousted tenant, his former self, were stationed in one of the corners, watching the antics of the new man in possession.

And suddenly he heard himself crying, "I'll see if science will help you then. I'll see if it will."

He lunged forward and wound his arms about her hard. Her head flung right and left, her body was stiff like something frozen, which melted suddenly.

"Crazy," Mabel faltered. "Crazy."

He had picked her up clear of the floor. He looked about the kitchen with a guilty eye flash, and then went through the door with her. He went under the apple trees.

Mabel neither made a move nor uttered a cry. He went downhill and heard Hiram's dory knocking against the flat blue stones in the cove where she was grounded out.

The tide was coming in. He put the girl into the dory and took the painter's bowline adrift from its tree on the bank. He shoved off, running alongside until the water was at his knees. He leaped in himself and jumped the oars between the tholepins.

"Maybe one man's ultimatum is as good as another's," he yelled, tugging at the oars like a madman.

A long ridge of iron-colored water sprang up to windward and passed under the dory, sending a vicious rain of spray in their faces. Against the menace of this background Mabel's face, clouded in flying strands of hair, was dense white.

"Where are you headed for—the coast of Spain, or only Davy Jones' locker?" she cried ironically but peered at him as if mystified.

He stared through the dark and gripped the oars hard.

"Where am I headed for, if it comes to that?" he muttered. "Perdition, I guess. Call it perdition, Mabel."

"I guess I can help out in that direction," the girl said. She stood up, and put her hands to the oars, and pushed as he pulled.

"I'm out of my wits," he muttered. The spray had drenched her, and he heard her coughing. He let go the oars and seized one of her wet hands. The oar to the left slid into the water and was lost, but Mabel kept hold of the other one. She dragged it aft and brought the handle up through the loop of the sculling rope.

"You give me the course," she said grimly.

She was tilted flat against his heart, her knees yielded to the motion of the dory, but she kept fast hold of the oar.

And suddenly Charles Gayley had a spasm of misgiving. "My soul and body, Mabel," he shouted, laying his hand over hers. "Isn't it past time for that old lady's nitroglycerin?"

After a second's tautness he felt the girl shudder in his arms. She twisted her head back savagely.

"Oh, yes; well past it," she cried with her mouth buried in his coat. "Charl, don't you honestly know? Don't you know, after all? I made certain they had told you."

"Know? Know? Look here, what am I supposed to know?"

Mabel took her mouth away from the cloth of his coat to say desperately, "She's dead, Charl; that's the sum and substance of it. Dead and buried."

"Dead?" whispered Gayley.

"Yes. It happened as far back as when you were away in the seiner. But I couldn't have her die, Charl. There was never anything came at such an awkward time as that old lady's death. I couldn't bear to see you go away; and she was all the hold on you I had. And then—I don't know what possessed me—it came over me that I could. Don't you see? All the man you ever saw to talk to was Allen Winter and Allen's a friend of mine."

"What are you trying to tell me?" the man said, lowering his face to Mabel's. "It won't—won't hold water. For one thing, I heard her ring her bell, now I come to think of it, just before we came away. I expect it was her ghost that did that."

"No. I rigged it," Mabel uttered faintly.

"You—rigged it?"

"Yes. I led a piece of string down the backstairs and out an inch or so at that keyhole where I could grab it with my back against it and give it a tug. Oh, Charl," she gasped, "there isn't any mortal thing I wouldn't tell you now. I've lied and connived enough already. I put it off on Jim Bartlett; all my love."

"Ah, you rigged him too?" said Gayley, twisting like a man in a trap. "He hasn't been near you all this time, I suppose?"

"Nobody would come near me, once they heard about me," Mabel Upham answered.

"I guess even a man with his head in the clouds like you, would come to hear about it in the end. So, I can tell you with my own lips. I'm only another woman—like your mother."

"Is that so? Is that so?" he said with stiff lips.

"I guess that's a kind of wild justice," Mabel dropped out with a babbling laugh, her face against his shoulder. "One erring woman gives you life, and another one gives it back to you when you had thrown it into the gutter as if it was a sucked orange. You didn't want it. It was 'Thank you for nothing' from the beginning. Better dead. Well, Charl, I guess I've swallowed your philosophy, that what I guess. One day would be a good deal like another from now on. And there isn't Traill enough in me to want to step into Aunt Hitty's shoes. What say? Shall we go on as we are going?"

The man saw that they were driving head on for the Forges. But Mabel's words had drained out of him every last ounce of wariness. He stood like a stuffed man, without pith or purchase. A lurch of the dory made him slip along her fishy bottom boards. He reeled and crashed down, his jaw clouting the side of the dory.

The blow paralyzed him, he realized later. He couldn't stir hand or foot for several seconds; he couldn't find his tongue. Mabel's body was weaving back and forth over him. He heard mysterious music made up of the drone of great water hammers, falling down there directly ahead, one after another, whitening and crumbling on those half-buried rock anvils. It was at half-tide that the power of the Forges was at its height. And it was half-tide now. A dory coming under those hammers would be struck into kindling in a second. And they could neither of them swim a stroke.

And then, "Starboard," he cried feebly. "Starboard."

"Starboard yourself," Mabel cried back with a strangled wind-torn laugh. Her rigid face hung over the butt of the oar, she pushed down with all her strength, holding the dory to the mark. He felt a surge, a shaking, a cold breath—and then the blood swarmed into his fingers, he seized the oar and twisted it sharply in the water.

The dory went quaking over the horn of the easternmost anvil without splintering. Charles Galey knew that he ought to be bailing water—he felt it almost to his knees; but instead he stood trying to make out the shine of those vivacious eyes.

"Humbug!" he heard Mabel shouting. He held fast to her. "Haven't I known it all along?" She cried. "Don't you ever tell me again, Charl Gayley, that I kept you in the world against your will. There must be some mysterious attraction somewhere, more than just force of gravity, I vow . . . I certainly gave you your chance to shake hands with the devil, didn't I? You wouldn't take it. Why wouldn't you, Charl?"

"Ask me something easier," he muttered. After one or two false starts, he plumped out. "I'm just my father's man, if you want to know."

"Your father's man is plenty good enough for me," Mabel said. "My goodness, it's your father's man I've laid in wait for!" With this, he lost his hold on the remaining oar, which promptly slid into the water.

"Crazy! Now we've lost the only oar we had," Mabel said, struggling in his arms. "You'd lose your head if it wasn't screwed onto you."

"What's the odds? We can't go wrong. We're in the Gulf Stream," Gayley murmured hypnotically. "Can't I tell it by this change in the temperature? Don't you feel yourself, Mabel, a different kind of a send-off in the wind? I bet a thermometer would show this water blood temperature at least. Don't you ever come to think that you have got a monopoly of science, Mabel."

"Oh, science!" Mabel answered huskily. "I guess that covers a multitude of sins. We little know, don't we? I wonder, though if you fully appreciate the fix you're in. I won't tread on eggshells with you, though. I never have, and it's too late now to make a beginning. But I guess if I do accept your advances now, at the eleventh hour—it'll only be to keep you out of prison on a charge of abducting a single woman without just warrant, if that's how the lawyers phrase it. I won't fall back on science. Mercy, no! I think—I think myself—truly I do—it's just a case, Charl, of where nobody, man or woman, can ever strictly have the laugh on God."

THE DEVIL TAKES CARE OF HIS OWN

From the *Saturday Evening Post* (December 17, 1932)

*John L. Sullivan played a huge role in the life of Richard Hallet—who wrote several stories with a focus on the heavyweight boxer, including "The Man Who Licked John L." (*American Legion Monthly*, June 1939), a colorful tale in which a drunken Sullivan knocks himself out as he fights the man in the mirror. "The Devil Takes Care of His Own," based on true events and Hallet's favorite of all his stories, depicts the clash of culture and sport in Boston, highlighted by a lecture by Oscar Wilde with truly ironic consequences.*

Billy Hogarty was setting off fireworks in Dover Street, from which it might be known that John L. Sullivan was home again, "in the hamlet of me birth," to use his favorite expression. He was a Boston man, and he was now champion of the world after thrashing Paddy Ryan to a fare-ye-well. It was time now to show the caution of a champion. "Come straight home and don't drink a blessed drop until you get here," Mike Sullivan had telegraphed his mighty son after the victory.

Now John was home, he could do what he pleased. He was coming out of Hogarty's barber shop when Captain Talbot saw him. The champion's plug hat—gray, with a black ribbon going halfway up its walls—was tilted to his brows. He wore a cutaway coat of shepherd's plaid, bound with wide black braid, a ship's cable of a watch chain and a boutonniere of violets. He threw a fistful of silver to the crowd, and the roar of applause, the scramble, reminded Captain Talbot of that roar when "the mighty wave of democracy breaks on the shores where kings lie couched at ease."

305

That was, originally, what Georgia Dahlgreen's poet, Wilde, had scrawled in the album of the Prospect House at Niagara Falls; and Captain Talbot thought darkly that he would have to meet the poet tomorrow afternoon at Georgia's house.

He walked through the crowd and put out his hand to Sullivan.

"The Cribb Club extends congratulations," Talbot said. "You will be a great champion, John."

"Haw," said John L. Sullivan in his bull-fiddle voice. "Who said the Irish couldn't fight? Come into Tommy Boles' and have a drink."

"I'm not drinking."

"You'll drink with me, me boy."

"If you're wise, John, you won't drink yourself."

"By Sancho, I can lick any man living, drunk or sober," John maintained.

There were men, members of the Cribb Club, who whispered that Hal Talbot, if he tried, could whip John handily. Talbot, a Back Bay swell to start with, but a sea captain by profession, liked better than anything to loaf in Dover Street saloons. Dressed to kill, dressed like Berry Wall in all his glory, Talbot would pick a quarrel by squirting perfume out of the cologne fountain in his cane; and he had no trouble flattening his man after he had hooked him. Now he good naturedly let Sullivan take his arm and shove him into Boles' saloon.

John's father, Mike, said to him, "Take the gentleman's word for it, John, and let the tanglefoot alone."

John picked his little father up and set him on one end of the bar. "Stay there now, father, where you'll not be underfoot. Rock and rye," the boxer shouted. "Name your poison, captain."

"A glass of milk," Talbot mildly stated.

Milk. The barman's eyes were gooseberries; Mike Sullivan himself looked apprehensive.

"Where are your ears? A tumbler of milk," Talbot repeated sharply. The barman filled it with a trembling hand, and John set down the rock and rye.

"Milk, is it? Milk is it, for a milksop?" he roared. Who before had ever ordered milk under the guns, the fists of John L. Sullivan; those dread fists hardened by dipping them every night of his life into a brine pickle? He seethed and glowered, his eyes grew vicious, and he seemed to shoot bolts of light from under shaggy brows. Talbot drained his milk.

"Thank you, John. Come into the Cribb Club some evening, and give us a lesson in the art."

"Haw," said John L. Sullivan.

In the street outside, Captain Talbot felt strong, solid on his pins. It might be that he could whip a champion. It might be that a champion was fearful of that very thing. Yes; but what would be the look on Georgia Dahlgreen's patrician face, if she could see what ruffian's tricks her fiance was up to?

Captain Talbot was a house guest at the Dahlgreen mansion in Back Bay. He could not possibly escape this infliction of the visiting Englishman. This apostle of the beautiful—the knight of the lily, he had been dubbed—was lecturing in Boston; and Georgia had met him in London. Captain Talbot, returning to the Dahlgreen mansion in the middle of a winter's afternoon, had the door opened for him by Georgia herself in white, with a pink sash. Lily Dahlgreen, her sister, was in white mull, with a green butterfly on one slim shoulder.

"What's the sofa doing, shoved in under the stairs?" he asked.

"It's horsehair. His lordship loathes horsehair," Lily whispered. "He doesn't like wax flowers, either, and he makes fun of antimacassars because they 'look like an eternal wash day.'"

"And so they do," Georgia said sharply.

"Say they do. I could be outspoken myself if I chose. He's even criticized our curtain poles. They're like ships' masts, he says."

Captain Talbot grinned, and squinted comically at the Dahlgreen curtain poles, from which "depended"—to use a word popular in 1882—the pale red-velvet curtains of the drawing-room. The forced tulips, he noted, were gone from the window seat, but on the mantel an innocent little Satsuma vase of white clover still held on.

Mr. Wilde's own choice of flowers was not impeccable, Captain Talbot reminded the two girls. It was known for a fact that he had sent wallflowers to Sarah Bernhardt. But it was agreed on all hands that he did know womanly beauty when he saw it. He had discovered Lily Langtry; she was now, by popular acclaim, the most beautiful woman in the world. Mr. Wilde's superlatives were at her service. He declared he would rather have discovered Langtry than America. America, however, he was willing to exploit, and already Mrs. Langtry had been photographed against the unpretentious background of Niagara Falls.

"The falls are incorrect in design, Wilde says," Captain Talbot chuckled. "He also finds the North Atlantic tame, on the strength of a smooth passage. I hope he gets a good shellacking going back."

"You are uncharitable, unfair," Georgia pouted. "If Mr. Wilde himself were here—"

"And by the way, where is he?"

"I have sent him with father to see poor Dennis O'Shaughnessy, the young sculptor who lives in an attic. A word from Mr. Wilde might help Dennis."

Mr. Wilde came with General Dahlgreen. The poet suffered this introduction to Talbot with a minimum of interest. He kept his fur coat on, although the house was warm; and asked that the shades be drawn and candles lit, since, like his mother, Lady Wilde, he could not endure the light of day. His thick hair, parted in the middle, hung to his shoulders; an orchid shriveled in his buttonhole.

Georgia placed him, still in his overcoat—for he would not take it off—on the window seat, under a hanging vase of hyacinths. "What is the verdict on my sculptor, Mr. O'Shaughnessy?" she asked.

"He is good. He is one of the few Irishmen who are not too poetical to be true poets."

"Will he succeed?"

"He has brains in his fingers and does beautiful things. But—success? Success means applause; and applause is a danger signal. It means that too many have grasped your point for it to have much significance."

"But Dennis—"

"Dennis will do. He will have his troubles, of course. We have all but annihilated the modern sculptor by losing all nobility in dress," said the apostle of the beautiful. "To see a frock coat done into bronze is only to add a new terror to death."

His voice dropped. He toyed with the idea of sculptors. He told Georgia a whimsical tale of a sculptor who dared to melt down an immortal bronze of Pain that Lasts Forever and remold it into an equally immortal piece entitled Pleasure that Lasts for but an Instant.

"That is the privilege of sculptors. They can choose an instant—say this very instant—and make it immortal. And instants are so much more worthy of immortality than eternities are. Where," besought Mr. Wilde, "is our sculptor-in-ordinary? Send for him, dear lady."

Captain Talbot said, "A poet ought to do as well. Wasn't it a poet who said, 'Make me immortal with a kiss'?"

General Dahlgreen, on the far side of the screen, said, "It appears, Mr. Wilde, you may have a competitor. There's talk of Sullivan's lecturing."

"Sullivan?"

"The boxer."

"Let him lecture with his fists."

"Are there any more convincing arguments?" Talbot asked.

"Not for the witless," the poet replied.

Mr. Wilde could not endure Sullivan any better than the light of day. In fact, the two men, champions in their kinds, were poles apart. The poet lit a gold-tipped cigarette, and with the ruthlessness of the visiting Englishman, pronounced, "What is the case of Sullivan? A ruffian from Boston and a ruffian from Troy stand up and pommel each other. What is proved? The Boston ruffian hits the harder. Well, he merely shows himself the greater ruffian. If Mr. Sullivan had killed Mr. Ryan and were going to be hanged for it, the public would bear his fate with resignation."

"Who can answer for the public?" Captain Talbot cut in sharply.

"I suppose I can, as well as any man living. I form publics. I am a dealer in publics. Publics are sheep and I am the shepherd. If I choose to say that Mr. Sullivan can do nothing against a gorilla, the public will believe me."

"I quite agree," Georgia said. Her brow had an embarrassed flush. "I do wish, Hal, you wouldn't show yourself so often at the Cribb Club. I know, of course, there are members who are gentlemen."

"Thank you," Captain Talbot bowed. "And there are members who are poets. There is, for instance, John Boyle O'Reilly."

"O'Reilly?" Wilde affected ignorance.

"The O'Reillys have been princes of Cavan for a thousand years," Talbot asserted. "He is as tolerant a man, as Ireland ever produced or America ever boasted," he continued heatedly, but quoting, in his effort to match the poet's wit. "Well, and I can assure you that O'Reilly speaks in glowing terms of Sullivan. He has even put on the gloves with him at the Cribb Club."

"There are poets, even among the Irish, who can see the stars no other way, perhaps," Wilde said insolently. "If he chooses to stand up to a man who rushes at him like a bull at a barnyard gate, that's his affair. I contend that no gentleman will go faster than a walk."

"And no gentleman will get a cross dog at his heels," Talbot savagely replied.

"Have I got one of them at mine, by any chance?" the poet wondered out loud.

Talbot was fairly turfed and knew himself to be so. Georgia detested scenes. He got himself in hand, went to the wine cabinet, and poured himself a nip of whisky. Lily called to him softly from the stairs. She had heard the finish of that clash of wits; and now she put her finger on Hal Talbot's mouth.

"You had nearly lost your temper, Mr. Talbot," she informed him.

"Stay with me here till I can get my second wind, Lily. Don't leave me, on your life."

She was in pink China crepe draped from her shoulders, where were pale green-velvet band and roses to support it.

"You are lovely." He took her face in his strong square hands and tilted it.

"You are nice, but not critical. Shall it be this, or black?"

"Black and without flowers or jewels, my charming redhead."

"Black will make me older—"

"But only just the necessary little—"

"Ruffian," Lily cried.

"Come in under the stairs; I'm not afraid of horsehair. I have just come off second best in a tilt with Mr. Wilde, and you are balm to my defeated spirit."

"Beaten at words. Well, words are women, deeds are men, I have heard you say myself," Lily murmured, sitting by his side. "Words will never banish Mr. Sullivan." She looked straight into his eyes. "It is common rumor at the Cribb Club that you can warm Mr. Sullivan's jacket for him, though."

"That isn't likely. He is world's champion," Talbot said. Notwithstanding, he felt a curious warm flood of strength and resolution through his members. Lily's praise was tonic, her kisses would probably be sweeter than the best canary. He had been two years away; her beauty had kindled, she had a new audacity, and her gray eyes, with their new lights, were more dangerous than danger.

"I suppose no lady will ever see a prize fight?" Lily submissively inquired.

"Naturally not."

"Still I should love to see one. I have an unholy interest in Mr. Sullivan. In whatever hits out. I could disguise myself in men's clothes."

That, he said, would be criminal, would be tantamount to carrying concealed weapons, which was against the law. No, it wasn't to be thought of. Blood might flow, and the sight of blood would make her faint. Lily had been shielded from the burly world. Hal Talbot couldn't so much as introduce a boon companion to her—say Mr. Sullivan—without first getting her ear, her parents' ear, permission all round. Mr. Sullivan's qualifications would have to be stated in detail. The Dahlgreens were the blues and the blues were the exclusives, who treated what they had built up as if it might be blown down in a breath; as indeed it might.

Behind the pierced-wood screen, the poet's voice went on and on, with only the briefest syllables from Georgia. Houses in America were atrocious, he told her. The carpets were hideous, the mirrors were crimes, the wax flowers horrors, the chandeliers, hanging from plaster vegetables in the ceilings, beggared description. The women, however, were oases of pretty unreasonableness in this desert of ugliness.

"Ass. How can Georgia swallow it?" Lily whispered. "It's true, of course, what he says. That makes it worse. All except about women."

Talbot said, "He is genuine enough. He is probably genius, Lily, but I must say I like genius better when it wears its invisible cloak."

"He was forced to declare his, he says, at the Customs," Lily laughed. "They should have confiscated the whole outfit. I'm dying to see what he looks like in his morning suit. His room at the Hotel Vendome is hung in dream of blue with lace over the bed, and the boudoir is all exquisite low art tones."

"If you go on in this vein, you will have me in a frame of mind to rob a stagecoach," Captain Talbot said.

"Captain Talbot, have you—have you ever really held one up?"

"Yes, ma'am, in company with Rocky Mountain Pete," Captain Talbot said grimly. "We were laying for the Overland, ambushed behind a nigger head, and when she did come, she took us too sudden. There she was on two wheels, girl, and gun barrels sticking out of her like quills on a hedgehog. The driver had the lines for his leaders in his teeth, and a pistol in each hand, and that Bill Cody hair of his streaming in the wind. You never saw a grander sight. There wouldn't be one in fifty would have the sand in him to hold up to a thoroughbred like that."

"But you did."

"I did not, Lily. I felt her shake the earth, and I just ducked my head and let her go. I couldn't stop that outfit single-handed."

Lily cried deliciously, "Captain, you are pulling my leg."

He looked down affrighted, but actually this highwayman had only put his hand upon her knee. The expression had just come in, along with telephones and Mr. Edison's electric light.

"It's just a slang expression," Lily, scarlet, told him.

There was no harm done, he said. Their lively talk was brought up short, as if their enchanted shallop had run upon a sunken reef. Lily, abashed, managed to say, "Seriously, though, you are enamored of the West?"

"I am quite in love with it."

He was carried away by her use of the current stilted English; yet he had an impulse to pick her up out of the cotton wool in which she came so charmingly packed. Lotta Crabtree, she said, had told her stories of the mining camps, where she had danced her way to fame.

"You are prettier than Lotta," Captain Talbot said, with a sense of new enveloping dangers. "I should like to see you tread the boards yourself. You have verve enough."

"I should be petrified."

"No. You could act. But that is not praise. Anybody can act. Most people do as easily as they breathe. They are conventional; and to be conventional is to be a comedian. It is to play the part assigned to us."

"Heavens, I recognize that sentiment. You have—captain, you have stolen it from Mr. Wilde."

"It is sacred fire. People before now have let poets break their bonds for them, strip them of their masks and show them to each other."

"Yes, we are hidden even from ourselves," Lily murmured. She thrust against him; she had been positively in his arms. Captain Talbot had a pang of contrition. It was Georgia, by hypothesis, to whose chariot wheel he was now chained. Lily, as if conscious of her treason, said hurriedly that she would go and change into the black.

Behind the pierced-wood screen, the apostle of the beautiful was telling a pathetic fairy story. He had warmed to his work and unbuttoned three buttons of his overcoat. His cravat of green silk bulged like a pigeon's breast; the amethyst on his finger sparkled; his hands were very fine; he had struck the pitch of a subtle emotion with a single note, drawn as if from a violin a master's hand. Georgia was fairly subjugated; her fine dark eyes glistened with sentimental unshed tears; Captain Talbot felt his gorge rise at the ease with which this charlatan fathomed the soul's chemistry. He went to his room rather than risk another fall with Mr. Wilde.

The lecture in the Boston Music Hall was at eight o'clock; at 7:30 Captain Talbot's coupe was in the street. The two girls came down the stairs together; Georgia in pale blue velvet, dream of blue and opal tinted, with a fern trail across her bosom, and scented white buds in her corsage; and Lily in low black with jet toilette and filmy deep Valenciennes. She was ravishing, like a portrait by Fortuny, and without flowers or jewels in the masses of her Titian hair. She had over her shoulders a yellow silk scarf with black moon and dragon—Captain Talbot's gift to her, direct from Canton.

No sooner was he clapped into the coupe with Georgia than she began upon him.

"You were disgraceful, really, in your attitude to Mr. Wilde," she said. "Why will you always and forever bring the talk round to that dreadful creature, Sullivan? You can't think those roughs that congregate on Dover Street should be encouraged."

"I flatten them at every opportunity."

"But that is so unlovely. Do you really think that beauty has no place in the world?"

"If I thought that, would I be sitting here?" he said playfully. "We must define beauty always in terms of its special manifestations."

"Copycat. That might be Wilde himself."

"Wit, itself, has evidently gone wild," Talbot chuckled. "But you should not expect too much of me. Mr. Wilde says that husbands and prospective husbands of beautiful women are really in a class with criminals. They steal away what should by rights belong to everybody."

Georgia sniffed. The coupe drew up at the Winter Street entrance to the Music Hall. The Dahlgreens were right behind, and Mrs. Dahlgreen in black corded silk, a very precise woman, introduced Stanley Mortimer, of the Meadow Brook Hunt.

"How is New York?" Captain Talbot asked him.

Wonders never ceased, Mortimer replied. He had talked only yesterday with Mr. Vanderbilt, who was thinking of turning Maud S. into a road horse in the spring.

"Nothing can be surprising anymore, since Mr. Wilde's advent," Mrs. Dahlgreen thought. Everything was queer and unsettled nowadays. It wasn't only Wilde. Women were listening more and more to Lucy Stone. The pull and haul over religion between Ingersoll and Talmage was disgraceful. Talmage had just advised Ingersoll to crawl into the rat hole of everlasting nothingness, and Ingersoll had said that he was not fond enough of Brooklyn to comply.

"I can see," Mrs. Dahlgreen said privately to Talbot, "that Georgia has had you on the carpet, young man, over something. But your shoulders are broad. And then, I remember dear Mr. Disraeli—Lord Beaconsfield, you know—telling me that nothing is of so much importance to a young man as to be well criticized by a woman while he is still young and malleable."

"What a town it is for quotation," Talbot thought to himself. "Nobody seems to back himself to win—or nobody but Sullivan." Even the epidemic of full beards had been brought about by physicians advising patients to protect weak throats. They wanted their very weaknesses to remain *in statu quo*.

Captain Talbot, with Georgia seated on his right, had contrived at first to have Lily on his left; but her mother would not consent to that arrangement and had shifted her to the other side of Mr. Mortimer. Captain Talbot felt the grind of the social machinery to his very bones. He was discontented with Georgia. To his dismay, he was finding that, even when tranquil, she didn't interest him. She pointed out a critic from New York, George Smalley, who had got famous overnight by cabling from London a eulogy of Lily Langtry's ankles. Talbot was in worse and worse humor. Critics and hackmen, he said, were exactly the two sorts of people who wouldn't come to lectures unless paid for doing so.

Georgia turned flat away from him in a pet. Talbot saw Lily's yellow scarf on the floor. It had slipped down there when she was changing seats. He picked it up and put it in his pocket.

Fifty or sixty Harvard students had just come in by the Winter Street entrance and, with the genuine Bunthorne gait, were filing up the aisle. The young men wore velvet coats, knee breeches, silk stockings and long-toed shoes with curling tips.

It was a take-off on Mr. Wilde. On their shoes, in their cuffs and in the lapels of their coats were sunflowers. They carried lilies in their hands and had languishing smirks on their fresh young faces.

Georgia Dahlgreen bit her lip and muttered "Shameful" behind her fan. Mrs. Dahlgreen said, "I should be mortified enough if a son of mine were in that procession."

Mr. Wilde appeared. He needed hardly any forewarning to gather himself for the attack. His wit was instant and killing; as much so in its way as a blow from Sullivan's fist. He was twenty-six, and two continents hung on his most casual word. His epigrams were barbs, which, once planted, like porcupine quills crept through the skin and worked always nearer the heart. He had the sap if not yet the fruits of genius. His approval worked miracles; his sneer was obliterating.

There he stood in his long hair, his high-waisted coat and clinging pantaloons, hut he carried no lily. He began calmly, "I consider it an honor to lecture in Boston first because you are the only city in America that has influenced the thought of Europe." That was true. Bronson Alcott had just said that actuality was the thingness of the here, and this was considered a good mark for Mr. Wilde to shoot at. After a devastating pause, he went on, "And also because I seem to see about me here certain infant signs of an artistic movement."

His insolence and grip were superb. Those bellied youths were staggered, as if they had been hit flush on the jaw. Mr. Wilde was going on, "A little levity is always welcome. Even to the dull, the dull are dull. I might breathe a silent prayer to be delivered from my disciples, but time presses. And so, as Wordsworth says in one of his sonnets, 'Turn we, turn we now from these boldly bad men.'"

Captain Talbot, infuriated, thought, "This fellow will carry the day yet. We shall all be carrying lilies."

Georgia's color was high, she breathed fast and had eyes for nobody but Mr. Wilde. Mr. Wilde was in the thick of things. He was complaining that America had no ruins, our lack of traditions would yet rob our roses of their bloom and our livers of their lives.

"The past," said the lecturer, leaning superbly on his pulpit, "does not mock you with the ruins of a beauty, the secret of whose creation you have lost." He let fall his manuscript, and broke into his lecture to say accusingly, "You have at this moment a great genius in your midst starving in a garret. You are surrounded with ugliness, with horse ears, wax flowers and electric lights, but you are not beyond redemption. In young Dennis O'Shaughnessy, of whom you know nothing yet, you have a man who can whip up the horses of the sun and yet know how to curb them. You have a man whose idlest thoughts are unborn bronzes, a man whose delicate fingers are brains, yet you prefer to adulate a brute whose brains are in his fists."

Lily Dahlgreen looked at Talbot, and her lips shaped the words, "Oh, poor Mr. Sullivan."

Mr. Wilde returned to his lecture, but for Talbot, the tilt of Lily's nose, the fall of her burnished hair, was more eloquent. Her new playfulness became her. They were the only two people in the world who had a sense of humor.

Mr. Wilde concluded his lecture and picked up his manuscript. There was vigorous applause—that danger signal—since many who had come to scoff remained to pray. Henry Mapleson came up to Georgia. His big, freshcolored face beamed. "Your poet did himself proud," he said.

"Isn't he marvelous?" Georgia asked him. "Wasn't it all too thrilling?"

"It was just too consummately too," Mr. Mapleson replied. "Have you heard what he called Niagara Falls?"

"The bride's disappointment," Captain Talbot cut in. "The report is that the falls kept on falling."

Georgia's icy profile was his reward for this sally. She said to Henry Mapleson, "Wasn't his contrast too devastating—I mean between the different use made of their hands by the sculptor and the prize fighter? Wasn't that perfectly crushing? The two are at such absolutely opposite poles."

Mr. Mapleson genially quoted St. Paul, "Every man has his proper gift from God." He asked to be presented to Mr. Wilde. He had, he said, a possible commission for the new-found genius, O'Shaughnessy. Georgia took Mapleson's arm. She said under her breath, for Captain Talbot's private ear, "You had better wait for me here. You have been abominable." In a still fainter voice, intense with passion, she added, "Rowdy."

Captain Talbot felt a red flash inside his head. He was abandoned. He stopped General Dahlgreen and told him that a matter of first importance had suddenly claimed him. Would the general see to it that Georgia got home safely? Captain Talbot scarcely waited for his answer. He went away with his head down like a blind bull. The Cribb Club would still be open. He collided with a party of youths, some still with draggled sunflowers in cuffs and shoes. They had dropped their lilies and were slinking out of sight like whipped curs.

The Tom Cribb Club on Avery Street had been organized by Back Bay swells. Boxing was growing in favor. Sullivan was a national hero, and public sentiment was all against him. Members of the Chicago Board of Aldermen had been discovered at the ring side: a Boston paper said that was to be expected of a city lit only for hog assassinations. Only last year, Sullivan had been forced to fight John Flood on a scow in the middle of the Hudson River, to escape from the authorities. The country hung breathless on the doings of pugilists—and forced them to flee to its very confines in order to get a chance to put their dukes up in peace.

The Cribb Club—up one flight over a machine shop—was equipped with a ring, a punching bag and a place to take a bath. The ring posts were dogged into iron plates let into the door. When Talbot entered, a group of members were watching a match between Joe Lannan and a tough marine. Captain Irish of Station Four was present to see that there was no blood and no brutality.

Captain Talbot felt that he had got into an air that he could breathe again. It was certainly very mixed company. The swells encouraged certain sporting men to make the club their stamping ground. Billy Hogarty was there; so was Ike Weir, a boxer and high kicker. The poet John Boyle O'Reilly asked if Sullivan would come, but Hogarty wouldn't answer for it. The champion had been applying himself strictly to the tanglefoot since his arrival home.

The fight between Lannan and the tough marine was tame. They were taking attitudes and administering light slaps under Captain Irish's watchful eye. Suddenly, like a bolt from the blue, Sullivan arrived, and slammed the punching bag with the back of his fist. He was in a black sweater, under a light-colored double-breasted reefer with smoke-pearl buttons. His cap was pulled well down, and the angle of his cigar boded no man good.

The cheer from his henchmen was spontaneous and inevitable. On the day of his mother's funeral, when he came out of the house to get into the mourners' hack, they cheered him to the echo. Then he glared for silence, now he solicited their cheers. He looked fit and formidable, but his domineering face was flushed and his eyes, under thick brows, had a wicked light.

"Haw," he roared in that more-than-ordinary bootleg voice of his. He walked into Captain Talbot, and shouldered him. "How's mamma's boy? Bring a glass of milk. Milk for the milksop. Milksop. Milksop. Haw."

Everything the captain had suffered tonight reinforced his present motive. He squirted cologne out of the cologne fountain in his cane, and said murderously, "You are in a gentlemen's club, my man. It is a good place for a pug to shut his trap."

"Haw," said John L. Sullivan.

The fighters in the ring now merely made dabs in the air with their fists. Nobody was looking at them. Captain Irish grew paler than the whitewashed wall. John had been drinking, but he was still a champion. He knew how to compress into his famous glare all the feral instincts of an animal intent on the kill. He was spoiling for a fight.

Captain Talbot felt gratefully that what Boston, and what he personally, needed was a touch of John L. Sullivan as an offset to Mr. Wilde. He reached out and deliberately pulled John's cap down over those infuriated eyes. It was like darting a harpoon into a whale. John spouted visibly. He backed against the outside of the ring ropes; they creaked under his weight; he was ready for the spring when Dan Gill and Snicker Doherty seized his arms.

"Captain Irish is here, John," Dan Gill whispered. "Get your man in the ring. In the ring, John. Let's get the togs on and try conclusions."

John nodded and threw his cap in the ring. The bone haircut with which he had affrighted Paddy Ryan had not grown out. He looked appalling and invincible. Ike Weir appointed himself as Talbot's second. Captain Irish said, "No bad blood, I hope, gentlemen?"

"Just a friendly exhibition," Dan Gill said soothingly. "The boys are just like kittens."

The two men stripped. A pair of fighting shoes and trunks were found for Talbot. John came forth in a green breechclout and long black stockings. Dan Gill called for colors. Captain Talbot took Lily's scarf out of his pocket, and Ike Weir wound this around the top of one center stake. John produced a silk handkerchief, with the harp, the shamrock, a sunburst and a flag in the four corners, and John himself in a fighting pose in the middle. Dan Gill wound this about the opposite stake.

Talbot stripped well. He looked hardly inferior to John himself in physical strength, but he was possibly not so round. There was less of him through the hips. John was by nature a well-rounded man;

round arms, round chest, round legs, round belly. He was thick all the way down; and now, kissed so recently by Southern suns, he looked bronzed and baleful. He swung again at the punching bag, and burst it like a rotten plum, with a single blow that shook the Cribb Club to its foundations. Flakes of plaster fell; the odds against the swell increased; and Captain Irish looked more apprehensive than before. The calm was ominous. A thunderhead was making up.

The storm broke with a cry from the referee, "Seconds out of the ring." The men had been led up to the scratch. At the word "Time," Sullivan came like a bolt of light, tough as white lightning, with all the sun's energies concentrated in his burly frame. Captain Talbot met the attack by side slipping to the right. His name was mentioned in the Cribb Club with more than respect. He was one of two or three men—Billy Appleton was another—who, it was whispered, might lick Sullivan, but that was before Sullivan had become champion of the world. Success was tonic; and Sullivan's true power, his magnificent physical strength, had not yet been called forth.

Talbot stood for a split second, waiting to get in his right on John's jugular. Failing in this, he threw the champion to the boards with a cross-buttock. This made one round, and Talbot, in his corner, was touched up by his bottle holder.

"Now you've hurt him, look out. He'll be worse than the Old Scratch," Ike Weir cautioned. "Keep out of the way of that left. It's like a ramrod, Mr. Talbot. It's knocking your head into the edge of a door in the dark, that's what it is."

"Chop it," Talbot muttered. "I'll get a harpoon into him."

Time was called again. Ten years later it would be a boxer who would weary John out by tactics that would have made a fish sweat; but in 1882 there was no boxer living who could stand up long against him. And it was ever John's opinion that a man, a champion, was not in the ring to defend himself, but to make a fight. The era of the dancing masters was not yet. A man in Connecticut had invented a machine to measure the power of a mule's kick; but Sullivan's fist, hardened in brine, would have given this machine short shrift.

For a big man, Talbot was elusive; he could ghost; but he immediately found that while some of John's blows might be strange—and Corbett said later that he did not understand them all—they nevertheless had wicked force.

Talbot, feinting with his right, led with his left, but his arm passed over John's shoulder. Instantly Talbot, with this same left, had the champion's head in chancery, hard against his flank. He punished John's ribs with his free hand. The blows sounded as if rung off a drumhead. The champion yelped and grunted and succeeded in breaking the hold.

He was hurt, and he had grown dangerous. The bronzed body dripped sweat, the hungry fists were backed by the fell purpose of the mouth; John's black eyes were intent, cruel and uncowed. He came like a crow lighting on corn, with no scarecrow in the field. Talbot felt his head rocked by an uppercut that sprang not out of the knuckles nor the elbow, but was incubated in John's heels, rippled up his spine, fluid and electric, and discharged itself in rainbow colors.

It wasn't going to be easy to wear out John's pelt for him. To the strong boy's natural strength was beginning even now to be added the strength of a popular legend. Genius does what the spirit of the time expects of it. John was invincible, because his fellow citizens expected him to be invincible. The onset now was vicious beyond anything. The air was full of claret-colored dogskin. Captain Irish had insisted on gloves, and this was lucky. Talbot had never known punishment like this. Once, coming from New Caledonia, in a ship loaded with nickel ore, he had foundered in an open seaway. There had been something tragi-comical in the fatal disintegration of the ship—masts, shrouds, skids, decks, deck houses splintering, crumbling and all going by the board together.

He knew now that he was foundering again, in the grip of forces he could not control. A crashing blow on the temple spun him round on his heels. Lily's scarf, that black moon and dragon on a yellow ground, fled across his vision. He had a thought. Perhaps he could draw an attack, and then, slipping away, trick the champion into swinging his fist into that stake. "You can warm Sullivan's jacket for him," Lily Dahlgreen seemed to be whispering.

But he felt numb. He had been inexcusably careless. He ought not to have taken blows as hard as that from Sullivan; and now it was harder and harder to take ground to the right to avoid that bull rush. The strong boy grew stronger with each blow, exactly as if he drew his strength from his exertions. He was all hard skull, bone haircut, pointed elbow; iron fist, brine-pickled.

Captain Talbot could think as fast as ever, faster; but he could not telegraph these thoughts to his extremities. Communications had been cut. He had all he could do to keep his eyes open, his mouth shut, his tongue out of the way of his teeth. He sank his right shoulder, thinking to spring in and get one home for nothing. But for that, against Sullivan, he would have needed springs in his boots. The champion, in fact, came like a bull at a barnyard gate. He was wound up, ready for the kill; he started his blow; Talbot saw the very inception of it in that masterful and cruel brain and, with arm raised, turned the palm of his hand out so as to take the force of the blow on the fleshy part of his forearm.

And then the friendly bout was over. It was like being struck by lightning. Paddy Ryan, who lost the championship to Sullivan, complained that he felt as if a telegraph pole had rammed him, butt end foremost. That was it, exactly. Captain Talbot opened his eyes. He had been poleaxed, and his head was on the knee of his bottle holder. Sullivan sprawled in the other corner, had his legs straight out in front, his arms hooked into the ropes. Tom Delay and Danny Murphy were rubbing him with a rough silk mitten as if his life depended on it. John had resumed his cigar, but his breathing was still a little stormy.

"Did I win?" Talbot grinned at Ike Weir.

"You were taking any God's legion of grief," Weir said, "and on top of everything Captain Irish hit you with his night stick. He won't stand for blood, not unless he has the spilling of it."

In fact, at the first show of blood, Captain Irish's club had descended, but it was on the head of the Back Bay swell, not on that of the newly crowned champion, that the blow fell.

"You whipped me fair enough, John," Captain Talbot said.

The champion answered in that accent of the bull fiddle, "Here's my flapper. The Irish can still fight a little. Go and get a beefsteak on that peeper."

Captain Talbot hardly knew how he had got into that street of Back Bay houses so bitterly criticized by Mr. Wilde. Horse carts didn't run there. He had walked, to clear his brain. The Dahlgreen house was dark, except for the red light in the hall. Everybody was in bed, no doubt; but the general had given him a latchkey.

Captain Talbot blinked. The misty aura provided with the impact of Sullivan's fist still persisted. Dream of blue. Well, Mr. Wilde by now must be in his lacy bower at the Hotel Vendome, dreaming of a time when the rose on England's shield should be no more crimsoned by the blood of battle.

Captain Talbot's eye was closing fast. His map, to use John's word for it, was altered for the worse. It wasn't in the least likely that Georgia would find him supportable at breakfast. Or, for that matter, any of the Dahlgreens. He was in a mood to crawl into that rat hole of everlasting nothingness prescribed for Robert Ingersoll by Talmage.

His best plan might be to get his bags and sneak away. His break with Georgia was fatal; this was a distinct gain; but Lily would not like him so well now that John L. Sullivan had beaten him. He did not like himself so well. He detested, in bitter truth, the very shadow that he cast. He opened the door with as little noise as possible. Lily Dahlgreen, near the stair bottom in a negligee of white Algerian and with her hair clubbed at her neck, was turning up the hall light inside its wine-colored shade.

"I saw you from my window. I hadn't gone to sleep. I really was waiting for you," she whispered.

"What made you think I would come?"

"I don't know. I did. Of course, you are *persona non grata* in this house now. Oh, Mr. Talbot, you are hurt," Lily said. She recoiled against the newel post. There was a faint waft of violet scent. Talbot knew now why he had returned here in person, instead of sending a messenger for his belongings. He had wanted to get into Lily's neighborhood, just as Mr. Wilde had been found—Langtry, very late, had stumbled over him—curled up asleep on Lily Langtry's doorstep in London, when he was writing the poetry to her that made her the most beautiful woman in the world.

"I'm still on my pins, as they say at the Cribb Club," Talbot said. "That fool poet of Georgia's complains that there are no ruins in America. He is wrong. And you were wrong, Lily, in saying I could warm Sullivan's jacket for him. I have tried. He warmed mine," Talbot said with a wry smile. "He wore out my pelt good. And now he's got your scarf. I put it up."

His head was spinning. That night stick of Captain Irish's had done him no good. He put his arm weakly across Lily's shoulders and trusted himself to her delicious strength.

"Hal, you are hurt cruelly," she faltered.

"Just an ordinary drubbing. The blow to my pride is worse. But don't misunderstand me, Lily. I didn't want to be champion, only master of a champion. Amateurs can't fly that high. Come in here, under the stairs."

Fatigue emboldened him like drink. "By heaven, you are fetching. Ravishing. You are more dangerous than Mr. Wilde and Mr. Sullivan rolled into one. You can hit harder. Right from the heels."

"Hush. Is this language for the middle of the night?" Lily asked. "What can we be thinking of? There isn't the least excuse for us—unless we might be putting beefsteak on that eye."

That eye. That physiological miracle, which, as Talmage often said, must have taxed the ingenuity of God; but it had been an easy mark for Sullivan.

"Beefsteak. You and Sullivan have the same remedies. You have a lot in common. Sit still, goose. How can I tell you that I love you with a beefsteak on my eye? I couldn't. I do. I am hopelessly your slave. Will you come West with me?"

"I feel so strange. Can it be me hearing you say this to me?" Lily whispered, bending her narrow body away from him, but not too far. "Mr. Talbot—are you asking me to marry you? It's—unprecedented; Georgia—"

"Georgia and I have quarreled fatally. She thinks me . . . rowdy. Not that she would use that word, perhaps"—he was willing to cover Georgia's indiscretions—"but still she thinks it and she may be right. The marriage wouldn't hold. The splice would draw. Lily, you must see that your people will never let me have Georgia now, after tonight."

"They won't let you have me, Mr. Talbot."

"I'm not asking them. I'm asking you."

"You are so fierce. You come at me like Mr. Sullivan."

"Like Mr. Sullivan. What better model? Boston needs this man. He can't be quoted, and Boston has been living by quotations. Sullivan settles something on his own account. Not much, but still something. I saw him pick his father up and perch him on the bar of Tommy Boles' saloon. Sit there, father, and don't be always underfoot, he said to him."

"And you think I can dispose of my father in that fashion?"

"No. It will come harder."

"There would be a scene. A rowdy scene. But it might be worth it. Hal—if you knew what a fierce ambition I've had just to call you Hal. Even from a time when you would pick me up and kiss me and put me down again. Hal, you didn't kiss me this time home. . . . Highwayman," Lily uttered after several breathless instants.

"Will you come West then?"

"Maybe. If there's enough tincture of the rowdy in my blood."

"It's only rowdies like yourself that can do anything for men like me."

With her head fallen back against him Lily murmured, "Ah, my own dear love." This was quotation at its best. She had given him unconsciously Lily Langtry's line to Claude in *The Lady of Lyons*. Langtry was really in the air that men and women breathed just then. Langtry and John L. Sullivan. Lily Dahlgreen echoed Langtry's tenderness, but she had much more than Langtry's usual abandon. But, then abandon, Wilde himself conceded, was never Langtry's forte.

"It's just too weird, but I do believe I owe my happiness to Mr. Sullivan," Lily whispered. "He does seem to have cleared the air. Now you will think me rowdy. I may end by putting up my dukes. And oh, Hal, have you heard how Mr. Sullivan has turned the tables on Mr. Wilde, but quite unwittingly? Of course, you haven't heard. It happened after you left the hall. It seems poor Dennis O'Shaughnessy after all was there, though he didn't come in until after the lecture. He was so very pale and shabby and tragic with those gloriously haunted eyes. Everyone was looking at him. Well, Georgia brought him forward; and on the strength of Mr. Wilde's praises Henry Mapleson gave him a commission. I suppose the poor boy's fame now must be assured."

"That was decent of Mapleson."

"Yes, but was it decent of Dennis to accept?"

"To accept? Why shouldn't he, poor devil?"

"Because—he really owed all his publicity to Mr. Wilde and"—Lily stifled a laugh—"the commission is from an athletic club. It is to make a statue of John L. Sullivan."

THE ASSES OF SAUL

From the *Saturday Evening Post* (May 2, 1936)

It is the first decade of the 1800s. Thomas Jefferson is president. British ships are menacing the east coast of the young republic. Aaron Burr is being accused of treason. This clever story, a rare focus on politics for Hallet, turns on the legendary courage and wit of then major general (later president) Andrew Jackson.

Applying his Harvard knowledge of the law, history, and the Constitution, plus a shrewd biblical reference or two, Hallet sets his story in a series of dramatic events and engaging conversations among distinguished guests at a Richmond inn, including the famed author Washington Irving. Wooed by a young southern belle who warns Jackson that her fiancé—who happens to be the general's own aide-de-camp—is about to be unfairly matched in a duel against a sharp-shooting soldier, Jackson applies all his own skills as a duelist and raconteur to save the day. In the process, he answers a repeated question among the guests: Could Andrew Jackson ever fill Jefferson's shoes?

In an attic room of the Swan Tavern in Richmond, Virginia, Major General Andrew Jackson, of Tennessee, was shaving with a hunting knife. Young Carter Chevalier watched him with fascinated eye from the bed. On a table lay that case of dueling pistols which the world had already heard about. If the General was known in the East at all, it was because of his affair with Charles Dickinson.

In that famous duel, Dickinson had been killed, whereas Dickinson's own bullet had only split on Jackson's breastbone. People said that

Jackson was immortal, or that anyway he couldn't die without his own consent.

Without his own consent, however, he had now been subpoenaed by the Government, by Thomas Jefferson, to attend the trial of Aaron Burr for treason. Young Chevalier was another Western witness. Aaron Burr was accused of a conspiracy to split the West from the East, seize New Orleans, conquer Mexico. Mr. Jefferson had rashly said, in advance of trial, that Burr's guilt was beyond doubt. Mr. John Marshall, the Chief Justice, before whom the case was tried, might have his legal doubts of that, and already, while the grand jury was still sitting, the air was full of obscure threats against the Court.

Chevalier said, "They want Marshall to issue a subpoena to bring the President into Court with a letter of General Wilkinson's which is said to be material."

"Let Jefferson bring his body into Court then," Jackson said.

"After all, the President is President."

"The President is Thomas Jefferson," the General affirmed.

"They have cited the case of the King of England," Chevalier advanced. "The Court's process can't issue against him."

"The King can do no wrong," Jackson said. "Is it claimed that the President can do no wrong? You know better. He can be impeached."

The General deposited lather on the razor cloth on his left shoulder.

"It is said," Chevalier continued, "that Jefferson will have the Chief Justice impeached if the subpoena issues. He has told the district attorney that Law is a jade that must be ridden with a hard bit, or it will fling a man in his position in the mud."

Andrew Jackson snorted. The President, in fact, from the turn of the century, had been in a fierce grapple with the Court. Nothing would mollify him. Not that Mr. Jefferson himself was lawless, but he liked law cut to fit, and he was never tired of asking pointedly if judges were made of better clay than other men.

Carter Chevalier opened the door, to a knock, and took a musk-scented letter from a Negro in a brown jacket and striped overalls.

"It's from Mr. Terrel Southgate's daughter Michal. . . . By the dried great toe of a dead saint, you have a captive dragging at your chariot wheel, sir."

"I had a feeling that something held me back."

"'Entreat the General to come and see me,' she says. 'He knew me once as a child in Washington.'"

"Southgate. I remember the father."

"You have had the daughter on your knee—and you remember the father!" Carter cried. "It's plain you're not one of these military men who sacrifice to Venus in place of Mars. I vow to God, sir, Michal Southgate is one of the loveliest pieces of crockery ever you set your eyes on."

"She's a curer, is she?" The General was dragging on his shirt.

"By heaven, there's no vision equal to her this side the jasper throne, General!" cried the lady's admirer. "If you had seen her last night, curtsying and tip-fingering, with her train stretching behind her like a sunset shadow, you would have said she could count four degrees of nobility at least."

"Strip away flounce and furbelow and I daresay the lady underneath will be found a trifle less tonish," the General said a little tartly. "Isn't she a drawn prize yet?"

Chevalier picked up one of the dueling pistols and aimed it through the window.

"Mr. Powhatan Carstairs, of Vengeance Ridge, considers that he has drawn the prize . . . These cursed eyes of mine, General! A man of honor is a fool to get himself born with bad eyes if he means to stay on the planet."

"I suppose if a man is killed for her every morning before breakfast, she only holds her head the higher for it," General Jackson said. He had got himself into pantaloons lined with buckskin from crotch to ankle to prevent abrasion of his bones in the saddle. Now, drawing on his blue dragoon's coat with bullet buttons, he looked sharply at his young friend, and led the way downstairs.

The travelers' room of the Swan was full of law characters and others. Burr's conspiracy was all the talk. Nearly everyone believed him guilty, except the silly women who had sent him fruits and calves'-foot jelly in his prison. Powhatan Carstairs announced that he had come from Vengeance Ridge to see Burr hanged.

"Thomas Jefferson says that Burr is guilty, and I believe him," Powhatan announced.

He naturally would. He ran a good many of Jefferson's political errands for him, and was supposed to have the great man's ear. Powhatan was a powerful young man, with a big ruddy face, the features crowded too close in the center of it.

"Thomas Jefferson has let slip the hellhounds of persecution against my poor friend Burr!" cried Luther Martin. This was one of Burr's counsel, in his cups. Mr. Martin's ruffles were dirty, his eyes red, his very wig had a thin, dingy, half-burned look, as if he had studied the case too close to the candle, and with a brandy bottle at his elbow. "Where," he went on, "is the act of levying war? There is none, sir. It was General Jackson here that built Burr's boats for him, and does anyone accuse the General of treason? I say it was Burr's intention to slip quietly down the Mississippi with his band of young men, and then, if there should be war with Spain—I say if there should be war, and in that case only—Burr had it in mind to attack Mexico. Thomas Jefferson has got the law wrong, if he thinks that this is treason."

"You must say for Mr. Jefferson that he does know a little law," Powhatan Carstairs insisted.

"Make it stronger, sir," came the clipped voice of Andrew Jackson, "and say he knows damned little law."

The arrival of the stage created a diversion. Ginery Twitchell came in, with a whalebone coach whip under one arm.

"Pour me a tumbler of 'fun'!" Ginery roared. This superb reinsman's bearskin cap was on at a fierce angle.

A Mr. Washington Irving, of New York, in a gray coat and white brocaded waistcoat, inquired gaily, "What's the news in Washington? Is it true that the French minister has an aide play the flute to drown his wife's outcries whilst he is beating her?"

"How should I know?" Ginery roared. "It rained like all scissors the only two days I went to school, and the teacher didn't come. They say in Washington, 'Hang Burr high as Haman,' and that's all they say. They say just the guard set over Burr is costing the United States seven dollars a day, and that's enough in time to bankrupt any nation. Landlord, three fingers of the strict-construction brandy."

He gulped it down, spun up sand with a snap of that whiplash with which he could decapitate fowls with his coach running, and would, if any gentleman would wager with him. He went outside at once.

"There's a man for you," young Mr. Irving laughed. "He's seen Mother Nature in her bed gown and morning smock, I'll warrant, as well as in her evening glory, lying like Venus in a grape arbor. Do you perceive, gentlemen, that he has a look of Thomas Jefferson about him?

When he takes the reins into that mighty fist, a man may as well say, 'There goes the United States of America.'"

"His horses are named after the states," Powhatan Carstairs thrust in. With a sidelong look at Jackson, he added, "He tells me Tennessee has gone a little lame this morning."

"That's from throwing herself against the harness then," the General said, drawing on his corncob. "In Tennessee we say there's more brandy being drunk than just the strict construction. Did Mr. Jefferson buy Louisiana from Napoleon under strict construction? When he ordered the Army to arrest Burr, a citizen, was that strict construction?"

"That was an emergency," Powhatan growled.

"Shall we let emergencies turn us over to the government of one man? Shall we own that 'consent of the governed' is nothing but a celebrated phrase from that man's pen?" Jackson cried.

"The Federal authority, sir," Mr. Irving said to the testy General from Tennessee, "is like the Arabian genie that, when the cork was removed, poured out of the poor fisherman's bottle in the form of smoke, and filled the whole horizon. Will the genie crowd himself back on invitation? Not, sir, while he has the shape of Mr. Jefferson, who, when he was in the bottle, declared the people free and equal. I think we should beware of these kindly great men who are too monstrously for the people. Lately they call this rascally paper money the people's money, merely because it is issued to the people, like Jefferson's orders."

"So, it is the people's money," Powhatan Carstairs said, with a black stare. "Manufactured for the people, issued to the people, and spent by the people, and who under the canopy of heaven is the worse off for it?"

"Why, the people," Mr. Irving said with his easy smile. "The people who think that governments are mints to coin golden promises into cash. And since the supply of such gold is inexhaustible, and the people's aptitude for spending holds out, all goes well, for so long as fools are willing to live in their own paradise."

"For so long," Andrew Jackson said, "as there is no Patrick Henry to touch with the spark of his eloquence the train of American courage, which is always ready laid."

"Do you mind, sir?" Mr. Irving asked, whipping out a tablet. "There's no thief like a writing man, who must take his rough gold where he finds it. 'The train of American courage.' They speak the truth who say that General Jackson can talk as well as shoot."

Ginery Twitchell bawled "Stage!" from outside and cracked his whip. "Where's the fat man that engaged two seats?" he was heard to yell. "I've got 'em for him! One's inside and one's on top!"

And with this hoary joke, known to all stage drivers, but delivered by none with better effect than by the redoubtable Twitchell, he was off again. Those for the stage left their breakfasts half eaten. It was an old trick of the landlord to have Ginery call "Stage" a little early. General Jackson left his friend Chevalier discussing a fried chub and walked outdoors. A six-horse bell team from the West went by, with bearskins on the horses' withers, and a tar bucket hanging from the axle tree. The General's gorge rose. It was Thomas Jefferson that kept him biting his thumbs here, with the West waiting for him. The very Lombardy poplars that shaded the Swan had been planted by Jefferson's orders. The Capitol on the hill, where the great trial was proceeding, was a replica of the Maison Carree, which Jefferson had brought from France on paper. Almost the print of Jefferson's foot could be seen in the Virginia dust.

The coach came tearing out of the stable yard. Ginery Twitchell's elbows were squared, he had the reins all buckled neatly into one fist. He saw Jackson, and wrapped the whiplash under Tennessee's belly.

"Body of death!" the General cried.

The Swan's black cook, Cyrus, overheard him.

"I hears 'em all talk and argufy, and what do I git out of it? I don't git nothing out of it, that's what I don't git," he said to his assistant. "But I'm thankful the Lord reigns."

"How come you is?"

"Because if the Lord didn't, the Gineral would."

General Jackson was in the Southgate drawing room, and Michal Southgate played her harp for him. She sang There's Nae Luck About the House and plucked chords like deep blooms of sound. Divine perfection of a woman, young Chevalier had called her, and fairest among ten thousand fair.

The young man might live to find that the bouquet was better than the flavor, as in the case of that celebrated Apple of our general mother. No matter, the girl was pretty, though she had airs of an aristocrat. She slept, Chevalier had hazarded, between Irish sheets of bareskin linen, her pillow stuffed with live-geese feathers. Shadows of harp strings trembled on her face.

"Gold-headed women look well beside a harp," Andrew Jackson acknowledged to himself. "I wonder what she wants of me?"

For this time, she had written him personally, asking him to dine. Chevalier was not included, but Powhatan Carstairs was here, and closer to the harp than the General. In a fantailed scarlet coat, the friend of Jefferson looked as if he might be guarding his prize. Had she ridden roughshod over Chevalier, with those coach horses of hers, blooded bays shod with German steel?

There was nothing to be got out of old Terrel Southgate on that point. Terrel was in black silk clothes, he looked sunken. He was one of the ancient lights of the dominion, but he had been deafened a little by the guns at Stony Point. The General's eye, cruising again, noted a sprig of geranium in the girl's gold hair.

Michal Southgate was in loose floating sarcenet that showed the nymph beneath to desperation, like an angel in a drifting and dissolving cloud. This was the French influence, which Jackson liked no better than the English. France, when she had mastered Europe, might give America a sweep with her tail . . . French swords, French dancing masters. . . . And at the same time, English frigates off our capes, nay, in our very harbors, impressing American seamen.

Michal swept the harp strings, and the General's eye shifted from General Washington's brass stirrup on the mantelpiece to the painting of Pocahontas in her wigwam by night. There was a chaplet of wild-flowers in her hair, brilliant hummingbirds hung from her ears. The thick fall of her black hair half covered the polish of a girl's bosom. She was on tiptoe, her lips pouted to blow that splinter of flame held out to her by the lover. Once blown, the lover was accepted.

Were the days of Chief Powhatan's wooden throne better? Would the General prefer that throne to Thomas Jefferson's whirligig chair? Benjamin Franklin's experiments had drawn lightning from the skies; Mr. Jefferson's had culminated in a chair that enabled him to look all ways at once, and cope with an argus-eyed constituency. The people. Was he their instrument? Were they not rather Jefferson's instrument of many stops, on which he played in place of that violin which was of no more use to him since he had fallen in France and shattered his wrist?

General Jackson threw out a bitter cloud of smoke from his cigar—one of Mr. Irving's long nines. He was exasperated. Could he not even hear a song from the throat of a pretty woman without thinking savagely of Thomas Jefferson and British frigates?

Michal's song had ended. The General stood up, pulled at his big nose with thumb and finger, made explosive little puffs.

"You sing well, ma'am," he said.

"My harp hardens the finger ends," Michal laughed and held them out to him.

"It melts the heart," Powhatan said, and seized the fingers a little rudely before the General could reach them.

Terrel Southgate exacted the General's attention:

"I hear that the Chief Justice has issued his subpoena to the President."

"But will the President obey it, sir?"

"Depend upon it," Terrel said, "we shall have a clever statement from Mr. Jefferson on the point. He is a good deal of a wit."

"No doubt, sir," Jackson flamed. "Wit must be original; judgment need only be reliable. We have a government of wits and pedants. God knows, they are original, but they will end by giving us the dirty end of the stick."

"Thomas Jefferson likes experiments," Terrel quavered. "He will spend half the night watching a tadpole in a glass of water, waiting for its tail to drop off."

"If I look for a tadpole's tail to drop off, I strike it off, sir, and then it's off," Jackson retorted. "Thomas Jefferson holds the two houses of Congress in the hollow of his hand. Now he attacks the judiciary. The Government's case against Aaron Burr is only Jefferson's way of giving the Supreme Court a taste of the cowskin."

"Montesquieu says the judicial power is next to nothing," Southgate murmured. "It has no guards, no palaces, no treasures, no arms but truth and wisdom, no splendor but the justice of its judgments."

"Let its judgments be just, and the Court's posse may grow big enough to overthrow a standing army," Jackson said ominously. "If I were judge—"

He stopped short. When he had been judge in Tennessee, he had kept the statutes open with his pistol that threw the ounce ball.

"If you were judge, General," Michal prompted him, sparkling.

"If I were judge, I should know how to keep the President from turning into a working majority of one," Jackson said grimly. "But I am not a judge. All I know is horses."

"You love horses!" Michal cried. "Let me show you my horse, if you please. He is called Alborak, after Mahomet's horse that took him from earth to heaven in a single night," she added, linking her arm in his. "Powhatan, will you mix father's toddy for him while we're gone?"

The stables were beyond the box labyrinth, which was usual in Richmond gardens. A stable light was burning, with a half-dried mullein leaf slipped into a lard-oil lamp for a wick. Alborak was a black horse with a blaze face, all his legs white to the knees. The girl brought the horse's head down to hers, the black mane dragged across her whiteness.

"Fancy blood," the General said, laying his powerful hand on the glossy haunch. "The neck a little short, perhaps. He'll go without a pepper pod under his tail. So, you can go from earth to heaven on this horse in a single night?"

"I have been," the girl whispered, and took her breath in sharply. "But I never shall again."

"The horse was a good bargain, if he took you once."

"Are there any bargains in this life?" Michal cried.

"Life itself is a bargain, ma'am."

"Can you call that a bargain in which we had no part, except to be sold into the chains of our slavery and the dungeon of our despair?"

"Hoity-toity," the General laughed. "Is it so bad with you?"

"Men call life a bargain, because they hold it cheap," Michal murmured bitterly. "You don't know, perhaps, that Powhatan Carstairs has challenged Carter Chevalier to a duel? No, I see you don't. Powhatan is a dead shot, and Carter's eyes are bad. He is doomed. Powhatan will kill him because I love him, and for no better reason."

"But they give a better reason, I hope."

"If I tell you, it is to be considered a privileged communication."

"You are a privileged character," the General said.

"Well, then, Powhatan said in Carter's hearing that you, sir, were in the conspiracy with Burr. He said that you and your friend Colonel Burr were bent, like Satan, on withering every bud of virtue."

Those forge fires that were the General's eyes began to blow up.

"The devil," he let fall unguardedly.

"Worse than anything, Powhatan said that in the—the duel with Mr. Dickinson, you wore loose clothes, to deceive your opponent as to the position of your heart. Carter, as a friend of yours, gave him the lie, and then Powhatan challenged."

Andrew Jackson plucked his nose as if it were a harp string.

"They fight in the morning?"

"No. Because Carter has still to testify for Burr, and if Powhatan kills him now, it might look as if he—as if Powhatan were nothing but an Administration bully. But it is merely postponed," Michal sobbed.

"I'll cut off his ears," the General asserted. "I'll cut off the scoundrel's ears."

Michal Southgate pouted her lips and deliberately blew the flame in the lard-oil lamp, with a look like Pocahontas.

"I can't bear to have you look into my cowardly eyes," she whispered. "You can't intervene, of course, without disgracing Carter. If I come to you at all, it must be—because Parson Blair told me you were like Saul, in the Bible, and I am named after a daughter of Saul."

"I have kissed the Book," Andrew Jackson said, "but I have never made a study of it."

"Have you forgotten," the girl faltered, "that Saul was sent by his father to find some strayed asses, and the Lord pointed him out to the prophet Samuel to rule over Israel? There was confusion, and people said they must have a king. So, Samuel detained Saul, and told him the asses he was hunting for had been found."

"The asses had been found," Jackson repeated.

He clapped his hands back of him and walked through the stable door into the shadow of a knotty oak that had been brought over from Africa in an acorn. Michal drifted at his elbow.

"Yes, you are Saul. You can find a way out of anything," she breathed. "If you merely open yourself to the people, you can be king. Carter has told me how they hang on your words."

"You would make a king of me, of all men on earth, when I would hang all kings by their heels," Jackson said.

"All kings but one king. That is the nature of kings," Michal whispered. Her fingers closed hard on the General's wrist. They were cold, he could feel, as in the article of death; yet her influence was hot on him, like flame from a scented lamp. "If you would only close your eyes, and wish Powhatan out of my path, he would be gone tomorrow, I am sure of it."

"Pouf," said Jackson. "As I would snuff a candle. . . . It's done then, ma'am."

A brook beyond the oak tree had been dammed into a little pond, in the middle of which a naked Venus lay in a ribbed shell. Jets of water played on her from a ring of frogs with open mouths. A man must be a fool if he supposed Venus born from a tiling as weak as water. Man ruled the world—and woman man. The General felt, irascibly, that he was being played upon, that he was yielding to a spell woven out of moonbeams and wet lashes.

He made that noise in his throat that suggested a hungering lion with its jaws against the ground. The sound evoked Sir Gilliatt, the fiddler, who came mincing between the brick piers of the carriage gate adorned with brass faicons. Gilliatt was a gingerbread man in a lilac vest and a brown wig with side curls. He looked fearfully at Mr. Jackson, who carried his red hair combed back into an eelskin sack.

"Well, sir, speak up. What's your message?" the General said sharply.

"My message is for Colonel Southgate," Gilliatt answered. "The British frigate *Leopard*, sir, has fired on the *Chesapeake* outside the Capes. Our ship was forced to strike her colors."

"To strike her colors," Jackson repeated. "Body of death!"

"She was not ready for the fight. Only one gun was fired, and that with a live coal brought from the cook's galley," Gilliatt said, trembling, as if he had been captain of the guilty frigate. The light in Andrew Jackson's gray eye was actually dreadful. He looked capable of tearing the *Leopard* to pieces with his fingers. Michal Southgate's lips were parted. She breathed softly, "Saul."

"If my judgment deserts me, I shall be the last man on earth to find it out," Jackson told himself.

Michal's arm was slipped through his; they began to walk together toward the house.

After a long day of wrangling in the House of Delegates, where the wolf pack, as General Jackson called it, had drawn closer round Burr, the horse racks on either side of the Capitol were still full. Inserted in the Richmond papers of that day was a notice that after court adjourned, Major General Jackson, of Tennessee, would address the people from the steps of the Capitol.

He stood forth suddenly, redoubtable in that coat with bullet buttons. The Lilliputian sickles of the law would be replaced now by the one Brobdingnagian scythe. Jackson's seagoing friend, Captain Tom Wintermaster, was in the front ranks, holding up an effigy of George III on a pole.

This was Jefferson's country, but General Jackson did not hesitate to fall tooth and nail on that celebrated man.

"Thomas Jefferson told us, when he was campaigning, that the world was too much governed," the redheaded upstart from Tennessee informed his audience. "Yet now he acts like George III himself. He is the best democrat in theory and the worst in practice that ever ruled the world. He adjudges my friend Burr guilty before his trial and spends thousands of the public moneys to dragnet witnesses. The two houses of Congress crawl on their knees to him over broken glass. Still he is not satisfied. He is like Aaron's serpent that swallows all the rest. He threatens the Constitution itself; and without that hoop to the barrel, what are we but a pile of staves?"

Powhatan Carstairs, planted not a dozen feet away from the orator, gave a jeering laugh.

"Do you laugh, sir?" Jackson roared.

"It's laughing that draws nails from coffins," Powhatan flung back at him.

"I have heard of laughs that put nails into coffins," Jackson answered. The people, stacked thick as pins in front of him, were as if turned to stone. Powhatan's face grew red in that furnace glare of the gray eyes. His guns, suddenly, were spiked.

Jackson was forging on. It was a bad day for the people, he said, when the aristocrats took up for them. What did Thomas Jefferson know about the people? His interest in them was nothing more than employment for a gentleman. He had never chinked his own cabin, much as he liked to show himself in the character of a simple farmer, and subject, like the poorest, to the bitterness of droughts, bugs, frosts and lazy slaves.

"If he has a fondness for the people, it's because the people are his stock in trade. The people are his tadpoles, and he sits up late to watch them under glass," Andrew Jackson cried relentlessly. "War he abhors, yet even war he knows only at secondhand. Where was he in the time of Tarleton's Raiders? Fleeing for his life, they tell me here in Richmond. And so, he never learned to tell a good soldier from a bad. He leaves James Wilkinson at the head of the Army and brings him here to bear false witness against his friend Burr. Wilkinson is a villain from bark to core. Where is he? Is he here? Let him stand forth, while I call him double traitor, and pensioner of Spain."

"The General is laying the foundation for a crop of duels!" a Yankee voice cried.

But Wilkinson did not stand forth. He had known that to linger in the neighborhood of Andrew Jackson would not be healthy for him. Wilkinson was a duelist himself, but he did not like the ugly rumor that Jackson had been practicing shooting silver dollars from between his friends' thumbs and fingers at fifty paces.

"He is in the city," Jackson continued. "Amuse him, some of you; with Jackson's statements in regard to him. Tell him that this trial is like the oozy bottom of a creek where a man may sink easy enough out of the sound of Gabriel's horn. If Aaron Burr is guilty of treason, then I undertake to be stretched on the same gallows with him. Burr? Burr? What kind of nightmare is it that holds us here, talking of Burr, when our ships are being knocked to pieces by the British guns? Thomas Jefferson is close enough to hear those guns, and he goes on inspecting tadpoles. He will lay an embargo, I am told. A man kicks you downstairs and you revenge yourself by standing in the street and making faces at him. Face-front or die will be a better policy."

That rotary devil in the General's eye was like a coiled spring imbedded there. The cords in his throat showed taut, like a ship's cables in a tideway. His left hand showed the scar that he had got as a boy, from a British dragoon's saber, because he wouldn't black the fellow's boots. It was then and there that he had vowed damnation and destruction to the British.

Fascinated, Mr. Irving said to his neighbor, "The old boy sets his triggers like a bird catcher behind a blind. Well, dangerous times call for dangerous men, I've always heard."

"It's the dangerous men that make the dangerous times," a Yankee voice informed the elegant stripling of the pen.

Mr. Irving had his tablets out again. History was making. Jackson's power was like the rush of a strong wind. A cheer was raised. A cheer for Jackson in Virginia, in Jefferson's Virginia. Power—personal power—hung there, like the red apple on its bough.

He seized it, making a fierce ending to his speech, "Must we turn skunks to save our noses? It is an old saying that the workman is known by his tools. This is true as Holy Writ. If you want to know what kind of a workman Thomas Jefferson is, look at James Wilkinson, look at Powhatan Carstairs. By the eternal, these men are not fit to carry guts to a bear!"

Men were used to the vitriol of horseblock oratory, but a speech in this vein they had not listened to, perhaps, since Patrick Henry's red wig adorned the hustings. They hummed and swarmed, like Hybla bees hanging in mid-air. Andrew Jackson clapped his hat on and stalked toward the horse rack. Powhatan Carstairs, he found, was walking with him.

"Did you say, sir, that I was not fit to carry guts to a bear?"

"Did I, sir? Then I retract. You are fit, eminently fit."

"There's no hill cat from the West can talk to me so," Powhatan raged. "My friend Horsley, of Rockfish Gap, will wait on you, sir, directly. You have the choice of weapons."

"Hill cats use claws," Jackson said at once. "I suggest hunting knives—and with our left wrists tied together."

No man better knew the proper use of frightfulness.

Buchanan's Spring was very pleasant at the crack of dawn. Its antlered oaks glittered with dew. General Jackson, first on the ground, stubbed his toe against one of the iron megs at which the Chief Justice, John Marshall, threw quoits, when he came here with the Barbecue Club.

"We had better pull these megs up," his friend, Captain Wintermaster, said.

But the megs were driven deep and couldn't be started.

"It's a good omen. It means that the Supreme Court will stand," Jackson said. "We can fight well enough between the megs. It's all in fun. I tell you privately," he added, "I don't mean to do this fellow Carstairs any harm. Pistols are very well, but the first flourish of a knife takes the bottom out of a man like this one. No blood will be shed, Wintermaster. I guarantee it. . . . Here come our friends. Good. They don't mean to keep us biting our thumbs here."

Peter Horsley came up.

"My principal will not indorse what I am going to say," he began, "but I must again protest this unchristian method of settling differences between gentlemen."

"If there is a Christian way of fighting, point it out to me," Jackson said. "Come; is it to be a fight or a foot race? It's knives or nothing, Horsley. I'm not one of these dandies whose lacy honor is satisfied with a drop of blood and the wound bound in a handkerchief."

Jackson laid aside his coat with a neat economy of movement, and stood, lean and formidable, in his ruffles. Captain Wintermaster opened the case of knives and held it out to Horsley to take his pick. He seemed reluctant.

"Come, sir," the General urged. "Lay hold of one of them. They won't bite. They are good steel. Specifications call for them to weigh one pound, the blade to be nine inches long, and so forged as to quiver like a bloodhound at the slightest touch. You see, sir?" went on the General, loud enough for Powhatan to hear him. "This knife can flay a buffalo alive, or cleave a human skull to the teeth, and at the same time it makes an excellent razor."

Powhatan Carstairs came forward, moistening his lips.

"Let the principals lay their left wrists together," Wintermaster said. He bound them with a rawhide.

"I still protest this method!" Horsley cried.

"Is it too close for comfort?" Jackson queried.

"It's well enough," Powhatan mumbled, but his lips were dry. The attitude was strange to him. It was familiar to Jackson, probably, and besides, he was remembering that Jackson couldn't die without his own consent. The General's hair was combed severely back from his temples, unpowdered, and gathered in a clubbed queue. He looked hard-favored, hard-bitted, and, kicking at the sod, sank his iron-plated heels into it to brace himself.

"Look at me," Wintermaster said sternly. "I am going to put the knives into your hands. Gouging and biting not permitted. If a knife drops, neither second shall pick it up, and if either does, the other second shall shoot him dead. Am I understood? Now then. You are to raise the knives when I flick my handkerchief between you."

The sun rose, wind stirred in the oaks, a cock crowed, a bird's wing fluttered, the principals stood like cast-iron men pegged into the soil. Morning, that had first whitened like the ash around an ember, now palpitated like that ember. Powhatan's heart, visibly, was in his throat.

At the snap of the handkerchief the knives flashed, the right forearms ground together. But at this game, Powhatan was a child in Jackson's hands. He had no footwork, but stood as if planted, in those stout shoes of his, with high quarters, designed to boost him up out of the loving red mud. Worse, Jackson maneuvered the sun into his victim's eyes. The top of the General's knife all but ticked the other's Adam's apple. Powhatan sagged, writhed, shuddered, his knees knocked together. Sweat dripped into his eyes. Blinded, he expected the worst. At his wits' end and carrying his life like an egg in a spoon, he felt Jackson's elbow gore him. He slipped to his knee, humped like a craw-sick bird.

Jackson's feet were planted wide, as if, like Antaeus of old, he drew strength from the naked earth. His leverage was torturing, and Powhatan toppled and fell heavily, with his free arm doubled under him. He dropped his knife.

Horsley, horrified, made a move as if to slip the knife back into his friend's hand, but Wintermaster's pistol, that threw the ounce ball, was raised against him.

"Does he yield?" Wintermaster asked Horsley.

"He yields, yes!" Horsley cried.

Jackson's knee was sunk now in Powhatan's belly, his knife raised, ready to rip his man from throat to bellyband, it might appear. He had, in fact, no such intention, but the unlucky Powhatan was left to draw his own conclusions from that bloody flourish. Powhatan didn't lack a share of courage; twice before now he had fought duels and braced himself against a pistol shot, standing calm enough to receive fire, even though he had himself fired first and missed.

Steel was different. The point of that toad slabber of Jackson's sickened him, as the General had known it would. The sun flashed horribly on it.

"I yield," he cried faintly. Now the words were out. He had begged his life of Andrew Jackson. His ruin was complete.

In the breakfast room of the Swan, guests for the stage were eating hoe cake and fried chub hurriedly and drinking Rio coffee. The morning was hot; a little Negro with a wire kept the red cloth fan moving against the ceiling. Nothing was talked of but Andrew Jackson's speech.

The Yankee voice said, "I see how it is. We shall be delivered over to the West when our Virginia masters are through with us."

"We might do worse," young Mr. Washington Irving cried. "Jackson has swept everything into the sea. It's flying news already that nothing under the blue canopy of heaven can keep Burr from acquittal, now that the General has spoken his piece. Sentiment has changed. Thomas Jefferson may still wear the red waistcoat and breeches of his friend Robespierre, but he can't tumble the Supreme Court in the dust. Mr. Jackson has taken a fall out of him."

"Brave words," said the Yankee voice.

"Words," Mr. Irving flashed. "The Italians say that words are like women, haunting and elusive in their fragrance—and in their double meanings. Words are women, deeds are men. The people are a thousand-stringed harp, and a man who touches it will do well, like Ulysses, to stuff his ears against that siren music."

"The Government have got enough of Jackson's harp," said the Yankee voice. "They've let him go. I hear he's leaving for the West."

"Stage," bawled Ginery Twitchell from the door, and snapped his whiplash. The travelers, as usual, jumped up and left half their breakfasts uneaten. Andrew Jackson pinched Ginery's elbow.

"How's Tennessee this morning, Twitchell?"

"Guaranteed sound of wind and limb, sir," the great Ginery said abjectly. "I might, say, Virginia has had a touch of colic, sir."

"Virginia's an old horse now," Mr. Jackson said. "File her teeth down, put sweet apples in her milk, brush her up, blow up the hollow's above the eyes, do what you will, still she's an old horse. You had better knock her shoes off and put her out to pasture."

The General filled his pipe and stalked into the empty breakfast room.

"House," he called, and brought his fist down on the table.

The landlord of the Swan appeared, with his carrot-colored wig sliding on his nose.

"Bring me a dish of crabs, picked and baked in their shells, hot, understand me, with butter and grated crackers," the General commanded.

"The stage is about departing, sir."

"Let it depart."

The landlord returned in person with the crabs.

The General had poured himself coffee and groped for a spoon.

"Where are your spoons, landlord?"

"Spoons, sir? There were plenty silver spoons about a moment since. . . . Why, bless my soul, sir, where are they?"

"Where, sir? Do you think travelers balked of their breakfast will not take something in exchange? Why a damned rascal do you stand and stare at me, man? Your spoons are travelers too."

The carrot wig was more than ever dislocated. The landlord vanished. Michal Southgate came in unattended. She wore riding boots and a green riding tunic. Tilted on her charming head was a long-haired beaver hat, reddish-gray, with an ostrich feather curling on its brim.

"If you are looking for Carter Chevalier," the General began, "he has marched away with the Richmond Blues for Lynnhaven Bay, to defend our coast from these cursed British frigates."

"It's not Carter I'm looking for. . . . Did you know that Mr. Jefferson has sent the district attorney that letter of Wilkinson's that the Court wanted?"

"He's knuckled, has he? Good."

"But the letter did not come in Mr. Carstairs' saddlebags, as others have. Powhatan can't be found. He's not—he's not at Vengeance Ridge, General."

"No, ma'am."

"Then where is he?"

"Pouf," said the General. "Didn't we wish him to the devil?"

"Wish him—"

"If wishes were horses," the General said, puckering his eye corners, "a man could go to heaven in a single night. Mr. Carstairs can go in the contrary direction, for all me. He has gone on the tide, for England, with my friend Captain Wintermaster."

"For England? Then there will be no duel?"

"No duel, ma'am, as the ship was sailing so soon. Mr. Carstairs has left it in my charge to convey his apologies to Mr. Chevalier."

No man knew better than the General how to cut the Gordian knot, or stand an egg on its end in the fashion of Columbus. He had solved this problem by knocking it on the head, and he would live to bulldoze destiny itself.

"I have you to thank for this in some way, I well know," Michal said, very low.

"Let you be thanking yourself," the General said testily, with a touch of the North Irish brogue he had from his mother. "It was you set me on to devil Thomas Jefferson, quoting the Book to me."

"Jefferson?"

"If I cut a cat hole in a door, I only cut it for the biggest cat."

"You mean, that Powhatan—"

"Went through the hole after his chief."

"You reasoned with him."

"I clapped the persuaders on him, ma'am."

"You see? Pistols are not the only weapons among gentlemen," Michal cried, suffused.

"So it seems," the General acknowledged, toying with a crab. He gave her his long Presbyterian look. Not Peter Hawkins himself, the tooth drawer, with his pullikins, would know how to extract this secret from him. The girl was in tears, plague take her; she was dropping tears into his breakfast.

"Was I to live a thousand years," she sobbed, "I could never—I could never thank you half enough. But you will be repaid. Men are saying that you will find yourself one morning in Thomas Jefferson's shoes."

The General thought he heard a rush of harp music past his ears. Could he crowd his feet into Jefferson's shoes? Michal was too close for comfort, he was rapidly concluding. She made a flourish with her arms; the tip of the ostrich feather got itself pushed into the General's eye. He swore slightly. . . . She was gone, but she had left a kiss on his lean cheek. Flame from the scented lamp.

That red seal of the double letter from his wife spoke him like a warning beacon to a mariner, who thinks that a bold shore permits a close approach. . . . Let you be coming back to Nashville, Mr. Jackson, to smoke your pipe with a calico woman that has a pipe of her own and loves it. . . . The General took tongs and picked out a coal for his pipe. . . . A certain amount of petticoats was good for the soul.

"House!" he roared. He tossed a pistareen to the fan mover. "My bags, boy. My portmanteau."

"Coach done gone, sir."

"Coach done come back. Coach done forget the General," said Andrew Jackson.

In fact, the landlord of the Swan had sent a man riding bareback on a stable nag to fetch it back. The horn blew. The stage was coming fast. Ginery Twitchell, superb reinsman that he was, cracked his whip. The leaders came jingling round the corner on the run, the swings at a gallop, the wheelers on a fast trot. The wool tassels on their head stalls shook, they picked up their knees pridefully, their necks were clothed with thunder.

Ginery pulled all taut with his shaggy fist, touched the brake with his toe, shouted "Ehe!" and the team stood still.

General Jackson, of Tennessee, threw out a cloud of Christian's Comfort—home twist—from that trans-Allegheny corncob.

"I thought the United States of America wouldn't leave me in the lurch," he said to Ginery.

The resemblance between Mr. Twitchell and Mr. Jefferson had never been more marked. The coach creaked in all its shacklings with Ginery's descending weight. He opened the door. There was a respectful murmur among the passengers. General Jackson had been left behind. . . . The General puffed at his pipe. He was thinking of Thomas Jefferson's shoes, and suddenly he knew what it was that haunted him, like a bat flying upside down in the brain's cave with its unfathomable dark. If ever he should find himself in Jefferson's exalted shoes, the Supreme Court should never take him by the nose.

He glared, implacable, irascible, and took that member in his own thumb and finger.

"General," the landlord of the Swan was pleading, "I'll thank you to point out the man that took my silver spoons."

General Jackson, gaunt in his linen wraprascal, mounted the stage.

"An excellent breakfast, landlord," he flung over his shoulder. "You set a good table, but you tolerate too many low characters about the premises."

"The spoons, sir," the landlord urged miserably.

"Spoons, landlord?"

"If your honor will condescend to point out the thief."

"You'll find them in the coffeepot," said Mr. Jackson. . . . "Touch off the nags, Ginery. Put them up to all they know at once. We are late. Come, give them a taste of the cowskin, man."

The shadow of Saul, tall and terrible, fell across the land. The asses, as the prophet said, had been found, but there was no mention yet of the kingdom appointed to the seeker.

ZIMBOLACI'S DAUGHTER

From the *Saturday Evening Post* (March 29, 1930)

Hallet wrote a dozen stories with a Salem (Massachusetts) sea captain, Arad Whitney, as the hero—sailing into one tough scrape after another from the Azores to Zanzibar. In this one, Whitney, once imprisoned by an Arab ruler, gets even when he purchases an attractive Arab woman in a sultan's slave market. The woman turns out to be the leader of a band of women who later rescue Whitney as he traipses across the desert as a prisoner again. This is the best among many colorful, sometimes overdrawn tales of derring-do in the far reaches of the globe.

Arad Whitney stood riveted to the ground in front of the slave cage in Zanzibar market. A lot of seedy Arab traders in flashy turbans and jeweled swords were bawling in his ears, inviting his attention; he saw nothing but the Georgian girl, Scharife, standing proudly in one corner of the cage. The very girl, with the Dog Star, Sirius, worshiped by Arabians, tattooed on her breast, who had stood back of his chair at the Sultan's dinner to the Salem mates and captains, and poured attar of roses on his handkerchief out of a Florentine flask. Then she had been a favored slave in green silk pantaloons with silver bells at her ankles, her black hair tucked under a scarlet cap.

Now her body was covered only by a single twist of ragged chintz, which left her arms bare and allowed the Dog Star to shine for all beholders. Captain Hassan bin Ibrahim, of the Arab navy, muttered in Arad's ear:

"A valuable property. The Sultan's Persian wife is jealous of her and has put her on the block. There is a good excuse, of course. A part of the north roof of the harem fell in last week and killed two wives, and the fair Persian laid that mischief at this girl's door. It is claimed she is a witch, a sorceress. You do not understand these things in Salem."

Arad knew the Persian wife. He had seen her in a blue velvet mask with oblong eyeholes. Mounted on a white donkey, she had been going to the mosque, attended by her runners, slaves, carpet spreaders, groom, bath servant and executioner. She was known to make free use of steel and poison. This girl was lucky, no doubt, to get off with slavery.

Tavaces, the auctioneer, seeing that Arad's eye was taken, took hold of the girl Scharife and, with his grimy thumbs at her jaws, tortured her into opening her mouth. "Observe. The teeth like camels' milk. This is a jewel. She has accomplishments. She copied the Koran for the Sultan on the bleached shoulder blades of camels. She taught horsemanship and spear throwing to the young princesses. Reis Whitney, buy; thou wilt gain. If this cursed Parsee in the calico hat buys her, she will die with burst lungs diving for pearls in the green waters of Oman. He offers fifty."

"Sixty!" Arad cried; and immediately he could have bitten his tongue out. He had no money of his own. If he prevailed over the Parsee he would have to use Lettie Shand's money, her adventure, a belt of gold round his waist, which she had charged him to lay out to best advantage, preferably in shawls of Canton crepe. And what would Lettie Shand, his love, say to the purchase of a woman quite as young and fully as good-looking as herself; and no doubt equally religious, to say nothing of her skill with spears? Arad himself had seen her stick three gold slippers in the sand, and then, at thirty paces, find the mark with two spears out of three. Lettie, at Mr. and Mrs. Mond's school for young ladies on Vine Street, Salem, had learned English, French, geography, the use of the globes, vocal music, and plain needlework.

Arad remembered, too late, the Arab saying that while a word is still unspoken you are master of it; once it has passed your lips, you are its slave. Well, perhaps the flowery Parsee would speak again. He did and raised the bid to seventy sequins. Arad, wresting himself away from the Georgian's brilliant eyes, saw his captain's grim chin forging through the crowd. Captain Amasa Webb was in a bottle-green coat with a stiff six-inch collar turned up around his ears, and a white beaver hat slanted on his thick brows. He had, obviously, a long flat bottle of whisky slipped into his stocking leg.

"What's this?" Captain Webb roared.

The woman in the cage, never taking her eyes from Arad's face, murmured, "Buy. Buy, my master. Ransom comes before alms. Let me be thy slave, oh, reis. I will spread thy carpets, I will spill perfume as of yore, guard thee against poisoners. Ransom comes before alms, and as you know, he who gives not alms daily will have a serpent knotted about his neck in the other world. Buy, as you yourself have been a slave."

Ah, so she knew that. Only two years before, Arad, wrecked on the brown shores of Arabia Felix, had been a slave, but luckily he had been sold in the Muscat market, and the Sultan had redeemed him, in accordance with the terms of the treaty of commerce then existing between Zanzibar and Salem.

"One hundred sequins!" he cried stormily. Something like a sob swelled the Georgian's breast; she cried, moving her throat painfully, "May God imparadise you!" And the Parsee knocked his knuckles against his calico hat in token of defeat. The master of the block swung the cage door wide and thrust Scharife bodily into Arad's arms. Her hair whipped into his eyes; he winked them, but he was not so blinded as not to see Captain Webb's face blazing within a foot of his own.

"You bring that woman aboard ship, and I'll wipe you down with a white rope's end!" old Webb thundered. Old Slobber-chops. He was an intensely moral man. When he dealt in slaves himself it was only in the black cattle of the pirate coast; this purchase of Arad's outraged him to the core. "I knew a man bought a white slave in Bagdad once for a keg of powder, and he had better have kept the powder. Once you get entitled with a foreign woman, you don't know what law ain't likely to be quoted flat against you. There was Tom Powers married a girl at Honolulu, and the law there said no foreigner that marries a native woman can ever leave the kingdom without her saying she's willing for him to go. He's there yet."

Arad said, "I'm not marrying this girl, and I'm not trading in her either."

"How you going to account for the money to Lettie Shand?" his captain asked, with a look at the new slave which forced from her lips the murmur: "O, reis, let me have clothes to shield me from the glances of demons."

"Clothes," Arad repeated, and began to see that the business had many angles.

"Clothes!" roared Captain Webb and increased the slant of his beaver.

"Clothes. I will clothe her for you," Captain Hassan bin Ibrahim said politely. "Seek her at my house at about the hour of the fifth prayer."

Arad, stooping to break the foot-long silver chain between the girl's ankles—badge of her service to the Sultan—heard Captain Webb advising him, "You come back aboard ship, and count it money lost. You can't sell again and show a profit. You've paid now twice over what any woman's worth—any foreign woman. You relinquish her, my boy, and I'll give you a two-ton trading privilege in ivory."

"Relinquish her. She is free already!" Arad said, but the look in Scharife's eyes was not that of a manumitted woman.

At the hour of the fifth prayer, when he stood outside Captain Hassan's gate, he was still examining his motives. Would he have paid one hundred sequins, out of Lettie's hoard, to free the black girl with a brass shirt stud in one nostril, who had stood in the same corner of the cage with the indomitable Scharife? Naturally not. Had the Arab in him then yielded to some spell of sorcery, was Scharife in fact a witch, was he the same man Lettie Shand had bidden adieu at Derby Wharf, or another— an Arabian, speaking the language of heaven, the very Arabic which he had learned in his captivity? Next, if he wasn't careful, he would be thinking that Scharife was one of the houris of Mohammed, those creatures fair as the sheltered egg, and appointed to lie on brocaded couches and be the reward of the faithful.

He stared at the passage from the Koran pasted on Hassan's gate. "Under thy Veil, O Veiler, happens all." He opened it and strode through piles of green hides, dirty jackasses and slaves to the first of two stone staircases. At the top of the second he stooped through a crooked Saracenic arch, and in a dozen steps, pushing aside a green baize curtain, stood in a great, cool, whitewashed room, with still another staircase of stone against the west wall. But since, through some religious or superstitious motive, there must always be something unfinished about an Arabian house, as if to show that the lives here are likewise still unfinished, the staircase stopped in mid-career, ten feet short of a little wooden door painted in green and yellow stripes. This gap was bridged now by a little crimson camel ladder—the sort of thing used by the old or the fat to mount camels. The room, hung with mirrors, clocks, swords, daggers, lances and Arabian fans, had nothing on its earthen floor but a rich Persian rug and a single chair of East Indian blackwood for any Salem captain who happened to be visiting. Ali Bey, a Turkish traveler, was here now, and Abd Errahman, captain of a dhow called the *She-Mule*, visible at her anchorage through one of the tall windows. Ali Bey had laid aside his French musket and double-edged sword and sat cross-legged on the rug in a robe of green and gold. In his turban was an aigrette of pearls from the Persian Gulf; diamonds gleamed in the gold haft of his dagger.

He looked burly, black, glossy and pious; his eye, under shaggy brows, had a world of concentrative power, and, in fact, he boasted that he could tell a man from a woman in the desert at three leagues. He was a sharif; the blood of Mohammed was in his veins, which made him technically blessed, but didn't prevent him from being a perfectly good and human rogue; and Arad had heard the whisper that Ali Bey had the power of metamorphosis, criminal in a lesser man, and might turn himself into an antelope under an unsuspecting fair woman's hand, or into a leopard or a hyena. It was asserted that twice, in the guise of a hyena, he had tasted human blood. But he was now on his second pilgrimage to Mecca.

A Sakalava girl—her hair between silk and wool—placed a cushion for Arad, and then, putting a black bottle of cherry brandy at his elbow, began indolently fanning him with a scented fan. Ali Bey took up his tale where he had left it off.

"Yes, by the Prophet's red beard, a grand robber, a miscreant, was this Zimbolaci. I met him first in his public house on the island of Cyprus, with his mustaches like palm leaves, a knife, two big pistols— it was Zimbolaci who taught me the policy of going armed," Ali Bey broke off to say, and stroked the stock of his musket lovingly.

"We sat together drinking, smoking and playing chess. His daughter served us, when she wasn't flirting with that Russian admiral who was carrying troops to the Black Sea. Her sister had been married to a Greek, one Constantin Ipsilanti, who had served in the Walloon guards in Spain, and could recite poetry in twelve languages."

"The Prophet detested poets," Hassan murmured. "He calls them liars."

"He does well. But this poet, it seems, in his spare time had taught his wife's sister horsemanship and the use of spear and pistol. Her name

was Djamila, and she must have proved an apt pupil, because when I
next saw Zimbolaci she had run away and got herself made captain of
the emir's guard at Harar, owing to her skill. That poor devil of an emir
had his guard made up of women trained to arms, thinking they were
safer and more loyal. Well, he was wrong. Since Adam made woman
out of a crooked rib, to try to straighten her is to break her. This Djamila
revolted and led that battalion of hers into the stony desert. Arabia the
Stony. I am told now that this band is the terror and scandal of those
parts. The desert tribes are unmanned at the very thought of them.
They are considered as jinn rather than women, although the Sultan did
manage to take one or two alive in a raid. Djamila was a big factor there
in that desert, where a white face is a strong fetish. And by the burning
souls of those wretches who hamstrung the she-camel of God, if she is
like her father, that miscreant, that poisoner—"

Ali Bey here showed emotion for the first time; and Captain Hassan,
turning his courtly face toward Arad so gently as not to shake the fly
fringes of his turban, said, smiling:

"The divan at Constantinople, Reis Whitney, had sent our friend here
on a pilgrimage to Mecca, and in the meantime had made this Zimbolaci chief of the sacred well of Zemzem. All pilgrims must drink of the
waters of this well; to refuse is impious."

"You cannot think with what winning grace and sweetness that devil
offered me my two pitchers a day," Ali Bey growled, with a menacing flash
of his powerful eyes. "I could not, of course, break off my pilgrimage."

"Naturally not," Hassan agreed. "You were watched. He was
watched," he added to Arad, "but knowing himself to be unpopular
with the divan, he had foresight enough to carry in his sleeve a paper
of vitriolated zinc, which he swallowed when he felt the first burning
touches of the poison, and so saved his life."

"He—this Zimbolaci who had kissed my beard several hundred
times a day on the island of Cyprus," Ali Bey breathed harshly, with
a movement of his arm which stirred the flame of the tall spermaceti
candles at his back. Abd Errahman, with his full coffee-colored face,
and body spare as a mummy, and clothed only in a puffy turban and
a string, got to his feet; the Sakalava girl's fan hung like a fantastic
bat from her limp wrist; Captain Hassan bin Ibrahim's luminous mild
eye wheeled with the others. All were looking at that little green-and-
yellow door above the broken staircase. The upper half of it had swung

out; and now Scharife, Arad's purchase, his slave, closer to him than his heart, his neck vein, cried fiercely:

"He is a liar—a poet and a liar! But even if the divan at Constantinople had decreed his death, there was just cause. This man had already changed himself into a hyena and eaten humans. It was discovered by his failure to rub off all of the hyena's tail against a tree when he returned into his human body."

Ali Bey's eyeballs moved strangely, his jaw slacked as if a kind of vertigo, a coup de soleil, had attacked him. He was not angered. It was rather as if the heavens had opened to reveal this houri wrapped in silk and stretched on a brocaded couch at the top of a flight of silver stairs infinitely long and protected by a silver roof.

"Thou—thy very self—fairer than the sheltered egg!" he cried. "Djamila!"

"Impossible!" Hassan bin Ibrahim cried. "Not Zimbolaci's daughter?"

"With Allah nothing is impossible. We are but feathers dropped from his wing," Abd Errahman reminded them gloomily. "Captain Whitney has bought her," Captain Hassan said. Ali Bey clutched the red Morocco case containing his Koran, and fixed his powerful eyes, with the burning devils of sin and piety fighting in them, full on Arad's face.

"Wilt thou sell?" he shouted. "I offer you four hundred sequins! Five hundred!" Arad felt his head in a vise. Five hundred. Five times Lettie Shand's lost adventure. How could he refuse? But Scharife, in a white turban and blue shirt to shield her from the glances of demons, ran down the camel ladder and halfway down the broken-off staircase.

"Do not sell me to this man," she implored.

"I sell? I give you freedom," Arad groaned out.

"I cannot take it. I am your slave."

Ali Bey poured on the rug out of a canvas bag a heap of sequins, Persian piasters, doubloons, Spanish dollars, gold Venetian coins, and some bearing the stamp of the Caliph Harun-al-Rashid's reign.

"Sell; thou wilt gain. Slaves are exacting. You are well rid of her. She has a sweet tooth; she will eat all your dates and honey. And she is the daughter of her father Zimbolaci. She will poison thy soul."

"I will not! May Allah seize him by his lying sinful forelock and drag him on his face into the midfires of hell!" Scharife cried desperately.

"It may be as well to sell," Hassan interjected mildly. "The Sultan is expected in a day or two. He is under the Persian wife's thumb, but it will not be well for the purchaser of his favorite slave to be found here. Unless you sell, you had better embark at once aboard this dhow—the *She-Mule* which is bound for Muscat and Aden."

"Embark—embark," Scharife whispered.

"I have no money."

"Pledge me, your slave, for the passage money. In Muscat I have friends who will redeem us both."

"Embark then!" Arad shouted, seeing his fate hung round his neck closer than his neck vein, in the person of this ravishing slave who could neither be sold, exchanged nor freed. Ali Bey motioned his slave to rake the impudent coins back into the bag.

Abd Errahman, sitting against a bale of cinnamon on the high poop of the *Baghalah*—*She-Mule*—drew smoke through the shank bone of a goat, and said quietly, "I saw a ship's topsail shine a moment since on the sea's threshold. Would it be the British frigate?"

The massive Ali Bey looked with contemplative eyes at the sand heaps in the dhow's open hold, where the fierce pilgrims were lighting individual fires to cook their evening meal. The *She-Mule* had been going round lately in this ocean like a hen with its head cut off. Near Muscat she had fled from the mere rumor of Johassem pirates—those rascals who cried "God is great!" with each head they cut off against a ship's rail, and afterward perfumed decks—and now she had lost the favoring monsoon, and the mighty breath of India, redolent of the spices of Trincomali and Coromandel, blew them day and night toward Aden. The dhow, in shape like a pear cut in two longitudinally, shambled before the wind, and Abd Errahman, who had charts printed on linen showing in detail the latitude and longitude of the infernal regions, had no sea charts and got his bearings here only by random glimpses of the shape of some distant headland, fogged in clouds of fine yellow dust which the northwest wind had swept up and carried here from Mesopotamian deserts.

"Even if it is the frigate," Ali Bey said at length, "she will not hold up a ship bound on a pilgrimage to Mecca." Abd Errahman, once the slave of a butter merchant at Mocha, and later a desert rider and Baloche mercenary, shook his head faintly. In the desert he could tell the print of a thief from that of an honest man in the sands, but on the sea he contented himself with listening to the creak of the giant steering tackle and calling five times a day on Allah.

"If we escape this fellow by running before the wind," he said now, watching the looming topsail, "it will only be to fall into the hands of these devils in the neighborhood of Sib. This coast is inhuman."

Arad Whitney, in brown linen coat and pantaloons, presented himself.

"Let me have the loan of your Koran, Ali Bey," he said sharply. "My slave wants to read in it."

"Your slave. Despise your slave or she will despise you," Abd Errahman warned him, but Ali Bey did not refuse him the Koran. The Salem trader had showed to great advantage in that business of outmaneuvering the Johassem pirates. He had somehow got the dhow into his hands without any formal transfer, and now many of the pilgrims were inclined to think of him as the master of the hour.

Ali Bey, giving him the Koran, murmured, "Allah give me only a little of what he has given you." But when the boy was out of hearing, Abd Errahman asked, "Which is slave, and which is master between them? Or is it love? Has he purchased a lump of sugar with a mountain of gall?"

"But if sugar be the mountain," Ali Bey suggested. "Certainly, she is beautiful. Her hair is black as feathers of the male ostrich, her neck is Allah's watch tower, her lips are rubies set in ivory, her arms are slender swords mounted in silver. But her eyes—her eyes are black as the muzzles of loaded pistols, warm with the flash of powder."

"Life is a sea, and men blind billows on its surface," Abd Errahman contended.

"The slave occupies the cabin, and the master stands guard outside. Three times a day he brings her dates and honey. He has given her a knife. You saw him yourself take it out of the hands of that foolish Persian who used it only for picking his teeth. And now, when the master sleeps, the slave watches," went on the captain of the *She-Mule* earnestly. "She is a sorceress, I hear, who can turn a man into a bearded goat."

"Night of power," Ali Bey said suddenly, "we shall have sand in our teeth before we know it. The beach is not far off."

"Allah make hard things easy," Abd Errahman said, without moving his shoulders from the bale of cinnamon. The man, clasped by his bare legs to the top of the great pole mast with its forward rake, cried down that the water was shoaling. But Arad, holding the Koran with both hands on Scharife's knees—she was sitting on a cedar chest bound with cords—had no thought of the razor edges of coral reefs.

He did not see the sun sinking between apple-green mountains, nor
the remote saffron-colored sands, with the rows of palms growing
darker and seeming to push their stems up directly out of a lilac ocean.
"Again. Read again," Arad urged his slave.

Scharife put the point of the Persian's silver-hafted dagger to her
teeth, dropped it to the Dog Star on her breast.

"This passage is well-known," she assured him. "Thus: 'And who
of you is not rich enough to marry free believing women, then let him
marry such believing maidens as have fallen into his hands as slaves.'
. . . Well, am I not thy slave—I, Andrea Zimbolaci's daughter?"

The dhow was filled with wind-driven bats and butterflies; a yellow
butterfly lodged on Scharife's breast, covering the Dog Star there.

"But I am an infidel!" Arad shouted. "You are commanded to marry
believing men."

Scharife lowered her face swiftly to his, and her great eyes searched,
entreated.

"You an infidel? Oh, my master Salem, how can you be an infidel—
you who speak the language of heaven so sweetly? Have you considered? What of that day when the summoner shall cry to hell, 'Art thou
full?' and hell shall answer, 'Are there more?' Tell me, is it easier to
believe, or to lie in hell forever with your right hand chained to the back
of your neck? Ah, no, by the veil of night, by the fig and olive, by earth
which openeth her bosom, by the star-bespangled heavens—"

"What are they all shouting at now?" Arad interrupted. He stood up
and recognized the *Bold Runner* by her cream-colored bulwarks, her
red-painted ports. It was Captain Webb's topsail that Adb Errahman had
mistaken for a frigate.

"Old Bullhead has got wind of me at last," Arad thought.

A puff of smoke at the *Bold Runner*'s bow was followed by a splash
of solid shot under the dhow's counter. But the beach, not half a
gunshot off, was black with horses, asses and wild dromedary riders.
The frenzied pilgrims babbled shrill prayers, asking, among other
things, to have the spirits of the drowned Egyptians lay hold of that
ship's on-coming keel.

But the *Bold Runner*'s second shot pierced the dhow's great right-
angled sail fairly. It burst like a pinched grape skin, but the *She-Mule*'s
forefoot was already in the sand, and the pilgrims pitching forward on
their faces in involuntary attitudes of prayer. Arad, with one arm round
his slave and the other clutching the carved head of an Egyptian god,

a poop ornament, saw the surf black with naked spearmen coming full tilt with knives in their mouths. "Old Bullhead will be taken in the same net," he thought, seeing the *Bold Runner*'s sails shaking in the wind. "He's certain to put a boat ashore after me."

And, in fact, the *Bold Runner*'s longboat was already in the water.

"What cock-and-bull story have you told this sheik?" Captain Webb— old Bullhead—croaked. It was the fifth night from the taking of the dhow and the *Bold Runner.*

The Sheik Bel Arab of Sib was encamped under a holy sycamore, with his slaves, women, wives and spearmen. Abd Errahman, late captain of the *She-Mule*, had covered himself with sand, but Captain Webb sat disconsolately in his underclothes—all that Bel Arab had left him—with his gouty foot swathed in dirty canvas. Old Bullhead was yellow as a lemon peel from his years of haunting the deadly mouths of the oil rivers of West Africa, but he still had that damn-my-eyes look of an old salt about him, even after three days on the back—the stern, rather—of the camel called El Harami—the Ruffian—whose spine was like the blade of an oar set on edge. The Ruffian's belly, too, vast and smooth by reason of the three barrels of water he had taken in at the last well, offered few fingerholds.

"I have told him to take us to Aden and get his ransom there," Arad said.

"Who from?"

"The sheik asked that very question, sir. He asked the man's name. I told him, 'Consul.'"

"Consul! Faugh! If I had a white rope's end handy, I'd make you turn your back to windward, big as you are. I'd skin your back. Consul!"

"What else was I to say, sir? His eye pierced me to the soul. 'You agree,' he said, 'before God most high, to pay one hundred dollars for each, and for me personally a double-barreled gun? This is a long desert, there is risk in the southwest, and I could sell you easier in another direction.' So, I swore, captain, by Allah, and by the authors of my days, and by the sacred stone, and by the burning souls of those wretches who—"

"That's enough," old Bullhead grated. "I don't doubt you piled the agony on thick enough. You've got that slave of yours gone, and that's one mercy. You don't even know which way they took her."

"I am thinking she was in the same caravan with Ali Bey," Arad said darkly.

Old Bullhead snorted. Abd Errahman, with only his head out of the sand, whispered, "These people are afraid. They have sniffed a war wind. They are keeping the fires low, and I saw them, a little while ago, feeding the camels opium to stop their grumbling."

Bel Arab's lampblack spearmen were in fact wakeful. They had finished buttering their bodies and their red heads, had eaten their shark meat—which would have baffled the product of Doctors Peabody and Fisk, those Salem manufacturers of incorruptible teeth—and now went about putting ear to the sand, listening, and then roaring like a lion or laughing like a hyena, to indicate to other possible desert voyagers that this well was not a place of social meeting.

Toward noon of the next day, confronted with a line of horseshoe-shaped sand dunes, the caravan stopped uncertainly.

"Behind these hillocks is—whatever is," Abel Errahman declared. "Yonder are tracks," he cried bitterly to Bel Arab.

"Tracks?"

"Tracks."

Abd Errahman put his very nose to the suspected sand, and the spearmen in secondhand wigs, formerly the property of English barristers, hemmed him in. Their oiled spears quivered, and their buttered bodies shone like lacquer. Herbs here were reduced to blackened cinders, and the horses' tails, full of electricity from the dry air, crackled as they beat off the flies, which, like slaves or camels, it seemed, feared to desert the caravan and take chances alone with such a dismal valley.

Abd Errahman stood up slowly.

"Your fears are justified," he said to Bel Arab. "These are women."

"Women?"

"Women—all women, by my neck and yours. To the last woman."

Even the old Baloche mercenary could tell at a glance whether the animals were loose, freighted, or mounted, and if mounted, whether by men or women, jinn or mortals.

"Well, in any case, they have passed—they have missed us," Arad muttered.

"He who sees the track sees the foe," Abd Errahman said sternly. "Well, life is a storm, and man only a handful of dust flung against it. These are not women to trifle with; they are—" But speech was choked in his throat with the advent of a burning sand shower which blotted out everything, or all but a dire shape, shrouded in this sand wind, mounted on a swift horse, and clad, it seemed, in some kind of bright calico wraprascal. Then the air in a twinkling was full of spears, gun flashes and fierce women's voices. Bel Arab was beaten to his knees; he was a captive with a spear driven through both cheeks, and his horsemen fled into the desert.

Arad, brushed by a horse's shoulder, felt his hand seized. Scharife, in a leather skull cap, with a lion's hide around her body and a shield of boiled hippopotamus hide on her left arm, was sliding toward him, shaking clear of the shield, freeing her big toe from the iron stirrup.

"Is there anywhere a mosque more beautiful than heaven's vault?" Scharife murmured from the turreted parapet of a house deep in the oasis of Ihrah. She was clad in a twist of red silk, with thirty-eight-ounce silver rings around her ankles, and an ugly red weal on her forearm where she had put a brand to remind herself, first by the burn and later by the scar, that a vow of love or hate was still unfulfilled. Her eyes were black; the lashes, touched with antimony, would have made the blackest bee envious, Arad thought. And then, her teeth—like camels' milk. Ali Bey was right. "Can you still think," Scharife cried, gripping Arad's arms, "that this blue sky is but an empty socket, lacking Allah's eye?"

"Not in Egypt, not in Norway, are the stars so fierce as over this Desert of Oman," Arad said.

"And who but Allah caused my women to attack the very revenue caravan in which I was a slave? It is true, Ali Bey escaped on a dromedary and notified them, but Allah directed his footsteps. And could you not believe that this oasis was the very paradise promised by the Prophet?"

"Yes. . . . If only I had not sworn an oath to get this old captain of mine to Aden."

"He shall be sent. Consider. This oasis is no bigger than my palm, my heart, yet all the riches of Oman are crowded here. Fig, olive, walnut, citron, pomegranate, sugar cane and coffee bushes. Let this be the fire where you warm your soul, O master Salem."

The desert wind, stirring in the inky palm fronds, was sweet as the music plucked from David's harp, mysterious, fragrant as the breath of love.

There was no noise. The women who had been wounded were quartered in the ground floor of this house. The rest had played with the great rope swings hanging from the palms—for Arabs love to swing; they had eaten of a leaf brought by camel loads into Aden, which produces hilarity; but their laughter had died, and they slept, wrapped only in oasis gloom, to the music of running water.

"This slave of mine may be a captain of thieves, but she is closer to me than my neck vein still," Arad was thinking. Aloud he said: "My captain won't be satisfied short of Aden."

"My troopers will take him to Aden."

"He won't go without me."

"Not if steel prods him? These desert riders of mine are merciless. Their flesh is like iron. They go for days on a diet of dates, sleep naked in the sand. I too already, since I have breathed this desert air, my arm is stronger, my aim is truer."

She hung her whole weight from his neck by her arm. Her eyes, lighted only by the glow from the coffee furnace, adored him. "I am a seaman," Arad faltered. "I know nothing of the desert. If, like Abd Errahman, I could tell a thief's track in the sand from an honest man's . . ."

"You can tell a snake's from a camel's. The rest will come. You can tell happiness from misery, and love from hate."

"I am an infidel, I tell you."

"So you are always telling me, but I do not believe that. You know that one day the sun will be folded up, and the stars will fall, and the seas dry, and the mountains crumble like carded wool. Children know this. Well, then, on that day when the sky shall be stripped away like a veil—nay, like the skin of a flayed animal—do you think Salem will give you fairer visions than this oasis? How can you convince me that you will prefer then to drink in hell as the thirsty camel drinks, and never satisfy your thirst?"

For whole seconds there was no sound but the bubbling of clove-scented coffee in the coffee furnace near the stairhead. Zimbolaci's daughter used all her sorcery, and the trader sank to his knees. The violent booming in his ear, like surf, was only, he became aware, the beating of Scharife's heart. Yet suddenly he had a clear vision of the *Bold Runner*, laden with coffee, ivory and spices; her sails white under a flying moon, her hull rising and dipping to the long seas that rolled green over the weather fence. Madness; the *Bold Runner* was in the Sheik Bel Arab's hands, Lettie Shand's adventure was lost, had slipped like sand through his fingers; he could neither recover it nor come into her presence without it. Yet, in this fierce yellow world, with only Allah's eye to watch him, his visions were still of Salem—the Haste, the Brimbles, Gray's Rock, and Marblehead fort.

Scharife, his slave, was the daughter of a poisoner, and had dripped cold poison in his veins.

"Let me drink in hell then!" he cried thickly.

"We can still be happy," Scharife reminded him.

"The only happiness is self-forgetfulness—so they say in Salem."

"Then death is the most satisfying self-forgetfulness," Scharife flung at him; and Ali Bey's description of her eyes as muzzles of two loaded pistols was never closer to the facts. "Well, you shall not die. I will make you my slave, since I cannot be yours. Do you hear? You shall crouch in the sand outside my tent, spread my carpets, polish my spears, read my prayers, load my camels. . . . Yes, by Allah, you shall be forced to scrub my neck and shoulders night and morning with sand, my hand-maiden. You are a slave henceforth, a slave from Zanzibar."

"Good! File my teeth then, slit my ears, slash my cheeks, choke me with flour and blind me with pepper," Arad grated. "Bury me standing to the neck in sand, I shall be a seaman to my last breath."

"Oh, may Allah blacken your happiness!" Scharife sobbed.

"May Allah break the legs of all your camels!" Arad stormed.

At this truly dreadful curse Scharife gasped and, vanishing into the tiled stairway, banged to the copper-ringed door at the stairhead. Almost instantly Ali Bey crawled over the parapet. He had, it seemed, climbed up a rope swing in a neighboring palm and swung himself onto the roof.

"Ah, friend of my soul," the celebrated Ali Bey murmured.

"You," Arad said savagely. "I thought perhaps you had turned yourself into a hyena again."

"It is true, I was within a hair of being eaten by a hyena," Ali Bey conceded. "But then, how to turn myself back into a man? There's the rub. Well, here is a choice for you. Shall we take these four knives and stand toe to toe until one of us is left remaining; or, on the other hand, will you see fit to sell this slave of yours for three hundred sequins, which is what these women have given me for my services in rescuing their leader?"

"This slave of mine," Arad repeated, "for three hundred sequins. I like this better. Put the knives up. She is yours. But how can she be made to follow you?"

"With you gone, I shall accomplish it. For the time being, I can give up my holy errand," Ali Bey announced. "Let her turn east or west, she will see nothing but the face of Allah, hear only the voice of love. Only relinquish her, escape, and these sequins are yours. Escape is easy. My camel is outside the thorn ring at the edge of the oasis, a rose-colored dromedary, very fleet, watered and provisioned. The old man, your captain, has been roused already. This camel will go three days and nights without stopping. You sleep and cook on his back and take turns at the neck position. I will describe the route to Aden. The sand showers will conceal your tracks, and furthermore, I will put them off the scent."

"Good. Put the sequins into my belt. This moon-faced beauty is yours," Arad whispered ironically. Ali Bey folded his hands over his heart in the usual desert salutation.

"This camel here—the miscreant—won't rise," Arad said in a dusty voice to Captain Webb.

"You have forgotten the words. Ikh! Ikh!"

"That makes him kneel."

"Knock him between the ears."

"That is only to stop him. He is stopped already. No, he has pricked a hoof," Arad groaned, and swept with one bloodshot eye the line of yellow desert which came like a grim sea in sand ripples up to their very ankles. The atmosphere was all on fire.

Far off, and still huge as ever, was the monstrous mountain called the Believer's Back, because in shape it was like one of the faithful praying with hands, knees and forehead on the ground. For two mornings Captain Webb, baking out his lame foot in hot sand, had shaken his fist at that mountain, at that implacable Believer. Yet he himself did not believe.

"We'll have to walk," Arad said.

"Walk? How can I walk with this cursed foot?"

"When you can't walk, I'll carry you." They limped away in frayed camel-skin sandals, and the abandoned camel followed them with his eyes and a babyish quivering of his flexible lips. The desert swallowed him, and the two fugitives stumbled across a vast sheet of isinglass which cut their worn sandals to shreds and struck sun into their eyes in blinding flashes.

"Maybe another time you will think twice before laying out money in a slave," Captain Webb complained.

"I could have had five hundred sequins for her at Zanzibar," Arad answered.

"And wouldn't take it. No, not you. Instead, you dally and lollygag, and put me to the trouble of getting on your trail. By the holy poker, if Lettie Shand hadn't made a point of getting me to swear by the bloody wars that I would keep an eye on you, I wouldn't find myself in this predicament. I'm covered with pink ants."

"I got three hundred sequins for her as it was."

"It weighs you down. You'll see. You'll have to drop it."

In fact, coin by coin at first, and then by the double handful, Arad was forced to throw his treasure to the sands. His mouth and tongue were coated with a wax-like crust; his lips cracked, his bones crumbled in the fierce heat. The sun was like a lion's flaming breath. He moved spellbound in an evil dream from which there was no escape, and which altered only for the worse.

When that night they camped under a dead tamarisk by a well choked with sand, they roared feebly like lions and laughed like hyenas, to frighten away wandering Arabs; and they were answered by an indifferent roar of a neighboring lion who evidently knew this well was dry, since he came no nearer. Captain Webb muttered that J. Chaney, in Water Street, Salem, who sold lion-skin overcoats along with his Petersham surtouts, ought to be along with them.

"Chaney would drive a hard bargain with the beasts," old Bullhead whispered grimly; and they licked dew from their knife blades, as once, becalmed in the Bight of Benin, they had licked dew from ship's iron and eaten tallow arming from the bottom of a ship's lead.

By noon of the next day they had no images in the brain except such as had to do with water. A phantom hand offered water in a bowl, and withdrew it. An oasis turned into a clump of dragon's-blood trees and sickly green acacias. A camel's-back cloud dripped rain in buckets, but the sun drank it in mid-air. A waterspout became a fiery pillar of sand, which made them kneel as low as the Believer, and let the flesh be grated from their naked bodies. They had lost all track of time. The celebrated Capt. James Riley, in his captivity, had marked the days on his leg with thorn pricks, but these captives had no thorns.

They could not tell, later, by what degrees they came into the valley of elephants, but there, soon or late, they found themselves. Elephants lay all about as thick as sand, but they lay on their leathery sides, capsized, hamstrung, and dead of thirst.

The sun flashed on their tusks.

"Here's trade at last," old Bullhead cackled feebly. "Here's prime ivory and heavy average, if I know ivory. The *Bold Runner* ought to make a saving voyage." He pulled at one of the tusks; it slipped from his hands and he rolled in the sand.

He was, he said, monarch of all he surveyed, and Arad, to humor him, crowned his captain king of this desert by dropping a few blackened gum leaves on his head. They staggered on, now falling like dry sticks from the camel fold; again, with curses standing each other up like ill-behaved manikins. The hides of these unbelievers were filled with flaming darts from the garrison of heaven, poured out of a sky of brass; and they could never wink out of their eyes the colossal shape of that mountain of a believer, eternally on his knees.

Arad's eardrums were tortured by the exaggerated sound of sand particles rolling down into his footprints when he lifted his raw feet. Ivory was everywhere, a king's ransom; it was like the vision of dry bones of Ezekiel; but the boy had Captain Webb on his back now, and he was forced to drop the last handful of his accursed sequins.

Old Bullhead fancied he was on the sea again.

"Take the wheel, you lazy ship's cousin," he croaked in Arad's ear. "Can't you see we're abreast of Little Misery already? It's the fourth Salem channel, you long fool. Stand to the westward till you bring the north part of Naugus Head onto the north part of Coney. West by south a half south."

"That'll leave the Cutthroats to the south'ard," Arad muttered.

"Say it does. Pass between the Middle Ground and the Triangles, and you can't come to any harm. Now, boy! Now you've got Hopkins' steeple well open to the south'ard of Crowinshield's lower store. Haul up for the anchoring ground. Lettie Shand has seen your topsails by this time, I wouldn't wonder."

Arad Whitney, sinking lower, heard the cluck of water under Derby Wharf. It was easy enough to think himself in Essex Street with a St. Iago cigar in his mouth, his throat cooled with a foaming draught of Newburgh amber and pale ale.

For a long while now he had not dared to look back at the Believer, but the noise of sand particles had turned into the thunder of horses' hoofs.

Coup de soleil touched his brain with its powder flash; horses were reined up on every side, brown women with aquiline noses and black hair fell out of the sky like curses, walled him in with their shields, barred his way with red-hot spears.

"O Allah," he shouted, flailing his arms, and using Abd Errahman's favorite formula, "shadow me in thy shadow on this day when there is no shade but thy shadow!"

"Thou art shadowed, thy prayer is answered!" Scharife cried, dismounting and pressing close against him in her lion skin, which the sun's rays had heated unbearably hot. "Allah hears his son."

The revolted captain of the emir's guard, this long-haired scourge of the desert, held the sinking trader up and moistened his lips with water from a prayer bottle.

"Why do you look here for me?" Arad muttered.

"Ali Bey has powerful eyes. I buried him in sand to the neck and asked him where you were. He looked once and saw you. Next, we found your camel. Again, on a patch of flint where there were no tracks, we found here and there a coin."

"Well, I am your slave. Bury me standing."

"No, by Allah. You are the knife, I am the flesh," Scharife murmured. As soon as a tent had been erected over them, she asked submissively, "Is it your will to return to the oasis? That is Allah's shadow."

"No. I go on my pilgrimage—to Salem."

"I am the slave of my slave."

"I have no ship!" Arad cried, inspired.

"But I love you better than myself. It beseemeth not me to take other lords than thee, oh, my master Salem. Since you cannot be free without a ship—and certainly a horseman without arms is nothing better than a plucked bird—I will get your ship back in exchange for my captive, the Sheik Bel Arab."

"But the ship is empty. My captain here has been robbed of the specie with which he meant to trade. If it was Canton, China, Houqua would trust him with half a dozen shiploads, but the trade with Zanzibar has just been opened. If we should return to Salem without the customary ivory . . ."

"Ivory? But here is a valley full of ivory. It is yours to the last tusk. I will stop a shark-meat caravan and compel transportation to Sib."

"As I am a child of sin, I do not deserve—I have not earned," Arad was beginning brokenly and piously.

"If Allah did not pardon sinners Paradise would be an empty place," Scharife reminded him. "You go, but this wretched little Salem cannot keep you always in its camel fold. You will come again."

"My beard is in your hand. They will send me again."

"That is what I think. My ivory will bring you. Well, God imparadise you both." "You both." He knew that Arab habit of speaking to a man as if he were two men, his erring self and his guardian angel, his familiar demon, the spectator in his blood. Sinking like a drowned man in Scharife's arms, Arad Whitney felt these two men locked together in his breast.

On a fall night in Salem, Arad came ashore from the *Bold Runner*. Some kind of festival was in the air, he inferred. Union Street, full of mud, was just one long stable, and even poor Mrs. Rust's garden was jammed with carriages and horses. Young Arad learned that there was a cotillion party in the supper room of Hamilton Hall, and that Lettie Shand was there. He sent Honeycomb's boy in to fetch her down to him at the back entrance.

Waiting, Arad stared through a lower window at Lucas Estes, who had exchanged his post horn for an elegant twelve-keyed silver bugle with gold trimmings, a present to him by popular subscription. The boy was playing an E flat solo with variations. "Cease, Rude Boreas," Arad thought the tune was. Suddenly he felt ghostlike, legendary, as always on returning home. Salem remembered him, stared at his adventures and absorbed his cargoes, but could he take Salem quite into his confidence? Could he impart, even to Captain Shand, his owner, the terms of that strange desert bargain? And then he thought, what if Lettie Shand should fail to recognize him?

"Arad."

There was Lettie, not a handspike's length away from him, her dress of sprigged muslin covered by an Indian Cashmere shawl festooned over her left arm. She wore, fetchingly, the very bell-crowned hat that Arad had brought her home from Wales, for no better reason than that Welsh women were the most beautiful and captivating in the world. But were they? he now asked himself. Had they enough elan, were they headlong, could they tell when to throw caution to the winds? Testa lunga, that was the Italian of it. How would they look, wrapped in a lion skin and nothing else besides? Or, for example, Lettie. "You can tell your father his ship's in," Arad said a little throatily. "The *Bold Runner* is tied up alongside."

He stepped forward impulsively in his red shirt and tar-smeared pantaloons. "Arad, no; not here." No testa lunga in the gold-haired Lettie's eyes. "Anybody might go by. . . . Well, one. . . . There. . . . It is you. You are thinner, but you look well. You have been sixteen months away, but I suppose to you it seems only yesterday. Tell me quick; how have you done with my adventure?"

"I bring you five for one, in ivory, from the Desert of Oman," Arad reported. "You would be surprised at the quantities and quantities of elephants there. They live by uprooting trees full of burning milk. I tried to drink the milk myself and blistered my lips."

"You are beginning your fairy tales early this time home," Lettie laughed, and tapped his nose with her sandalwood fan. "How do you kill your elephants, pray?"

"They are killed for us. An Arab on a white donkey lures the elephant past a bush where another man is waiting to hamstring him with a knife or shoot a poisoned arrow into the sole of his foot. Naturally, after that, in time he sinks down and dies of thirst. He has my sympathy," Arad added, staring.

"And you have his ivory. A fair exchange," Lettie said, frowning and moving her fine shoulders under the shawl. "But these infidels can never be anything but base and cruel. They will poison a man, I suppose, as quick as an elephant. And their terrible religion. I remember how eloquently Doctor Bentley once preached on the infidels. He said eternity to them was just lolling on a green silk cushion with some dark-eyed, improper, foreign woman."

"I don't know that it speaks well for the lady in the case, if that's eternity," Arad said somberly. What if he told Lettie now that the *Bold Runner*, as she stood, with all tackle, apparel and furniture, to say nothing of a priceless cargo of ivory, was just a heart gift of one of these same infidels? What if he told her that henceforth the fortunes of the house of Shand were founded on one cunning prayer to Allah from his own lips? Instead, he said, "Eternity to me was waiting for old Southwick's cowhide to fall when I was one of the johnny-cake-and-ashes boys in Southwick's Alley."

"I can't have you trafficking any more with this terrible Arabia," Lettie Shand decided for him. "What if you were taken slave again? It set its mark on you before. It did truly. You were like a stranger when you made love to me in Arabic. And then these fights with Northwest

Indians, and Fiji cannibals and those awful yellow Chinamen. It's coarsening. Next you'll be dickering in slaves—creatures made in God's own image."

"In God's own image," Arad repeated, with certain reflections of his own.

"There is blood on trade, we can't deny it!" Lettie Shand cried. "I vow, if I had not been born a trader's daughter, I couldn't stomach it at all. I can't as it is. I've got news, Arad. I've got father to agree to take you into partnership. You're needed here."

"He'll never think so now. I've opened a new market."

"Others can develop it. You're not indispensable, I'm sure."

"Nowhere but there," Arad replied with an enigmatic laugh.

"Let's not discuss it now. This is not the time or place," Lettie said swiftly. She shivered; the warmth was out of her eyes.

"I think I had really better go back in. You can't come with me, Arad; you're not dressed for it. Perley Poore's Newbury riflemen are being entertained. The poor fellows slept on the common last night in tents with just a single blanket apiece; imagine—and only oysters to eat."

"That was hard."

"I'll come see my ivory tomorrow."

She left him abruptly. Arad felt himself a stranger in the earth, so situated that only things hull down, remote, could have reality. Such as now, the stars shining over Oman. "Voyaging was victory," the Arabs were always saying to justify their wanderings; but what, looked at closely, was this victory? Queer that the two men in him would never let him come to rest. In the end, no doubt he would be caught between pilgrimages; there was probably no escape from his dilemma except to founder in an open seaway. The Salem band, inside, played Come Where My Love Lies Dreaming, and Arad, standing stock-still, saw the veil of heaven stripped away "like the skin of a flayed animal," offering the vision of Scharife, his slave, in Captain Hassan bin Ibrahim's house at Zanzibar, dropping her sweet poison almost with her father's art, from that queer stone staircase ending nowhere, broken off in midcareer, unfinished, like the house of dreams.

MY UNCLE'S FOOTPRINTS

From the *Saturday Evening Post* (March 30, 1946)

While a correspondent for Maine newspapers covering World War II, Hallet realized a lifelong ambition to visit the Marshall Islands and the site of his uncle Will Jackson's 1884 shipwreck and heroic actions to save the captain and crew of the ship Rainier. *His account here, one of only two articles in this book, is a rollicking story of cross-cultural interchange and personal discovery in the remote Pacific.*

My uncle, Will Jackson, of Bath, Maine, was a legendary sort of man, and in his short life as a seafarer he had many narrow squeaks. Once while going round the Horn, he was washed overboard, and the next wave washed him back on board again. Shipwreck topped the list of his adventures. In 1883, while en route for Kobe, Japan, aboard the new Bath ship *Rainier*, he crashed on the windward reef of the atoll of Ujae in the Marshall Islands, ninety miles west of Kwajalein. He survived—only to be stamped to death a few years later by a runaway horse on a peaceful Sunday morning in San Francisco.

Growing up with the legend of my fabulous uncle, I never wearied of hearing family tales about his sojourn among the cannibals of Ujae—who were not really cannibals at all—and I had a sneaking wish to ship before the mast and fall among cannibals myself, although I hoped that they would be friendly cannibals, as his had been.

I finally did ship on a British windjammer out of Bayonne, New Jersey, bound, in oil, for Sydney, Australia. But adventure cannot be contracted for. Either it happens or it doesn't happen, and in due course—124 days—I arrived in Sydney via the Cape of Good Hope without having been cast away at all or even faintly threatened with shipwreck.

More lately I had about reconciled myself to the fact that I was never likely to catch up with my legendary uncle, when suddenly a way opened for me to set my feet all but in his footprints, and walk through the scenes of one of his most startling adventures.

At Pearl Harbor, last summer, I stopped over on my way to a forward area as a correspondent. I thought perhaps I might at least fly over Ujae en route and, getting the ear of an admiral, I spun my yarn. I painted the picture of this Maine ship crashing down on that remote reef, the native outriggers swarming all round her, the ship's company looking dubiously at those wild fellows tumbling in the surf, with yellow flowers hanging from the holes in their ears.

Ujae was uncharted and was believed to be a cannibal island when Uncle Will landed there; a liking for long pig on the part of the inhabitants was certain to have disastrous consequences for shipwrecked men. (I could see the admiral was interested and continued with my uncle's story.) As it turned out, they were not cannibals, but they might well enough be killers, for white men had often come in "snatch-snatch" ships to kidnap their youth and set them miserably to work on foreign plantations.

That was not the mission of the *Rainier*, but the Ujaens could not know that. Kabua, the paramount chief of the Marshall Islands, was notoriously fond of tobacco and killed whole ships' companies to get it. He made other errors too. Once, by mistake, he had drunk a little kerosene, thinking it to be the white man's beverage, and once, lured on by the agreeable smell of soap, Kabua had eaten some.

Luckily, Kabua did not visit the atoll of Ujae during the period of Uncle Will's shipwreck. Fortunately, the King of Ujae, Nejeke, was a more sympathetic soul, or perhaps he was just more canny.

"S'pose king good to Will Jackson," he said once. "Man-of-war no bum-bum king?" By "bum-bum," I told the admiral, Nejeke probably meant "bombard."

Here was, at least, the beginning of a shrewd foreign policy.

Will Jackson was a diplomat too. He replied, "S'pose king good. Give Will Jackson plenty *kai-kai* (food). Man-of-war no bum-bum king."

King Nejeke went away and sent back plenty of coconuts by a boy messenger.

The ship's company turned to and built a small schooner out of the wreckage of the *Rainier*, King Nejeke contributing a breadfruit tree for a keel. It was not a donation exactly; the crew were forced to barter most of their clothes for it. And while they toiled naked in the fierce sun, the king sat watching, dressed in an ulster, and with a pair of detachable celluloid cuffs hanging round his spotted ankles.

The new schooner was about two months building, and in her the captain of the *Rainier*, who had suffered a stroke and was speechless, sailed for Jaluit with Will Jackson and about half the members of the crew. The rest of the crew waited at Ujae. At Jaluit, the schooner was confiscated by a German trader, as part payment for the food he furnished her crew.

One day while things were in this ugly pass, the schooner *Lotus* dropped anchor at Jaluit. Formerly of San Francisco, she now belonged to paramount chief Kabua, the old killer of ships' companies, who had his main establishment on the atoll of Ailinglapalap. Kabua's son was skipper of her. He said he must first take medicine to Kabua, who was sick, but after that he would go to Ujae and bring off the rest of the shipwrecked people there.

Will Jackson thereupon shipped in the *Lotus*, and thus got back to Ujae, where he found King Nejeke strolling on the beach in the uniform of a United States naval commander. This uniform, he explained, had been given him by the commander of the U.S.S. *Essex*, which had just lately taken the stranded men off Ujae. The king handed Will a letter signed by the commander, saying that the *Essex* was sailing for Jaluit to pick up the captain and the rest of his men, and would then continue on to Yokohama.

"Man-of-war go. No come again," King Nejeke said. "Never mind. King good to Will Jackson."

King Nejeke and the young Maine seaman became good friends, though always with certain reservations. Will stayed in his tent on the beach, and the king sent him daily gifts of baked breadfruit and coconuts. Three months dragged by. Will grew impatient and demanded that the king send him to Jaluit.

At this point the king consulted a familiar spirit named Libogen. This spirit was that of a woman who had died forty years before and was now fluttering in the thatch of the king's palace. She spoke in a bird's voice. Libogen had the gift of prophecy.

Consulting this useful spirit, Nejeke held up his hand with fingers spread far apart: on the fifth day a trading schooner would drop anchor in Ujae lagoon and take Will Jackson to his people.

Libogen spoke truly. On the fifth day the schooner came.

As I finished my story, I could see the admiral was impressed. I told him I would like to fly over Ujae and look down from the air on those historic islands. He thought I might be able to do better than that. He looked in his files and found that there were no Japs on Ujae now. There had been seven, in charge of a weather station, but when the marines landed, these Japs, after a little formal resistance, blew themselves to pieces.

"Perhaps the atoll commander in the Marshalls may be able to set you on Ujae with an interpreter," the admiral said.

The atoll commander put me in touch with the head of his military government for the Marshalls, who arranged my itinerary. So we came, after some days, to the fabled atoll of Ujae, which, like all atolls, consists of a shallow oval lagoon bound in by coral reefs, with white surf beating all round and a fine trade wind drawing through the island palms.

We entered about noon through a break in the reef on the leeward side and cast anchor about a mile offshore. Outriggers took us to the beach; our party included an American dentist with his chair, young American doctors with their instruments and medicines, an education officer with his records, and me with nothing more than a legend of shipwreck.

It looked like a fatal blow to my prestige when it appeared that I must come ashore on the shoulders of a squat, muscular Marshallese, who stood chest-deep in water at the prow of the outrigger, and invited me to clasp my legs round his neck. Ens. Mike Rooney, the education officer, said I had better do as I was told. The islanders expected it; they would not think too highly of a white man who presented himself to them drenched to the skin, and with his shins barked on coral. Rooney's explanation comforted me.

I, therefore, Will Jackson's nephew, came into Ujae piggyback, and was dumped down on a coral beach of dazzling whiteness, lapped by a light green sea and backed by tall palms.

The natives of Ujae, 132 of them, were drawn up in a straight line from the water's edge up into the palms. With Rooney, I passed along this line like a political candidate, and shook hands with all—men, women, children and babies. The men were mostly in blue cotton shirts and pants; the old women still clung to Mother Hubbards, or rather Mother Hubbards clung to them; the young women's skirts compromised by going halfway between knee and ankle. Some were wearing dresses made of netting which the military government had sent as a protection against mosquitoes at night.

I asked my interpreter, Rudolph Capelli, of Likiep, to gather them round me; and then I told them of the wreck of the *Rainier*, of the fortunes of the crew and their final rescue. I asked if any man or woman present was old enough to remember these events. Sentence by sentence, the interpreter turned my words into Marshallese.

There was a moment of silence. Then an old man, very shrunken, his eyes blue with incipient blindness, his bald bead shining in the hot sun, stepped forward and spoke briefly.

"This is Lami," the interpreter told me. "He says that he was special boy to your Uncle Will Jackson. He was told by the king to bring him coconuts to his tent."

FOR AULD LANG SYNE

A great cry of surprise and joy went up from the natives. Their bare toes grasped excitedly at coral pebbles.

"How big were you when you were my uncle's special boy?" I asked Lami.

The old man's fading eyes searched the crowd; then he put his withered hand on the head of a boy of twelve.

"I was as big as this boy. No bigger," he said.

As it was possible that old Lami was claiming acquaintance with Will Jackson merely to save me from disappointment, I tried to get him to say something positive, something that would check with my own knowledge.

"Can you remember the name of the captain's daughter?" I asked.

It was a thousand-to-one shot. Who could expect him, after sixty years, to remember the name of that young white woman who had descended on him out of the struggling cloud of white canvas of a doomed ship pounding to pieces on the reef?

"Emma," he finally said.

Exactly so. It was Emma. Old Lami spoke the name with affection, as if she still lived warmly in his memory.

There was a great stir, but old Lami, sunk in the past, only lowered his head and said "Emma, Emma," twice over.

"She was the age of this one," he added, getting up and putting his hand on the shoulder of a young woman of twenty-five whose black hair was stuck thick with yellow flowers.

"Tell me this, Lami, are there any traces of the ship left on the reef?"

"There is only iron," Lami said regretfully. "The wood is all gone."

"There is iron!" Rooney and I shouted together.

"Does it lie far under water?" I asked Lami.

"Coral has grown up around the windlass and anchor," Lami said, "but there is other iron which the seas have lifted over the reef into the lagoon. The young men can take you there in canoes. They know where it is as well as I do."

Rooney, rising to the occasion, cried, "I proclaim tomorrow, June ninth, a national holiday! Three outriggers will go to the wreck, and afterward there will be games and dancing! Let this be known in Ujae as Will Jackson day!"

THE AMICABLE SHARK

Morning dawned clear with a fresh wind, and our three outriggers slipped along like water skaters. I scanned the reef, which stretched away for twenty miles, a band of brilliant yellow; beyond it was a band of tumbling surf whiter than any mortal pigment, and beyond that a band of blue sea.

Presently a cry was raised, "Keero-sin." We had arrived at Kerosene Ridge, so named because the *Rainier*'s cargo had been chiefly kerosene.

The outriggers dropped their sails; their crews jumped overboard with towing ropes and tugged the canoes closer to the windward surf. Soon they touched on coral. Lying on the central arch of my outrigger and looking down through a crack between the slats, I saw, between trees of coral, an underwater gully rippling with white sand; through the gully drifted a seven-foot shark, his back black as the very iron we were seeking.

Five men jumped overboard, including my interpreter, Capelli.

"Don't you see the shark?" I shouted to him.

"They have talked to him before," Capelli said. "He is a friendly shark. Does not bite."

The shark moved on into the lagoon, and the natives swam for the reef.

Ensign Rooney jumped from his outrigger to mine and handed me a camera protected from spray by two white wool socks. He was stripped to shorts and shoes. He dived in, keeping his shoes on as a protection against coral, and swam for the reef. If this had been a hunt for hidden treasure, Rooney could not have shown more zest.

He swam perhaps an eighth of a mile and stood up in water that came to his waist. The five natives beyond him were grouped in less than two feet of water; and I saw two of them dip their arms under water and bring up a v-shaped object, perhaps four feet long. It showed black against the chalk-white background of surf. Iron. Here was evidently one of the bones of the wrecked *Rainier*, and Rooney signaled his joy by shaking his two hands over his head like a boxer.

Our signalman began signaling our ship to come up. She was invisible in the land haze, but we saw her answering spark.

Now it was a race against the rising tide. We inched the outriggers closer to the salvage party, who came on with the water chest-high. Rooney got very close to us, then suddenly disappeared.

He had slipped off his coral perch. Looking straight down, I saw him, eight or nine feet under the outrigger's keel, rolling over and over on clear sand, and hugging against his ribs a precious lump of iron.

He stood himself up, braced himself against the tide, and then began to climb a coral growth, looking cautiously for footholds. He got his head above water within four feet of the outrigger. He still had the iron.

"Take it," he gasped. "It's only a trinket; heavy stuff coming. I think we've got a set of her bitts."

I swung his trinket inboard, and Rooney went back to help.

The tide was now boiling at the necks of the men bringing the bitts, and we reached them only in the nick of time. Standing on a shelf of coral, they hoisted the bitts as high as they could, and we on the outrigger swung them inboard.

The bitts were lumpy with coral. We dumped them down on their side, and a huge white crab with brilliant red markings ran out of one of them. It was his tough luck to lose the house that had been made for him in Bath, Maine, sixty-odd years ago.

"We had a piece of the ship's bell," Rooney said, "but only the bottom half, and no name on it. We dropped it to get the bigger stuff. Boy, this really is Will Jackson Day."

Half an hour later we hoisted our salvage to the ship's deck. One brace of bitts, an end of the ship's cable, another part that we couldn't identify, and Rooney's "trinket," which turned out to be the lower block of the lanyard rigging.

Back on the island of Ujae, the natives listened with joy to our tale of recovery.

At six o'clock the chief magistrate came to tell us that the banquet in Government House was ready. It was enormous. Outside were ten baskets filled with coconuts and breadfruit. Inside at our table were five boiled chickens.

Rooney said to the interpreter, "Hallet and I can't possibly eat more than one chicken between us. Would it be better to pass the other four around or to spoil five chickens?"

The interpreter said gravely, "It would be better to spoil five chickens. It would please them better. These are official chickens. They are for you."

So, Rooney and I spoiled the five chickens, while the islanders squatted on coral pebbles and ate breadfruit. After the banquet, twenty-five or thirty girls came serpentining past our table. Their hair gleamed with coconut oil; their lips wore the friendliest of smiles, and they sang in stiff English their song of welcome.

"Meester Hollot, we are very glad to see you. We kiss our lips to you," they chanted in unison. Each, as she came opposite the table, plumped down some gift—a shell, a hardwood paper-cutter, a cigarette case woven of leaf fibers, or a native fan.

I thanked the women for their gifts and the men for their heavy exertions on the reef. I said that their ancestors had been good to Will Jackson and his mates in their day of misfortune, and that they themselves now proved by their hospitality that their feelings for Americans were as kindly as in the old days. I expressed the profound hope that this historic occasion might not be forgotten, but rather that it would be handed down to their own descendants as a bond between them and America.

Then came the dances, outside the hut. Some were mild, and some were wild—at least the native preacher thought they were wild. The girls danced in a circle, with arms across one another's shoulders. They spun round in the coral, uttering weird sounds, and then, coming close to my chair—the only chair on the island—this circle of girls turned like a millwheel. Each girl, in turn, jounced hard against me, and ran away shrieking. The native preacher disappeared inside his house while this was going on.

Afterward, crowded inside the Government House, we had an exchange of songs. The Marshallese sang hymns which Boston missionaries had taught them. Rooney and I sang—after a hasty conference—"Old MacDonald Had a Farm." They sang "America," and "God Bless America;" and I responded with a chantey, "Yankee Ship Comes Down the River."

It had been a long day and Rooney and I felt exhausted. There was a man at the party named Bugwin, a former chief magistrate of the island. His real name was Libogen, but he was no relation to the spirit Libogen who used to prophesy for the old king, Nejeke, in my uncle's time. Bugwin disclaimed all supernatural powers.

Rooney and I were directly in the white glare of a patent kerosene lamp and could not sleep. I was thinking vaguely of the farmer who, on a similar occasion, said to his wife, "Ellen, I think maybe we had better go to bed. These good folks may want to go home." But Rooney said that we must sit it out; island courtesy demanded it.

And the natives couldn't leave, because that would look like walking out on us. A very old man, a preacher—the island had two—finally broke the deadlock. He sang a hymn, solo, and then announced in English, "Now I go home."

Within two minutes Government House was empty, and Rooney and I fell into our cots and slept like dead men. Will Jackson Day had been an immense and unqualified success.

The day following on Ujae was Sunday, and we attended services. The sermon was double-barreled, both preachers working. *To ene* was the basis of the second sermon. The interpreter worked it out for us. *To ene* is the heart line that attaches a man to his friend, and the preacher said that just as Ujae's heart line went out to Will Jackson's nephew, inspiring them to receive him as a friend when he came to their island, so if they should come to America, his heart line would attach to them, and protect and enlighten them in that strange land which has now taken the sovereignty of their Marshall atoll.

Late that afternoon I told the people of Ujae that a plane would come very soon and take me away. The words were hardly out of my mouth when Bugwin, who had been staring seaward, lifted his arm and cried *"Balloon,"* which is the native word for plane.

All heads were lifted in amazement. How could I know that the unseen plane would suddenly appear in the heavens?

Bugwin leveled a finger at me and cried, "You—you, Meeeter Hollot—you Libogen!"

Actually, I am not. It had all been arranged that way. But I didn't want to disillusion Bugwin. After all, I was Will Jackson's nephew, wasn't I?

ACKNOWLEDGMENTS

My reasons for putting this selection together are explained thoroughly in the preface. But I want to say I could not have completed this mission without the outstanding and unstinting cooperation of Patricia Burdick, assistant director of Special Collections & Archives, at Colby College, Waterville, Maine.

All of Richard Hallet's papers, from original manuscripts to most of his short stories and magazine and newspaper articles, and his published and unpublished novels, went to Colby after his death. His wife, Mary, made the decision, and I suspect Uncle Dick (as I knew him) was a close friend of Richard Cary, the late professor of American literature and then head of Colby's Special Collections. Cary was the author of the marvelous profile of Hallet in the fall of 1967 edition of the *Colby Quarterly*, which I have excerpted as an introduction in this volume.

Hallet's papers constitute a massive file; he wrote a half-dozen more novels than the five that were published. He also wrote more than two hundred short stories and thousands of newspaper and magazine articles during his career. While I made a few trips to Waterville from my home in Arrowsic, Maine, I was saved hundreds of hours and miles of driving by Pat Burdick's timely assistance in forwarding various copies, by email and normal mail, and her assistance in tracking down others not in their files.

I also appreciate the valuable assistance of Carmen Greenlee, research librarian at Bowdoin College's Nathaniel Hawthorne Library, and Leilani Goggin, always there to help with tricky computer issues.

This work could not have been pulled together without the outstanding support, editing, and technical skills of Lauren Leatham, a very talented Cornell University student who was instrumental in helping me organize this material and readying it for publication. Lauren provided brilliant support for an earlier book, *Dereliction of Duty: The Failed Presidency of Donald John Trump* (2020).

I am indebted to Trove, the National Library of Australia, and a good friend, Joan Wilcox, of Sydney, for unearthing Hallet's remarkable fifteen-part series of stories for the *Melbourne Herald*, encouraging steps in his writing career, and published in 1913 after he had left Australia. I also appreciate the assistance of Lindl Lawton, of the South Australia Maritime Museum, for locating images of the ships Hallet arrived on and departed from Sydney.

My thanks likewise go to Tom and Ash Kahrl, proprietors of the Bath (Maine) Printing Company. They printed copies of dozens of short stories as I struggled to select what I determined were the most appealing of Hallet's tales to include in this collection—and they skillfully converted the old, faded, and jagged texts of these stories into modern typeface. Choosing sixteen pieces out of some two hundred stories and articles was a daunting task.

I could not have completed this project without the moral support and sharing of family photographs from Richard Hallet's two granddaughters: Susan Hallet Witt, of Boothbay Harbor, and Jennifer Hallet Chipman, of Rockland. I wish to thank Bob Keyes, an outstanding reporter at the *Portland Press Herald*, for his assistance in locating old photographs, as well as Julia McCue of the *Press Herald* and Sophia Yalouris at the Maine Historical Society.

As always, I am grateful for the outstanding professional care and oversight of Michael Steere, editor at Down East Books, and the superb production team at Rowman & Littlefield, in this case led by Patricia Stevenson, assistant managing editor.

Lastly, I am indebted to continuing and crucial editing help and encouragement from my patient and lovely wife, Marty, and from our daughter, Sarah Hill Schlenker, and son, Alexander Jackson Hill, both outstanding writers and editors.

A BIBLIOGRAPHY OF RICHARD MATTHEWS HALLET

Compiled by Richard Cary

BOOKS

The Lady Aft. Boston: Small, Maynard & Co., 1915. Also, London: T. Werner Laurie, 1915.

Trial by Fire. Boston: Small, Maynard & Co., 1916.

The Canyon of the Fools. New York: Harper & Brothers, 1922. Also, New York: Grosset & Dunlap, 1924.

The Rolling World. Boston: Houghton Mifflin Co., 1938. Also, London: Eyre & Spottiswoode, 1939; Toronto: Thomas Allen, 1939.

Michael Beam. Boston: Houghton Mifflin Co., 1939.

Foothold of Earth. Garden City, NY: Doubleday, Doran & Co., 1944.

BROCHURE

"The Boothbay Region Story," Boothbay Region, 1764–1964. Boothbay, Maine: Boothbay Bicentennial Committee, 1964.

IN ANTHOLOGIES

"Making Port," in Edward J. O'Brien (editor), *The Best Short Stories of 1916* (Boston: Small, Maynard & Co., 1917), 162–180.

"The Razor of Pedro Dutel," in Frederick Stuart Greene (editor), *The Grim Thirteen* (New York: Dodd, Mead & Co., 1917), 201–228.

"Rainbow Pete," in Edward J. O'Brien (editor), *The Best Short Stories of 1917* (Boston: Small, Maynard & Co., 1918), 307–325.

"To the Bitter End," in Edward J. O'Brien (editor), *The Best Short Stories of 1919* (Boston: Small. Maynard & Co., 1920), 178–199.

"Harbor Master," in Edward J. O'Brien (editor), *The Best Short Stories of 1921* (Boston: Small, Maynard & Co., 1922), 207–239.

Hallet's comments on the techniques of writing, in Arthur Sullivant Hoffman (editor), *Fiction Writers on Fiction Writing* (Indianapolis: Bobbs-Merrill Co., 1923), passim.

"The Anchor," in Charles W. Gray (editor), *Deep Waters* (New York: Henry Holt & Co., 1928), 213–240.

"Stories Everywhere," "Foot-Loose," in Henry Goodman (editor), *Creating the Short Story* (New York: Harcourt, Brace & Co., 1929), 160, 161–192.

"Misfortune's Isle," in Blanche Colton Williams (editor), *O. Henry Memorial Award Prize Stories of 1930* (Garden City, NY: Doubleday, Doran & Co., 1930), 143–169.

"Misfortune's Isle," in Raymond Woodbury Pence (editor), *Short Stories of Today* (New York: Macmillan, 1934), 195–223.

"Thoughts on Writing," in Thomas Page Smith (editor), *Cordially Yours* (Boston: Boston Herald Book Fair Committee, 1939), 78–80.

"The Razor of Pedro Dutel," in Boris Karloff (editor), *And the Darkness Falls* (Cleveland: World Publishing Co., 1947), 314–328.

"Maine's Champion Fiddler," in Nathan C. Fuller (editor), *The Down East Reader* (Philadelphia: J. B. Lippincott, 1962), 169–175.

PERIODICALS

"The Handkerchief," *Cosmopolitan* XLVII (July 1909), 191–196.

"The Hired Man," *Designer* XXXV (March 1912), 305.

"The Black Squad," *Saturday Evening Post* 185 (August 24, 1912), 3; (August 31), 17.

"Beyond the Tides," *Harper's* CXXVI (May 1913), 840–847.

"With the Current," *Smart Set* XL (July 1913), 9–40.

"The Foreign Voyager," *Harper's* CXXVII (September 1913), 578–585.

"On a Calm Sea," *American* LXXVI (September 1913), 34–40.

"Stradivarius and the Food of Love," *Everybody's* XXXII (May 1915), 609–622.

"Southampton Bill and the Siren," *Everybody's* XXXIII (July 1915), 105–118.

"The Family Tree," *Everybody's* XXXIII (August 1915), 218–229.

"Shooting Off the Solid," *Saturday Evening Post* 188 (January 1, 1916), 13.

"Archaeology for Amateurs," *Atlantic Monthly* CVII (March 1916), 319–328.

"Making Port," *Every Week* III (March 20, 1916), 5–7.

"The Sea Adventurer," *Every Week* III (October 2, 1916), 7–9.

"Bos'," *Everybody's* XXXV (November 1916), 564–578.

"The Quest of London," *Everybody's* XXXV (December 1916), 697–708.

"The House of Craigenside," *Saturday Evening Post* 189 (February 10, 1917), 3; (February 17), 23; (February 24), 21; (March 3), 21.

"Fashioning the Hollow Oak," *Century* XCIV (June 1917), 161–176.

"Rainbow Pete," *Pictorial Review* XIX (October 1917), 31.

"Ticklish Waters," *Saturday Evening Post* 191 (September 7, 1918), 17; (September 14), 17.

"Go Down to the Sea in Ships," *Saturday Evening Post* 191 (February 22, 1919), 11.

"The Anchor," *Century* XCVII (March 1919), 577–590.

"Blue-Water Law," *Saturday Evening Post* 191 (May 3, 1919), 8.

"Limping In," *Saturday Evening Post* 191 (May 17, 1919), 10.

"To the Bitter End," *Saturday Evening Post* 191 (May 31, 1919), 8.

"Everything in the Shop," *Saturday Evening Post* 192 (August 9, 1919), 16.

"Beef, Iron and Wine," *Saturday Evening Post* 192 (August 16, 1919), 16.

"The Shackling," *Saturday Evening Post* 192 (August 30, 1919), 42.

"The Interpreter's Wife," *Saturday Evening Post* 192 (October 11, 1919), 42.

"Inspiration Jule," *Saturday Evening Post* 192 (November 8, 1919), 58.

"The First Lady of Cranberry Isle," *Saturday Evening Post* 192 (November 29, 1919), 18.

"Wake-Up Archie," *Collier's* LXV (February 14, 1920), 7.

"Bluebeard Shadrach," *Saturday Evening Post* 192 (March 20, 1920), 20.

"Local Color," *Saturday Evening Post* 192 (May 8, 1920), 29.

"The Mountain and Mahomet," *Harper's* CXLI (November 1920), 735–750.

"A Whale of a Story," *Pictorial Review* XXII (November 1920), 20.

"The Harbor Master," *Harper's* CXLIII (June 1921), 36–45; (July), 198–206.

"The Canyon of the Fools," *Saturday Evening Post* 194 (October 22, 1921), 5; (October 29), 22; (November 5), 22; (November 12), 22; (November 19), 22; (November 26), 22; (December 3), 22.

"The Gulf Stream," *Saturday Evening Post* 196 (April 5, 1924), 16.

"A Streak of the Mule," *Saturday Evening Post* 196 (May 3, 1924), 24.

"The Transient Woman," *Saturday Evening Post* 197 (January 31, 1925), 8.

"The Kitchen Democrat," *Saturday Evening Post* 197 (May 30, 1925), 10.

"Tame Crow," *Saturday Evening Post* 197 (June 13, 1925), 14.

"The Winter Kill," *Saturday Evening Post* 197 (June 27, 1925), 10.

"El Parrett's Luck," *Saturday Evening Post* 198 (December 5, 1925), 28.

"The Point Where All Sails Shiver," *Saturday Evening Post* 198 (December 12, 1925), 20.

"The Horoscope," *Saturday Evening Post* 198 (May 29, 1926), 22.

"Nothing but Blue Chips," *Saturday Evening Post* 198 (June 19, 1926), 10.

"The Unwatched Light," *Everybody's* LV (July 1926), 100–107.

"Husband in the Dark," *Saturday Evening Post* 199 (September 4, 1926), 20.

"Tick-a-Lock; Iron Bars," *Saturday Evening Post* 199 (October 9, 1926), 16.

"Beyond a Reasonable Doubt," *Saturday Evening Post* 199 (November 6, 1926), 8; (November 13), 38.

"Theed Harlow's Cadenza," *Saturday Evening Post* 199 (April 2, 1927), 42.

"Makeshift," *Shrine Magazine* II (November 1927), 14.

"Bottomless Pond," *Saturday Evening Post* 200 (November 12, 1927), 42.

"A Privileged Communication," *Shrine Magazine* III (January 1928), 26.

"Foot-Loose," *Saturday Evening Post* 200 (March 10, 1928), 8.

"One Shirt and One Soul," *Saturday Evening Post* 200 (May 12, 1928), 14.

"A Bad Washing," *Saturday Evening Post* 200 (May 26, 1928), 26.

"Local Time," *Saturday Evening Post* 201 (September 15, 1928), 12.

"Gambler's Gold," *Saturday Evening Post* 201 (November 10, 1928), 10.

"March Hill," *Saturday Evening Post* 201 (December 8, 1928), 12.

"Trader's Risks," *Saturday Evening Post* 201 (March 16, 1929), 16.

"The Tiger's Mouth," *Saturday Evening Post* 201 (May 25, 1929), 16.

"Walk in the Water," *Saturday Evening Post* 202 (August 17, 1929), 33.

"Demons of the Sand," *Saturday Evening Post* 202 (August 31, 1929), 8.

"The Interloper," *Saturday Evening Post* 202 (September 21, 1929), 49.

"Railroad Speed," *Saturday Evening Post* 202 (October 12, 1929), 22.

"Misfortune's Isle," *Saturday Evening Post* 202 (November 9, 1929), 18.

"The Earthquake," *Saturday Evening Post* 202 (February 1, 1930), 10.

"Zimbolaci's Daughter," *Saturday Evening Post* 202 (March 29, 1930), 20.

"The Soul Killer," *Saturday Evening Post* 202 (May 3, 1930), 46.

"The Frigate," *Saturday Evening Post* 203 (August 23, 1930), 16.

"Tumble-Down Dick," *Saturday Evening Post* 203 (December 13, 1930), 22.

"Conjurers of the North," *Saturday Evening Post* 204 (September 12, 1931), 14.

"The Devil Takes Care of His Own," *Saturday Evening Post* 205 (December 17, 1932), 12.

"Throw Him Down, McCloskey," *Saturday Evening Post* 205 (January 21, 1933), 10.

"The Last of the Romans," *Saturday Evening Post* 205 (April 8, 1933), 14.

"The Cloud Shooter," *Saturday Evening Post* 205 (June 10, 1933), 6.

"Bushed," *Saturday Evening Post* 206 (September 16, 1933), 8.

"The Dog-Eye," *Story* III (October 1933), 45–55.

"The Golden Horseshoe," *Saturday Evening Post* 206 (December 9, 1933), 10.

"Cuba Libre," *Saturday Evening Post* 206 (December 23, 1933), 8.

"Cheese It the Cops," *American Legion Monthly* XVI (January 1934), 22.

"A Man of Many Bells," *Saturday Evening Post* 206 (April 21, 1934), 18.

"Sudden Johnny," *Collier's* XCIV (December 29, 1934), 16–18.

"The Silent Act," *Collier's* XCV (May 18, 1935), 16.

"The Hidden Rooster," *Saturday Evening Post* 207 (May 25, 1935), 20.

"The Crowbar," *Saturday Evening Post* 208 (February 8, 1936), 18.

"The River's Gift," *Collier's* XCVII (February 15, 1936), 7.

"The Asses of Saul," *Saturday Evening Post* 208 (May 2, 1936), 22.

"The Figurehead," *Saturday Evening Post* 209 (October 10, 1936), 24.

"The Path Master," *Saturday Evening Post* 209 (March 6, 1937), 18.

"Blonde Demeter's Land," *Technology Review* XLI (May 1939), 307.

"The Man Who Licked John L.," *American Legion Monthly* XXVI (June 1939), 5.

"I Lived Mine," *Writer's Digest* XIX (September 1939), 13–16.

"Mopping Up the Thoroughfares," *Technology Review* XLII (December 1939), 68.

"Blind Man's Bluff," *American Legion Monthly* XXVIII (January 1940), 3.

"Saturday's Whale," *Adventure* CII (February 1940), 61–68.

"Net Returns from the Banks," *Technology Review* XLIII (December 1940), 70.

"Foreword," *Maine Maritime Academy Catalog* (1941), 5.

"Destroyers," *Technology Review* XLIII (May 1941), 299.

"Destroyer, a Million a Minute," *Science Digest* X (July 19, 1941), 1–4.

"Wooden Ships and Maine Builders," *Technology Review* XLIV (November 1941), 24.

"Answer, Echo, Answer," *Technology Review* XLIV (May 1942), 311.

"The Trail of Bambi," *Collier's* CX (October 3, 1942), 58.

"Dark Kingdom," *Argosy* CCCXV (May 1943), 48–58.

"My Uncle's Footprints," *Saturday Evening Post* 218 (March 30, 1946), 34.

"Famous Figureheads," *Yankee* XII (September 1948), 31.

"A Forgotten Maine Genius," *Down East* I (September 1954), 17–19.

"The Wreck of the *Rainier*," *Down East* I (October 1954), 16.

"A Frontier Courthouse," *Down East* I (November–December 1954), 17.

"The Great Quoddy Gold Hoax," *Down East* I (Winter 1955), 18–20.

"Destroyers Every Other Friday," *Down East* I (May 1955), 16–20.

"Bill Nye, Humorist of the Gay Nineties," *Down East* II (October 1955), 18–20.

"Maine on the Silver Screen," *Down East* II (October 1955), 28–31.

"Maine's Champion Fiddler," *Down East* II (November 1955–January 1956), 37–39.

"Hiram Maxim of Sangerville," *Down East* II (April 1956), 29–31.

"When Baseball Belted the Earth," *Yankee* XX (August 1956), 36.

"Sir William Phips," *Down East* III (September 1956), 23.

"The Happy Warrior," *Down East* III (November 1956–January 1957), 30–34.

"The Inmate of Cell 67," *Down East* III (February–March 1957), 22.

"Trail Blazer and Statesman, Ralph H. Cameron of Southport," *Down East* III (April 1957), 26.

"Hannibal Hamlin—Foe of Slavery," *Down East* III (May 1957), 30.

"Lily of the North, Madame Nordica," *Down East* IV (September 1957), 28–31.

"Apache Peacemaker, Maine's General Oliver Otis Howard," *Down East* IV (October 1957), 24.

"Elijah P. Lovejoy," *Down East* IV (January 1958), 24.

"Gene Tunney—A Forelaying Champion," *Down East* IV (June 1958), 35.

"The Deep Roots of Boothbay Harbor," *Down East* IV (August 1958), 36.

"Elijah P. Lovejoy, Martyr to the Cause of Freedom," *Club Dial* XXXIII (February 1959), 12.

"Doc Rockwell, King of Whim," *Down East* V (March 1959), 21–25.

"Kenneth Roberts and His Water Dowser," *Down East* V (June 1959), 32.

"Cyrus Curtis, A Maine Export," *Down East* VI (July 1959), 36.

"Artemus Ward," *Down East* VI (September 1959), 30.

"The Fightingest Maine Stock," *Down East* VI (October 1959), 24.

"Two Dead-Locked Inventors," *Down East* VI (November 1959), 27.

"King of the Road," *Yankee* XXIII (December 1959), 40.

"The Fabulous Story of Sir Harry Oakes," *Down East* VI (January 1960), 12–15.

"Holman Day," *Down East* VI (April 1960), 36–40.

"A Lady in a Gentlemen's Club," *Down East* VI (May 1960), 22.

"Bixler and the New Colby," *Down East* VI (June 1960), 32–36.

"Boothbay Harbor, Maine," *Yankee* XXIV (July 1960), 48–55.

"Lincoln County Pilgrimage," *Down East* VII (August 1960), 40–43.

"When Prohibition Came to Maine," *Yankee* XXV (February 1961), 38–41.

"Lobsters and Lobstermen," *Down East* VII (April 1961), 28.

"Captain Richard Quick, Hom Voyager," *Down East* VIII (April 1962), 16–19.

"All Finished with the Engines," *Down East* VIII (June 1962), 44–47.

"A Great Maine Opera Star—Emma Eames," *Down East* X (August 1963), 50.

"The Conqueror of Louisburg," *Down East* XIII (May 1967), 23.

NEWSPAPERS

"Making Port," *Boston Sunday Post Magazine* (March 19, 1916), 5–7.

"Transcontinental," *Chicago Sunday Tribune*, Graphic Section (November 19, 1933), 7. Also, *New York Sunday News* (November 19, 1933), 54C–55C.

"The Cast of the Mighty John L's Arm," *Boston Sunday Herald* (January 15, 1939), B-3.

"Too Many Seamen?" *Christian Science Monitor*, Weekly Magazine Section (July 27, 1940), 1–2.

"Fritz Kreisler, and What's in Him," *Christian Science Monitor*, Weekly Magazine Section (December 7, 1940), 5.

"He Builds Good Ships," *Christian Science Monitor*, Weekly Magazine Section (March 8, 1941), 5.

"Maine Is Still Mother of Ships," *Christian Science Monitor*, Weekly Magazine Section (June 28, 1941), 8–9. Also, Congressional Record—Appendix (June 30, 1941), A3408–A3409.

"Booth Tarkington: At Sea at Home," *Christian Science Monitor*, Weekly Magazine Section (December 20, 1941), 7.

In his fifteen years with the Gannett newspapers (1937–1952), Hallet appeared anonymously and under his by-line in the editorial, feature, and general news sections of the daily *Portland Press Herald* and weekly in the *Portland Sunday Telegram*. His reports, interviews, and expositions—ranging from global events to local issues—are far too numerous to docket here; they are available on microfilm in several of the larger libraries in Maine. However, these five series and four articles bear particular interest here.

"Windjammer," *Portland Press Herald* (April 19–29, 1937).

"On the Gorges Banks in an Otter Trawler," *Portland Press Herald* (July 23, 27, 30, August 3, 6, 1937).

"German Submarines on the Atlantic Coast in the Last War," *Portland Sunday Telegram* (April 13, 20, 27, May 4, 11, 18, 1941).

"The Story of Maine," *Portland Press Herald* (November 1, 1948–June 27,
	1949).
"Men of Maine," *Portland Press Herald* (November 5, 1951–May 2, 1952).
"Boiling Down Three Generations (John Gould)," *Portland Sunday Telegram*
	(March 17, 1946), D-5.
"Maine, Touchstone of Famed Writers," *Portland Sunday Telegram* (April 14,
	1946), D-3.
"Maine Authors Convert Hallet to Dowsing," *Portland Sunday Telegram* (Sep-
	tember 25, 1949), A-19.
"Diviner Tries Art in Predicting Sex of Unborn Babies at Maine General Hos-
	pital," *Portland Press Herald* (October 6, 1949), 1–2. [Kenneth Roberts]

* * *

"The Book of Swag; An Overland Cruise: Sailors on the Wallaby." A fifteen-
	part series of stories by Richard M. Hallet published in the *Melbourne
	Herald*, 1913. TROVE, The National Library of Australia.

ABOUT HALLET

"Richard Matthews Hallet," *Saturday Evening Post* 191 (May 17, 1919), 65,
	69. Autobiographical.
Esther Brock Bird, "The Literary Coast of Maine," *Lewiston Journal*, Maga-
	zine Section (August 22, 1925), 2. Reproduced from the Harvard Decennial
	Report, 1908.
Janet Mabie, "A Rolling Stone Who Became an Author," *Dearborn Indepen-
	dent* XXVII (November 6, 1926), 3, 27.
"A Maine Reverie," *Portland Sunday Telegram* (July 5, 1936), D-1, 5. Auto-
	biographical.
Hallet's comment on his story, "The Figurehead," and his portrait, *Saturday
	Evening Post* 209 (October 10, 1936), 116.
Sam E. Connor, "'Dick' Hallett—Adventurer," *Lewiston Journal*, Magazine
	Section (June 4, 1938), A-9.
"Hollering 'Uncle' in the Pacific Causes Echoes," in the pamphlet "Inside
	Information," *Saturday Evening Post* VIII (March 26, 1943), 4.
Franklin Wright, "Peering into Yesterday," *Portland Sunday Telegram* (No-
	vember 28, 1948), 5.
Edith V. Campbell, "Writers Can Be Rovers," *Yankee* XV (February 1951), 26.

Kenneth Roberts, *Henry Gross and His Dowsing Rod* (Garden City, NY: Doubleday & Co., 1951), 142–145.

"Richard Matthews Hallet's Great Christmas Editorial," *Boothbay Register* (December 25, 1958), 6.

Terry Lewis, "Richard Matthews Hallet," *Boothbay Register* (April 30, 1964), 6.

Caroline Norwood, "Writer's Travels Inspired Stories," *Portland Press Herald* (August 16, 1966), 10.

ABOUT THE EDITOR

Frederic B. Hill was a reporter, correspondent, and editorial writer for the *Baltimore Sun*, including tours as bureau chief in London and Paris, covering Europe and southern Africa. He then served as foreign affairs director for Senator Charles McCurdy Mathias Jr. (R-MD) in 1985 and 1986. He helped establish and then headed an office in the Department of State that conducted policy planning exercises (wargames) and senior-level discussions on national security and global issues from 1986 to 2006.

A native of Maine and graduate of Bowdoin College, Hill is the author of *Ships, Swindlers and Scalded Hogs: The Rise and Fall of the Crooker Shipyard in Bath, Maine* (2016); coeditor of *The Life of Kings: The Baltimore Sun and the Golden Age of the American Newspaper* (2016); author of *Dereliction of Duty: The Failed Presidency of Donald John Trump* (2020); and coauthor (with Alexander J. Hill) of *A Flick of Sunshine: The Remarkable Shipwrecked, Marooned Maritime Adventures and Tragic Fate of an American Original* (2021).